BEYOND SPRING

BEYOND SPRING

Betty Brady

Copyright © 2005 by Betty Brady.

Library of Congress Number: 2004094338
ISBN :   Hardcover   1-4134-6085-2
                Softcover   1-4134-6084-4

All rights reserved. No part of this book may be reproduced or transmitted in any form or by any means, electronic or mechanical, including photocopying, recording, or by any information storage and retrieval system, without permission in writing from the copyright owner.

This is a work of fiction. Names, characters, places and incidents either are the product of the author's imagination or are used fictitiously, and any resemblance to any actual persons, living or dead, events, or locales is entirely coincidental.

This book was printed in the United States of America.

To order additional copies of this book, contact:
Xlibris Corporation
1-888-795-4274
www.Xlibris.com
Orders@Xlibris.com
24623

Lovingly dedicated in honor of my beautiful granddaughter,
Amy Marie Reynolds, the role model for my heroine,
Amy Marie Bradshaw.

CHAPTER 1

February 5, 1783—Amy's breath floated like a faint cloud in the frosty air as she scurried along the narrow sweet fern bordered lane that led to her home at the south edge of Charlottesville, Virginia. Hurrying winds snatched at her homespun skirt and blew her perky bonnet askew. Fence-enclosed yards looked ragged and unkempt littered with dead twigs, leaves, and a skiff of snow.

Amy Marie Bradshaw, a petite and slender fifteen-year-old, faced the afternoon sun, now dipping toward the mountains to the west, and was touched by its glow.

Sunlight misted her bouncing and shiny honey colored braids, bronzed her heavy dark lashes, and the cold February air flushed her cheeks crimson. Her small vulnerable mouth was transformed into a smiling rosy flower in her heart-shaped face as she entered her house through the back door. A blast of warm air from the cast-iron stove and blazing hearth in the kitchen embraced her. She closed the door and quickly slipped out of her wool cape and hung it on a peg behind the kitchen door. The air was resplendent with various mouthwatering aromas of cooking food, mingling with the sharp scent of cinnamon, cloves, and wood smoke.

Amy was happy to be home and she was filled with a sense of peace and tranquility indicative of the sounds and smells of her parents' house. This was the only home she had ever known and her mother kept it spotless and shining. The big family kitchen was the hub of the Bradshaw house; the room where everyone congregated and where friends and family members were usually entertained. A Victorian lamp, placed in the center of the huge oak table dominating the kitchen, and the fire in the hearth cast a warm rosy glow about her.

Margaret's cotton gown brushed the spotless floor as she went about her supper preparations, humming absently to herself. Thirty-four-year-old Margaret Bradshaw was a striking woman. She was slender and slim-hipped, with a saucy sprinkling of light freckles across the bridge of her nose. Her smile was quick and warm and the movements of hands and arms graceful as she tucked a stray lock of tawny brown hair under a side comb.

Amy's heart quickened as her mother turned expressive brown eyes upon her.

She gazed into Amy's eyes, twin reflections of her own, and smiled warmly. Amy gave her mother an impulsive hug and walked over to the wash basin to wash her face and hands.

"How was school today, ummm?" Margaret asked, her eyebrows raised inquiringly. Using the folds of her white apron she lifted a pan of cornbread out of the hot oven and set it to the back of the stove.

Standing before the washstand Amy rubbed yellow soap over her hands. "Just glorious!" she nodded emphatically. "Arnold Drexler asked if he could walk home with me after church Sunday." Amy cocked her head and looked imploringly at her mother. "Would that be alright with you?"

"I think Arnold is a very nice boy and I see no reason at all why he couldn't walk home with you after church. As long as the weather is nice," she added, inclining her head in compliance, a trace of laughter in her voice.

"I know the weather will be just grand, Ma," Amy said, her eyes serenely compelling. "I saw my first robin in the schoolyard today. And, Ma," Amy exclaimed with intense pleasure, "Mr. Freeland called on me to read the Scriptures this morning."

"That's nice, honey," Margaret said, eyes searching Amy's face as she reached into her own thoughts, smiling in remembrance of her own days of schooling. She understood the privilege it was to be called upon to read the Scriptures.

"Where's that brother of yours?" Margaret asked as she glanced idly out of the kitchen window, wiping the perspiration from her face with the bottom edge of her apron."

"Just wait 'til I tell you, Ma! When I got up to read the Scripture, Billy Joe started teasing me. You should have heard him. Bold as brass, as only *he* can do!" Amy retorted in cold sarcasm. "He did it right in front of everybody as I was walking to the front of the classroom. Mr. Freeland caught every word he said and called him down for it, too," she said indignantly, rolling her eyes. "He was really embarrassed when Mr. Freeland said he had to stay after school an extra fifteen minutes." Amy wagged her head. "I sure hope it teaches him a lesson!" she declared dramatically, her lips puckering in annoyance. "There are times I wish I didn't have a brother, especially one like Billy Joe!"

"Amy Marie Bradshaw, what a terrible thing to say!" Margaret chastised sharply.

Amy bristled as her mother scolded her impatiently, but then quickly settled when she saw the soft smile that flickered over her mother's mouth and touched her somber brown eyes. Amy knew instinctively what her mother was thinking before Margaret spoke again.

"That boy is fond of mischief, that's for sure," Margaret clucked, shaking her head, her voice losing its steely edge. "But don't be too hard on him, honey. Boys who like you best will be the ones who pull your pigtails the hardest and say the meanest things to you at times. Your brother, in spite of his devilish ways, loves you dearly." There was a lovely resonance to her mother's voice, full of nuances and feeling.

"So you keep telling me!" Amy said emphatically and shook her head. "But I think I know Billy Joe better than anyone else, and a little brat is lurking beneath the sweet exterior he shows you and Pa!"

Amy dried her hands on a clean linen towel and in better spirits walked over to the stove where Margaret was busy slicing a potato into a hot skillet for frying. She reached into the pan and grabbed a thick slice, dipped it into the salt cellar, and started munching on it. Sniffing the air, she glanced at slabs of pork that were crisping in another skillet and a hot apple pie cooling on the table. "Ummm, Ma, it sure does smell good in here," she said eagerly. "Looks like you've been cooking all day and I'm mighty hungry. What do you want me to do to help?"

"You can set the table, honey. Your pa will be home before you know it and then we'll eat, and not a minute before. Now scoot!" Amy obediently reached into the massive oak sideboard and began removing their willowware china.

John Bradshaw walked in the door fifteen minutes later, eleven-year-old Billy Joe tagging at his heels wide-eyed and breathless, his hair hanging in his eyes and his faded blue shirttail hanging down his backside. A myriad of gleaming pieces of copper and brass hanging on each side of the huge cast-iron stove caught and held distorted images of Margaret and Amy as they moved about the room.

Glancing at Amy, Billy Joe rolled his dark brown eyes mockingly. He snickered as he pushed aside a stray lock of sandy-brown hair that framed his brow and emphasized the baby-roundness still evident in his cheeks.

The warmth of the kitchen, after the cold blast of winter winds blowing and whistling around every corner of the house, beckoned to John as he entered the kitchen. He breathed deeply, relishing the familiar scents and sounds of his home. He smiled, feeling truly blessed as he planted a resounding smack on Margaret's lips.

"That wind sure has a bite to it," John said, rubbing his hands together and shrugging out of his knee-length great coat, "and that's God's truth!" His piercing green eyes swept over Margaret and he cast a melting smile in her direction. Glibly he said, "You look good enough to eat, my dear little wife. Mighty pretty!"

"Pretty is as pretty does," Margaret answered coyly, her eyes warm and alive with interest. Her voice was vibrant with delight at hearing the complimentary words John had spoken. She tried to hide a smile as she stretched a bit to take some of the kink from her back. Amy glanced at her father, her velvet-brown eyes sparkling as she bustled about helping her mother set bowls of steaming hot food on the table.

"How's my girl?" John asked, finally giving his daughter his undivided attention.

"Just glorious, Pa!" Amy answered, basking in her father's attention, thinking just how wondrously handsome he was. Amy loved her mother dearly but her father was the most special person in her life. She idolized him. John was thirty-seven-years old, had a spare, but well-knit five-foot-nine-inch frame, and a cleft in his chin. Strong white teeth, penetrating gray-green eyes and coal-black hair added to his ruggedly handsome face. Margaret had always said that her father's infectious smile could charm the birds from the trees, and Amy had always found that statement to be true.

"Is anyone around here interested in eating?" Margaret demanded jovially, hands on hips. Amy fingered a loose tendril of hair on her cheek and hurriedly took her seat at the table.

"Do you need any help from me, Ma?" Billy Joe asked politely. Amy snickered and rolled her eyes knowing full well that Billy Joe was just buttering their mother up.

"No, son, I don't believe I do, but thanks anyway. Amy pitched in right after she got home from school and I do believe we're ready to sit down. Just wash your hands and right after supper we're going to have us a little talk, young man!"

Billy Joe's face clouded with uneasiness. He frowned, ducked his head and the tips of his ears turned a bright red.

"You in hot water again, my lad?" John's voice cut the air. He stared at his young son and shook his head.

Billy Joe stiffened and looked quickly up at his father. Amy had been hoping his mischief just might do him in this time, but she caught the wink from her father aimed in Billy Joe's direction and noted the smile that creased his face. She could visibly see Billy Joe relax when he realized that once again he was off the hook as far as his father was concerned.

Glancing uneasily over his shoulder at his mother, Billy Joe saw the faint glint of humor in her dark eyes, and turned and made a quick dash to the wash basin. A big grin was plastered on his face as he dipped his hands into the water basin and then quickly wiped them on his pants. Dipping one hand back into the water, he wet his hair and smoothed it down with his fingers.

Amy tensed as Billy Joe passed behind her chair, leaned down close and chanted in her ear, "Amy's sweet on Arnold! Amy's sweet on Arnold!" She glared fiercely at him as he sat down across the table from her. She continued to glare at her brother until her father hitched his chair to the table and bowed his head to say the blessing. After the "Amen" John sat and stared at his empty plate.

"Better eat while it's hot, Pa," Amy said, eyeing him speculatively. Her father seemed so preoccupied and serious. She was rewarded with a half-smile as her father filled his plate and took one bite of meat and potatoes. Amy kept darting glances his way as he chewed slowly for several seconds and then swallowed. Taking a sip of coffee John absently wiped his mouth on his napkin and pushed his chair away from the table. Amy followed her father's every move as he rose to his feet and started pacing up and down the length of the kitchen floor. She took quick notice of the look of alarm on her mother's face and glanced quizzically at her brother, curious as to what was troubling him. Billy Joe shrugged his shoulders and continued shoveling food into his mouth.

"What's the matter, Pa?" Amy finally asked, regarding her father with somber dark eyes. "You're acting mighty strange tonight."

John stopped his pacing and took a deep breath. His expression was tight with strain as he faced his family. As casually as he could manage he said, "I was talking to Howard Tippett today. His brother Sam and family went with Lewis Craig to Kentucky back in '81. Now Sam is back in these parts getting up another group to go back to Kentucky with him." Hesitating for just a moment, John glanced nervously to where Margaret sat watching every move he was making, and listening to every word he was uttering. Tentatively he said, "Howie's thinking of going with him."

"Fine and good for Howie," Margaret countered, setting her jaw. "But why, my dear husband, has that bit of information turned you so inside out that you can't even sit at the table with us and eat your supper? Howie's business doesn't concern us, does it?"

Amy took a bite of pork and began to chew slowly waiting for her father to answer her mother's question. She caught the air of excitement about her father as he started to explain. "In a way it does, sweetheart," John said quietly, as his green eyes pierced the distance between them. "He tells me more and more permanent settlements are being started from here clean out to Kentucky almost every day. People are opening up stores and stables and blacksmith shops, and I hear tell that carpenters and masons are just flocking to Kentucky."

John stopped pacing long enough to look straight into Margaret's eyes and waved his hands in the air dramatically. "Our nation as we know it is composed of thirteen colonies on the Atlantic coast, but the vast lands beyond the mountains is just waiting for those who are venturesome enough to go claim them. All the talk about town is that Kentucky is thinking of separating from Virginia and becoming a free and independent state. Thomas Jefferson is agreeing that separation for Kentucky is coming in time."

John started pacing the kitchen floor again, his arms still waving in the air. The excitement in his voice did not abate, but Amy just wasn't the least bit interested in hearing about political matters. What her father was saying about Kentucky becoming a free and independent state from Virginia was going in one ear and out the other. When John mentioned that Daniel Boone, Simon Kenton, and George Rogers Clark were all making names for themselves in the land that lay west of the Alleghenies, Billy Joe's ears perked up.

Daniel Boone just happened to be his favorite hero and Amy had to smile as he turned his eyes on his mother and commented; "If Daniel Boone thinks Kentucky is good enough for him, then it must be a pretty good place to be!"

"That it is, son," John interjected, happy at last to get a positive opinion from at least one member of his family to all he had been saying. "I've been told Kentucky holds claim to the richest and most fertile land our country has ever had to offer!"

Margaret quietly placed her fork beside her plate, slowly wiped her mouth with her white linen napkin, and dropped her hands into her lap. She looked up at her husband of seventeen years and frowned. "Why would you be interested in land that lies hundreds of miles from here?" she asked softly but firmly. "That land, for the most part I believe, belongs to the Indians!"

"Indians!" Amy exclaimed excitedly. "Mr. Freeland has been expounding on different Indian tribes that live in the vast regions of our world for the past several days, Pa!" Amy watched with interest and now listened intently as her father pulled his chair as close as he could to her mother's chair.

Looking directly into Margaret's steady brown eyes, John's voice was husky as he stated emphatically, "Land speculators will soon be pouring into Kentucky and more and more brave souls will be heading out that way. I've been told that when sowed to clover, timothy, barley and corn, it promises the best hay and crops to be had in our whole country. We could be rich beyond our wildest dreams!"

Margaret squared her shoulders and blurted, "We could be rich? Phooey, John William Bradshaw, have you gone daft? You make a good living right here in Charlottesville," she interjected quickly. "You're the best shoe cobbler in all of Virginia."

Amy's supper was forgotten as she gazed helplessly at her parents bickering back and forth. She licked her dry lips nervously and finally butted in. "We have everything we need right here, Pa, don't we?" she asked hastily, a high, nervous pitch to her voice.

John's smile was something to behold as he looked around the table at his family and then let his eyes come to rest once again on Margaret's pale face. As casually as he could manage he stated, "In Kentucky we could sink down roots and become one with a new land! I could become a farmer."

The word "farmer" fell from John's lips softly—almost

reverently, and Amy was as bewildered as her mother seemed to be. *Why on earth would my father want to be a farmer?* she wondered. *A farmer was a man who worked in the fields all day, plowing and planting and taking care of stinky cows, sheep and goats. A farmer was so removed from her father's trade as a shoe cobbler, as to be totally ridiculous.*

John's emotions seemed to burst out of control and with an exciting pitch to his voice he continued to badger his wife. "I could still cobble shoes if I had a yen to, Maggie, but I've always had a hankering to work the ground, you know that. In Kentucky the land would practically be ours, just for the taking."

"Have you taken leave of all your senses, John? We've got our home here in Charlottesville bought and paid for, so just settle your thoughts!" Margaret's voice steadily rose in volume. "Surely you wouldn't just walk away from all we hold dear here in Charlottesville to go traipsing off into a wilderness that we know absolutely nothing about!"

Margaret was on the verge of tears and Amy could see that her pleas were falling on deaf ears. Her own heart started beating erratically and her eyes narrowed thoughtfully. "Are you really serious about wanting to leave our home here in Charlottesville and move to Kentucky, Pa?" Amy couldn't keep her thoughts to herself one more minute.

Looking at Amy sheepishly and with a slow half-smile softening his face, John replied stoically, "You bet I am, honey, and that's God's truth! I happened to quote a price on our house today and Jim Cobb jumped at the chance to buy it. And better yet, a price well above what we have invested in it." John's comment hung in the air for a moment.

"But I don't want to move away from our house, Pa," Amy interrupted, a flash of wild grief ripping through her. Her hands clenched into tight fists. "I couldn't leave Kristy and Nikki, and especially Grandma and Grandpa Johnson!" Amy tried to swallow a huge painful lump in her throat.

"Amy's right, John," Margaret chimed in. "Amy only has one more year in school and Billy Joe has years of schooling still ahead of him. Our church is right here in Charlottesville, not out in the wilderness, where schools and churches are practically unheard of. And my parents aren't getting any younger, John! I . . . I just couldn't abandon them!" Margaret cried out in anguish.

Amy was in a fit of despair as her mother's voice broke, and tears she had been holding, cascaded down her pale cheeks. She felt an involuntary clutch of fear and glanced helplessly at her father. John was adamant and kept right on pleading, now looking directly into Amy's eyes. "You know your grandma and grandpa wouldn't stand in the way of this family's happiness, don't you, Amy?" John asked reprovingly.

A fast denial sprang to Amy's lips but her father had already turned his attention back to her mother. Her father said gently but firmly, "We'll build our own schools and churches in Kentucky, Maggie, and we'd be taking God with us if we move, you know that."

"But, Pa, there's Indians in the west. You just said so yourself," Amy stated apprehensively and with deep emotion. She glanced at Billy Joe and then back to her father, a faint thread of hysteria in her voice. Unconsciously Amy's brow furrowed, as she queried, "You wouldn't want to take me and Billy Joe out to Kentucky just to be . . . to be scalped, would you?" Fear, stark and vivid, glittered in her eyes.

Smiling indulgently at his daughter John continued speaking as though he hadn't heard a word she said. "Where's your pioneer spirit, Amy?" he asked lamely. Before that question sank in and could be answered, Amy heard her father say in a hushed, almost prayerful tone of voice, "We could leave as early as next month."

John's words fell like hammer blows and as an assault to Amy's ears, so much so that she visibly winced and cried, "Oh, Pa, no!" Her eyes, showing the tortured dullness of her disbelief, knocked Amy back in her chair. Her chest muscles were so tight she could hardly breathe.

Still smiling, John glanced from Margaret to Amy and back to Margaret again. Combing his hair with his fingers John pleaded, "Won't you at least think about it, sweetheart?"

Amy was brushing tears from her eyes when her mother jumped up from the table and rushed into her bedroom, slamming the door behind her, sobs filling the air. Amy winced at the dejected look of helplessness that appeared on her father's face. His eyes brushed hers briefly as he quietly rose from the table and followed his wife into their bedroom.

"Surely Pa isn't serious, is he?" Amy whispered to Billy Joe, as the door to her parents' bedroom closed softly behind her father. She was sober and subdued and cast an imploring glance in Billy Joe's direction. "He . . . he wouldn't take us away from Virginia to go trudging off into the . . . the . . ."

"The wild, wild, west, and miles away from your precious Arnold Drexler?" Billy Joe playfully finished for her while he kept right on eating. He caught his sister's eyes fixed on him with an expression of contempt and disillusionment, and felt for just a brief moment the slightest tinge of remorse for having teased her.

Biting her lip, Amy rose dejectedly from her chair and began to clear the table. "But he just can't do that!" she declared indignantly, not letting the matter drop. "Ma won't let him! And besides," she whined, "he could never make me leave Grandma and Grandpa Johnson!" Amy sniffed and tried to hold back tears that had quickly formed. "I'll simply die if I had to leave Kristy and Nikki. You know that's true, Billy Joe. Pa just can't be serious, can he?" she asked plaintively. Amy looked at her brother for reassurance, her sense of sudden disaster potent and aching within her.

"You're a bird-brain!" Billy Joe drawled in a mocking tone. He rolled his eyes in disgust and brushed the hair from his eyes. "What would it hurt anyway? I think it might be fun and adventuresome living right next door to Daniel Boone! I'm willing to give it a try if that's what Pa wants to do."

Hot tears rolled down Amy's cheeks as she watched Billy Joe reach for another piece of cornbread. He buttered it as he watched Amy out of the corner of his eye. Stuffing the whole piece into his mouth at once he asked sarcastically, "Why don't you act your age and quit being such a crybaby about everything? The problem with you is that you just don't want to leave your beau, Arnold!"

"You . . . you just don't understand!" Amy spoke with quiet, but desperate, firmness. Her fears were stronger than ever and her voice quivered.

"What's there to understand? You're in love with Arnold Drexler and you just can't stand the thought of leaving him."

Stamping her foot, Amy glared at Billy Joe disgustedly. She clenched her fists into knots and cried, "You're *horrid*, Billy Joe Bradshaw, and I *hate* you! I just *absolutely hate you*!" she plunged on carelessly. "Arnold isn't my beau and you know it! I could *never* ever love him, you little beast!" she shouted. Amy immediately chastised herself for screaming at Billy Joe but her little monster of a brother always seemed to bring out the worst in her.

Shrugging his shoulders indifferently, Billy Joe gave Amy a withering glare as hot tears spilled from her eyes and rolled freely down her pale cheeks. Billy Joe was unmoved by her tears, and he turned his back on his sister. "Makes no difference to me how you feel about Arnold," Billy Joe flung over his shoulder. "And just for being so hateful you can do the dishes by yourself!" Billy Joe turned to face a defiant Amy, stuck his tongue out, and ran from the room.

Tremulous thoughts roamed at will through Amy's head as she washed and dried the supper dishes. Of one thing she was certain, she would *never* forgive her father if he took their family away from all they held dear in Charlottesville and led them into a fearful wilderness. Her determination was like a rock inside her.

. . .

That night, lying snug and warm in the deep confines of her goose-down mattress, Amy glanced around her familiar room. The moon was shining through the window glass and cast dancing shadows over the hand-rubbed cherry-wood bed and dresser. It would all have to be left behind: the bedroom furniture, the cheery wallpaper with tiny pink roses that bloomed year round, her favorite rocking chair, and the brightly colored rug her Grandma Johnson had braided for her that covered the white pine flooring.

Tossing and turning that night Amy found herself crying bitterly one minute and praying hard the next. She fancied running away, hiding in her Grandma Johnson's attic, or simply refusing to budge out of the house if her parents chose to move to Kentucky. She fingered the gold heart-shaped locket that Kristy had given her for her twelfth birthday, and that always hung around her neck. Life would not be worth living away from her best friends Kristy and Nikki.

The next morning Amy found to her utter dismay that everything had been decided. Her mother's eyes were red-rimmed and swollen, her head bowed and her shoulders slumped. Listening with unbelieving ears Amy was told of their decision. "It's all settled, honey," Margaret said dejectedly as she stood before the stove, absently stirring a pan of oatmeal. "Heaven help us, but we're leaving Charlottesville the first week in March."

"Oh, *no*! Please tell me you don't *mean* it, Ma!" Amy implored. This is the only home I've ever known and Grandma and Grandpa Johnson live here, and my best friends, Kristy and Nikki!" Gulping, Amy took a fresh breath of air before ranting on. "If Pa takes us into the wilderness to live I know that I shall never see them again! Please, Ma. Please talk to Pa again," she said softly. "You can surely make him change his mind."

"I'm sorry, honey." Margaret set the pan of oatmeal to the back of the stove and turned her glazed eyes toward Amy. She shrugged her shoulders helplessly, walked woodenly to the table and sat down hard on her chair. "I talked to your father last night until I was blue in the face. He is certain this is the right thing to do for this family." Margaret spoke calmly and shook her head regretfully. Her sorrow was a huge painful knot inside of her, and her eyes showed a wretchedness of mind she'd never known before.

Amy's brown eyes darkened like angry thunderclouds as she realized her mother had given in to her father's wishes and that would be the end of it. Without another word, she flew from the kitchen, tears blinding her eyes.

Broken into small, bitter pieces, Amy's dark thoughts tormented her in the days that followed. She shared her grief with her best friends and they held each other and cried. At times Amy would stamp her foot and cry out bitterly, "I shall *never* forgive you, Pa, for what you're doing to us! *Never!*"

CHAPTER 2

"Surely this one small item can't make that much difference, can it, John?" Anxiety flushed Margaret's fair skin and strained her voice.

John shook his head sadly and Margaret reluctantly removed her ecru lace crocheted tablecloth from the 'Wilderness Pile' and placed it on the 'Virginia Pile'. Amy looked at her mother's face as she lovingly fingered the tablecloth. She knew how many hours of work it had taken her mother to crochet it and her heart broke for the harsh decision her father had made in asking her to leave it behind.

Margaret's thoughts were jagged and painful and she had to blink back tears that threatened to fall at any moment as she turned her back on her husband. Her crestfallen face revealed the turmoil that she was still going through. Amy sobered and chewed on her lip, fighting back tears of her own. She knew her effervescent mother loved everybody and she was seldom cross or troubled. Her exceptional magnitude of accepting life's little changes with eagerness and enthusiasm had always been heart-warming up to now. In her mother's defense Amy addressed her father tartly. "I didn't know one little old tablecloth could make that much difference, Pa," she said smartly, picking up the tablecloth from the discard pile and holding it to her breast.

"I'm as sorry as all get-out, Amy, and I know you and your mama feel I'm heartless and unmerciful in my decisions, but you'll see that I'm right, once we're in our new home. I'll be carving our furniture from our very own trees, and all these little necessaries you're so set on taking along, well, I'll try my darndest to make it up to both of you some day—I promise."

"That's easy for you to say, Pa, but you bought a mighty big wagon and two big horses to pull it," Amy muttered uneasily, trying to maintain her curtness. "Why would this one little . . . ?"

"I don't think either one of you are even *trying* to understand what I'm set on doing for this family!" Disappointment rang in John's voice as he cut his daughter off in mid sentence. He sighed, weary of the arguments. His voice sounded hallow and his usually lively eyes were dark and unfathomable as he said sharply, "There's lots of things I'd like to tote along to Kentucky too, but you have to remember that once we get to Martin's Station, we'll be leaving our wagon behind. What we pack now will have to be carried on our backs a mighty long way. I'm just trying to be sensible," John said, his brows drawn together in an agonized expression. "Somebody in this family has to be."

Amy flinched at the tone of her father's voice and was instantly contrite. She swallowed hard and said apologetically, "I'm sorry, Pa. I'm just not thinking. It's still such a shock to me to even be thinking about leaving Charlottesville that I've not tried to see your side of it. I know you wouldn't do anything to harm our family and . . ."

Quickly dropping the tablecloth Amy ran to her father. She put her arms around his waist and hugged him tightly. John lovingly patted her on the back and returned her hug. Amy looked up into his eyes that flickered with pain and said softly, "I promise, Pa, that from now on I'll do my very best to help you and not hinder your plans. And I'll not pack anything that I just don't absolutely have to have. Cross my heart."

"Thanks, honey," John said simply. "Don't think for a minute that I don't feel some regrets and recriminations about attempting such a move. Taking my family away from all that is near and dear to their hearts isn't coming easy for me. But I've prayed long and hard about my decisions and feel like the Lord is leading me to step out in faith for a brighter future for all of us." He sighed and kissed Amy on the forehead, and gave her another tight squeeze.

Releasing her, John pulled his gold watch from the pocket of his shirt and asked evenly, "Either one of you want to come with me to the meeting at the schoolhouse? Sam's supposed to be there about four o'clock and he's going to be answering questions about the drive to Kentucky."

Glancing expectantly at her mother, Amy saw her shake her head and frown. "I'm sure you can think of enough questions to ask for the two of us, John. I've got my hands full right here." Margaret stared at the chaos before her, a grim expression on her face and fatigue settling in pockets under her eyes.

"Would you mind terribly if I tagged along with Pa?" Amy asked hesitantly. "I'd like to see who all is planning on making this trip with us."

"Fine with me, honey," Margaret said softly, her energy flagging. "You've been helping me for hours and I know you're just as sick of it as I am. You go along now and enjoy yourself. I'll just keep sorting for awhile yet." Margaret's mouth curved into an unconscious smile, but her eyes were unresponsive.

Running to her mother, Amy planted a kiss on her cheek. Turning to her father she said, "Just let me get my cloak and muff, Pa." A smile played across Amy's mouth. "Billy Joe will be mad as a wet hornet when he comes home and finds we've gone without him."

John chuckled knowingly as Amy ran to get her cloak. He put his arms around Margaret and whispered soberly against her hair, "Please don't be cross with me, sweetheart. I won't be gone long. And if Billy Joe comes home and sets up a howl, just send him on down to the schoolhouse."

・・・

Amy's expressive brown eyes sparkled like diamonds as she

and her father entered the cavernous one-room schoolhouse that smelled of varnish, wood smoke and chalk. "Have you made up your mind for sure that you're goin'?" Howard Tippett asked as he walked up to John and Amy in the crowded schoolroom.

John's mind was a crazy mixture of hope and fear and his face was clouded with uneasiness as he faced Howard. He straightened his shoulders and cleared his throat. "My wife and daughter have sorted and packed for three solid weeks, Howie, and I've resorted and repacked so many times all our heads are swimming. I've got an eleven-year-old at home that seems to think Daniel Boone is just waiting for him to reach the western frontier and help him settle the land that lies over the mountains." John removed his hat and scratched his head. "I'm afraid if I didn't go now I'd be in a whale of a lot of trouble from him." John's face melted into a buttery smile.

Howard snickered and shook his head. "Know what you mean, John. My wife was dead set against our goin' at first, but the longer I talked about it the more the idea grew on her. Our kids are too young yet to realize where we're goin', but that's about all they've talked about for weeks now."

John looked a little dubious and exclaimed, "I just wish I knew for certain that I'm doing the right thing, Howie." He looked down at Amy and then back to Howard. "Are you sure your brother can find his way back across the mountains?"

Howard grinned and patted John reassuringly on the shoulder. "Don't you fret yourself about Sam none. His family is waitin' for him back in Kentucky and he'll get us there, as sure as God makes little green apples," Howard said confidently. "And don't you fret yourself none either, little lady," Howard said, giving Amy one of his engaging smiles. "Most girls your age would give their eye teeth for a chance to do what you're goin' to be doin'."

Glancing over his shoulder Howard exclaimed, "Here comes Sam now, and from the looks of him, I'd say he's primed and rarin' to go!"

A giant of a man, dressed in fringed hunting shirt and deerskin leggings, filled the doorway with his massive frame. Amy was awed by the size of him. He was strongly handsome, she thought, and she liked the way he carried himself with a commanding air of self-confidence. His powerful, well-muscled body moved with an easy grace as he walked quickly to the front of the room, his heels drumming a quick tattoo on the bare floor boards. His piercing blue eyes swept quickly about the room and he seemed pleased that so many people had come.

Every eye was on Sam as he folded his arms across his chest and leaned against Mr. Freeland's desk. "The good Lord willing, I'll be leaving Charlottesville for Kentucky in a week." Sam's voice rang with command.

A loud murmur arose, but the gabble of voices soon stilled as Sam continued speaking. "From all the talk I've heard, I believe the general feeling among you is that Kentucky is the Garden of Eden—the Promised Land, so to speak. Well, that's my gut feeling too," he said, his voice crisp and clear. "The land *is* generous, but not without toil. And I will be the first to remind you that it's also a bloody wilderness, full of roving Indians and thieving and conniving land speculators. The only way Kentucky can be turned into a Garden of Eden is by the sweat of our brows!"

"Gad, Sam, sounds to me like you're tryin' to prejudice us agin our goin' to Kentucky, not promotin' it," a man in the front row of seats quickly interjected. Amy stood on tiptoe and strained to see over the person standing directly in front of her. She didn't know the gentleman who had spoken, but the tone of his voice seemed warm and friendly enough.

Sam smiled down at the man and said in a matter-of-fact tone of voice, "I assure you my good man that was not my intention. But I would be remiss not to warn all of you right up front of the dangers involved in an expedition such as I'm contemplating. During the past two years I've lived in Kentucky, we've had no Indian trouble to speak of in my valley. But I do want to remind all of you that the Cherokee and Shawnee, among other Indian tribes, laid claim to this rich land long ago, and are still fierce in their determination to keep their hunting grounds."

Icy fear twisted around Amy's heart and she shivered just

thinking about the dangers they may be walking into. Her father was standing right behind her, his hands on her shoulders and she knew he had felt her unease because he squeezed her shoulders gently.

"The Shawnee were defeated back in the fall of '74 and signed a treaty saying they would stay north of the Ohio and no longer hunt in Kentucky," Sam continued. "But whether they will abide by this treaty is anybody's guess. Times could change and troubles could be a'plenty. Congress has barred further settlement north of the Ohio river and has told us that we can't take up arms against the Indians, except to defend ourselves within our own borders. If they harry us, we can call in the Militia, but we dare not cross the Ohio on the north or the Tennessee on the south to invade Indian towns in retaliation. It's my gut feeling from what I can piece together that the Indians understand our dilemma and they will at some time or another seize the opportunity to harry us."

"What route you fixin' to be takin' to reach this wilderness?" Amy looked behind her and saw that Thornton Decker, a young man who worked at the livery stable south of town, had posed the question. Thornton was six-feet tall and his massive shoulders filled the coat he wore. His piercing blue eyes dominated a face bronzed by wind and sun; his shock of flaming red hair reached to his collar. Well educated, Thornton knew daylight from dark and he was known as a peaceful man who wanted no trouble and made none. He held by the Good Book and attended the Methodist church that Amy's family did.

She was excited to think that perhaps he was entertaining thoughts of going to Kentucky.

Sam smiled. "Many people say taking a boat down the Ohio is the only way to go, but I have my own feelings about that. Even though the Wilderness Road is not one hundred percent safe from attack, I believe it is a far safer route to be taking at this time. I've made two trips so far with no problems whatsoever."

Clearing his throat, Sam said seriously, "Since the area I've claimed is not too thickly settled as yet and the land lies pretty far from the nearest fort or village, it could still be risky. So if you have any doubts about taking your family into the wilderness, now's the time to air those doubts or drop your notion of going altogether."

"I venture we've all taken risks in this life, Sam," his brother Howard countered. "Just getting out of bed in the morning poses a slight risk, I dare say." Amy laughed along with everyone else at Howard's jesting.

"Where's this land of yours to be found?" someone else called out.

"I'm located on the Green River in a valley rimmed in by hills. Never have I seen a land so lush or so bounteous. It has a blue-green carpet of thick, luxurious grass stretched over the richest and the blackest soil I've ever seen. It stretches in every direction as far as you can see. There are trees of every description and numerous rivers and streams. Deep springs are abundant and the breezes blow ever so soft and sweet day and night..."

Amy heard the longing in Sam's voice and was convinced that he was thinking about his family that was waiting for him back in Kentucky. She smiled knowingly and shook her head when Sam threw back his head and laughed. "Excuse me, folks. For awhile there I found myself back home with my family." The women all nodded their heads in understanding and Amy felt that Sam had endeared himself to every one of them.

"The title to my land is unquestionably clear and I'm willing to sell the families that go back with me a hundred acres each," Sam said, the warmth of his smile, echoing in his voice. "There will be more to buy if and when you decide you will remain in my settlement."

"What's the charge for this land of yours?" a voice rang out.

"Forty dollars a hundred—just what I paid for it. My interest is getting a settlement started, not in profiting off the land I've bought."

"Seems fair to me," his brother Howard called out, and the crowd cheered heartily.

"When did you say you were leaving, Mr. Tippett, and what's the best way to travel?" Amy was happy to find that her father had finally found his tongue.

"My plans are to head out next Monday morning," Sam answered quickly.

"Those that plan to go with me should be at the southwest edge of town in line and ready to roll at first light. A wagon pulled by mules, horses or oxen is a must, especially for those of you with little children. However, the wagons will have to be ditched at Martin's Station. From there on in to Kentucky there's no wagon road, and what supplies you'll be taking into the wilderness will have to be toted on your back or on pack animals."

Her father's wise words came back to haunt Amy, but she had no time to dwell on it because her father had posed another question. She listened intently to all that her father said. "Any items in particular my family will be needing that perhaps I haven't thought of, Mr. Tippett?"

"Let me see now," Sam said, rubbing his chin between thumb and forefinger. "A tent comes in mighty handy, especially for folks who don't hanker to be sleeping out under the stars for the next few months. I imagine you'll want your kids taking up all the sleeping room in the wagons. As for guns and ammunition, take the best and plenty of it. I can't stress this fact enough. Our very lives may depend on how well armed we all are."

There were nods and comments of approval from everyone in the room. "You'll need a keg for carrying your drinking water and iron cookware," Sam continued. "Take metal plates and cups. Axes, shovels and plenty of rope are a must. You'll need proper tools for tending your crops but remove the metal from your plow and crosscut saw and just pack them along. You can make new handles and wooden parts once you're in Kentucky. A family with children should take their schoolbooks, as there'll be plenty of time for book learning on the way."

Sam scratched his head and sighed. "Might be your heads are swimming right now thinking of all the paraphernalia I'm telling you to be toting along. Just use your heads and cut out all the extras."

"Reckon we'll be eating off the land most of the way won't we, Sam?" Howard interjected.

Sam laughed. "We'll find wild life a plenty, little brother, but I'm still encouraging you to pack non-perishable food aplenty: sugar, flour, cornmeal, salt, dried fruit, beans, corn and vinegar. Salt pork would taste mighty good on the trail, too, and keeps well."

"How many womenfolk are there back in your valley, Mr. Tippett?" A strong voice drifted back to those standing at the rear and Amy strained to hear every word the woman spoke.

Sam looked down upon a woman sitting on the front bench. Amy couldn't see who it was from where she stood at the back of the room, but she could hear the woman's voice and thought it sounded familiar.

Giving the woman a smile, Sam asked, "You are . . . ?"

"Ruby Myrtle Willis," the woman said, her voice carrying very nicely throughout the room. "And this is my husband, Roscoe Thomas."

Amy turned to her father and whispered excitedly, "That's Reverend Willis and his wife, Pa! Do you suppose they're intending to go to Kentucky?"

"Could be," her father answered softly.

"Wait until Ma hears about this!" Amy said excitedly. John laughed good-naturedly.

"There are fifteen families already homesteading in my valley, Mrs. Willis," Sam said pleasantly. "My wife, Abigail, and our three children are counted among them. Are you thinking of becoming one of us?"

Ruby found it impossible not to return Sam's disarming smile. "My dear husband and I were privileged to meet John and Charles Wesley many long years ago, and consequently Roscoe has been in a Methodist pulpit nigh on forty years now. It's been his dream to share God's Word with those who live on the other side of the mountains before the good Lord calls him home: white, black or red. He just never knew the day would come when he would actually be able to fulfill that dream." Sam nodded his head thoughtfully.

"My husband is blind, Mr. Tippett. I want to set you straight on that, but it makes him no less of a man. A finer gentleman or harder worker, you'll not find in a man of the cloth on God's green earth."

"There, there, now, my dear," Roscoe said lightly. "Might I have a chance to speak on my own behalf?" Everybody laughed good-naturedly, including Ruby, as Roscoe spoke up. "If you're not thinking we'd be too old for the journey, young man, or a hindrance in your travels, we'd be obliged to tag along."

"The way I see it, Reverend Willis, there's folks that's young at eighty and folks that's old at thirty. If you were of a mind to settle down next to my brood and me, we'd be purely honored," Sam said humbly. Those nearest Roscoe pounded him on the back.

"You men be sure and look favorably on your women. Make sure your missus has a little room for her yard goods, needles and thread, her linens and flower seeds. We want to keep our women contented." Sam looked down at Ruby Willis and winked broadly.

"Another thing," Sam said, swiping at a beading of perspiration on his forehead, "tote your medicine along. Minor irritations will consist mostly of blisters, ticks, fleas, chiggers and mosquitoes. Just so you're prepared for the worst, but not necessarily expecting it. I'll not tolerate a drunkard in the bunch, but it wouldn't hurt none to have a little whiskey on hand. Best thing to mix with honey for a cough and it's a good remedy for snake bite."

"Are we free to take our livestock, Sam?" Howard inquired.

"Good question, little brother. You folks will certainly want to bring your cows along to provide the children with fresh milk. Extra mules, horses, sheep and goats can go, but everyone pulls his own weight and will be responsible for his own wagon and livestock. You men will be expected to take your turn standing watch of a night, too. I want no fighting and squabbling amongst us. You have a disagreement about something that affects us all, you bring it to me. Just remember to go light on perishables and no heavy furniture or frills. You'll have to be practical; I'm insistent on that."

"What's the procedure if we do meet up with Indians, Mr. Tippett?" Amy had wondered the same thing and was glad her father had posed the question. "If we're attacked by Indians, we all fight—men, women and every boy and girl who can aim and shoot straight. But only on my say so. I don't want any hothead shooting at every little phantom or shadow. I hope you men will have time to show your women how to load and shoot by the time we leave. And in case you're wondering, when we stop for the night, the lead wagon goes to the end of the line. It's the fair way that we all take turns at eating dust. Any more questions?"

Hearing none, Sam smiled broadly. "Before you leave, I'd be obliged to have you sign my register with names and ages of everyone in your family that is planning to go along. Oh, and one thing more. We won't be traveling on the Lord's day. There'll be repairs to be made and chores to do, but we take our rest on Sundays, as much as for our animals as for ourselves. If you want to know where you'll be hanging your hat, I call my Kentucky valley New Hope. Anything comes up between now and next Monday, you can find me at my brother's place." Sam walked behind Mr. Freeland's desk and proceeded to greet each person in turn as they signed his register.

John felt like he had been run through the mill, and his head was swimming with everything he had seen and heard. "Never figured moving could be so complicated, Howie," John said lightly after signing Sam's register. "But the Lord has laid my pathway straight and clear and in it I intend to walk. And that's God's truth!"

Howard slapped John on the back and winked at Amy as they walked out of the schoolhouse together. "Our days are numbered, John. The sap's gonna rise and our hopes will become certainties!" Howard laughed richly. "If you need help with anything this week, partner," he said jovially, "just holler!"

Amy's heart quickened. Her father was smiling again and her heart, for days bound deep within her chest now broke free and soared.

CHAPTER 3

Sunday, March 2, dawned cold and blustery with heavy black clouds tumbling across the sky, blocking out the sun. After church Amy visited one last time with her friends, Kristy and Nikki, her mood perfectly befitting the bleak day that stretched before her. While she chatted with her friends, Margaret and John said their own sad farewells to their church family before going to the Johnson home to spend the night. Billy Joe strutted around the churchyard like a cocky rooster, parlaying with friends and joking about joining up with Daniel Boone and helping him settle the entire country west of the Alleghenies.

That night after supper John and his family settled in the front parlor of Margaret's parents' home for what they knew could be the last time. John sat on the green velvet seat next to Margaret, all of his conversations starting with "when we get to Kentucky," and ending with "after we're in Kentucky." William Johnson rocked gently to and fro, listening politely to every word his son-in-law uttered, his eyes sharp and assessing. Billy Joe sat in his Grandma Pearl's wooden rocking chair with the ecru crocheted covers on back and arms, the sandy shock of hair so like his father's, tumbling over his forehead. Amy sat on the green brocade divan, attached to her Grandma Johnson's ample frame like a burr.

Pearl's face, indicative of a weather vane, showed clearly in every line the grief she was feeling. Amy breathed deeply of the delicate breath of lavender as it floated in the room about her, mingling with the many sweet and subtly individual odors that dwelled in her grandparents' home. Closing her eyes she prayed fervently that even now God might somehow provide a miracle, preventing her father from whisking them all away from these familiar surroundings, into a vast unknown country laying to the west.

"Billy Joe, I have a favor to ask of you." Everyone's eyes focused on William and Amy was all ears as she heard her grandfather's deep resounding voice addressing her brother. She despaired at how old and haggard he looked, but marveled at his calmness when he spoke.

"Yes, Grandpa?" Billy Joe looked into his grandpa's eyes and quirked his eyebrows questioningly.

"I'd like for you to take my paint, Foxy, with you to Kentucky. Without you around to ride him, he wouldn't be worth a plug nickel to me. Do you think you could handle that?"

Rapture showed plainly on Billy Joe's face and Amy had to smile when she saw it light up like a jar full of fireflies. Billy Joe went flying across the room and threw himself into his Grandpa Johnson's waiting arms for a strong hug. "I don't know what to say, Grandpa. I . . . I . . ."

"That's a first, I must say," Amy quipped. "I never knew you to be at a loss for words before!" Billy Joe turned to his sister and stuck out his tongue.

Amy paid Billy Joe no mind as her grandfather turned his full attention upon her. She couldn't believe her good fortune when he said, "I would be honored if you would accept my mare, Midnight Belle, Amy, to be your very own. And I pray she will carry you in grand style into your new homeland."

Jumping up, Amy ran to her grandfather, fell on her knees, and put her head in his lap, tears blinding her. Her misery was so acute that it was a physical pain within.

William sighed heavily, his voice filled with anguish as he tried to comfort Amy. "There, there, now my child," he said gravely. "I didn't mean to make you cry."

Lifting her head, Amy looked gravely into her grandfather's dearly beloved face. *How,* she wondered, *can I ever live without his presence in my life?*

"You're an experienced rider, Amy, and I know I can trust you to love Belle and care for her as I have tried to do the past four years. You will do that for your old Grandpa, won't you?"

"I would be so proud to have Midnight Belle as my very own, Grandpa. I will love and care for her always, but I know how... how very much you love her and...."

"Then it's all settled. Take her with my love and blessing." Unbidden tears ran down William's wrinkled cheeks.

Amy was startled when her mother suddenly burst into tears and ran from the room, her grandmother following close at her heels.

"What's wrong with everybody?" Billy Joe asked in bewilderment, looking toward his father for an explanation of everyone's tears.

John's misery was like a steel weight in his chest. Floundering in an agonizing maelstrom, he looked at Billy Joe and put his finger to his mouth and shook his head sadly. He felt a warm surge of sympathy for his aging father-in-law.

Biting her lip, Amy buried her face in her grandpa's lap once more as her father walked over and grasped William's trembling hands in his own.

John's face was tightly drawn, his broad shoulders slumped, and his eyes were filled with pain. There had always been a special bond of love and friendship flowing between the two men, and Amy was relieved to know that it was as strong as ever. Knowing how her own heart was breaking at the thought of leaving her wonderful grandparents, she realized for the first time that it wasn't going to be easy for her father either, and she felt his pain as warm tears stung her eyes.

. . .

The March wind hurried over the mountains with the leafless trees offering little restraint. There was a definite nip in the air and heavy frost covered the white canvas tops of the wagons. As daylight strengthened, so did the birdsong, as every bird in every tree in Charlottesville seemed to be singing. The sparrows and the slate-colored Juncos sang as though it were the first dawn that ever was and they must celebrate.

The departure from family and friends for Amy and her family had been a very heart-wrenching scene of tearful communings and painful embraces. When their wagon pulled away from her grandparents' home, Amy closed her eyes to the agonizing scene of her grandmother and grandfather huddled together on their front porch, their arms entwined, valiantly waving as the Bradshaws' wagon passed out of sight.

A great tide of responsibility rolled over Sam Tippett as he sat astride his massive sorrel gelding and watched solemnly as wagon after wagon load of men, women and children took their places in line with surprising little confusion. Lanterns bobbed in the predawn chill. Each family had their belongings strapped to pack animals and bunched tightly into carts and wagons. There were dogs, cows, goats, sheep, mules and horses, and a few families had brought crates of hens, roosters, geese and ducks, strapping them to their wagons.

At precisely six o'clock Sam put his gold watch into his vest pocket, lifted his hand above his head, wheeled his horse and called loudly over his shoulder: "Let 'em roll!"

John's voice drifted upon the frigid air as he cracked his whip and cried, "Git up, Duchess! Git up, Dolly!" Amy was only faintly aware of the horses' hoofbeats as they lumbered past the smiling, waving onlookers standing in small clusters along the roadsides. Shadows were chill and deep as the wagons rolled past the last farmhouse at the southwest edge of Charlottesville. Suddenly Margaret cried out. She pressed her face against John's shoulder and bitterly sobbed out her grief and frustration.

Amy felt utterly miserable as grief and despair tore at her own heart. Her eyes filled with tears and she put her hands over her ears hoping to keep out the sound of her mother's heartbreak, as icy fingers seeped into every pore of her trembling body.

Long minutes later she wiped the tears from her eyes and blew her nose. She sat silent and withdrawn while Billy Joe chattered like a magpie at her side.

Amy was only vaguely aware of all the strange sounds that filled the wagon as they slowly ate up the miles, plodding uphill and down. Little by little, warmth crept back into her body and likewise, Margaret's tears were finally spent. She sat stiff as a board on the seat beside John, not saying a word.

Billy Joe was up and then he was down checking on Foxy and Midnight Belle, tied behind their wagon with lead ropes. His constant jabbering had Amy sorely vexed. A few miles out of town Amy heard a familiar lament, when Billy Joe asked for about the tenth time, "When can I ride Foxy, Pa?"

Giving Billy Joe a hostile glare, Amy couldn't believe how indulgent her father was with him when John answered patiently, "I've told you, Billy Joe, a dozen times or more, you have to wait until Foxy's used to the noise and confusion around him. I don't want him running off with you first thing. So please just settle down back there and behave yourself."

"Yes, Pa." Billy Joe answered glumly, but obediently, much to Amy's surprise.

The constant rumble of wagon wheels, the clip clop of horses' hooves and the swaying of the wagon had soon hypnotized Amy and she felt herself drifting into sleep.

The sun's warmth had begun to beat back the frigid forces and Billy Joe was livelier than ever. Suddenly Amy was rudely awakened when Billy Joe leaned down close to her ear and shouted, "Indians!"

A shadow of annoyance crossed Amy's face as Billy Joe doubled over with laughter. She found a perverse pleasure in hearing him shriek in pain as she reached out and grabbed a fistful of hair in one hand and pulled—hard.

"Try to get along now, kids," John said firmly. "We've a long way to go today and I have no intention of listening to your scrapping all the way."

"Billy Joe started it," Amy complained.

"Did not!" Billy Joe answered defensively.

"You did too, you little dim-witted brat! Take that!" Amy grabbed another hunk of hair and Billy Joe let out another blood-curdling scream.

Sudden anger lit Margaret's eyes. She turned around on the wagon seat and glared at both Amy and Billy Joe. "Stop your nonsense this instant!" she shouted, much to everyone's surprise. "I will not tolerate another ounce of behavior such as the two of you have just demonstrated! Just because your father has a rambling fever to take this family into the wilderness to live side-by-side with uncivilized heathen savages, gives you no right to act uncivilized!"

Appalled at the sound of anger in her mother's voice, Amy stared with unbelieving eyes and ears. She had never heard her mother use that tone of voice with them before. She cringed and moved as far away from Billy Joe as she could get in the crowded wagon bed and burst into fresh tears of her own. Sobbing uncontrollably Amy was further devastated when she heard her mother say with a voice of authority to her father, "Stop this wagon this instant, John William Bradshaw!"

Margaret gave her husband a hostile glare as he pulled hard on the reins and hollered, "Whoa, Duchess! Whoa, Dolly!" Margaret gathered her skirts in one hand and although struggling a bit, managed to step down from the wagon without help. She pulled her shawl tightly about her shoulders and started walking along the trail with a determined step, head down.

Amy was shocked at the depth of her mother's feelings, and had no idea what she had in mind, but something told her that she and Billy Joe had been way out of line. But Billy Joe always brought out the mulish worst in her. Rising to her feet, she carefully made her way to the back of the wagon where she knelt down on the wooden planks of the wagon. She craned her neck as far out of the wagon as she could so she could watch her mother.

"Isn't Ma coming with us to Kentucky, Pa?" Billy Joe wailed.

A tumble of confused thoughts and feelings assailed Amy at the sound of fear in her brother's voice and her own head swirled with doubts. John clucked to the horses and snapped the reins.

"Don't you fret about your ma, son. She just needs to stretch her limbs awhile. Why don't you crawl up here and keep your old pa company; give Amy more room to stretch out in. We've a piece to go today, but when we stop for the nooning maybe you and Amy can ride your horses for awhile."

Billy Joe brushed at his tears and grinned widely at Amy before making a B-line to the front of the wagon. As far as he was concerned their scuffle was forgotten.

The sky was a fresh-water blue and the land slightly rolling, looping gracefully through alternating stretches of woodland and open fields. The horses kept up a steady plodding gait, kicking up red dust swirls with every step they took. Amy had a strong desire to get out of the wagon and walk with her mother, but she was afraid her mother wouldn't welcome her company. So she stayed in the back of the wagon where she could keep a close watch on every step her mother took.

Margaret looked so dejected walking all alone, her heels digging into the hard rough ground, and Amy was moved to bow her head and pray that her mother's anger and heartache would soon fade.

It was a wonderful day for traveling Margaret decided. Gratefully she looked up at the sky, now dotted with fat clouds reminding her of downy white geese floating on a clear blue lake. The warm rays of the sun felt good beaming down on her head and shoulders, and she drew in deep draughts of fresh air as she walked briskly in the wake of her family's wagon. She murmured softly to herself: "This is the day that the Lord has made, and I will rejoice and be glad in it." She smiled and glanced skyward again. "I know that you make them all, dear Lord," she whispered, "but it seems that you make some days a whole lot better than others."

Deep in thought, Amy kneeled on her knees at the back of the wagon, and studied her mother's face unhurriedly as she walked resolutely behind the wagon. *She is so beautiful,* Amy thought. Amy had always been told that she had her mother's eyes and she had accepted those comments as a compliment. Her mother's eyes had always flaunted her emotions: teasing and taunting one moment, angry and piqued the next and then tender in an instant.

With her knees aching from kneeling on the hard wooden flooring of the wagon, Amy sat down and leaned her back against the tailgate. She was perplexed by her mother's earlier outburst, but was satisfied with a certainty that her mother's heartache over leaving Virginia would heal in time, just as her own would.

Suddenly Amy was jolted from her reverie as the wagon directly ahead of them came to a grinding halt and her father pulled his own horses up short. Amy heard a husky voice call out a friendly greeting to her father as the two wagons pulled along side of each other. "Howdy, neighbor. Nice day to be up and about!"

"That it is," John answered with a smile.

Amy quickly crept back up to the front of the wagon so that she could see to whom her father was speaking. She was quite impressed with the man's clean, light look and friendly voice. "My name's Theodore Carpenter," he said smiling, "and this here's my wife, Kitty." Kitty Carpenter was as plump and firm as a partridge and she had a friendly smile that defined the dimples in her plump cheeks.

John tipped his hat. "Pleased to meet you, Theodore. Ma'am."

As Margaret approached the two wagons John quickly made his own introductions. "John Bradshaw here and that beautiful young woman in the yellow sunbonnet is my wife, Margaret. This young scalawag is our son, Billy Joe," John said, ruffling Billy Joe's mop of unruly hair. And to Amy's delight her father said proudly, "The beautiful young lady in back of me is our daughter, Amy."

Smiling broadly, Amy's interest picked up when she heard Mr. Carpenter say with a note of pride, "Our son Matthew is riding at the head of the line. He's eighteen and wanted to watch Sam and learn just what a wagon-train master does all day long."

The families exchanged a few more pleasantries and then Theodore clucked to his horses and slapped them gently with the reins. Amy gave a sigh of contentment as she watched the Carpenter wagon move out slowly ahead of them.

Satisfaction pursed John's mouth and he said, "Billy Joe, time you was getting in back. I'd venture to say we're about to pick up a stray."

Billy Joe obediently hopped into the back of the wagon and Amy sent a swift prayer heavenward as her father patted the empty seat beside him. Grinning mischievously John said, "Could I interest you in a ride, ma'am? Be more than obliged to take you in exchange for the cranky gal I lost over an hour ago."

Joy bubbled in Amy's breast and shone in her dark eyes as she watched her mother scramble aboard the wagon and lean over and kiss her father on the cheek. Amy couldn't help but overhear her mother's soft whisper, "Forgive me?"

"I wouldn't have sense enough to crack a walnut if I couldn't forgive a handsome woman such as yourself now, would I?" her father exclaimed with intense pleasure.

Breathing a sigh of relief, Amy sent a quick prayer of thankfulness heavenward. She knew the heartache her mother was feeling—she felt it too. But a spirit of adventure was building slowly but surely within her breast and she was now looking beyond the simple comforts of home and family in Charlottesville; beyond the greening, reviving tobacco land; beyond the hickories, the mountain laurel and ferns. With a heart full of love and hope for the future—Amy looked beyond spring.

CHAPTER 4

Ben Grier, dressed in a coarse cotton shirt and baggy broadcloth breeches, opened his cabin door and shivered in the pre-dawn chill of the day. Ben was over six feet tall with powerfully built muscles, large hands and feet and a short broad nose. His mahogany colored skin glowed smooth as satin and his thick lips parted over large white teeth in a deep yawn.

He had awakened before dawn's first spangled streaks had lit the eastern skies. Once awake, he heaved a vast sigh, flung back the light cover and swung his feet over the side of his cornhusk mattress. He yawned and ran his hands through the curly black stubble of hair on his head and dressed quickly. There was work to be done and the sun was due to pop over the mountains at any minute. He shivered in the dawn chill, closed the door softly behind him, and walked out into the yard. He felt the indefinable pulse of March that touched the hillside and the verdant woodland. His legs and back were stiff and sore from the previous day's toil, and he worked the muscles in his lower back gently with his hands as he walked toward the small roped-in area that held his livestock: one skinny black and white cow and one doe-eyed, floppy-eared mule.

Faint sounds of neighing and the pounding of horses' hooves reached his ears. He quickly turned, cocked his head to one side and gasped as he saw three hooded riders, blazing torches held high over their heads, bearing down through the brush toward his cabin.

Sudden fear flashed in Ben's obsidian eyes, and panic welled in his throat. A paralyzing fear gripped him but before he could react, the men were upon him. One of the riders gave out with a whoop of triumph. "He's come out to greet us, fellas! Fancy that!"

Rough hands and burly arms seized Ben, pinioning his arms behind his back. He twisted and wrenched, trying to free himself. A shot rang out. Ben fully expected to feel the sting of hot lead, but one look toward the corral, as his cow slowly slumped to the ground, blood pouring from a hole between her eyes, assured him the bullet hadn't been meant for him.

At the sound of gunfire, Ben's wife appeared in the cabin door, fear, stark and vivid, glittering in her jet black eyes. She was a tiny woman, almost child-like in appearance. Her face was delicately profiled: eyes wide set, nose straight and finely nostriled, lips full and coffee-brown skin under a close skullcap of black wool. Seeing the hooded men she whispered faintly, "Lord, hep us."

"Git back inside, Gilda!" Ben screamed, struggling once again to free himself from the strong arms that held him captive. Immediately he felt a strong blow to the back of his head. His spine turned to jelly as he slumped to his knees, pain and dizziness engulfing him.

Flying to his side, clad only in a thin and faded cotton gown, Gilda flung her arms about Ben, tremors shaking her whole body. Her mouth was tight and grim as she glared with hate-filled eyes at their hooded intruders. Sourness rose in the pit of her stomach as fearful images built in her mind.

Slowly and painfully Ben struggled to his feet as sick fear boiled in his stomach. His mouth was dry and he felt as though the top of his skull would burst. Ben gasped, his voice thick and unsteady, a wave of apprehension sweeping through him. "Wha . . . what you fellas want?"

"We want rid of you, black man!" one man cried contemptuously. He jabbed his torch at the two frightened people trembling before him, and guffawed cruelly as they drew back in alarm. The stranger's voice hardened ruthlessly. "We don't cotton to your kind around here, understand?"

Ben's whole body was taut and the cords stood out in his neck. "But I's a free man. Got my papers t'prove it. Signed by Mr. Jefferson hisself. The law done changed last year, surely you done heard 'bout it. It was plumb legal for my master to set me free."

"Set free! Bah!" The man spit a stream of brown tobacco juice on Ben's bare feet, swiped his sleeve across his lips and sneered, "Settin' you free just made you elegant and uppity, sounds to me like!"

Ben quickly positioned himself between Gilda and the menacing trio. "But what'll you have me do? This's my home. Built it with my own two hands. Ain't intendin' t'bother nobody."

"You bother me by just livin' in these parts!" the man spat, his voice exact and cold as steel.

Desperation rang in Ben's voice as he begged and pleaded. "But Mr., I got me a chance to smithy...."

"The only thing you got a chance to do is get that mangy beast harnessed up to that buckboard and head out. You got five minutes or we're goin' to have us a little hangin' party. Ain't that right, fellas?"

The other two men laughed. It was not a happy sound. There was a deep-toned threat in its depths and Ben's blood pulsed fast in fear. Taking a step in their direction, Ben extended his hands in desperation. One of the hooded men struck him on the cheek with the butt end of his gun, drawing blood. "Four minutes," he barked harshly.

Leaping upward, Gilda clawed at the man's covered face and beat wildly upon his chest with all her might. Her eyes were blinded by tears and fury choked her voice as she cried out, "No! No! No!"

She was halted by an iron grip on her wrists. "Better watch it, little gal," the man said coldly as his fingers dug into her soft flesh. "I don't take kindly to strangers touchin' me—male or female!" He twisted her arms cruelly, then roughly thrust her away from him.

Dusting off his hands he raked her with cold, gray eyes. Turning, he mounted his horse and loped toward his two friends who had started riding toward the cabin, brandishing their torches.

Gasping, Gilda's body stiffened in shock. "Ben!" she screamed. "Hattie Lou an' little Arliss are still sleepin'!"

Gilda's warning cry stirred Ben to action. He ran to the cabin door, leaped to his daughter's pallet and snatched the sleeping child up in his arms. Running to the cradle beside his own straw mattress, he grabbed up his sleeping son and rushed back outside. "Grab what you can!" he cried as he ran toward the buckboard with two very frightened and screaming children held tightly, one under each arm.

Ben made several frantic trips into the burning cabin in a fruitless effort to save all his worldly possessions. He was only vaguely aware of the sound of the crackling flames and the stench of smoke in his nostrils as he labored.

The roaring grew louder in his ears and his lungs slowly filled with smoke as the flames ate their way up the walls and into the roof beams. Gasping and struggling for breath, Ben and Gilda had to finally admit defeat. They stood back and watched helplessly as the greedy flames ate their home and the contents that they hadn't had time to salvage. In just minutes all their dreams lay dying in the smoldering ashes before them.

Carelessly pulling off his sweat-stained shirt, streaked with blood and soot, Ben tossed it into the glowing embers. His muscular shoulders and stocky torso shone like burnished copper in the light from the fire. His face was swollen and already a purplish bruise was showing on one cheekbone and blood ran from the edges of a cut on his forehead.

There was a salty taste in his mouth as he absently raised his arm and wiped away streams of blood and sweat as they ran down his face. Beside him Gilda sobbed brokenly. Smothering a groan, Ben licked his thick, dark lips and reached out and clutched Gilda to him. Slowly they turned their backs on what was once their home, and walked toward their frightened, still sobbing children.

. . .

The wagons rolled to a stop beside a small creek for the noon meal. The day had grown mild and the sun's warmth was welcome. John and Billy Joe quickly unyoked their animals and led them to water, and Amy helped her mother prepare a cold dinner. While they rested they gobbled their food, hardly taking time to chew. Dogs were barking, young children were running about laughing and shouting, and babies cried or lay sleeping in boxes or crates in the wagons.

Sam watered his gelding and then hobbled him for grazing while he took a quick stroll through the encampment, answering questions and checking on each family.

"Harness is too tight, Howie," Sam said as he saw his brother struggling with one of his mules. Sam reached out and loosened the leather that was binding the shoulders of the animal. "The harness was rubbing the hide right off, but I don't think you'll have any more problems."

Howard grinned and shook his head. "Much obliged to you, big brother."

"You'll soon get the hang of it." Sam turned to his sister-in-law who was feeding her youngsters. "Howdy, Nancy," he said politely. "How's little Bobby today? Howie told me he was feeling poorly last night."

"Yes, he was, Sam, but he seems in fine fettle now, thank you kindly," Nancy smilingly replied.

Sam continued walking along the line of wagons until he had spoken to at least one member of each family. Going back to the head of the column, he was stopped by a friendly voice. "Like to sit a spell and have a sandwich with us, Mr. Tippett?"

Sam stared hard at the smile on the leathery, wrinkled face of Roscoe Willis, thick white hair skimming the top of his shirt collar. Roscoe stood before him, busy cutting thick slabs of ham and placing them between slices of bread as deftly as any sighted person—and Sam marveled. "How did you know it was me, Reverend Willis?"

Roscoe laughed heartily. "Wouldn't want me giving away all my secrets now would you, young man?" Roscoe added with mock severity. His sightless blue eyes pierced the distance between Sam's green eyes with a wide smile.

"I appreciate the invite in any event, so don't mind if I do," Sam said, chuckling. "I'm sure going to miss my wife's cooking on this trip. Just hope I can survive on my own," he said, dropping down on the tailgate of the wagon.

"Know what you mean. I'd surely be lost without my mate." Roscoe's smile was bright. "How about a cup of coffee while we wait? Ruby's on one of her mercy errands, taking some food to the Grier family that just joined us an hour ago. Would be a terrible thing to be burned out of house and home," he said sadly.

"She certainly has an eye for the needy and it's mighty nice of her. It's folks like you that I've dreamed would build next to my family and me. Folks who truly care and use the brain and brawn the good Lord has given them to get along in this world."

"I'm afraid the good Lord, in his wisdom, didn't allow me much brawn, young fella. I stand five feet and four inches in my stockinged feet, but I've never wasted regrets on my lack of height nor strength. Short people must be hardy to survive in a world among the tall ones, and by His grace, I'm hardy. In place of eyes to see the world about me, God gave me eyes to see through the windows of the souls of those I meet along the way."

When Ruby returned a few minutes later, Sam gratefully accepted the plate she handed him and ate hungrily. "You're more than welcome to put your feet under our table anytime, Mr. Tippett," Ruby prodded gently, pouring him another cup of coffee. "I have to fix for Roscoe and myself anyway and it's always a treat to be having company."

After the noon meal was eaten, Margaret sent Amy to the creek to wash their plates and utensils while she started shoving bags and boxes into place on the wagon. Rubbing her aching back, she turned to John. "How far do you suppose we've come?"

John removed his hat and scratched his head. "A fair piece I'd say. Maybe nine or ten miles. We're making real good time Sam told me. Take a few days to get the kinks out and everybody pulling together, but Sam says he's more than satisfied."

Rising slowly John glanced to where he had hobbled the horses and said, "I guess I better get Belle and Foxy saddled. The kids want to ride this afternoon and it'll soon be time to start rolling again."

Dressed in a long-sleeved white cotton blouse, a full riding skirt and jacket to match in soft brown suede, and brown leather boots, Amy sat astride Midnight Belle. Her bonnet hung loose at the back of her neck as she rode to the rear of the wagon train. Lost in thought she jumped when a male voice interrupted her reverie. "Mind if I keep you company for a spell?" The voice was courteous and impressive, the gaze steady and sent a ripple of awareness through her.

Amy shaded the sun from her eyes with her hand and stared in fascination at the young man mounted straight and tall on a beautiful palomino mare. Her breath caught at the sight of him and a massive sandy brown dog running eagerly at his side. The stranger wore a faded blue cotton shirt that stretched across his broad shoulders and revealed arms muscular and strong. He wore a dark blue neckerchief knotted around his neck and his taut-fitting breeches emphasized his well-muscled thighs. Slowly Amy lifted her head until she was looking into a face creased into a smile, the laugh lines splintering from the corners of compelling blue eyes—the most beautiful blue eyes she had ever seen, and the mystery shining there beckoned to her irresistibly.

Funny little darts of pleasure raced through Amy's entire being as she looked at his mouth—wide and sensual. Unbidden thoughts of what it would feel like to be kissed by those lips flitted through her mind. She glanced sideways at him, immediately ashamed of her thoughts and mutely shook her head affirmatively, dropping her eyes.

"My name's Matthew. Matthew David Carpenter," he said as he tipped his wide-brimmed, black felt hat. His blue eyes shimmered brightly in the sunlight. He removed his hat and ran his arm across his sweating forehead and gazed at Amy intensively with a significant lifting of his brows. "And you're John Bradshaw's daughter, right?"

As though drawn by a magnet Amy's eyes were observing Matthew through lowered lashes before they came back to rest on his face and found him staring at her. A faint light twinkled in the depths of Matthew's eyes as she dropped her gaze in embarrassment. Mutely shaking her head, Amy had to hold tightly to Midnight Belle's reins to keep her hands from trembling.

"Cat got your tongue?" Matthew smiled with beautiful candor.

Starting to shake her head again, Amy blushed. She fervently wished she could think of something clever to say but her mind was utterly blank. Matthew threw back his head and laughed fully, his voice warm and friendly. "Do you have a first name?" he goaded good-naturedly. He was unable to hide the amusement in his voice and was completely taken with her incredible brown eyes, ringed with thick dark lashes that seemed to glow with an inner fire.

"Uh-huh. My . . . uh . . . Christian name is Amy Marie."

"Well, I'm pleased to meet you, Amy Marie." Matthew's lips parted in a dazzling display of straight, white teeth. An undercurrent of bubbling excitement flowed between the two of them. "That your brother riding the Paint?"

"Uh-huh."

"Very nice," Matthew said quickly. Then giving Midnight Belle a quick look-see he added, "Your mare is quite beautiful, too."

"Thank you," Amy whispered hoarsely. She took a deep breath and relaxed as a small puff of wind fanned loose tendrils of hair against her face. "She was a gift from my grandfather. You have a pretty horse, and quite an impressive looking dog. He's so . . . so big."

Matthew leaned down and patted his mare on the neck. "Honey is one whale of a horse. I raised her from a colt. Broke her myself and she'll do anything I ask her to do. And Sandy's the best dog in the whole wide world. If he's only a year old and so smart, I wonder what he'll be like when he gets some age on him?"

Hearing his name spoken, Sandy looked up inquisitively at Matthew and cocked his head. Deciding he wasn't needed at the moment he went bounding off into the trees along the side of the trail, sniffing and searching out the underbrush, his tail wagging joyfully.

Billy Joe spied his sister talking to Matthew and his inquisitiveness got the better of him. He rode toward them grinning wickedly. He was holding to Foxy's reins with one hand and had one hand held behind his back. Reaching Amy's side, Billy Joe reined in close and before she knew what was happening, he whipped out the hand hidden behind his back and thrust it into her face.

Amy blanched white and screamed, drawing quickly on Belle's reins, and almost toppled out of the saddle. There, dangling from her brother's fingers, just a few inches from her face, was a squiggling, squirming snake.

"You little beast!" she raged. "Just you wait until I tell pa on you!"

Shrieking with laughter, Billy Joe swung Foxy around and trotted off in the direction from which he had just come. "You're just a scardy-cat, Amy! A scardy-cat baby! Afraid of a little old snake," he called over his shoulder.

"He's a brat!" Amy said, shaking her head in disgust. Her scare over seeing the snake had diminished, and now all she felt was embarrassment and discomfort at having Matthew witness her altercation with Billy Joe. She wondered if he, too, thought she was a scardy-cat.

Matthew offered her a sudden, arresting smile, thinking to himself, *she's as pert and feisty as a kitten, but the woman in her is beginning to show, and as beautiful as she is she will take the eye of every single man in the wagontrain.*

Amy glanced furtively at Matthew's face and caught his warm, beautiful smile and was relieved to find no recrimination showing. Matthew shook his head. "I know the breed," he said jovially. "But boys will be boys, and I'd say your brother is all boy."

"He certainly is," Amy agreed wholeheartedly. "I'd gladly trade him for a sister."

Matthew's smile quickly turned into a chuckle.

Seeing that he carried a pistol at his waist and a Winchester rifle in a scabbard, Amy asked pensively, "Do you think we're in any danger of being attacked by Indians on our journey?"

"There's always that possibility," Matthew said, nodding his head. "Sam keeps prodding us to be alert and I've got no quarrel with that. We've a lot of good stout men along that can shoot clean and straight, and I'm sure Sam and the rest of us will see to it that you get to Kentucky safely." He patted the stock of his rifle. "You best leave the worrying to us."

Licking her lips, Amy's heartbeat thundered in her ears. If she had been feeling any fear at all about their trek into an unknown wilderness, it was gone; replaced by a warm feeling of security and trust that her newfound friend had just instilled in her.

Matthew 's fingers curved around the reins as he nudged his boot heels against the flanks of his mount. He turned in the saddle, gave Amy a bold wink and waved to her as he sped away. With a flick of her wrist, Amy reined Midnight Belle and followed in Matthew Carpenter's wake. A covey of quail broke and ran from cover in the sweet grass beneath her feet.

CHAPTER 5

Hattie Lou Grier kneeled on the pallet in the back of the buckboard, clutching her rag doll to her breast. The Grier family had met and joined up with Sam Tippet's wagon train going to Kentucky early on the morning of March 4. Ben now patiently waited to take his place at the end of the line of wagons. Hattie Lou solemnly inspected each wagon as it slowly rolled by.

When the Bradshaws' wagon passed the buckboard, Amy waved to the little girl and Billy Joe followed suit. Hattie Lou grinned shyly back at them and then ducked out of sight. Smoothing her dress with her hands and hugging her doll close, she rocked back and forth, emulating her mother, while her strawstack of tight curls bobbed.

Gilda sat stiffly on the seat next to Ben, clutching baby Arliss in her arms. "They won't cotton t'us," she said matter-of-factly.

"Where'd that queer notion spring from?" Ben countered, not failing to catch the note of sarcasm in her voice.

"Be just like every other place we've ever been, Ben. Nobody's got any real use for us. Mark my words, Ben Grier, 'tis goin' t'be the same ol' story in Kentuck. We should never of joined 'em."

Ben sighed with exasperation. "What a bunch of gloomy nonsense! Mr. Tippett was right nice when I asked 'im if we could join 'em, an' he allowed we'd be more'n welcome. He said my smithin' would come in handy on this here trip and he assured me when we reach Kentuck I'd have all the smithin' I could handle. When we get to Kentuck, honey, why we'll more'n likely have 'nough comin' in to live mighty high on the hog. With all my mendin' an' makin' . . ."

"Sam might of said we'd be welcome, but what 'bout all these other high an' mighty white folks makin' up this here wagon train?" Gilda interrupted sarcastically. "You think they be wantin' the likes of us taggin' along clean t'Kentuck?"

"Who don't want us?" Hattie Lou interrupted, her curiosity piqued by her mother's nagging.

Gilda paid no attention what-so-ever to Hattie Lou's question. "You just cain't face facts, Ben Grier, or don' want to." Gilda bit her lip. "We got dark skin in case you've forgotten. Always have, an' always goin' to have! White folks jest don't rightly cotton t'black people, exceptin' t'do their fetchin' an' totin'. We be a hated race an' people on this here wagon train'll take t'us liken they would a pack of thievin' coyotes. *You mark my words!*" Her words were loaded with ridicule.

"There's a mighty big country west of them mountains, woman, an' I'm here t'tell you there'll be room for a whole slew of folks, white an' black. You mark *my* words, Gilda, honey." An easy smile played at the corners of Ben's mouth.

"Who hates us, Pa?" Hattie continued to pester.

"Don' you fret none 'bout folks hatin' us, chile. The Lord has special need for all folks. Just so we be the best we can be, that's all that matters t'him. Nobody better think this here fella is sneakin' in a white man's heaven like a licked houn' dog with his tail done tucked betwixt his hin' legs! We'll be right welcomed!" Ben slapped the reins and called out, "Gee up there, mule!" His mule continued its slow, but steady plod forward.

The sun looked like a golden ball in the western sky and the misty peaks of the towering Blue Ridge wall was standing tall before them when the wagon train finally stopped beside the Tye River in Amherst County for the day. Brush and trees choked the place Sam chose to spend the night. The willows, their long limber withes the color of amber, glowed with promise, as though some kind of golden sap was rising. The squeak and squeal of wooden axels and jingling harness slowly receeded as the column of dust-furred wagons jolted to a halt and pulled into a light circle.

As the last wagon completed the circle, Sam whooped joyously, lavish with his praise on the progress they had made their second day on the trail.

"Fantastic!" Sam boomed heartily, smiling in satisfaction. "I swear if every one of you hasn't handled yourselves like seasoned pilgrims today! Not a greenhorn in the bunch!"

The weary travelers, their muscles quivering and aching, were delighted with the respite from the interminable jolting of the wagons and were elated with Sam's compliments. They laughed and joked and slapped him on the back as he went about the camp, shouting instructions and giving a ready hand where needed.

Amy munched on an apple as she meandered down to the river for water. Billy Joe scurried about gathering wood for a fire. Soon the pungent smell of strong coffee and cooking food drifted throughout the camp, assailing every nostril, and everyone soon forgot just how tired and sore they were.

Walking back from the river with her bucket full of water, Amy gazed around the circle of wagons, watching and listening to the various sounds of the people as they busied themselves making camp. Fires burned brightly in front of each wagon, filling the air with smoke and various appealing wood scents.

Amy stopped before the Willis' blazing fire to chat a minute with Ruby as she bent over the fire, a long-handled wooden spoon in her hand, stirring her kettle of ham and beans. "It's been a beautiful day for traveling, hasn't it?" Amy asked her brightly."

"That it has," Ruby readily agreed. She stood to stretch the kinks out of her shoulders and rubbed her backside. "And I felt every mile!" she laughingly added.

"Good to have you and your folks along, Amy," Roscoe said. He sat on a log near the fire, his hands stretched toward its warmth. "I'm looking forward to getting in a little fishing with that young brother of yours on this trip. Tell him I said to get himself over to our wagon whenever he has a few extra minutes and we'll talk about it."

"That will pleasure him to no end, Reverend Willis. And it will get him out of my hair for a while anyway." Amy grinned and wagged her head.

"He's a mighty fine lad and I think his sister thinks so too," Roscoe added with a chuckle. "Sure smells good around here doesn't it?" Roscoe asked, sniffing the air. "It's truly a blessing," he added jovially. "A welcome rest after a good day's journey and a beautiful wife to serve me meals fit for a king."

"Eloquence flows as rushing waters from your lips, my dear husband," Ruby said gently. "I don't know if supper will be fit for a king or not, but I guarantee it will be filling."

Amy was touched as she witnessed the gaze Ruby had turned on her husband. It was indelibly clear that Roscoe and Ruby were two very fascinating and special people. The sun faded slowly in the western sky and a cooling wind gusted off the river. Amy shivered. "The sun's going down mighty fast so I better get back to the wagon and help ma with our supper. Have a good evening."

"Give our best to your parents, dear, and stop by any time," Ruby said, as she started cutting her cornbread into generous helpings.

After supper was over Amy took the tin plates and cups to the river and scoured them with sand. While she was gone, Margaret made up the beds in the wagon and then folded quilts and made pallets inside the tent for John and herself. As soon as his bed was made up Billy Joe climbed into the wagon and they didn't hear another peep out of him. John checked on the horses once more and they all went to bed as soon as Amy returned from the river.

Not used to riding Belle for such a long time at a stretch, the muscles in Amy's legs ached and she had a few burning sore spots along the inside of her thighs. Her muscles screamed from the strain. "Goodnight, Ma. Goodnight, Pa," she said with a long exhausted sigh. "Sleep tight and don't let the bedbugs bite."

"Goodnight, honey. Rest well and God bless," her parents chorused.

As night closed in, nocturnal animals began to crawl from their nesting places in the dense underbrush to hunt. They drank from the river and peered at the humans who had invaded their territory. Amy was oblivious to the chirping crickets' song and the bullfrogs' clamorous and unmelodic voices from the river, as she heaved a heavy sigh and climbed into the back of the wagon. The temperature had dropped considerably with the setting of the sun and Amy shivered as she hurriedly undressed and slipped into a warm woolen gown. She paid little attention to the noise the other campers were making or their horses as they champed grass at the side of their wagon.

Breathing deeply of the fragrant night air, Amy stared through the curtains at the back of the wagon and into the blackness that surrounded her. How different and mysterious to be sleeping on the floor of a covered wagon instead of in her comfortable featherbed back in Charlottesville. There was no bed, and no solid roof above her now; only the stars and a small disc of moon that was slowly creeping up on the darkness. The steady breathing of Billy Joe told her he was fast asleep. Curling her aching body into a tight knot, Amy quickly said her prayers and dropped off to sleep, Charlottesville and her grandparents, forty odd miles to the northeast, completely forgotten.

A fierce, lonesome howl, like the wail of a lost spirit, came eerily from close by, bringing Amy upright and trembling. Hoo-ooooo! Hoo-ooooo! The call of the owl rent the stillness of the night and was answered by the echoing hoot of its distant mate. Amy clutched her homespun quilt close, trying to convince herself she had nothing to fear. "Hoo . . . oooh . . . oooh!" it came again, louder and nearer this time it seemed.

A dog, a few wagons away, started barking and soon other dogs followed suit. Following sharp commands from their owners, the barking soon stopped and Amy relaxed somewhat. Billy Joe turned over in his sleep but didn't waken, and Amy leaned on one elbow and gently tucked his quilt more tightly around his slumbering form.

Settling back on her pallet, Amy was acutely aware of the silence all around her now. The rise and fall of voices had died away; telling her that most of the weary travelers had gone to sleep. Although Amy was totally exhausted, sleep was a long time in coming the second time around. Her mind refused to cease its scurrying from one thought to another as she lovingly traced each room of her home in Charlottesville, as familiar to her as the image of her own face in a mirror. The only home she had ever known and she knew in her heart she would never see again. Finally she drifted into a deep and dreamless sleep.

Each morning found the camp a bedlam of sound and a maze of movement. The men fed and yoked the animals; the women served breakfast, packed cold lunches, tended to children and helped the men repack the wagons.

As the Blue Ridge came nearer, the road, a winding rocky trail now, became narrower as the woods closed in and isolated farmhouses dropped behind. It was Friday, March 7, and off in the distance appeared the towering sentinel Peaks of Otter. The long blue wall was a panorama of scenic beauty. Cresting a hill, Sam spied the long winding James River and it wasn't long before the roll of heavy wheels and the steady clip-clop of hoofbeats ended for another day.

The ferns along the margin had pushed their curling fronds through the rich earth and there was just a promise of wild flowers in the tender green. A strong wind was blowing through the trees and the woods were enlivened by the sounds of a multitude of birds. Happy at the early rendezvous, the women and young children bustled about gathering firewood as the men and older boys unyoked the animals, hobbled them, and turned them out to graze. Voices of hundreds of young frogs and insects, just awakened to life, rose in varied chorus from the singing river and lush meadow. High clouds reflected the sun's rays and a mist of humidity cloaked the meadow in a gold-tinged gray. The delicious odors of stewing meat and coffee soon blended with the sharp, eye-tingling, but pleasant smell of wood smoke.

While Ben staked out their mule, Gilda, dressed in a bright flowered cotton skirt and white blouse, frantically searched through their meager fare for enough food to feed her family supper. Her face showed the strain she was under when Ben returned.

"Fin' somethin'?"

Gilda shook her head and looked at Ben with wide, liquid-dark eyes. "Narry a hunk of dry cornbread," she said forlornly. "Ben, what's we t'do? No food an' our babies hungry?" She rigidly held her tears in check.

Ben forced a smile. "I got me a gun," he responded quickly. "Give me a hour an' I be rustlin' us up a rabbit or squirrel for the pot." His arms went around his wife and he pulled her close. "God'll provide. Iffen he sees the sparrow when it falls, he ain't goin' t'let Ben Grier's family down!"

"Like he's been doin' lately?" Gilda said mockingly, spitting out her words sarcastically. She tore herself away from Ben's arms with a choking cry and turned her back on him, shoving boxes this way and that in their buckboard. "Don' go talkin' t'me 'bout God an' his goodness an' how he's carin' for the sparrow when my babies are goin' hungry 'fore my very eyes! You know what you can do with your God!" she cried angrily. Her fingers clawed at her skirt as tears rolled down her dark cheeks.

Ben pulled her back into the circle of his arms. "Please, honey, don' blaspheme. Ain't goin' t'be easy. You knows it an' I knows it. But we be young an' strong an' we got each other an' our babies." Ben stared into her eyes, shining with tears. "I loves you, Gilda, honey—I loves you a heap. I be workin' hard for Mr. Tippett an' for some of these other good white folks. I be workin' 'til I drop to earn . . ."

"Don' you dare go beggin' or askin' for handouts, Ben Grier!" Gilda interrupted angrily. "From Mr. Tippett or any of these other hypocrites 'round here! We bowed an' scraped all we is goin' to in this life!" Gilda set her jaw stubbornly and punctuated her words with guile. "White men robbed us of our home an' most everythin' we owned, an' I ain't forgettin'! *Do you hear me, Ben Grier?!*"

Gilda's black eyes were snapping, but Ben saw tears swimming in their depths, and it cut him to the quick knowing what misery she was suffering. "I's a thinkin' the devil hisself has heard you, honey." He grinned, cupped her face between his two big hands and kissed her lightly.

Gilda swallowed and looked at her husband in wonderment. *How like him t' take my fits so calmly,* she thought.

"I ain't goin' t'be long," Ben told her. "You get that fire a goin' 'cause we is goin' to have stewed rabbit for supper—or better yet, some squirrel! Um . . . umm, I can shore taste it now!"

Ben's voice was cloaked as a huge flock of crows, numbering in the hundreds, gathered in the tops of the trees close to the bank of the river. Their noisy, croaking clatter soon began. Gilda looked uneasily into Ben's eyes and said, "'Tis a bad omen. Means death, Ben. Yessuh, my mammy done always tole me."

Ben hesitated, measuring her for a moment. "They's a heap of them old sayin's that ain't never come true. Crows got t'gather here, there or yonder, an' they's bound t'croak an' clatter some. Stop yore frettin' now."

Gilda's mind was congested with doubts and fears and in a quivering voice she said, "Be careful, Ben, an' watch out for the snakes and such."

Ben squeezed Gilda's hand, went over and picked up his gunnysack and rifle and loped toward the woods. "God'll provide!" he called gaily over his shoulder.

"I's powerful hongry Mammy."

Gilda jumped. "Land sakes, chile, don't sneak up on me like that!"

"I didn't sneak, Mammy. I's jest hongry. When do we eat?"

"You go an' play," Gilda hedged. "I be fixin' supper soon as yore pa gets back. An' don't be wakin' Arliss up, neither. Jest now got him t'sleep. He's been cross an' cranky t'day." Gilda couldn't look her own child in the eye. She hadn't the heart to tell her that if Ben had no luck hunting, they would all be going to bed hungry this night.

Hattie Lou looked up at her mother wistfully. "Please, Mammy, just one piece of cornbread?"

"I said go play, Hattie Lou! We stopped early t'day an' it ain't goin' t'be suppertime for a long spell yet. Iffen you don't want t'mind, then you can jest go on t'bed!" she said sharply.

Arliss cried out and Gilda turned to Hattie Lou in vexation. "Now see what you gone an' done? Go play this very minute 'fore I whup you with a hickory switch!"

"Yessum," Hattie Lou said dejectedly. She hung her head and a tear escaped and rolled down one soft cheek.

. . .

"You want fish for supper?" Billy Joe asked his mother excitedly. "Preacher Willis is going fishing and he asked me if I wanted to tag along."

"I think that would be just fine, son. We haven't had fresh fish for a coon's age. If your pa doesn't need you to help him, that is. You must ask him first."

Billy Joe's face glowed with delight. "Done asked. He said he'd manage just fine without my help, especially if I was to be bringing in the meat for supper. That's important, ain't it?" Billy Joe squared his shoulders proudly.

"Isn't it?" corrected Margaret as she looked lovingly at her son, at his sweet freckled face and innocent brown eyes.

"I'll cut me a willow pole and dig some worms while you get the fire going," Billy Joe said, grinning at his mother.

"You just be careful that you don't fall into the river, and use caution in cutting your willow pole. We don't need any fingers cut off! And Billy Joe," she admonished, "mind what Reverend Willis tells you, and be back here in a couple of hours. It looks like it might rain."

Billy Joe was already out of ear shot, headed for the Willis' wagon. Margaret's voice died away as she realized her words of caution had fallen on deaf ears. She shook her head and smiled after him.

With a long exhausted sigh, Ruby Willis sank down wearily onto the tailgate of her wagon. It was surprisingly warm and she absently fanned the air about her flushed face with her handkerchief. She was delighted to see her husband and the Bradshaw boy fairly fly from camp on their way to the river. They seemed such an unlikely pair, but they thoroughly enjoyed one another's company.

Ruby was grateful to Sam for calling an early halt to their travels. She wasn't getting any younger and it was good to be free of the interminable jostling of a moving wagon and the weight of the heavy reins on her hands and wrists. Tomorrow promised to be a tough day of mountain climbing and Sam wanted animals and people alike to be rested and ready.

Sniffing the air, Ruby caught herself glancing uneasily at the sky. The smell of dust clung to the air. She sniffed again. There it was, ever so faint, but the distinct smell of rain! She glanced at the sky again. The clouds seemed thicker, grayer somehow as they scudded along rapidly, swirling as they traveled northeast.

The aches in Ruby's joints rarely played her false. That might mean one thing and it might mean another, but the rapid rise in temperature, in Ruby's mind, could only mean one thing—the clouds were getting ready to let go.

Glancing around the light circle of wagons, she could see everyone was finding chores to do. The men were working in their shirtsleeves and the women were busy in their homespun dresses. Margaret Bradshaw was humming happily as she headed for the river, a reed basket of dirty clothes in her hands. A newlywed couple, holding hands and with rapturous looks on their faces, was headed in the same direction, each carrying an empty red-cedar bucket.

A number of the men and older boys with guns in hand, headed toward the woods, seeking rabbits and squirrels for their wives' cooking pots. One man and two of his sons worked diligently on a broken spoke on a wheel and at cleaning and oiling their harness.

Two women sat on the ground, thread and needles in hand, talking quietly as they kept strict watch over some little ones playing tag nearby. Several small boys were chasing a couple of dogs through the camp, their squeals of laughter carrying over the excited yelps of the dogs. Sam, conscientious as always, seemed to be everywhere at once, helping wherever necessary or giving out with a few kind words to everyone.

Ruby deemed Sam a man devoted to the safety and well being of his charges, always there, at the head of the caravan—a natural-born leader. He was the man who bore the responsibility of every man, woman and child on the train: seventy-two people in all, on his broad shoulders, and he was ever vigilant to have a scout report to him regularly on straggling wagons or breakdowns.

Ruby's ears picked up the shrill cries of a baby. *Poor little tyke. Must really have something bothering it to make it cry so,* she thought. Putting her hands on her aching knees she slowly pulled herself to her feet. It would be awhile before Roscoe and the Bradshaw boy was back from fishing, so she would go and see if she couldn't give the mother a hand, whoever she might be. *Sure wouldn't be easy traveling with a baby,* she reasoned.

Ruby ransacked her food box until she had filled a small basket with bread, jam, sliced ham, half a raisin pie and some dried fruit. Satisfied that she was well armed with food, she started out, breathing a quick prayer: *Dear Lord, most of us who are well off take for granted our daily existence and our possessions. Help me this day to find someone less fortunate than myself, thus allowing me to be able to express my love to you, because it is when I am feeding the hungry, that I am truly serving Christ.*

Gilda sat on a worn and ragged quilt beneath a willow sapling, hugging her feverish and fretting baby close. She rocked him back and forth and crooned to him softly. After a few sobs he grew quiet and she unbuttoned her blouse and offered him her breast. Arliss sucked greedily for a few seconds, then screwed up his face and cried even louder.

Gilda kissed his feverish cheeks as his chubby arms flailed the air. "Poor little ole black chile." Gilda choked on her words and reached up and swiped at the tears of frustration that rolled down her own brown cheeks.

"Can I give you a hand with your youngster?" Ruby asked pleasantly, motherliness written all over her face.

Gilda jumped and threw Ruby a startled glance. Raising finely arched eyebrows she protested. "Don't need help, ma'am," she said, rubbing quickly at her cheeks, trying to dispel the telltale tears. "Ain't wantin' t'be beholdin'."

"Fiddlesticks!" Ruby's blue eyes met Gilda's black ones. "Fate may have denied me children of my own, but common sense tells me that on a trip such as we are undertaking, even the littlest ones will tire a body out."

Setting the basket of food down in front of Gilda, Ruby reached her arms out for the crying child. "By the way," Ruby said pleasantly, "I'm Ruby Willis. My husband, Roscoe, is a Methodist minister."

Gilda hesitated a moment, her face clouded with uneasiness. Seeing nothing but pure kindness written on Ruby's face, and feeling she could surely trust a minister's wife with her tiny son, she reluctantly relinquished her crying baby into Ruby's outstretched arms.

"You're a bouncer, you are," Ruby chuckled as she lovingly cradled the baby in her arms. Eyeing Gilda she said, "You're no bigger'n a minute yourself and I imagine he's done wore you to a frazzle today. Let me walk with him a bit and see if I can't quiet him down some." Ruby gestured with her hand toward the basket of food she had brought with her. "You can put that food away. I fixed too much as usual. Sure hope you can use it up before it spoils."

Filled with loathing and offended by Ruby's interference, Gilda none-the-less eyed the basket of food hungrily. *Just the way with white folks,* she thought to herself. *Always in the middle of a gale, stirrin' things up!*

Gilda sat silently, the sun warming her face, and watched with rebellious dark eyes as Ruby walked back and forth along the edge of the perimeter of wagons, cradling the whimpering baby in her arms, crooning all the while to him.

Suspicious thoughts flirted with Gilda's mind and she grimaced. "White woman," Gilda said with a tremor in her voice, "yore the first ever t'touch my chile, let alone hold 'im in yore arms. An' yore lookin' like yore enjoyin' ever minute of it!"

Ruby grinned and continued to croon to the child in her arms. The minutes passed by slowly and Gilda could hardly believe what her eyes were telling her. She was still suspicious, but she couldn't help but sense the simple goodness in the older woman.

When Ruby finally laid her sleeping son on the pallet in the shade, Gilda gave her a searching glance and asked, "Ain't you the one that left some vittles the other night?"

"That's right. I'm hoping another time your family will be able to pleasure my husband and me with your presence at our supper table."

"Cain't..." Gilda groped for words, her eyes meeting Ruby's searchingly, looking for an assurance that she could trust her. "Cain't thank you 'nough," she finally blurted, a look of total bewilderment showing on her face.

"No thanks needed, my child." Ruby's sincerity and warm smile penetrated Gilda's guard.

In a little rush of words, her eyes downcast, Gilda spoke softly, "Thank you kindly for the food you done give us t'day. No way we can ever pay you back though."

Ruby held up a hand to silence her. "Lord love you, child. You need pay no never-mind to that," Ruby reassured her. "I just wanted to help in some small measure. Sam mentioned some of the difficulties you and your family suffered at the hands of those terrible men a few days back. I hope you know that not all white people agree with such brutal tactics. But, put all thoughts of your misfortunes behind you now. God saw fit to protect you and for that we're all grateful. And your presence among us is surely welcomed."

"Yessum." Gilda said, nodding her head, her mood suddenly buoyant.

"I just hope you don't hold what those terrible men did to you against those of us in this wagontrain. I won't pretend it would be easy to lose everything you had worked so hard for, but whenever the Lord allows a hurt, he always puts a cure near by. Earthly setbacks just tend to bring us closer to the dear Savior."

"A real Bible banger ain't you?" Gilda's golden skin turned ashy and her eyes narrowed and hardened. "Well, I done heard all the preachin' I want t'hear from you," she said tartly, her hands clenched into tight little fists at her sides. "Iffen there's a God, which I shore rightly doubt, he's much too busy doin' what it is he does all day long, t'be pestered with the likes of us!"

The light went out of Gilda's eyes as she continued her tirade to Ruby. "We done git put in place no matter what. Belittled—denied—an' lynched. I's seen black men hangin' from trees jest for lookin' at a white woman. Our babies are tol' that God made 'em to shovel white men's manure an' tote their freight." She sighed and gave a resigned shrug to her shoulders. "Once believed in God—loved 'im with all the heart I got in me, but . . ."

Gilda stared mutely at Ruby, the things that she had dared to say to her rolling over her mind like a storm. She looked wretchedly unhappy and desperately hopeless.

She might, for a time have lost sight of you, Lord, and *her soul's been warped and twisted,* Ruby pondered sadly. *But dear God, I know you haven't lost sight of her. Of that, I'm certain.*

A breath of wind caught Gilda's thin and faded cotton skirt and molded it against her slender legs. Pathetically childlike, her eyes filled with tears and she swiped at her cheeks with the back of her hand.

"Don't you underestimate the Lord, young lady," Ruby said, summoning a smile and squeezing Gilda's hand. "I believe he put you folks in our path to let Sam be your Moses, leading you to your Promised Land. It's clean and big in Kentucky and it's fitting for you to go there. Perhaps once there your neighbors will look at you and not the color of your skin. God's hand is always at work in our lives, my child, using for good, even what appears to be evil."

Ruby placed a hand on each shoulder, and holding Gilda at arm's length she looked into her tear-dimmed eyes and said, "Now, you get some rest while your little one's napping, and I'll mosey on back to my own wagon and try and mind my own business." Ruby glanced toward the sky and at several campfires nearby. "The smoke from the fires is sticking close to the ground. Sure sign of rain." To herself she thought, *Something is ominous and disquieting about the sky, Lord.*

Turning to leave Ruby said lightly, "You just remember, my child, trying times are not the times to stop trying. Faith can move mountains, but sometimes it has to do it an armload at a time."

Gilda watched Ruby slowly pick her way across the campground, an empty basket in her hand. All her loneliness and confusion welded together in one big upsurge of devouring yearning. A stranger had come to visit her this day, but a friend had departed.

CHAPTER 6

Amy and two of the Dobbs' sisters, Rebecca, sixteen, and Miriam, fourteen, decided to take a walk. Checking out the camp, the three girls found five youngsters who wanted to tag along. Amy instructed the little ones to link hands and off they went. It wasn't long until three-year-old Bobby Tippett started to fret. He was tired and he wanted his mother. Amy squatted before him. "Come on, Bobby, I'll ride you piggyback," she offered, smiling sweetly at him.

The little boy needed no coaxing. He put his chubby arms around Amy's neck, locked his little legs around her waist, and smiled blissfully at his stroke of good fortune.

Rebecca and Miriam walked with their arms locked around each other's waists, talking and laughing with Amy and all the children behaved beautifully.

A hazy sun shone in the afternoon sky as Amy and her new friends, Rebecca and Miriam, herded their young brood through the woods. Leaf mold lay thick on the ground, making a soft carpet on the little-used path they were treading. The children skipped purposefully along, twigs and briars snatching at their clothes.

The hillside was crowded with birch, maple and oak, all still wearing the dull brown dress of winter, with only the evergreens standing out in bold contrast. Halfway up the hill, and around a turn in the path, they came upon a clearing where sloping banks of green grass led down to a small stream. The children ran eagerly to the edge of the clear, running water, which was only inches deep. The breeze, blowing off the water, felt cool on their bare arms.

"What a heavenly spot," Amy whispered as two little boys fell to the ground and started turning somersaults. The other children soon followed suit, laughing and squealing in splendor, their sweet voices carrying on the wind. Amy kneeled down in the soft green grass and loosened Bobby's hold on her neck. She deposited him on the ground before her, and started tickling him in the ribs with her index fingers. Bobby giggled wildly and the other children, hearing his wild shrieks, stopped what they were doing and gathered around Amy, vying for her attention.

"If you will all sit down I'll tell you a story. Would you like that?" The children clapped their hands and laughed in delight. For the next half-hour, they sat spellbound as Amy told them stories about Noah and the ark, Daniel in the lion's den, and Moses and the Israelites crossing the Red Sea.

The children were so engrossed in the stories Amy was telling that they didn't see the doe and her fawn that had crept up to the water's edge, just a short distance from where they were sitting. Rebecca was the first to catch sight of the deer and she put her finger to her lips. Amy quieted and looked in the direction that Rebecca was pointing. She then cautioned the children into complete silence, and they watched wide-eyed as the gentle animals drank thirstily.

As the wind shifted, the doe threw up her head, her ears pricked tall above her luminous eyes, and her nostrils flared. She had traced their scent. She wheeled, and with a great bound, the animals sped away, much to the chagrin of the children.

The sudden wind disturbed the quiet surface of the water and whistled in the branches of the trees overhead. Miriam glanced up and scanned the sky. "I don't like the looks of the sky," she said dubiously, looking first to Rebecca and then to Amy. "Maybe we should be starting back to camp."

"It's spring—you've got to expect rain in the springtime," Rebecca said calmly, trying to put her sister at ease.

"I don't like it either, Becky," Amy murmured in sudden anxiety, as she glanced at the gray sky. "It looks like we might be in for a bad storm."

Miriam's face wore a frown as she grasped her older sister's arm. "Come on, Becky, let's go back," she cried, "I'm scared!"

A cold rain started falling like driven nails, and they were all wet and shivering in just moments. Trying to hide her growing concern Amy jumped up and said brightly, "We're going to play follow-the-leader now. Everybody has to do what I do, so pay close attention." Amy quickly picked Bobby up in her arms. "Miriam, you take the two boys, and Rebecca can handle the twins. Let's all stay together now," she said as they all started running, everyone obedient to her quiet command. A dark curtain of cloud moved to cover the sun and Amy could hear the chattering sparrows and noisy crows as they flew helter skelter throughout the forest.

As they raced for camp, the clouds overhead lowered and the sky darkened and an uneasy stillness filled the air. Then lightning flashed and thunder rolled, drowning out the screams of the children. So fast and furious was the rain falling that at times Amy became disoriented. The wind fought the wet branches of the trees, and she almost fell several times trying to dodge the whipping limbs. Out of breath, Amy finally dropped to the ground as another blast of thunder exploded around them as they all huddled together. Bobby was crying hysterically and holding so tightly to Amy's neck she thought he would strangle her.

The intensity of the storm increased and lightning was driving into the earth, striking trees to their left and to their right, popping and crackling until Amy didn't think she could endure it a moment longer. "Dear God, please help us!" she screamed. Amy put one arm around Becky's shoulder and one arm around Miriam's shoulder and they crouched over the children, groveling in the sodden grass as the storm swept over them.

. . .

The forest was alive with bird song, the air humming with insect sounds and the meadow lay unbroken and beautiful with short, lush grass, and bearberry willows.

Sunlight filtered through a hazy sky to cast a rosy glow over the trees that were vast, round and countless.

Father and son jogged along a beaten path, moving in rhythm, feet lifting high, Sandy dogging their heels. Suddenly Ted saw a flash of movement in the meadow ahead and cautioned Matthew. Matthew signaled that he, too, had seen the buck and two whitetail does. Sandy whined softly, his body trembling, as he picked up the scent.

"Sandy, down!" Matthew commanded softly. Sandy dropped into a crouch and his cold, wet nose found Matthew's hand. For several minutes they crouched and watched the animals' movements at a respectful distance.

The deer finally broke free of the meadow and darted into the brush. Ted and Matthew followed through a path thick and tangled. Almost abruptly, the sprouts and scrub thinned and the earth grew more sandy and rocky. Up ahead they saw the deer clamber up a steep incline. A trickle of sweat found the top of Matthew's nose and he blew it away with a puff of air. Ted met his gaze and smiled broadly. *What a lad!* He thought proudly. *Eighteen and as tall as myself and still growing!*

A gust of wind blew down the mountainside and fanned their sweat-dampened faces. They were almost within shooting range when one doe bounded over the ridge, quickly followed by the others. Ted and Matthew cleared the underbrush and came to the steep, rocky grade up which the deer had scrambled.

They started their climb that was steep and treacherous in places. Ted was in the lead about twenty feet and more than halfway to the top when some loose gravel slipped beneath his feet. He felt himself slipping, but neither his agility nor sense of balance could keep him from falling. He clawed the air and with a cry tumbled sideways. His gun flew out of his hands and landed with a resounding thud on a large boulder half buried in the ground. There was a deafening roar as the gun discharged.

Sharp rocks gouged and ripped at Ted as he slid head first, flying faster and faster down the steep incline. His head hit a half-buried rock, then his shoulder and ribs. He twisted around but kept sliding down the incline until his right leg slammed up against another boulder with agonizing force.

Ted now lay on his back, willing nausea away. It hurt to breathe and the blood in his mouth tasted like copper. The pain in his leg and groin was like a red-hot poker as he tried to turn onto his side. Blood had soaked through his pants and was staining the ground red.

Matthew flew down the incline recklessly in an urgency to reach his father. In a matter of seconds he was looking down at his father lying in a pool of blood. Matthew sucked in his breath and his face turned white as bile rushed from the pit of his stomach into his throat.

He sucked in a breath of air. Instinct served Matthew better than reason as he quickly unbuttoned his shirt and removed it. He carefully eased his father's pants down until he could put the shirt over the bleeding wound in his groin. He then applied pressure to try and staunch the bleeding. Still holding the shirt on the open wound with one hand, he pulled his father's belt from its loops with the other and buckled it around his father's thigh to try and hold the shirt in position.

A moment later Sandy came hurtling down the rocky incline. He whined and whimpered and nudged Ted with his nose. Matthew grabbed the thick fur at Sandy's neck. "Easy, boy," he said and Sandy dropped to the ground and flattened his ears. He put his nose between his two front paws, looking from Ted to Matthew with sad amber-colored eyes.

Matthew's heart was thudding loudly in his ears, and fear closed his throat. His father was lying so still, his face like hickory ashes. The boulder held him firmly in position so there was no danger of his falling further down the incline. He was still conscious and winced as pain shot through his body and a deep moan escaped his lips.

"I'm here, Pa," Matthew gasped, tears blurring his vision. "Is the pain real bad?"

"Pretty . . . bad . . . son," Ted gasped weakly. His face was gray, his eyes glassy and pinched into slits against the glare of the late afternoon sun.

Matthew cringed at the extent of his father's injuries. "I'll have to go for help, Pa, but I'll leave Sandy here with you. Please, Pa, just lie still. You're going to be fine and I'll be back before you know it."

Turning before the words were barely out of his mouth, Matthew slid down the rest of the embankment, cautioning Sandy to remain behind. The big shaggy dog sniffed Ted thoroughly, then gave out a long, low sigh and settled himself comfortably at his side, his massive head tucked between his giant paws.

The day was warm and close as Ben Grier loped on a path through the shadowy woods until he was out of earshot of the camp and its confusion of noise. This particular belt of timber was thick with sugar maples and oak. Grapevines and poison oak, springing from piles of old leaves, climbed up the trunks of the tall trees. The brush undergrowth of green briers and scrub, and tangle of creepers, made the path he was on hard to follow.

He stopped now and then and waited patiently, his eyes and ears straining for the least little sound or movement. A throaty clucking began nearby and then he heard the slurred squeaky bark of a young squirrel off to his right. He left the path and moved silently toward a large oak, vaguely aware that the wind had picked up and it was getting cloudy.

Catching a flicker of movement above his head, Ben raised his gun and as a sharp crack exploded the air, a fuzzy gray form fell end-over-end from a high, lofty branch. It plopped into the leaf mold a few feet in front of him. "Nice shootin', Ben," he said, to himself, grinning from ear-to-ear. Stalking quietly, deeper into the maze of trees, Ben soon had two more plump grays.

Pushing hurriedly through the underbrush, Ben slung the gunnysack with his squirrels over his shoulder. Farther along, he laid the squirrels down beside some fat-stemmed stalks of poke. Visions of fried squirrel and poke and lamb's quarters made his mouth water, and for the next few minutes he helped himself to all that he could find.

The wind was singing through the trees and two Jays in a maple tree were hollering and squawking. Glancing up through the boughs of the trees to the southwest, Ben tried to judge the time of day by the angle of the sun's rays. The clouds were now so thick and dark that the sun was quickly being blotted from view.

Ben could see threads of lightning in the dark clouds overhead and heard the rumble of thunder as a few scattered drops of rain fell. He grabbed up his sack of squirrels and his greens and started loping in the direction of the camp, taking giant kangaroo leaps.

He hadn't gone far when he heard someone shouting. Then he saw him. It was the Carpenter boy, running and waving his arms wildly and yelling incoherently. Ben changed directions and ran to meet him.

"For God's sake," Matthew sobbed like a child, "come and help me! Please . . . it's my pa. He's hurt bad! Come quick, help me . . . ." Matthew tried to take a deep breath, but his side hurt and his lungs burned as though they were on fire. He was trembling as he grabbed Ben's arm and started pulling on him.

"What happened?" Ben asked quickly.

"Pa fell and . . . and his gun went off. He's been shot and maybe his leg is broken. Just hurry!" Matthew turned and started running back the way he had just come.

Dropping the gunnysack with the squirrels in it, Ben dashed after Matthew. A flash of lightning filled the sky and then the storm hit in full force. The rain drummed down and bushes were quickly flattened to the ground.

Directly overhead, wisps of gray cloud extended down from darker masses and were whirling ominously. Ben had a prickling sensation on the back of his neck as a roaring sound filled his ears. He stopped running and cocked his head and listened. There it was again. He turned and looked in a southwesterly direction and froze. A long gray tail extended from a blue-black shelf of cloud. It curled slightly near the ground and Ben could see whole trees being sucked up into its maw. The wind howled, sucking, blowing, bending and twisting everything within its reach.

It seemed to Ted as though he had been lying in the rain for hours. Intense pain was gnawing at him constantly. Sandy nosed his hand, whining softly and pleading for his attention as the rain continued to beat down with force, biting and stinging. A moan escaped Ted's lips as he tried to move.

Dipping his muzzle, Sandy licked Ted's hand and then his face with his rough, swiping tongue. He whined deeply as water poured down his massive head and he nudged Ted again. "Down . . . fella . . ." Ted whispered. Sandy immediately dropped to his haunches obediently.

Ted continued to move in and out of consciousness, only faintly aware of the hammering rain, the roaring wind and his pain. He thought he heard voices over the roaring in his ears, and then he felt the movements of Sandy as he made a forward rush.

"Down, Sandy!" Matthew gently kneed the animal aside and dropped down beside his father. Sandy moved aside, his amber eyes following Matthew's every move. All around them lightning flashed and pulsed blindingly and the heavy rain pounded them unmercifully.

"The . . . the noise, son. Wha . . . what's happening?" Ted rasped.

"It's a cyclone, Pa! But I found help!" Matthew screamed trying to make his father hear above the roar of the wind. He held his father's hand and squeezed it. "When the storm passes, we're going to take you back to camp! Hang on, Pa . . . just hang on!" Matthew's eyes were pleading.

Ben and Matthew watched, mesmerized as the low swirling cloud, with its dark finger, swept through the meadow below them. It moved through the grass, breaking trees and tossing up handfuls of grass and brush with contemptuous ease.

Lightning flashed and thunder still rolled as the tornado moved on another dozen yards, then, as if tired, it raised itself off the ground and shrank up into the parent cloud and trundled off to the east.

As soon as the storm passed, Ben stooped over and picked Ted up in his arms gently, as though he were a child. "Oh, God, please," Ted groaned and then went limp.

Matthew stared at his father petrified. "Pa?"

Ben shot Matthew a reassuring glance. "Don' you worry none, young fella. Yore pa's just restin' his eyes."

The bodily suffering of Theodore Carpenter had been no greater than was the mental suffering of his son. Blinded by tears, Matthew stumbled on the trail ahead of Ben and his precious load. Sandy ran before them, unusually wary and skittish, constantly scenting the air. Suddenly he moved into the center of the path down which Matthew and Ben would have to proceed. He growled and bared his teeth.

Taken aback by the dog's behavior, Ben stopped in his tracks. "What's wrong with that there dog?"

"I have no idea." Matthew gently kneed Sandy and attempted to shove him from the path, but Sandy wouldn't budge. "Git!" Matthew cried, sorely vexed. "You git to going!" Sandy cringed at Matthew's reprimand and his tail swept the ground abjectly before he tucked it between his legs and lowered his body to the ground. He whined and looked at Matthew with mournful eyes, but refused to move as commanded by his master.

Matthew saw something large and red with fire, coming across the wet meadow towards them. The object was about ten feet tall and threw off bits and pieces of flame, like a pinwheel, as it rolled toward them, a wild, errie humming sound accompanying it.

Matthew's hair stood on end and his scalp prickled, his heart beating like a trip-hammer in his breast. Sandy whined piteously and cowered at his feet. Large forces of electricity surged through and around them as Matthew, his eyes as big as saucers, looked to Ben for encouragement.

The flaming ball rolled closer, looming larger and more brilliant. As it rolled, it began to change shape. It became taller and thicker and consisted of pure crimson fire. The musical humming changed pitch and became a growl. It sizzled and narrowly missed them, as sparks showered down around them.

Matthew hunkered down and wrapped his arms around Sandy. Tears were streaming unashamedly down his cheeks as he praised his faithful dog for saving their lives. "If we had gone just a few feet farther . . . !" Matthew said in awe to Ben.

CHAPTER 7

After they arrived at the river it hadn't taken Billy Joe very long to catch three good-sized catfish. Then the bites began to slacken. After five minutes with no further bites Billy Joe was chagrined. "Think we can find another spot better'n this, Preacher Willis?"

"Whatever suits you, my lad. I haven't had a good bite yet. And while we're at it, why don't you call me Rock? I'll feel no disrespect on your part and that's what all my close friends back home called me. I trust you're one of them now."

"You bet your britches I am!" Billy Joe answered joyously.

"I'll call you B.J. for short. How does that suit you?"

Billy Joe beamed. "You're all right, Preacher!"

The wind suddenly increased sharply, feeling hot and humid on their skin. Roscoe swiped his forehead with the sleeve of his shirt. "Perhaps we can find a cooler spot too. The air's thick as warm molasses and my clothes are sticking to me tighter than bark does on a tree." Roscoe rolled the sleeves of his shirt up to his elbows, and wiped his brow again. "I sure don't recollect such a sultry day this early in March before. Tell me, B.J., what does the sky look like?"

Billy Joe scanned the sky in every direction. "The clouds seem to be in a mighty big hurry, Rock." He glanced upward once more and said, "Yep! They're moving awfully fast."

"Watcha doin'?"

Billy Joe jumped and stared at the small girl that stood at his side, her big brown eyes fastened on his face imploringly. She peered inquisitively into the bucket and saw the catfish that Billy Joe had caught. "You fishin'?"

"Appears that we are," Billy Joe said lamely, concentrating on his fishing line.

"We loves fish!" Hattie Lou squealed, her eyes shining with wide-eyed innocence. "Specially catfish. Pappy fishes a lot back home."

Billy Joe swung his head around and looked at her seriously. "You want some fish for your supper then?"

Round-eyed, Hattie Lou stared at Billy Joe in wonderment and wagged her head. "Oooo, how divine! What's your name?"

"Billy Joe. But preacher Willis calls me B.J. for short. What's yours?"

"Hattie Lou," she answered happily. How old you be, B.J.?"

"I had my eleventh birthday just last month. How old are you?"

"I's seven, goin' t'be eight."

"This here's my special friend, Rock," he exclaimed with intense pleasure. He's a preacher and he's blind. He's letting me be his eyes today," Billy Joe said proudly, his chest puffing out just a smidgin.

With a glint of wonder in her eyes, Hattie Lou turned her attention to Roscoe who had been listening with interest to every word the children had been saying. "You talk t'God every day, mister?" Hattie Lou asked wistfully," looking at Roscoe in awe.

Roscoe smiled indulgently. "That I do, child. Every day."

Hattie Lou studied his face intently for a moment, then satisfied she had discovered a kindred spirit, addressed Billy Joe again. "You have other chillen, B.J.?"

"Yeh. I have a sister, Amy. She's fifteen and thinks she knows it all. Do you?"

"Arliss. Jest a baby. Had a sister once. She's dead now," Hattie Lou said uneasily, and then a huge smile curved her mouth and her black eyes clung to Billy Joe's. "I's goin' to Kentuck to live. Where you headin'?"

"Everybody in this wagon train is going to Kentucky, silly goose!" Billy Joe said matter-of-factly, then laughed and shook his head.

With a woeful expression on her face, Hattie Lou hung her head. "You hate me, don' you, B.J.?" Her voice was soft, innocent and pleading. Roscoe was taken aback by Hattie Lou's comment and wondered just how his small friend would answer her question. But he needn't have worried. Billy Joe did him proud in his own inoffensive way.

Billy Joe cocked his head and regarded Hattie Lou quizzically for a moment. "Now why the dooce would you say a thing like that for? I don't have any reason to hate you. I don't even know you!"

Hattie Lou flinched at the tone in his voice. "Mammy says all white folks hates us cause we's black," she said dolefully as a look of despair spread over her face.

"What's wrong with being black?" Billy Joe asked, staring at her, baffled.

Hattie Lou shrugged her thin shoulders, her face wistful, and managed a feeble answer. "Don' rightly know, but must be somethin' awful wrong in it. Mammy says . . . ."

Billy Joe interrupted her and said with resolve, "Don't matter a lick to me cause you're black. So your mammy's wrong in thinking everybody is going to hate you. Don't you fret about it none." The matter was closed as far as Billy Joe was concerned.

Billy Joe's mood seemed suddenly buoyant. "Rock and me are going to change fishing spots now cause we've caught all the fish in this here river. You can come with us if you want to. I'll even let you carry my fishing pole if you promise to be real careful with it," he remonstrated.

"I be mighty careful with yore fishin' pole, B.J. Promise," Hattie Lou said, all of a sudden looking like she had swallowed a ray of sunshine.

Carefully handing Hattie Lou his willow pole, Billy Joe picked up his bucket.

"Hold tight to it now," he admonished again.

"Ain't went fishin' in a long time, B.J." Hattie Lou exclaimed breathlessly. "Cain't wait t'tell my mammy!"

Roscoe rested his right hand on Billy Joe's shoulder as they followed the river, using an old Indian trail. Hattie Lou skipped happily along behind them, proudly carrying Billy Joe's pole. She was being very careful with Billy Joe's pole and looking for all the world like she had never had a worry or care.

As they walked, Billy Joe watched the trail carefully for ruts or holes that Roscoe could stumble over. He was very adept in describing the terrain to Roscoe as their path led through a fresh and breathing forest of pine and cedar. The river continued on course, but the path they were using suddenly cut downhill through a clump of bare oak trees, to a small lake. The encroaching shrubbery almost hid it from view. Wild vines grew in profusion, choking everything in their path. Scores of Birch trees graced the edge of the still water, their reflection white and pencil-slim. Beyond the lake was another opening where the path picked up again and wound uphill.

"This looks like a good spot to me," Billy Joe said, very pleased with himself for finding the lake. "All right with you, Rock?"

Gaining the shade of the trees, Roscoe sighed with relief at the sudden coolness.

"Fine with me, B.J., just fine. But I should caution you to keep your eyes opened to any intruders—two legged or four."

"Are we in danger from Indians around here, Rock? We're not even in Kentucky yet!" Billy Joe asked in astonishment.

"Never let your guard down, my boy. We must practice before the fact. Danger has a way of creeping up on you when you least expect it," Roscoe said wisely.

Glancing around them with wary eyes, Billy Joe carefully led Roscoe to a broad sandy bank of the lake, lined with marsh grass. A male red-winged blackbird, perched on a low limb of a birch tree, arched his black wings. The crimson epaulettes on his shoulders flashed as he warbled in a long-drawn "konkereeeeee," before he flew a short distance away where he could watch them out of small beady eyes. A cottontail leaped out of the long marsh grass, studied the intruders for a moment in time, and then ran for the safety of the nearest brush.

Finding a firm spot along the bank, stippled here and there with the prints of small animals, the trio settled themselves comfortably. Billy Joe set his bucket of worms down very carefully and leaned over and dangled his hand in the water. It was very cold and very clear and through the ripples he could see small fish darting here and there on the white-pebbled bottom.

Kneeling on the bank, Roscoe splashed his face and forearms with the cold water and then took a large red handkerchief from his hip pocket and wiped himself dry. Hattie Lou proudly handed Billy Joe his willow pole. "I took good care of it didn't I, B.J?" she asked, an expression of satisfaction showing on her face from the obvious confidence he had placed in her.

Billy Joe grinned and wagged his head as he reached for his bucket of worms. He dug around until he had found the biggest worm he had in it. Hattie Lou squirmed and made a face as Billy Joe forced the squiggly worm onto the sharp barbs of his hook, and tossed the hook and worm into the water. He watched dreamily as his worm-wound hook ducked below the surface the minute it hit the water. "Lookee there, Roscoe, a bite already! I told you this would be a good place to fish didn't I?"

Roscoe laughed at Billy Joe's exuberance, enjoying himself immensely.

Every time Billy Joe's line moved the least little bit, Hattie Lou would get excited. "Pull, B.J.! Pull!" she would cry, clapping her hands and jumping for joy.

"Hold your horses, Hattie Lou. I gotta wait for him to take the bait," Billy Joe cautioned, time and time again. He finally pulled and caught a small bluegill, but he carefully removed the hook from its mouth and threw it back into the water. He baited his hook again and waited patiently. In just minutes his line jerked the pole hard and his luck improved. Soon he was in perpetual motion; baiting his hook and catching fish. After he had caught half-a-dozen beauties, the excitement had subsided for him. "You can fish now if you want to, Hattie Lou."

Hattie Lou's black eyes danced. "Oooo, B.J., thank you," she said gleefully, clapping her hands and hopping about wildly. Billy Joe gallantly baited the hook for her and threw in the line before he handed her the pole.

Hattie Lou sat in silent rapture until Roscoe spoke. "We'll have to be getting back to camp pretty soon, kids. Won't be long before suppertime and your folks will be worrying about you. Feels to me like it's going to rain soon anyway."

Gray clouds were rolling along very fast and it was getting dark. They could hear the wind singing overhead. "Guess maybe we better be headed back," Billy Joe said glumly, giving the sky another quick look-see. "Ma will start fretting if I'm caught out in a storm."

"Oh, please wait 'til I catch me a fish, B.J.," Hattie Lou pled mournfully. Won't'cha?"

Glancing up into the late afternoon sky once again, Billy Joe said uneasily, "You better hurry up and catch one then. We've got a piece to go you know, and we're liable to get soaked if we dally too long."

Hattie Lou concentrated real hard on watching her line. At the least little nibble on her hook she would give the pole a jerk. Suddenly the pole was almost torn from her hands and she cried out in triumph. Billy Joe jumped to his feet. Hattie Lou had caught her fish. It took all her strength, plus Billy Joe's, to pull the fish out of the water and onto the sandy bank, where it lay panting and wriggling, but it was completely hers.

Literally dancing with excitement, Hattie Lou squealed ecstatically. "Caught me a fish! Caught me a fish!" Roscoe and Billy Joe couldn't have been happier for her.

"Rock!" Billy Joe suddenly shouted in alarm.

"What is it, my lad?"

Only a glance was needed to tell Billy Joe that the air was in a good deal of turmoil, with clouds scurrying every which way. "It's the sky!" he gasped. "Everything looks funny—sorta dark and green all at the same time!"

Billy Joe stood transfixed, staring up into the towering gray clouds. Those closest to the ground had a pearly-green quality. A sudden hot and moist wind gusted, shaking the trees, and scattered raindrops spattered the ground about them. Hattie Lou leaped toward Roscoe and grabbed one leg, her eyes as big as prunes. "I's scared, Mr. God man!"

Roscoe wrapped his arms around her. "I'll admit I'm a bit frayed at the edges myself, child, but my trust is in the Lord."

It started raining and small hailstones pelted down on them. In the distance they heard a roar which gradually increased in volume. Roscoe knew at once what was happening. "B.J.," he cautioned, "listen to me, lad. Look around us. Do you see a ravine or deep gully nearby?"

Billy Joe gazed frantically about and shook his head.

"Speak up, lad! Speak up!" Roscoe shouted.

"No! I don't see any gully, Rock, but while we was fishing I think I seen a hole in the side of that hill over there." Forgetting for the moment that Roscoe couldn't see, Billy Joe pointed to a spot to the north of them.

It was getting darker and the roaring had built to a thunderous level. Wind lashed at the trees and they whipped in agony as Hattie Lou's grip grew stronger on Roscoe's leg. "What's happenin', Mr. God man?" she screamed.

Roscoe quickly grabbed Hattie Lou's hand and groped for Billy Joe's. His heart was pounding in his chest with such force he thought it would surely burst. Wind buffeted them and set every blade of grass impotently bending. It whirled a hail of sand from the bank of the lake with a stinging assault on their faces and bare arms. The rain, driven by the screaming wind, was smashing down around them and was shockingly cold. "Head for that hole in the hill, B.J.!" Roscoe shouted. "Just take my hand and lead me!"

Fishing pole and fish were completely forgotten. Billy Joe ran as fast as he could, his temples pulsing and his chest so tight that he could hardly breathe. "This way, Rock. It's not far now!" he screamed, pulling on Rock's hand.

Thunder crashed, lending wings to their flying feet, as they raced up a slight incline, slipping and sliding in the wet grass. Finally the three of them were crowded, but safe and sound within the confines of a small cave. They were soaked to the skin. Their teeth chattered, and their limbs were shaking as Hattie Lou and Billy Joe clung tightly to Roscoe.

In mute terror the children watched as an inferno of whirling debris and sand flew in all directions before them. A huge black cylinder, outside the mouth of the cave, extended out of the clouds to the ground and was twisting sinuously, like a snake. A tremendous bolt of lightning smashed to the ground in front of them, blinding them temporarily. Their eyes were closed against the brilliance of the flash of lightning and they didn't see the black funnel whip viciously once more and then lift up off the ground.

The roar was like nothing they had ever heard before. Hattie Lou put her hands over her ears and kept her eyes closed, trying desperately to shut out the sight and sound of the nightmare she was experiencing. Roscoe sat with head bowed, arms tightly wrapped around his charges, and prayed to the One who controls even the storms.

Slowly the darkness faded. The funnel was gone and the rain began to slacken. After a seeming eternity, the trio crawled from the cave and carefully picked their way around up-rooted trees, broken limbs and other debris that littered the ground before them.

As they neared the spot where they had been fishing in splendor just minutes before, Billy Joe gasped in utter astonishment.

"What is it my lad?" Roscoe asked anxiously.

"It's my bucket, Rock," Billy Joe said incredulously as his mouth dropped open.

"What about your bucket, B.J.?"

Billy Joe gave Roscoe a sidelong glance of utter disbelief. "It's right where I left it and all our fish are still in it!"

CHAPTER 8

As Margaret passed the Carpenters' wagon on her way to do her wash, Kitty stuck her head out of the back. "Headed for the river?" she asked pleasantly.

Margaret nodded. "Want to come along? I'd be happy for the company."

Kitty shook her head. "Thanks anyway, but I just mixed some flour and water with my potato shavings to start some sourdough. Maybe next time. Sam told me earlier that since the river's muddy, I might want to get our drinking water from a little creek over that-a-way. You just might want to do your laundry in it. Be cleaner."

Margaret thanked her warmly and went her way, humming softly. She found the stream with no difficulty and with great delight, discovered it was beautifully clean and clear. The sun was bright and hot and just a few dark clouds hung low in the sky to the southwest. The breeze, blowing off the water, felt cool on her bare arms.

She washed her clothes, soaping them well and then rinsed them; watching as the suds quickly flowed with the current, until they disappeared altogether and the water ran clear again. She then shook the garments and spread them on some bushes in the sun to dry.

How wonderfully still everything about her seemed. Sitting down under the comforting shade of a spreading oak she gazed about her. The forest, dressed in its winter fare, was pleasing to the eye, but how much more beautiful it would be in the weeks to come, she reasoned.

The laurel would cover hill and cliff with its bell-shaped, rose-purple flowers, and the mountains would bloom with purple trillium, violets and yellow and pink ladyslippers. There would be the waxy gloss of leaves and huge, but delicate, pure white sweet-scented blossoms of the magnolia, and the dainty chalices of green and orange tulip trees, blending with the lacy, tinted draperies of dogwood and redbud.

Leaning back against the trunk of a huge oak tree, Margaret pulled the skirt of her dress down over her legs and hugged her knees. Her mouth curved into an unconscious smile and her eyes had a burning, faraway look in them as she thought of her family and friends back in Charlottesville. Her memories came full circle and she mentally scolded herself. *Face facts, Margaret. Every mile you take draws you farther from the place of your birth. What once was, can never be again. You must begin anew and not bury yourself in memories of the past.*

Margaret's body jerked and she became fully aroused. She had been dozing in the warmth from the late afternoon sun. Her glance fell on some of her clothes that had blown off the bushes onto the ground, and she jumped up and ran to retrieve them. The clouds had covered the sun and she could hear the faint rumble of thunder and the chattering sparrows and noisy crows as they flew here and there.

Quickly she gathered up her clothes just as big drops of rain touched her nose and then her cheek. The wind blew harder, wrapping her skirt around her legs, and chilling her to the bone. In seconds the rain came in sheets, soaking her to the skin. She was running over the wet terrain towards the camp, fighting the wind every step of the way.

The wind had torn her hair loose from the combs that held it in place, and the wet strands lashed about her face like a whip as she ran. It had grown dark right before her very eyes and apprehension engulfed her. Lightning seemed to dog her flight, driving into the earth just behind her. With a popping and cracking lightning struck trees to her right and to her left. Margaret finally dropped her basket of clothes, put her hands over her ears, and ran for her life, hot tears mingling with the rain on her face. Another bolt shook the ground and she heard a tremendous roar. She found herself running wildly, having lost all sense of direction as low-hanging limbs and briers raked at her clothing.

A bolt of lightning lit the sky, stopping Margaret dead in her tracks. Sheer black fright swept through her and she breathed in shallow, quick gasps. That's when she saw Amy and her friends. Because of the raging storm, she would never have heard their cries. Crouching on the ground beside her daughter and her friends, and the small children in their charge, Margaret's arms trembled as she gathered them as close as she could to herself. She was weak with fright. With her eyes closed, she cried out fervently, "Dear God, please help us! If it be your Will, let us come through this storm unscathed . . ." A calmness passed through Margaret as she knelt in the face of the storm and continued to pray, "Our Father, Who art in heaven . . ."

. . .

The sky had been a bright blue with only a few scattered clouds when Kitty had bid Margaret Bradshaw goodbye and had started mixing her sourdough. Setting the sourdough aside she decided to take a short nap before Ted and Matthew returned from hunting. Glancing out the back of their wagon, her eyes were drawn toward the now darkening sky. The wind whistled through the trees and a jagged line of lightning flashed across her line of vision. The horses, hobbled in the meadow, whinnied and nervously pawed the ground.

Sighing, Kitty drew the back curtains together. Lying down on a cot she relaxed fully and was soon sound asleep. Fifteen minutes later she was rudely awakened by a profound sense of foreboding.

She listened to the now frenzied whinnies of their horses, the shouts of the men in the camp, and the cries of frightened children. Kitty arose from the cot she had been lying on and shook her head, as if that simple act could dispel her gloomy thoughts.

Chiding herself, Kitty thought sourly, *Every woman in the whole camp has probably been working her fingers to the bone while I've been sleeping the afternoon away.* What will Ted and Matthew think, coming in from their hunt, and not even finding a fire started? Again the foreboding she had felt earlier niggled at her conscience. She drew the back curtains aside and scanned the meadow that separated their camping grounds from the woods. She saw neither beloved form of husband or son. The sky had rapidly changed from mildly threatening to a lightning-filled ebony. A wild wind blew and rain and hail suddenly blasted the canvas cover like bullets. The wagon swayed beneath the on-slaught.

Kitty's skin crawled, as she suddenly realized just how fragile her temporary home was. Rain and hail blew through the front and back openings, soon drenching everything within reach. The whole canvas top pulsed in and out as though it were a living, breathing monster. Kitty clawed the air as a multitude of sounds exploded in her ears simultaneously: frantic shouts, the whinny of horses, a baby's cry, and the incessant sound of the wind. "Oh, God," she breathed aloud, "Where's Ted? Where's Matthew?" Groping blindly for the ties holding the canvas flaps at the back of the wagon she finally managed to get them down and secured.

Running to the front of the wagon, a stout wind whipped violently through the open curtains and catching her off balance, almost knocked her down. Crouching behind the seat, her eyes, sharp and accessing slid out across the circle of wagons. Two women were crouching beneath one of their wagons, hovering over their children. Another woman was braving the storm, trying to rescue her chickens as they ran clucking to and fro. Wet and bedraggled dogs slunk under the protective shelter of their wagons, shaking their wet coats. Cooking pots hanging from tripods danced madly in the wind. The wagons on the far side of the circle were obscured by the diagonal sheets of rain that fell with a heavy roar and rose in a spray from off the ground.

"Ted! Matthew!" Kitty screamed as the wind again buffeted the wagon. Wiping her face with the hem of her white apron, she watched in a daze as the wind billowed out the sides and top of the Bradshaws' tent, jerked the pegs out of the ground, and with one mighty surge, ballooned it across the circle. Belongings, stored in the tent, were scattered in every direction. The wind howled like a banshee and lightning zigzagged across the darkened sky. In desperation, soaked to the skin and her teeth chattering uncontrollably, Kitty clawed at the ties that held the front curtains. Lightning was continuous, the sky a greenish blue flame. The roar was deafening as the evil wind blew the curtains out of Kitty's hands. She was hurled into the depths of the wagon. Her world went black when she struck her head a forceful blow on the corner of a large trunk stored inside the wagon.

. . .

Kneeling beside the inert body of Kitty Carpenter, Sam carefully pulled the skirt of her sodden homespun dress down to cover her legs. Picking up a blanket he shook it free from its folds and covered her body. He could think of nothing more to do for her at that time.

The whole camp was in a state of chaos. The force of the storm had blown clothing and other small articles away. Many sacks of staples such as sugar and flour were ruined. Tents and canvas tops had been ripped open and torn, and wagons tossed about. Cattle and horses had broken free of hobbles and tethers and had run in fright before the storm.

Husbands and wives clustered about, hugging their children and each other, and it seemed as though everyone was talking at once. John stood beside his wagon, assessing the damage done to their belongings, and wondered where his wife and children were. Their wagon was still in one piece, but their tent had been blown away along with their blankets and clothes that had been stored inside. He had spent thirty minutes rounding up their horses and they were now tethered and calm.

With a sigh of relief John spied Margaret and Amy walking toward him. The ground was soaked and it pulled at their boots with a sucking sound with each step they took. An involuntary shudder ran through him as he realized his family could have been lost to him due to the storm. *My beloved wife, Maggie, of almost twenty years—his soulmate. And Amy, his first born. High-spirited, with a bubbling personality, and the spitting image of her beautiful mother.* John ran to welcome his wife and daughter with open arms.

Amy looked pale and drawn and was holding tightly to her mother. When she saw her father she ran toward him with her arms flung wide. John crushed her body to him and when Margaret reached him the three of them clung together.

"Thank the good Lord you're all right!" he cried, searching Margaret's face anxiously.

"But I must look a fright, John," Margaret said, tucking a lock of loose hair behind one ear and smoothing the folds of her linsey skirt with trembling hands.

Amy was frazzled and dirty, her pretty dress splotched with ugly dark stains, and torn in numerous places. John hugged her again. "I was so worried," he whispered, "when I thought you might be hurt. Are you hurt, honey?" he asked quickly, thrusting Amy away from him, and giving her a quick look-see.

"No, I'm fine. Really I am, Pa. But it was dreadful!"

John held his daughter close. "I know, sweetheart, I know." Amy clung tightly to her father as anguish seared her heart and she started to sob. *Almost a woman,* John thought to himself, *but still very much the child.* "There, there," he crooned, patting her back. "It's all over, honey."

Amy wiped her tears and searched her father's face with an intensity that reminded John so much of Margaret. "Is Billy Joe all right? Was our wagon hit?"

"The wagon is in good shape but our tent was blown away." John looked at Margaret expectantly. "Wasn't Billy Joe with you?"

"Why, no," Margaret said, growing weak in the knees. "He went fishing with Reverend Willis. With a sinking heart, Margaret whispered, "John, don't tell me . . ."

"I'm not telling you a thing but to settle yourself! I'm sure Billy Joe is fine. He's probably back at Roscoe's wagon cleaning a whole parcel of fish right this very minute. You go and rest up and I'll find Billy Joe, and that's God's truth!"

The words were no sooner out of John's mouth than Billy Joe ran breathlessly to meet them. His clothes were muddy, his face and hands grimy, but he was grinning like a Cheshire cat. Margaret crushed his small body close until he finally groaned and squirmed free. "I just gotta tell you what happened today, Ma," he cried excitedly.

But Margaret had no time to listen to her son's tale, as a young boy came running up to her, the expression on his face grim. "Miz Willis says for you t'come quick."

Shivering, Margaret looked hastily down at her clothes that were soaked and plastered to her body. "Please tell Mrs. Willis I'll be there just as quickly as I can change into dry clothes."

"Yessum, I'll certainly do that," he said as he turned and loped off.

Sighing, Margaret turned her attention on her children. "I need to use the wagon to get into dry clothes, but as soon as I'm through I want you both to change into dry clothes. It will be a wonder to me if the whole camp doesn't come down with the croup or catch pneumonia."

Amy smiled, knowing what a worrywart her mother was, especially where she or Billy Joe was concerned. Now she had a whole wagon train to worry over.

"Will you please fix your father and brother a bite of supper, Amy?"

Billy Joe was pulling on Margaret's arm, trying to get her undivided attention. "Ma, I want to tell you about . . . ."

"I'll have to listen to your story later, son," Margaret interrupted. "I'm sorry I have to leave you right now honey, but it sounds like Ruby needs me in a hurry. You eat whatever Amy fixes without growling, you hear? And then off to bed with the two of you. You've both had quite a day."

Disappointed that he would have to wait until morning to tell his mother about his exciting day, Billy Joe knew full well his father would listen to the tales he had to tell before making him go to bed.

Gazing at her mother thoughtfully, Amy asked uneasily. "Wouldn't you like for me to accompany you, Ma?"

"Thanks, but no, honey. I'll feel better knowing that you're seeing to your father's and brother's needs at the moment." Margaret leaned over and kissed Amy on the forehead. Lightly she fingered a loose tendril of wet hair on Amy's cheek. "I'm so proud of how well you've handled yourself today, honey. So very proud." Sighing, Margaret frowned and said, "I don't know how long I'll be gone, but it must be very important or Ruby would never have called for me."

After changing into dry clothes Margaret kissed Billy Joe and gave him a hug, holding him much longer than necessary. "Mind what your sister tells you, young man, and no nonsense. I'm counting on you."

"If you need me, you know where to find me," John said, his face grave as he gave her a strong hug. I love you, sweetheart. More than you could ever know."

"Thank you, dear. I appreciate hearing that." Margaret kissed him quickly and whispered, "and I love you too."

John watched intently as Margaret wrapped her cloak around her shoulders and went on her way. Mist and fog hung low and the soggy ground sucked at her feet, as familiar night sounds echoed all around her: frogs croaked, dogs barked and horses whinnied in the meadow.

Every nerve in Margaret's body screamed as she bore witness to the storm's devastation that lay about her. *My loss is so much less than anyone's Lord,* she prayed silently. *I feel almost ashamed. My family wasn't harmed, our wagon suffered little damage and I just wish with all my heart that everyone else had fared as well.*

Shivering, Margaret pulled her cloak close about her shoulders as vivid images of the storm and its horrors played over her mind. *In everything give thanks, for this is the Will of God.* Margaret could hear her own dear father's voice echoing through the recesses of her mind, quoting the verse he so often applied to his own trying situations. *But I'm finding it so hard, Lord, in this instance, to give thanks,* Margaret thought to herself.

A bright shaft of lantern light slipped through a large tear in the canvas cover of the Willis' wagon as Margaret sighed heavily and heaved herself up onto the tailgate.

The faint fragrance of wintergreen met her nostrils as she opened the canvas curtains and entered the wagon. Roscoe was coatless, his sleeves rolled up to his elbows. His face looked gray by the light from the lantern he held in his hand, but his voice was calm when he spoke to her. "Thank God you've come, Mrs. Bradshaw! The missus can surely use another pair of hands."

Slipping off her cloak, Margaret laid it aside and went to stand over Ruby as she knelt beside the body of a man lying on one of their cots. "It's Theodore Carpenter, Mrs. Bradshaw," Ruby exclaimed softly. "Matthew and Ben Grier brought him in just a short while ago. He's been hurt—bad!"

Ruby soaked a cloth in a pan of soapy water as she talked, wrung it out and gently washed Ted's face and neck. There were thick encrustings of congealed blood that had caked his right cheekbone and lips. Next she washed his chest and arms, carefully cleansing his cuts and bruises as she went.

After applying salve and bandages where needed, she asked Margaret to hand her the scissors. "They're in my sewing box on top of the grub box right behind you, dear.

I'll be needing some more clean towels, too," she added quickly. They're in the box just under the pile of blankets.

Margaret gathered up the scissors and towels as Ruby had asked her to. Handing Ruby the scissors, Margaret moved to the end of the cot. "Hold the lantern a little lower, dear," Ruby admonished Roscoe, snipping deftly away at Ted's trousers. Ruby looked at Margaret, a flicker of apprehension coursing through her. "If you will kindly assist me here, we'll see if we can get the shirt and pants off of Mr. Carpenter without disturbing him unnecessarily."

A clammy hand squeezed at Margaret's heart as she and Ruby tugged gently to free Ted's bloody clothes from his body. She gasped at the sight of so much blood and the torn flesh sickened her, but she was quieted before Roscoe's calm repose.

Ted moaned and shivered uncontrollably. Ruby grabbed up a bottle of whiskey and handed it to Margaret. "Give the man as much as this as he can drink and wrap a blanket around him as best you can."

The light was dim and the shadows moved with flickering confusion on the canvas walls, but Margaret could see Ted wince in pain as Ruby tried to cleanse the wound in his groin. "Kitty?" he whispered hoarsely, opening his eyes with great difficulty, and fighting hard to remain conscious.

"Don't try to talk, Mr. Carpenter, just save your strength," Margaret coaxed.

"Open wide for me, and try to drink as much as this fiery liquid as you can. It will help fight the pain." Ted took a small swallow of whiskey and gagged.

As Ruby worked cleansing the wound, Ted moaned and flinched away from her probing fingers. Her brow was knit with determination and Ruby barked, "Get some more of that whiskey down him! The poor man has suffered enough and I'm going to have to probe deeper to find the shell and try to remove some of the bone chips I'm finding as I go."

"Drink, Mr. Carpenter," Margaret whispered as she cradled Ted's head in her arms and held the bottle to his lips. "It will help ease your pain." Ted took another swallow of the amber liquid and choked. Following a fit of coughing, Margaret propped him up higher, using all the strength she had. She again held the bottle to his lips. "Drink, Mr. Carpenter! Drink!"

Groaning, Ted managed another few sips before falling back weakly on the cot as Ruby worked quickly and efficiently. Margaret was terrified at what the end result of Ted's extensive injuries would be but yet was awed by Ruby's deftness in cleansing and bandaging his wounds.

Ruby finally found the ball of lead that had lodged in Theodore's thigh. Having boiled what herbs and leaves she had on hand, she dipped a clean white towel into the hot mixture and wrung it out before applying it to the wound. Ted screamed in agony as Ruby repeated the process several times and then wrapped his leg as best she could in clean bandages.

"Now go to sleep," Ruby crooned, "and God love you for having had to put up with my clumsy doctoring."

"I . . . I'm so . . . cold . . . ." Ted mumbled and Margaret grabbed yet another woolen blanket and covered him. He blinked several times, then closed his eyes and sighed deeply before falling into a fitful sleep.

Margaret passed her hand across her eyes, trembling in an agony of fatigue. She looked at Ruby's ragged appearance and her heart went out to the older woman. "You're exhausted," she stated simply.

"A bit down in the haunches, my child," Ruby admitted, "but who of us should complain when we still have our loved ones with us." She caught hold of Roscoe's free hand and squeezed it gratefully. "You may set the lantern down now, my love. Mr. Carpenter is asleep, thank the good Lord . . . ."

" . . . And a woman by the name of Ruby Myrtle Willis," Roscoe said kindly. A shadow flickered across his face. His startling blue eyes looked straight ahead as he sighed. "It is at times such as these that I miss most what I don't have—my sight. But only to have been a better help to you, my beloved."

"How can God stand by and let such awful things happen?" Margaret asked in her bewilderment.

"Life must be opened to grief and pain, child," Roscoe said kindly. "But never forget that no matter how much we suffer in face of such tragedy, the Lord suffers more than any of us."

"By the way, where is Mr. Carpenter's family?" Margaret asked. "His wife and his son?"

Ruby straightened, easing her back, and gazed thoughtfully

at Margaret for a moment. "Then you haven't heard?" Ruby's brows drew together in an agonized expression.

"Heard what, Ruby?" Margaret spoke in a weak and tremulous whisper.

"Sam came and got Matthew a few minutes before you arrived. Kitty is dead," Ruby said softly. "Near as Sam could tell, she was in her wagon when the storm broke. She must have fallen and struck her head."

"Oh that poor, poor woman." Margaret's face drained of all color and tears immediately filled her eyes. "And Matthew—whatever will that poor boy do if his father . . . ?"

"Hush, dear," Ruby interjected, laying a quieting hand on Margaret's arm. "We must pray that Mr. Carpenter comes through this terrible malady." The tense lines on Ruby's face intensified. "There was another tragedy too, Mrs. Bradshaw. That young newlywed couple, Bundy, I believe their last name was. Word came to Sam just a few minutes after he found Mrs. Carpenter that they had been crushed beneath a fallen tree. Must have taken refuge under it to escape the storm, more's the pity."

"Oh, Ruby, how dreadful!" Tears spilled down Margaret's pale cheeks as Ruby's words sunk in. "Oh, God, why?" she murmured, sobbing brokenheartedly.

Roscoe put one arm around Ruby's shoulders and groped for Margaret's hand with the other. "I've been praying silently all the while you were working on Mr. Carpenter. Now let us lift our hearts to the good Lord in unison." Margaret looked solemnly at Ruby and wiped the tears from her cheeks. They clasped hands and bowing their heads, made their petitions to the Almighty known.

CHAPTER 9

Saturday dawned gray and sober. At first light the men began to stir, and one by one they rose from their bedrolls, stiff and bleary-eyed. They pulled on their boots, built up hot fires and then went to feed their animals.

Soon smoke from all the fires hung in the misty air, carrying a delightful fragrance of burning wood, bacon and strong coffee. After everyone had eaten, bedding and supplies were removed from the wagons to air and dry. Within an hour, every bush was spread and blooming with sheets and blankets and assorted items of clothing. Eating utensils were washed, dried, and put away. The whole campground was fragrant with the tantalizing aroma of fresh-baked bread. Life had to go on.

"I am the resurrection and the life, saith the Lord . . . ." It was mid-day, and the sun was shining down from a sweep of bright blue sky. A whippoorwill, perched on a bough of an ancient cedar tree, sang its lonesome song. The gray-green branches hung like a lacy curtain over the crowd of people who stood in clusters, listening intently as the Reverend Willis recited the words of the burial service. The men stood sober as judges in their Sunday broadcloth, hats in hand, while their womenfolk stared dully into the yawning deep holes that held the blanket-wrapped bodies of Ned and Jessica Bundy, and that of Kitty Carpenter.

The women's faces were gaunt with fatigue and they shrank toward their husbands, reaching and drawing their younger children nearer their spreading skirts. Amy stood rigidly between John and Margaret, trying to listen to what Reverend Willis was saying, but her thoughts kept drifting—back to the moment she had first heard the grim news about Matthew's mother and Ned and Jessica Bundy. She had fixed supper right after her mother had left to help Ruby, and they had just started eating when Sam stopped by to tell them the sad news.

Sam's face was pinched and grim as he told how he had been checking on everybody after the storm, and had stuck his head in the Carpenter's wagon to call out a greeting when he saw Kitty. She had received a mighty blow to her head and was lying in a pool of blood. "There was nothing I could do for her," he said solemnly. "She was already dead."

No sooner had Sam covered Kitty's body with a blanket than Thornton Decker had come with the bad news about the Bundys. They had been seen earlier walking in the woods and evidently they had stopped beneath an oak tree during the storm to take shelter. The tree was hit by lightning and the two of them were killed instantly, their bodies pinned beneath the fallen tree.

A shaft of sunlight pierced through the branches of the boughs of the cedar tree, and startled Amy into attention. Her gaze completed the circle of those gathered for the burial service and came to rest on Matthew. He stood as if on wooden legs, dry-eyed, and his sad blue eyes never blinked or wavered from the sight of the cold, dark grave before him. Matthew's mother had been dressed in the flowered silk she had been married in and then wrapped in a thick, warm blanket, and placed in that grave.

Reverend Willis stopped talking. There was a brief pause and then in unison the people joined their voices: "Our Father, Who art in heaven...." As the voices drew to a hushed "Amen", Amy raised her head and watched dismally as Matthew clamped his broad-brimmed hat down on his head. For a fleeting moment, she had seen the fear in his eyes, and the muscle in his cheek that had begun to twitch. A wave of pity washed over her. She wanted to go to him, to hug him or say something to bring back the sparkle in his sad eyes. But when the rest of the people had paid their respects, and she was finally standing before him, she was struck dumb, her knees weak and wobbly.

His face blank, Matthew dutifully held out his hand toward her. Amy grabbed his proffered hand into her own trembling one and squeezed hard, her thick dark eyelashes fluttering against her pale cheeks. They stood close together for one tense moment, then Matthew, pale and drawn, thanked her politely for coming to the service.

Clearing his throat, Sam drew the attention of the people to him. "In all due respect, I've decided we'll remain right here until Monday morning. That will give Mr. Carpenter more time to mend from his injuries, and we've all got things that need to be looked after due to the storm."

Looking forlornly at the three gaping holes, Sam shook his head sadly. "In keeping with the customs, I'll be holding an auction of Ned and Jessica Bundy's effects tomorrow at one o'clock. I'll send the money to Jessica's parents, being they're the only kin I know of."

Gazing at Matthew somberly Sam said, "Guess we've done what we could for these folks. I just wish it could have been more." He then took Matthew's arm and steered him in the direction of the wagons. As soon as everyone had left the area, Howard Tippett and Thornton Decker took shovels and returned the freshly shoveled reddish-brown dirt back into the open graves. They carefully mounded them and covered the mounds with rocks to protect the graves from scavengers.

. . .

The bright glare of morning sunlight streaming through the canvas flaps struck Margaret full in the face. She was stiffened by the cramped position in which she had slept fretfully all night.

She sat straight up and glanced hastily around her, then smoothed back her untidy hair with both hands. With every bone and muscle screaming in agony, she rose shakily to her feet. She glanced at the cot where Theodore Carpenter was lying and gasped. He lay so still she thought he must be dead. He looked dead and she was overcome with panic, until she caught the faint rise and fall of his chest. Sighing, relief flowed through her. "Thank you, Lord, for allowing him to survive the night," she whispered.

She glanced down to where Matthew was curled in a blanket on the bare boards of the wagon floor beside his father. Her heart went out to him. His face was swollen, his eyes puffy and every now and then he would moan in his sleep. Roscoe was propped against a wooden crate, his head sagging on his chest, and snoring softly. Ruby was nowhere to be seen.

Margaret's legs trembled with fatigue and her eyes felt like two burned holes in a blanket. Having had nothing to eat or drink for over eighteen hours, her stomach clamored for food.

Reaching for her dark blue cloak, she wrapped it around her shoulders, and with a groan stepped out of the wagon and onto the ground. She brushed at her dress, now crushed and wrinkled and glanced around her. A stillness hung over the camp, as few people were yet up and about. Even the dogs were strangely quiet. The fire glowed red before the Willis' wagon, and the air was filled with the fragrance of coffee and bacon.

Margaret's stomach tightened and growled.

"Good morning," Ruby said jovially squinting her eyes against the smoke that swirled around her head. She laid another small handful of twigs to the fire before turning to face Margaret. "Did you finally get a few hours rest?"

Margaret took note of Ruby's pale face and the dark shadows under her eyes, but noted that she seemed in good spirits. "It was a little after four when I finally went to sleep. Did you stay up with Mr. Carpenter all night?"

Ruby smiled. "I managed a few winks. When you get my age you don't need much sleep. You sit yourself down here and get something to eat. So much going on around here last evening

I plumb forgot to fix any supper. I imagine you're starved by now."

"I really should be getting back to our wagon and see to my family, Ruby. Mr. Carpenter seems to be in a deep sleep, but he looks . . . ."

"I gave him several doses of laudanum so expect him to sleep awhile yet." Ruby's voice was resigned.

Margaret's voice caught in her throat. "He isn't going to make it, is he, Ruby?" she whispered, biting down on her lower lip and pain filling her huge brown eyes.

Ruby glanced up at Margaret and blinked. Straightening up slowly she put her hand against the small of her back. She was tired and her back ached, but forgetting her own aches and pains she put a comforting hand on Margaret's shoulder. "He's in God's hands," she said wearily. "What will be, will be. Now, you run along and check on your own little family." Ruby smiled reassuringly and said gently, "I'll manage alone here for awhile."

Margaret frowned. Her head was throbbing. Merely holding herself erect required a strong effort on her part, and hunger pains gnawed at her empty stomach. She looked at Ruby with a feeling of admiration and tribute. There, beneath her calm exterior and gentle voice, lay an unbreakable steel band of courage.

"I'll be back just as soon as I can." Margaret hugged Ruby and kissed her on the cheek. "You try and rest while I'm gone."

The fresh air was like a balm to her soul as Margaret breathed deeply of it. The Willis' wagon had reeked with the accumulated odors of sweat, blood, whiskey, wet clothes and strong medicinal odors. Emotions swirled within her as she gingerly made her way past the other wagons in the campground to her own. *It's a harsh reality, Lord, that Kitty, Ned and Jessica are dead and already buried, and that Theodore Carpenter now lies at death's door. And Matthew, that sweet and stalwart young man now sleeping fitfully back in the Willis' wagon, has so much misery facing him.* Margaret shook her head sadly. *Such a high price to pay for a dream, Lord,* she thought sadly.

After fixing breakfast for her family and tidying up the wagon,

Margaret took a quick sponge bath, and then rubbed herself with a coarse, sun-dried towel until she glowed. Dressed again, she brushed and combed her long brown hair, coiling a thick rope of it and pinning it high on her head.

A narrow mote-filled beam of Sunday morning sunshine drifted into the wagon as she lifted the curtains to throw out her bath water. Amy had finished with the breakfast dishes and was peeling potatoes, carrots and onions for a stew. Billy Joe had gone with his father to feed and curry the horses.

Feeling rested and like a new person, Margaret hummed softly as she stowed the clean dishes into a crate at the back of the wagon. Finished with that chore she looked about her with satisfaction. It was almost impossible to tell a devastating storm had entered their lives at all. Glancing in Amy's direction, she said, "I'm going back to help care for Mr. Carpenter, and I'll be staying just as long as I'm needed. Maybe I can talk Matthew into coming over and going for a ride with you this afternoon. He's hardly moved from his father's side since his mother's funeral."

"I don't know how he can stand it," Amy said, looking at her mother out of fear-filled eyes. "I'd simply die if anything was to happen to you or Pa. Don't ever let that happen to us. Promise me, Ma." Amy's voice quavered, caught between a deep breath and a sob.

"As much as I would like to do that, honey, I can't begin to promise such a thing. Each of God's children must accept what the Lord sorts out for him, and live each day as though it could be his last. Life is a very precious commodity—one that most of us take for granted I'm afraid." Margaret stared into space then shook her head. "We must not get morbid. I'm off. Take care now." She leaned over and kissed Amy on her forehead.

"I love you, honey."

"And I love you." Amy stood and wrapped her arms around her mother. "If I can be of any help, please let me know," she whispered. "I would so like to help Matthew and his father."

"I know you would, dear. But the wagon is so crowded as it is. We have barely enough room to move around in it. I promise I will send for you if I need you." Amy smiled and sat back down. She picked up another potato and started peeling it.

In spite of all Margaret and Ruby had done, Ted had lost a lot of blood and his leg had become badly infected and continued to swell. His skin was hot to the touch. Matthew was fanning his father when Margaret entered the wagon. Ruby was changing the dressings, and had applied more hot compresses. She had also made some tea out of the roots of the butterfly weed and boneset, and every few minutes she would try and get a few drops into Ted to help reduce his fever.

Ted was barely conscious. At times his eyelids would flutter in his swollen and bruised face, and he would moan. He continually moved his head from side to side. Ruby's clear blue eyes caught and held Matthew's. "I've done everything humanly possible for your father," she said quietly. "His pain is intense and I feel that I should be honest with you." Ruby swallowed the lump in her throat and put a hand on Matthew's shoulder. "The leg should come off, but even then . . . ." Ruby's words hung heavy in the air.

Icy fear twisted around Matthew's heart and tears glistened in his eyes.

"But . . . but . . . who, Ruby?"

"I don't believe there's anyone here could do it," Ruby said simply, shaking her head.

Matthew looked down at his father's flushed and swollen face and dropped to his knees beside him. He gently took his father's hand into his own and cried out brokenly, "Please, Pa, fight with all the strength you have. You just gotta get well," he pleaded. He squeezed his father's hand as tears cascaded down his pale cheeks.

Margaret was standing behind Matthew, and leaning down she put her arms about his shoulders. Matthew turned to her and grabbed her about the waist until she was cradling him tenderly in her arms. "Go ahead and cry, son," she said laying her face against the top of his head. Margaret rocked Matthew back and forth, crooning to him, as thought it was Billy Joe she held in her arms.

Catching them all by surprise, Ted moaned and raised himself up off the cot. He opened his eyes and looked about wildly. "Kitty?" He whispered. "I . . ."

Matthew quickly brushed his tears away with the back of his hand and gently eased his father back down on the cot. "It's Matthew, Pa. Just rest now. You're going to be all right. Do you hear me?" he begged, his expression one of mute wretchedness.

"I . . . I thought . . . I heard your mother calling to me. Where . . . where is your mother, son?"

"She's . . . she's not here right now, Pa. She's . . . she's . . ." Matthew couldn't continue speaking. His throat had tightened as though a rope choked him. Ted sighed and Ruby checked his pulse and gave him another few drops of laudanum. She laid an arm on Matthew's shoulder and when he looked up at her beseechingly, she shook her head sadly.

With a muffled sob, Matthew crumpled. "I can't go on without you, Pa," he sobbed. "I don't want to live if . . ." Matthew choked on his words. Wiping his nose on his shirtsleeve, he lay his head on his father's chest, and wrapped his arms as best he could around his body. "Why did it have to be you?" he whispered. "Why, Pa? I love you so."

"Hush now . . . son." Ted licked his lips and reached out a shaking hand and laid it on Matthew's head. "I love you too . . . so much, son. You have always made me and your mother so . . . proud." Ted's voice grew faint and tears glistened in his eyes. "You're the man of the family now, son, and if you . . . live . . . then I live too. Be sure and take good care of your mother." Ted mumbled a few incoherent words and then his face slowly broke into a beautiful smile. He held out his arms as though he was going to embrace someone. "Kitty," he breathed softly, "you did come."

CHAPTER 10

    Sunday evening, an hour before sunset, as the sunlight sifted through the branches in shifting patterns on the ground beneath the giant cedar, the people gathered once again at an open grave. A small wren broke the silence with a trickle of song as Roscoe spoke kindly: "Many of you may be asking in your hearts, 'If God is a God of love, why did he allow these tragedies to happen? Well, I can't answer that question. I only know that he promises never to leave us, in life or in death, if only we believe and trust in his dear name.

    "Jesus said: 'I am the Resurrection and the life. He that believeth in me, though he was dead, yet shall he live. And whosoever liveth and believes in me, shall never die.' "Jesus said these words to comfort his people in their sorrow. He was well acquainted with sorrow and grief. When his beloved friend, Lazarus, died we can only imagine his grief and pain as he looked into the accusing eyes of his beloved friends, Martha and Mary. 'Lord', they accused, 'if thou had only been here, our brother would not have died.' Then they witnessed his tears.

    "Did Jesus fail Martha and Mary that day? Has Jesus failed those of us who stand here in sorrow today? No! Not then and not now! He can always be trusted. He cared for Martha and Mary in

Bethany many years ago and he cares for Matthew and everyone else here in Virginia who has been left to mourn our departed sisters and brothers. Jesus wept then, and Jesus is weeping now.

"It was my privilege to speak with Theodore and his lovely wife, Kitty, shortly after we started this journey together. They were stedfast in their faith, having been saved by grace and baptized with the Holy Spirit many years ago. They wisely instilled their beliefs in their son, Matthew, and he in turn has chosen to walk the straight and narrow path, following in their footsteps.

"As he stands here before us this day, his heart is heavy with the loss he suffers. But he is not without hope. Matthew rejoices today. Not as those who have no hope, but as a child of the living God. The dreams that were alive and full of promise just a few days ago for Matthew now lay crushed and broken beneath his feet. As the days and years pass, he will always wonder what might have been. But some day he will be reunited with his beloved parents through the One, Christ Jesus, who provides us with victory over death.

"I pray those of us who have had faith and trust tested the past two days can repeat the words of Job: 'The Lord gave, and the Lord has taken away: blessed be the name of the Lord.'"

As Roscoe ended the service, Amy's eyes rested on the rise of ground between the laurel bushes where the bodies of Ned and Jessica Bundy and Kitty Carpenter now lay at peace. Then her eyes traveled to the open grave where Theodore Carpenter's earthly remains had just been placed next to his wife's grave. *Why? Oh why, dear God?* She pled silently.

The women about her cried softly; the men cleared their throats and swallowed tears as they stood with heads bowed. Matthew stood tall and serene at the side of the open grave, hat in hand, a faint breeze blowing his hair. John and Margaret stood on one side of him and Ruby on the other.

There was a radiant look on Matthew's face as he reached down and picked up a handful of thick red clay and threw it into the dark hole where they had minutes before gently laid his father.

Amy's heart was broken as she watched Matthew closely. He

went from one huddled group to the next shaking hands and thanking all that had come. At last he stood before her and reached for her trembling hands. He looked deep into her eyes and managed a smile and squeezed her hands until they ached. "I want to thank you for all you and your family have done for me, Amy. I will never forget it."

Amy agonized over Theodore and Kitty's death and tried to share Matthew's grief. And yet she was filled with a great relief in-so-much-as she had not yet been afflicted with death. "Losing a loved one must be the worst ache we can know, Matthew," Amy said as she gazed at him in utter despair. She wanted nothing more than to throw her arms around Matthew and will his pain and heartache away, but all she could muster was a weak, "I'm so sorry." Matthew leaned down and gently kissed her on the cheek, dropped her hands and made his way slowly back to camp.

Thornton Decker was standing next to Roscoe, dressed in his buckskins and linsey-woolsey, his red hair glistening in the sunlight. Amy listened raptly as he put his harmonica to his lips and started to play a simple melody. His eyes squinted into the rays of the setting sun, and the notes he played were sweet but sorrowful, and tear welling, yet they soothed and lulled.

Several people offered bed and board to Matthew, but Matthew's choice was to continue the journey with Roscoe and Ruby Willis. He would drive their wagon, freeing Ruby from this very tiresome and trying chore. And it was his decision to give Ben and Gilda Grier his parents' wagon to use in place of their buckboard that had been badly damaged in the storm. This gave the Grier family much-needed shelter and more comfortable living quarters until they reached Martin's station in Powell Valley. It would be there that they would all rendezvous with Captain Martin and abandon their wagons before heading through the Gap.

As a thick ebony blanket settled over the camp that night Amy realized just how tired she was. Her mother looked at Billy Joe and said, "You need to get to bed, honey. We start moving in the morning and it will mostly be uphill all day. And Amy looks as though she might drop at any moment."

"I am tired," Amy agreed. She hugged her parents. "Are you going to bed too?"

Margaret smiled tiredly, her eyes bright with warmth and love. "I might sit here before the fire with your pa just a little while longer," she answered.

Her mother's smile and the sweet lilt to her voice was like a warm fire in Amy's heart. There was a communion between her parents that was stronger than anything she had ever seen before. She did not understand it nor did she question it; all she knew was that it was there, and she was thankful.

As Amy was stepping up into the wagon, her father reached out and gathered her mother close, glaring impatiently at Billy Joe. Billy Joe looked at his father and grinned. "I'm going! I'm going!" he said lamely and hopped into the back of the wagon, right at Amy's heels.

The spring night was filled with fog and the thickening mist crept silently over the entire campground. Once again the hustle and bustle of a busy day had subsided and a semblance of tranquility had been restored to the faint-hearted. A coyote howled in the distance and several dogs bayed loudly from the circle of wagons.

Amy's fingers twisted a broken thread in her patchwork quilt as she lay on her pallet on the floor of the wagon. She could hear her father's voice as he talked quietly to her mother. "Have I told you lately how much I love you?" Amy smiled to herself as she heard her mother answer coyly, "Maybe once or twice lately, but I wouldn't mind hearing it again."

Turning over and snuggling deeper into the confines of her quilt, Amy whispered, "You could charm the birds right out of the trees, Pa." The rosy glow surrounding them deepened as the day ended and sleep stole into the Bradshaws' camp as silently as a thief in the night.

CHAPTER 11

It was an hour past dawn. The rays of the sun peeked through a frosting of mist, sparkling on wet thickets, and water dripped from the roof of the one-roomed cabin, forming many large puddles on the ground. Cheeley McCabe stepped out of the door, a whiskey jug in his hand, and with bleary eyes gazed about him.

Cheeley was a big burly man, broad-shouldered and with a coarse, dirty red beard, long shaggy red hair, and small beady-black eyes. His clothes were wrinkled and mud-stained, his face, deeply marked by the seasons of the year. He lifted a hand, fingernails black as coal, and throwing back his head, his Adam's-apple bulging, took a generous gulp from the jug he held in his hand. He swiped at his mouth with his dirty and frayed shirtsleeve and cursed as three skinny pigs nosed about the yard in search of food. "Git out here ye lazy slut!" Cheeley yelled in a surly tone. "What's a man gotta do 'round here to git somethin' to eat?"

A young girl appeared at the door of the cabin, a bucket in her hand. She looked about her, her green eyes, dull and lifeless. She was dressed in a drab brown homespun dress and barefoot. Strings of light honey-colored hair straggled over her hollow cheeks and a drift of freckles crossed the delicate skin of her nose.

"Don' ye be dawdlin' at the spring neither, ye hear? Ye'll feel the weight of my strap iffin ye do!" Cheeley took another swig of whiskey and stumbled back into the cabin.

Once at the creek, Sally quickly filled her bucket and then sat down on the cold, damp ground and leaned back against the trunk of a willow tree. She closed her weary eyes and rubbed her hands over her swollen belly. With a glad heart, she felt the baby stirring within her. It would not have seemed strange to her had it died, so sick and weak she had been the last few days. *And how much better had the child died,* she thought, *like the three before it—before she had a chance to see it and to love it.* But this baby seemed stronger somehow than the other three had been. More active. "I wonder what you'll be, little one?" she whispered softly, still rubbing her belly in a round, circular motion. "A little tow-headed lad or a little blue-eyed maid?"

Sally sighed and shivered in the cold morning air. "In three month's time I'll be knowin'," she said out loud to herself. Taking a deep, unsteady breath, she heaved herself to her feet, picked up her bucket of water, and reluctantly headed back toward the cabin. She walked dejectedly, her head down, unaware of the blanket of reddish-gold light spread on the grass and bushes before her by the sun's bright rays.

Her thoughts rambled. *Her mother and three younger sisters had all died of the cholera when she was twelve years old. The next two years were bitter and bleak. When she was fourteen, her father remarried. Her stepmother had four children of her own and begrudged every bite of food or penny spent on Sally's care. During one of their endless arguments, her father gave in to his wife's tirades and agreed to trade Sally to Cheeley McCabe for an old rack-of-bones horse and a side of bacon. Cheeley promised to marry her and Sally was whisked away from the only home she had ever known, and forced into a life more wretched and miserable than she could have ever imagined.*

Cheeley had taken her to his drafty one-room cabin in the hills, boasting one window, a dirt floor, and walls so full of holes you could see daylight through them. Sally was immediately plunged into a living nightmare. Cheeley assured her he'd hunt her down and kill her if she ever tried to run away.

Sally tolerated the days and nights as best she could. The hard work, bad food, and demands made on her body only helped to wrap her into a cocoon of resignation and defeat. It was only when she was lying on her pallet on the dirt floor at night that she allowed the tears to come. The one and only time she had balked at Cheeley's advances, he had hit her so hard her ears rang for days. He threatened her with worse, and Sally had learned the hard way that Cheeley didn't make idle threats.

Sally's spirits sank lower each day. In time she learned to hate Cheeley McCabe, her father, and her way of life. If ever the opportunity presented itself, she had sworn to herself that she would kill Cheeley McCabe. And then she would go in search of her father. When she found him, the man who had abandoned her to this wretched way of life, she would kill him too. These thoughts were the only thing that kept her alive.

Gnats began buzzing around Sally's head and she shook herself out of her reverie. She felt weak and light-headed, and was afraid she was going to faint. She rolled over onto her knees and took several deep breaths until the dizziness abated. As she tried to get to her feet, a wave of nausea filled her. She weakly crawled to a nearby stump. She leaned against the stump, breathing hard, until the waves of nausea passed. In spite of the chill in the air, and the fact that she wore neither shoes nor coat, Sally was perspiring. She crawled on hands and knees to where she had left the water bucket, and dipping her hand into the bucket, she scooped up a handful of the cold spring water and doused her face.

It was then she heard a shot, or what sounded like the blast from a gun, coming from the direction of the cabin. The sound was repeated a few seconds later and Sally knew she was not mistaken—someone had fired a gun. She was almost paralyzed with fear. *Cheeley was probably drunk by now and riled because she wasn't back,* she reasoned. Lifting the hem of her dress she wiped her face with trembling fingers. Forgetting her bucket of water, she silently crept through the wet grass until she was within sixty yards of the gloomy and forbidding cabin. She squatted behind some gooseberry bushes. Two horses, a sway-backed gray and a rangy sorrel, were hitched to a stunted apple tree in the front yard, a few feet away from the cabin door.

Huddled in the weeds, her heart beating erratically, Sally was more frightened than she had ever been in her life. A man was lying face down in a mud puddle in the yard. Two men, holding guns, were standing over his body talking and pointing to the cabin. The man on the ground wasn't moving. Sally rubbed her eyes and stared for several minutes at the man on the ground. From his clothes and scraggy thatch of red hair, she knew it was Cheeley.

One of the men stooped over and removed Cheeley's boots. The other man rolled him over and cleaned out his pockets. Sally closed her eyes to the horror before her. When she opened her eyes, she saw that the front of Cheeley's shirt was covered with blood. The two men glanced furtively around them, jumped on their horses, and rode off at an easy trot.

Sally remained hidden for several minutes, her eyes never leaving the stiff form of Cheeley lying in the mud, three pigs snorting and rooting about his lifeless body. It was when the pigs started playing tug-of-war with Cheeley's clothes, that Sally felt the bile rise in her throat. She kneeled in the dewy grass until her spasms were spent and then wiped her mouth on the hem of her dress. Rising on two shaky legs, her skirt so wet it was plastered to her legs, she made her way slowly to the cabin. She carefully avoided looking at the grizzly form lying in her front yard.

Going swiftly to her pallet, Sally picked up a thin, ragged quilt and tore a piece of material from one end of it. She picked up a hunk of cornbread, pretty well nibbled on by mice, and wrapped it up. She placed the cornbread, along with her only pair of shoes in another square of the cloth. Tying it all into a bundle she glanced around the empty room. Quickly she grabbed up another quilt and wrapped it around her shoulders, picked up her bundle, and bolted out the door. Sally walked as quickly as she could in the opposite direction the two strangers on horseback had taken, never once looking back.

The sun was easing out of the day. Sally had no idea how far she had come but she had been walking for hours through a wilderness of deep forest. The path she followed was an old Indian trail—a trail also used by wild animals. She followed a stream through the foothills where groves of oak and birch stood side-by-side and trembling aspen and elm intertwined their branches with maple and ash. The landscape changed often, the steep slopes of the hills dense with masses of wild roses and dog hobble, intertwined with trailing arbutus, azalea and mountain laurel, making an almost impenetrable thicket.

Long-eared rabbits ran hither and yon in front of her feet while flocks of birds flew over her head. Coming to an open glade where crabapples and wild plum trees grew, Sally found a fallen tree trunk that lay like a bridge across a small stream. Here she sat and rested, ate the last crumbs of her cornbread and drank her fill of sweet cold water from the stream. The water was so clear she could see to the bottom, and the last rays of the setting sun seemingly turned the sand into glittering gold. Tree frogs began their nightly choruses from the edge of the stream.

Walking on a short distance, Sally spotted a herd of grazing sleek-antlered deer with light red fur and short white tails. At her intrusion the fleet-footed deer, their heads held high and their tails tipping up and down, fled swiftly. She walked on, up hill and down, moving among pungent foliage and dried leaves. Purple and white violets blossomed in profusion as far as the eye could see.

Although she was in a foreign place, with only a rag of a quilt wrapped tightly about her shoulders to ward off the chill, Sally felt truly at peace for the first time in five years. Never would Cheeley look at her in lust or scorn and never again invade her privacy or make lewd jokes about her femaleness.

Night was fast approaching and Sally had no way of knowing what lay hidden beneath the forbidding cloak of forest which now draped itself about her, but she felt no fear. Feeling her strength fading, she made haste to gather enough moss and pine needles to make a soft bed. She was hungry and cold, and every muscle in her body screamed, but she hummed a happy little tune.

Clutching the tattered quilt to her chin, Sally lay on her forest bed listening to the night sounds all around her: the hoot of an owl, the rustle of trees and shrubs, the buzzing of mosquitoes, and the chirping of crickets. Unmindful of the dangers surrounding her, Sally drew a long sigh of contentment, pressed her hands lovingly on the mound of her belly and fell into an exhausted sleep.

CHAPTER 12

Thursday dawned sunny and pleasant with soft, cool breezes blowing across the land. A good solid trail was before them as Sam and his wagon train made its way slowly up the eastern side of the Blue Ridge in Bedford County. Trees, in their boundless multitudes, covered the mountains like a living quilt. Shafts of bright sunlight filtered through a thick canopy of branches of huge black oaks, giant towering beeches, yellow pines, hemlocks, columnar tulip trees, magnolias and sweet gums.

In places the forest was so thick as to be almost impenetrable and the trail curved to avoid a twisted laurel thicket that would soon be ablaze with orange flowers. The birds chirped, tweeted, cawed and trilled in chorus, and the squirrels scolded at the intruders, tails whipping and hind legs kicking in time to their raucous invective.

Matthew sat on the seat of the lead wagon next to Roscoe, reins and whip in hand, his heavy rifle leaning beside him against the seat. Sam rode at a slow canter to the head of the caravan. The uneven rhythm of the creaking wheels of the wagons on the hard ground, the steady clip-clop of hooves, and the incessant chorus of voices soothing to his ears.

He was well aware of the feelings of nostalgia that had begun to affect most of the women. The loss of civilization was bearing on them more than they had previously admitted. Many tears were being shed for friends and relatives that had been left behind in Albemarle County.

Some of the weary travelers were afflicted with a variety of physical and mental disorders. It seemed to Sam as though the storm, and consequent deaths of four members of their entourage, had strained their nerves to the breaking point. Arguments broke out over the most trifling of disagreements. Husbands and wives stopped speaking to one another, only communicating through their children. Riding up and down the long line of wagons, Sam couldn't help but eavesdrop on conversations, and he shook his head sadly as the family disputes continued.

The women were tired of their endless chores and the lack of privacy weighed heavily on them. They had three meals a day to cook, laundry and dishes, kids to care for, animals to help feed, water and wood to carry, and their menfolk to please. They were also in fear of the wilderness and its unknown dangers.

Men were more suited to a life in the wilds: living unfettered, in all types of weather, listening to the constant roll of heavy wheels and the clip-clop of horses' hooves. Preying wild animals, breakdowns, and the ever-present threat of Indians farther down the line, didn't seem to faze their strong constitutions.

At noon a pale haze lay thick in the valleys and wreathed the tops of the hills. The wind sang in the treetops. The trail narrowed and threatened to lose itself in a maze of rocks and tangle of grapevines and blueberry bushes. Ferns crowded the path and the sound of water bubbling over rocks grew louder until it reached Sam's ears.

They finally came to a fast-running stream, one of hundreds that threaded their way through the steep ravines and cascaded down towering cliffs. They had crossed the Otter River and now Sam pulled his gelding to a halt beside the west bank of the river. While he waited for Matthew to catch up he glanced around him, marveling at the tall and stately sourwood trees that were growing in abundance in the area, along with cottonwood, dogwood, oak and hickory.

"Water your horses and take a rest under those cottonwoods," he instructed every wagon as it rolled to a stop before him. We'll have our nooning and get some rest." The horses pulling the Willis' wagon had stopped in the middle of the shallow stream and were drinking with long, noisy pulls at the cool water.

The remaining wagons followed suit one right after the other, their iron wheels grinding on the gravel and splashing water onto the horses' legs. After all the animals had their fill, the men popped their long whips, and drove their heavy wagons up the opposite bank. They came to rest in a small glade where the sun dappled the ground with dancing shadows.

The women prepared cold lunches of ham or bacon and cold-egg sandwiches. After eating their fill and personal needs were attended to, the men filled their water jugs and canteens with fresh water from the stream, and it wasn't long before the shout of "roll 'em" rang out loud and clear.

Sam was feeling the indefinable pulse of March, a slowly rising beat that touched the hillside and the woodland. It was like feeling his own pulse, his own growing strength; it was a good time to be alive. Darkness comes early to the canyons and ravines under close-growing trees so about an hour before sunset, Sam brought the caravan to a halt beside a heavily timbered creek bottom; an ideal place to camp. Grass was abundant, as was firewood for cutting.

The horses and mules were unhitched and turned loose under guard to graze. The sound of axes soon rang out and fires sent up blue smoke. Soon the tired and hungry travelers sat cross-legged on the ground eating a hot meal. After supper, Amy and Billy Joe went upstream a short distance to wash their eating utensils, knowing the water would be cleaner and clearer. As the sun sank behind the western horizon, the air chilled considerably. By the time they had scoured their utensils with sand, then rinsed and dried them, the ever-lengthening shadows and accompanying teeth-chattering, goose-bump cold, had chilled them both to the bone. Even the birds had fallen silent.

"I'm cold," Amy said, shivering violently. "Let's get back to camp."

"Just a minute," Billy Joe replied, looking back over his shoulder. "Look at that opening over yonder in the side of that hill. Let's go see what's in it."

Amy was shivering as much from fright as she was from the cold wind that blew around them, but she inched along the side of Billy Joe and crouched to peer into the blackness of the small cave. "I want to go back to camp, Billy Joe" she insisted, pulling on his arm. "There just might be a bear or wolf in that hole." She wrinkled her nose. "Phew! It stinks something terrible in there, Billy Joe!"

"You old scardy cat!" Billy Joe boasted. "There ain't any bears around here!"

Suddenly Amy screamed and she grabbed for Billy Joe's arm as a dark object brushed by her head. She grinned sheepishly when she realized it was only a bat. Billy Joe picked up a long stick and beat about the mouth of the cave. The stick struck a soft object and they both heard a low moan.

Grabbing Billy Joe's arm, Amy again tried to pull him away from the opening, but he refused to budge. Billy Joe tapped with the stick once again and the hair on the nape of Amy's neck began to rise as another moan wavered in the cold night air. Amy's feet turned to stone. She grasped Billy Joe's arm in alarm.

Slowly they backed away from the mouth of the cave. "Ghosts!" they cried simultaneously and turning raced for the camp their utensils forgotten. When they reached their wagon they stood panting and shivering telling their story to anyone who would listen.

Sam, John, Ben, and Thornton Decker armed with guns and holding lanterns before them, retraced the path Amy said they had taken. Light from Thornton's lantern turned the blackness of the cave into a pale gray. There on the floor of the cave, wrapped in an old ragged quilt, lay a young girl. Thornton had to stoop to get his large frame through the mouth of the cave, but once inside he easily picked her up in his arms and duck-waddled his way back out of the cave.

Sam held a lantern close to the girl's face. There was a bluish tinge to her skin and she shivered uncontrollably as she lay in Thornton's arms, moaning. "She's as skinny as a hoe handle and wouldn't weigh as much as a pound of soap after a week's washin'," Thornton admonished. I think we found her just in the nick of time."

When the men got back to camp, John instructed Thornton to take the girl to his wagon. "Amy and Billy Joe won't sleep a wink all night if I don't prove to them it wasn't a ghost they heard."

Thornton eased his burden gently onto a pallet in the Bradshaws' wagon, and then quietly backed away as Margaret, Amy and Billy Joe crowded around the unconscious girl. After wrapping her in warm blankets, Sally slowly opened her eyes and gazed about her. Seeing so many strangers, she cringed and pulled back in alarm. The men quickly turned and took their leave, taking Billy Joe with them.

A shadow of alarm touched the young girl's face. She stared at Margaret and Amy out of eyes half-defiant, half-piteous, her gaze clouded with tears. She was barefoot and bareheaded, and clad only in a faded and ragged homespun dress. The thin material clung to her body, outlining the distinct mound of her stomach. Her face was thin and pale; her hair lank and full of tangles, and the quilt she hugged about her scrawny shoulders was filthy and in tatters.

There was eagerness mingled with tenderness on Margaret's face as she asked questions of the girl. "Who are you and where do you hail from? And what were you doing all alone in that cave?" The young girl looked around her searchingly as though seeking an avenue of escape. Seeing none, she sighed heavily and answered in a tight voice filled with despair, "I'm . . . I'm Sally."

A pain squeezed Amy's heart as Sally stared at them, her green eyes big and round. She worked her jaws but no words would come, and she suddenly started to cry. Amy stood hesitantly, wanting to do something for her. Margaret was filled with pity as she whispered, "There, there, Sally. Nothing can be all that bad. I never meant to ply you with so many questions. It's just that we would like to help you, that's all. We'd like to be your friends, Sally."

A slight flush touched Sally's cheeks and pain came to her eyes. "I . . . I'm . . . so hungry," she wailed. "I . . . I ain't had nothin' to eat for days now exceptin' for a hunk of cornbread an' what water I could find in the creek." She looked about her in a daze and her eyes grew misty. "I could surely use somethin'. Anythin' would be grand if you have it to spare, that is?" she asked hesitantly.

Staring at Sally in horror, Amy recalled the delicious supper she had eaten just a short time before she and Billy Joe had found Sally. She had never known anyone who had nothing to eat for days and her heart melted at the thought.

Soothing Sally as best she could, Margaret quickly began to give orders to Amy.

"I want you to go to the grub box and rustle up a plate of food. Also bring me one of your clean shifts and some fresh drawers. She's about your size and I think your things will fit her just fine. While you're busy with that, I'll get some soap and water and see if we can't get a layer or two of this grime off this girl."

Amy was still staring at Sally with her mouth open. Margaret caught her eye and said, "Scoot, now!"

Margaret bustled about gathering a clean wash cloth and towel, a basin of hot water, and soap. She gently removed Sally's filthy, ragged clothing. "We'll be burning your clothes and blanket in the morning—with your permission, that is. I don't believe you'll be needing them any more, and they sure wouldn't wash up." Sally silently nodded her head.

Amy brought the clean clothes her mother had asked for. She stood mute and watched as Margaret gently washed and towel-dried Sally, and then dressed her in Amy's sweet-smelling clothes. Margaret's skin crawled and her eyes filled with tears when she saw the bruises and scars on Sally's scrawny arms and legs. She looked helplessly at Sally's mop of hair and shook her head. "We best let her eat before I tackle that head of hair, Amy. That might take awhile, and I know Sally must be most starved to death right now."

Amy brought a bowl piled high with beans and ham, and a plate with two slices of cornbread lavishly smeared with butter and a cup of buttermilk. With a glint of wonder in her eyes, Sally started eating with her fingers, shoveling everything into her mouth at once. She swallowed hunks of ham without taking time to chew, and couldn't drink the buttermilk fast enough. Seeing the bottom of the empty cup, Sally looked up at Amy shamefaced. Holding out the empty cup she asked timidly, "Cou . . . could I have just a tiny bit more? I ain't had any buttermilk in years, an' it tastes better than I ever remember it tastin'."

Amy scurried to refill the cup and Sally started once again shoveling in the food as fast as she could. "There, there, child, take your time," Margaret admonished, reaching out and clutching at Sally's hand. "There's plenty more food where that came from. I'm afraid you're going to make yourself sick eating so fast!"

Sally exhaled a long sigh of contentment and felt a warm glow flow through her. "I'm rightly sorry, ma'am. I guess my manners escaped me." Margaret and Amy stood back and watched Sally in dumb fascination. Pity shown in Amy's eyes, remembering a starving puppy that Billy Joe had once brought home for their mother to feed. The puppy had the same haunting look in its eyes that Sally did now.

After Sally had cleaned her plate, she lay back on the cot, her hands and fingers sticky, crumbs on the bedclothes, and a big moustache of white foam outlining her upper lip—but there was a beautiful smile on her face.

Dipping the washcloth in the basin of warm water, Margaret wrung it out and wiped Sally's face and hands, as she would have a child. Sally smiled at her dreamily, showing even white teeth. "I guess you saved my life, an' I'm beholdin' to you. I don't think I'd a made it another night in that there cave with no food an' too weak to crawl to the creek for water. I was afeared of goin' out an' dyin' from the cold, an' afeared of dyin' all alone in that there cave. I had the weary dismals, let me tell you. My mind was startin' to ramble. I was hearin' voices and seein' things I knowed warnt there."

"Why were you in that cave to begin with, dear? Did you run away from home? Do your folks live around here?"

Quickly Sally shook her head. She glanced at Margaret, met her eyes, and smiled. "I don' rightly have no folks. My ma died when I was twelve. Cheeley McCabe had come to trade my pa for some beaver skins right after we laid my ma to rest. Pa and Cheeley got to talkin' an' my pa give me to Cheeley. Traded me for a horse an' a side of bacon, he did. Chee... Cheeley... he treated me jest like he felt like, an' iffin I didn't move fast 'nough to suit 'im, he... he took a strap to me. He's dead now though."

Sally saw the look of alarm that crossed their faces. "Not by my hand," she added quickly, "but I'm plumb happy 'bout it. I hated 'im." Her eyes filled with tears. "An' I hate my pa for givin' me to Cheeley in the first place. An' iffin I ever find my pa, I'll... I'll rightly kill 'im too, if I'm able."

Amy was shocked into silence at Sally's words, but Margaret awkwardly reached out, put her arms around her shoulders and drew her close. "Shhhh," she whispered incredulously. "Those kind of thoughts aren't good for you—especially... well... you know..." She glanced down at Sally's belly, and then she glanced at Amy, her face turning red. Sally looked at Margaret's red face and she smiled. She rubbed her hands over her swollen belly and continued to smile.

"You *are* going to have a baby," Margaret stated flatly.

"Oh, yes, ma'am." Sally stated quickly. "That's the only fine thing to come out of this whole shebang. I'm goin' to have me a baby on down the line a piece. A wee little baby that I can hold on to an' love. Now that I'm free of Cheeley my baby will have a chance to live. The others died of beatin's I got from Cheeley. Died 'fore they had a chance to live."

"But you're no more than a child yourself, Sally. You don't look a day over twelve right now." Margaret peaked her eyebrows.

"I'm nineteen years," Sally stated firmly. Ma always tol' me I was born on January 11 in the year 1764. So you see, I'm all of nineteen years."

"Where are you wanting to go, Sally? You can't stay out here in the mountains, all alone, with no shelter, and no man to provide for you," Margaret stated emphatically. "Especially since you'll be having a little one soon."

"Don't rightly know," Sally said, her face shining with a steadfast and serene peace. "I ain't exactly had time to think that one clear yet, but it ain't troublin' me none."

"Would you like to go to Kentucky with us?" Amy blurted.

Sally looked doubtful. "Now why would you folks want to saddle yourselves with another mouth to feed? Yore ma's done been kind to me an' I'm beholdin', but I know they wouldn't want to take me in like they would a . . . a stray dog. I can make it by myself I guess, if I have to. Now that I've had somethin' to eat . . . ."

"Nonsense! My daughter does me proud by asking you," Margaret stated in a firm voice. "We'll make room for you and our family will be glad for the company. That is, if you would consider it."

"Oh please say you will, Sally," Amy coaxed. "We'd love to have you go to Kentucky with us. I'll share my clothes and things with you. Please, you will go with us won't you?"

Sally looked from one to the other of them in awe, a glimmer of hope shining in her compelling green eyes. "You really mean you'd want me to live with you? To sup with you an' tag along clean to Kentucky?"

Amy and her mother nodded in agreement. "There ain't a lazy bone in my body, an' I'd try an' earn my keep, iffin' you . . . " She looked at both of them once more, her eyes searching. Seeing the beautiful smiles lighting their faces Sally sighed. "You . . . you really want me?" she asked incredulously.

Amy tossed her head. "We really want you," she said simply.

"We'll do some more talking and planning in the morning," Margaret said, smiling. "You need your rest right now. You can sleep right where you're at, honey. Amy will make her pallet on the floor close by your side, and Billy Joe can start sleeping under the stars with his pa and me."

Drawing a big sigh, Margaret said with a gentle softness to her voice. "And I believe I'll leave off washing and brushing your hair tonight. That's going to be a chore. You just get some sleep now—tomorrow's another day." Margaret leaned down and kissed Sally on the forehead and patted her on the shoulder before tucking the covers tightly under her chin. "Goodnight, Sally. May the Lord's angels continue to watch over you." Catching her breath, Sally screwed up her face and burst into fresh tears.

"Why, Sally, dear, whatever did I say to hurt you so?" Margaret asked in alarm.

Sally wiped at her tears frantically and finally quieted and looked up at Margaret, disbelief shining in her eyes. "It's nothin' you said, ma'am. It's jest . . . jest that I've wondered all my life wha . . . what it would be like to . . . to be tucked into bed an' kissed goodnight." She sniffed and shuddered, then whispered, "An' now I know. Goodnight, ma'am," she said sweetly, brushing at the tears still running down her cheeks.

Margaret kissed Amy and hugged her close, biting her lip to keep from crying, then made her way slowly out of the wagon.

CHAPTER 13

It took four days, in fair weather and foul, to climb the eastern side of the Blue Ridge, to where the wagon train reached the main divide at Buford's Gap. Then another half day of leisurely riding down the western slopes had brought them to level ground again.

Saturday morning they followed an old Indian trail that led to the Big Lick, on a branch of the Roanoke River. Here, salt springs welled up in the mud, and from the hoof prints, Sam could tell it was a place of rendezvous for buffalo, elk, deer and smaller wild game. Vast canebrakes and a rich and luxuriant growth of trees marked the course of the Big Lick. Sam gladly turned toward it.

The stream ran swift and clear as crystal. Here, beside the bright woods and sparkling water running musically over the rocks, Sam called a halt to the day's travel. Small water birds splashing in the shallows filled the air with their cries and flutterings. Squirrels, quieted a moment by their coming, began to bark and chatter in the treetops. A flock of turtledoves whirred in to drink briefly, and then flew away to their roosting places.

"Be a good chance to go hunting, men. From the looks of all the tracks around here, I'm sure we can all dine lavishly on turkey and grouse tonight. Maybe we can even scare up an elk or two if we're lucky. So hop to it." Sam was grinning widely.

Matthew approached John, holding his rifle in the crook of his arm. John was staking out the horses, Billy Joe close at his side. "Like to take a ride in the woods with me, Mr. Bradshaw, and see if we can scare us up some game? If tracks are any indication, there's a crossing on the river over there that looks like it's frequently used by animals."

John smiled at Matthew, and a good feeling passed through him. He was happy that Matthew had singled him out from all the other available men to go hunting with. John hadn't found an occasion since Ted and Kitty's tragic deaths to really talk to Matthew, and he jumped at the chance to spend some prime time with him.

Easing into a smile, his eyes bright, John answered quickly, "Fine with me, young man."

Glancing at Billy Joe, Matthew grinned. He had noticed the hangdog expression on the boy's face. "Would you like to come with us?" Before Billy Joe could answer, Matthew suddenly turned his attention back to John. "That is if you don't mind, sir. I didn't mean to be so presumptuous."

"Quite all right, young man. I need to ride herd on this young fella anyway to keep him out of trouble and out of his ma's way." He reached out and laughing good-naturedly ruffled Billy Joe's hair.

"Oh, Pa," Billy Joe said, the tips of his ears turning beet red, but so full of happy feelings he could hardly speak. "Can I ride Foxy, Pa?"

"If you promise to stay within calling distance." John agreed. "If anything was to happen to you your ma would skin me alive and that's God's truth!"

Billy Joe rode out leisurely ahead of John and Matthew. They followed the game trail down a narrow path close to the Big Lick. Sandy broke away from the trail and was into the heavy brush, nose close to the ground, when Billy Joe topped a knoll grown up in scattered pines. Riding into an opening he pulled on Foxy's reins and gazed about him.

Suddenly the pine straw started moving. Sandy started barking furiously and ran about in all directions. Foxy shied at the unexpected movement and pranced sideways. Billy Joe jumped from his back and held tightly to his reins, trying to calm the excited animal.

Billy Joe had accidentally wandered into the middle of a herd of bedded deer.

There was at least a dozen deer now running in all directions, just as startled as Billy Joe and Foxy had been.

John and Matthew loped into the clearing just in time to see Billy Joe jump from Foxy's back. They both dismounted and quickly tied their mounts to a tree branch. Matthew raised his gun and quickly searched for a doe in his sights, but just about the time he was situated for a good shot, another doe jumped up and Foxy reared again.

The doe bolted and tore across the clearing, Sandy close at her heels. Seeing that Billy Joe was once again in full control of Foxy, John and Matthew took up the chase on foot. The doe darted into a thicket with Sandy nipping at her heels. She then jumped a small ditch and broke into open timber. Nimbly dodging tree limbs and briar thickets, she was soon out of sight. Matthew gave up the chase, the shrill barking of Sandy off in the distance, assuring him that his dog had not chosen to do likewise.

John was huffing and puffing when he reached Matthew's side. They looked companionably at each other and broke into grins. "The old man isn't what he used to be," John said, dropping to the ground. He leaned his head against the trunk of a tree, trying to catch his breath.

Matthew laughed and sat down heavily on a fallen tree trunk, aware that John looked completely done in. "Take awhile before Sandy realizes I'm not in the chase, but he'll be back directly. While we're waiting for him we'll have a chance to catch our breath."

They could hear the branch water trickling along somewhere to their right. They took deep breaths, relishing the wild, damp, sweet smell of pine. Except for the sound of running water, and their heavy breathing, silence was all around them. They sat comfortably together, regaining their strength, finding no need for idle talk. A chipmunk chittered, gave out with a little squeak at catching sight of them, and disappeared in the brush. Suddenly screams filled the air, bursting in on the silence of the woods, shattering John's nerves completely. "Billy Joe!" he cried, jumping to his feet. His skin prickled and he went cold. A shadow of alarm touched his face as he grabbed up his rifle and ran in the direction of his son's piercing cries, Matthew close at his heels. Visions danced in John's eyes of Billy Joe being mauled by a grizzly, or being scalped by an Indian, and his heart almost failed him. *If anything happens to that boy . . .* John could not give credence to his thoughts.

Finding Billy Joe was easy. When John and Matthew reached the edge of the thicket, they realized Billy Joe's outcries were but an ebullation of joyous excitement. He had tied Foxy to a bush, and had chased two half-grown wolf pups to their burrow. He was now on his hands and knees, grubbing away like a dog at the mouth of their hole, trying to get to them. By the time John reached his side, Billy Joe had hold of one of the pups by the hind leg, and was attempting to pull it free of its burrow.

"Drop it, Billy Joe!" John cried out, his expression clouded in anger. John darted a worried glance around the area, sure that he would see the mother wolf lunging at them from the shadows at any moment.

Billy Joe managed to get the young pup out into the light of day. It was dark gray in color, with perky ears and very large paws. It was yipping, snapping and snarling. "I said drop it!" John yelled, his accusing voice stabbing the air. He jerked Billy Joe by the shoulder with one hand and brushed angrily at his hands as they tightened around the animal's leg with the other.

"Do you want to lose a hand?" John admonished; shaking Billy Joe roughly as the wolf pup broke free of his grasp and ran. John stood stock still, his hands on his hips, glowering down at his young son. Billy Joe shuffled backwards on all fours and then stood erect, facing his father's furry and matching it with his own.

"Don't you ever let me catch you pulling such a dumb, foolhardy trick like that again!" John said, taking a deep breath and letting it out slowly. "Now, let's get out of here before the female gets back and tears us limb from limb for disturbing her young."

"Aw, Pa, I could have had me a dog if you hadn't butted in," Billy Joe whined, kicking out at the mound of dirt at his feet.

"That was no dog, son! That was a wild animal—a half-grown wolf!" John scolded.

"It looked like a dog to me," Billy Joe said sullenly.

John reached out and shoved Billy Joe ahead of him. "Looks don't count, son."

"Dang it anyway," Billy Joe said sourly.

"What's that you said?" John asked sternly.

"You say it," Billy Joe countered, cowering beneath John's stern gaze.

"Don't do as I do, do as I tell you, young man! And don't let me hear you say anything that even sounds like a cuss word, ever again! Do you hear me?" John said crossly, forbidding any further argument.

Billy Joe's face was set in a sullen, stubborn frown. He said nothing and John repeated, "Do you hear me, young man?"

"Yes, Pa," Billy Joe answered quietly.

John looked at Matthew who stood aside and watched as Billy Joe mounted Foxy and rode off ahead of them. Matthew shook his head. "As a lad of eleven, he's in a ferocious rush to grow up, sir."

John's anger abated somewhat under the warm glow of Matthew's smile, and he grinned. "I reckon I ought to have shook more sense into him, but a boy isn't a boy too long. My own pa was stern and allowed no boyhood pranks by me. I loved and respected him, but we had no close times that I can remember. I vowed it'd not be that way with me and my son."

Suddenly realizing where their conversation had taken them, John put out an unsteady hand and touched Matthew's shoulder, looking him in the eye. "I'm sorry as all get out, Matthew, for getting carried away with my speech. Didn't intend reminding you that, well, that . . ."

"It's all right, Mr. Bradshaw. Folks can't weigh their words before speaking just because it might remind me I have no pa—or ma for that matter. My folks are gone, but as my pa said to me there at the last, if I live he lives, and I know that life must go on."

"I'm sorry anyway. Your pa was a good man, and your ma was a lovely woman. Such a heritage will stay you well, and that's God's truth!"

. . .

That night Margaret sat beside John on a log close to Sam Tippett's fire, her eyes tracing the low-burning fires around the camp. They glowed brightly, the flames dancing in the wind. Above the tops of the trees, the stars blinked down out of the dark night sky.

Quite a few fellow travelers sat about Sam's fire, listening intently as he told stories about his first trip into the wilderness just two years before. Sam sat on a cottonwood log, his hat pulled down over his eyes, and his Mackinaw hunched about his neck against the cold. He held a cup of hot coffee tightly in his hands as he leaned toward the fire. The fire blazed, popped and crackled, and shadows danced on Sam's face and on the faces of those sharing his fire.

Margaret pulled the edges of the blanket that she had draped about her shoulders, closer. The cold was deepening fast and Sam's voice droned on: "Lewis Craig told the story straight and clear, just as it happened back in July of '55," Sam said quietly. "Less than thirty miles from where we're a-sitting tonight. The grain fields were turning to gold in Draper's Meadows that bright sunshiny day. The meadows were lush, the vegetable gardens green and luxuriant, and the settlers were ready to harvest their grain.

"The little group of cabins that made up Draper's Meadows was deeper into the mountains than any other white community in Virginia, and William Ingles and his wife Mary had lived there in prosperity and peace since 1748. They had two little boys," Sam added, "Thomas, four, and Georgie, two. Mary was expecting another baby in a matter of days."

Margaret could hear the inflections in Sam's voice and knew

he was thinking of his own wife and children who waited for him, over the mountains and far to the west.

"In the cool of that Sunday morning, William Ingles and his brother-in-law, John Draper, went to their separate grain fields. Ingles' close friend, Colonel James Patton, was at his cabin, writing. Ingles' wife, Mary, and Draper's wife, Bettie, were busy at chores. Mary's mother, Elenor Draper, had Mary's two young boys in her care as they picked berries in a nearby thicket."

Taking a swig of coffee, Sam continued speaking. "Hearing screams, Ingles rushed home and saw a band of marauding Shawnee Indians assaulting his settlement. It was a force much too large for him to try and oppose, as he was unarmed, having gone to the fields that morning without his gun. Chased into the woods by two of the Shawnee, Ingles was lucky enough to escape with his scalp intact by successfully hiding from the Shawnee."

Sam dangled his hands between his knees and picked at a clump of grass, his brows drawn together in a painful expression. "When the war hoops died down, Ingles ventured from hiding, and accompanied by Draper, scratched in the ruins of the smoldering cabins. Draper's baby had been killed and Colonel Patton had been scalped, but not before he had killed two warriors with his sword. One man was seriously wounded, but was able to tell the tragic details of the massacre.

"Bettie Draper had been shot in the arm just minutes before her baby had been killed, and Elenor Draper was killed and scalped right before her two grandsons. Mary Ingles, her two young sons, Bettie Draper and a neighbor, Henry Leonard, were all taken captives. The settlement had been completely wiped out, the homes plundered, and burned, and the horses stolen. The other livestock was killed or scattered. The savages beheaded one kindly neighbor, put his head in a bag and gave it to a Mrs. Philip Lybrook, and then left with their captives."

The smoke from the fire circled in the air above him as Sam's voice trailed off. "I must apologize to the ladies for speaking so frankly. Plumb forgot myself once I was into the telling of it."

"That's quite all right, Mr. Tippett," Margaret said as casually as she could manage. "If it gets too hairy we can leave, but I think we're all aware of the dire deeds that Indians are capable of. I can only speak for myself, but since there aren't any of our children within hearing distance, I would like for you to continue, if you please. I'm anxious to hear from you how things turned out for the Ingles' family."

Kicking the fire into a blaze, Sam warmed his hands. "Anybody have any objections?" Hearing none, he continued with his story. "Mrs. Ingles gave birth to a little girl three nights after being captured. Bettie, who only had the use of one arm, was her only help. Mary had to bite off and tie the cord herself because of Bettie's crippled hand. Mary's boys were later separated and taken to Detroit, I was told. Bettie was taken to Chillicothe and adopted into the home of an Indian Chief.

"Mary escaped her captors with another white captive—an old Dutch woman. She had to abandon her three-month-old baby girl and it about broke her heart, but she knew it would be impossible for her to make such a long journey through the wilderness, carrying a tiny baby. Mary's thoughts were, at the time, that by leaving her baby behind, at least the baby would have a chance at life.

"She and the old Dutch woman traveled through cane-brakes and marshes, across streams and rivers and over the mountains. They lived on nuts and berries, papaws, roots, and even ate the tender bark from the trees. Then the mind of the Old Dutch woman snapped and she tried to kill Mary. Mary was able to escape her, and after forty days and nights, she found her way back home." Sam shook his head in disbelief.

"Remarkable woman, that Mrs. Ingles. A very remarkable woman."

"Did they ever learn what happened to her three children, Mr. Tippett?" Margaret asked, shivering from the cold, but wanting to hear of a happy ending to Sam's story before retiring for the night.

"Mrs. Ingles did recover from her ordeal I was told. Had four more children I believe it was. But she couldn't forget her other children. The family finally received word about her two little boys. Little Georgie died soon after being taken from his mother, but young Thomas lived for a time in a Shawnee village, and was adopted by an Indian family. He was finally reunited with his parents when he was seventeen years old.

His parents paid about 150 shillings for his release. Mr. Ingles died just last year, a very prosperous man. He had succeeded in building a ferry across the New River. Also a tavern, a general store, and stables to care for the teams of wagoneers. As far as I know, Mary is still working in the store at Ingles' Ferry, her family all close by. Bettie was ransomed in 1761 by her husband, John, and had seven children before she died in 1774."

The fire had ebbed and Margaret was chilled through. She pulled her blanket close to her neck and yawned. "I think it's time to turn in, John. Morning will be here before we know it."

"If you're waiting on me, you're backing up," John answered nonsensically as he rose to his feet and extended a helping hand to his wife. They bade Sam a hasty "good night" and strolled toward their wagon.

A piercing cold wind disarranged Margaret's hair and she smoothed it absently. "Whatever we face on this trip, John, I'm sure of one thing. It can't be any worse than what that poor Mrs. Ingles faced. Can you imagine keeping your sanity through such trials and tribulations?"

"Would be hard," John agreed quickly. "I guess it's a blessing from God that none of us knows what we'll be called upon to bear in this life."

CHAPTER 14

Flinging back his woolen blanket Sam Tippett slowly rose from his bedroll to his feet. He yawned deeply and pulled on his heavy boots, slipped into his fringed buckskin jacket, and left his tent. He was greeted by a cold and crisp dawn, ice around the edges, and the first muted morning noises of the New River. He stood for a moment looking about him.

Fires burned brightly in front of several wagons and dark figures moved noiselessly around them. It had rained during the night and from the packed look of the ashes of last night's fire, Sam knew he would find no live coals. He ran his hand over the rough stubble on his jaw and for a moment wished he could forgo his morning ritual of shaving. Needing hot water for his morning coffee he sighed heavily and scattered the ashes with the toe of his boot, scraping down to the dryness of the ground underneath.

Sam's breath twinkled in the frosty air as he broke some small dead limbs from a nearby tree and soon coaxed a small flame from shavings. Squatting, he nursed the flame patiently, blowing into the shavings until they caught fire and glowed a flickering orange. When the blaze was high enough and he had a steady blaze, he added larger pieces of wood taken from a weathered cottonwood log he had sat on the night before.

Smoke boiled thickly around his head and he squinted his eyes against it. The damp wood spewed and sputtered. "Burn, drat you!" Sam muttered, "and keep on burning until I get me some hot water and grub!"

The ground was wet underfoot as Sam made his way to the river, a bucket in his hand. Fog shrouded the campground, twisting over and under and through the wagons. It laced and swirled in the top branches of the trees and lay like a bank of white wool over the river. He could see nothing beyond the river but a white wall of fog. The hills that had stood solidly before them yesterday had disappeared as though they had never been.

By the time Sam got back from the river, the camp had come to life. He savored the comfortable morning noises of clanking pots and pans as the women made preparations for breakfast. A wave of homesickness for his wife and children washed over him as their voices floated on the air coaxing sleepy children from their warm beds.

A rooster crowed and a coyote howled in the distance setting up a loud baying from the dogs in the camp.

By the time he had shaved and eaten breakfast, the fog had blown away, and the sun had risen on wisps of clouds, like wings of pearly fire, lighting the eastern sky. A jay flew to a leafless maple, and twittered his spring-song, and two redwing blackbirds, fluffed fat against the chill, talked hoarsely to each other in a willow whose catkins were still half-sheathed.

Sam carried his gear to where his sorrel gelding stood grazing and placed the saddle blanket and then the saddle on Sonny's back. Howard suddenly appeared before him. "Mornin' big brother," he said brightly, handing Sam a cloth-wrapped package. "Nancy wanted you to have these sandwiches. Thought maybe they'd come in handy for your noonin'. With ham an' gravy an' biscuits for breakfast we..."

Sam accepted his brother's offering and groaned. "Spare me the details, little brother," he interjected quickly, an expression of mock anger on his face. "Dang it all, Howie, some pal you turn out to be! Coming over here lording it all over me, knowing I'd be eating warmed-up mush while you're dining on fancy fair!" Sam stated flatly.

Taking a sip out of the coffee cup he held in his left hand, Howard shook his head from side-to-side, a whimsical expression on his face. "Well, in that case, I'll just go back and tell Nancy you declined the offer." He made a playful grab for the parcel that Sam now held tightly in his hand.

"You try taking these back and I'll break every bone in your arm!" Sam said and laughed good-naturedly.

"What kind of ground we gonna be coverin' today?" Howard asked, sobering.

"I'd like to make twenty mile every day for at least the next six days. We're about a hundred and twenty miles from Gate City located on the South Holston. I'd like to be there by Saturday evening. Be some hard pushing, but I believe we can do it. It'll be another hundred miles or so on to the Gap from there. Sound good, little brother?"

"We'll more'n likely lose some time at Martin's place gettin' rid of our wagons and all," Howard said, taking another swig of coffee. Glancing around the circle of wagons he said, "Sure goin' to miss those babies and that's a fact!"

Sam shook his head in agreement. "It won't exactly be a picnic from Martin's place. Guess that's where we'll separate the men from the boys."

Howard drained his cup. "I'd better get back and see if Nancy needs any help with the kids. I've got everything else of ours packed up and ready to go. See you later, big brother!"

Howard turned on his heel, and Sam stood and looked after his receding figure. How he envied him his Nancy right now. He missed his own Abigail so much and his three children. It had been months since he had left his wife and kids to make the journey to Virginia.

Desire for his family swept through him like a rushing tide. In his mind's eye he saw Abigail as she had stood at their cabin door waving goodbye to him. She had smooth, pale skin, and her mysterious dark eyes were flecked with gold and fringed by long black lashes. Her ruby-red lips were full and in his estimation, made for kissing. But it was her waist-long and naturally curly brown hair that grabbed his attention. It was heavy and sometimes unmanageable, with tendrils escaping and surrounding her head like a halo.

Abigale usually wore her hair in a chignon and Sam gloried when at night she would brush it and let it cascade down her back. It made her look sixteen again. Not at all like an old married woman of twenty-eight years with three children and another due in July.

Sam reached into his vest pocket and pulled out his gold watch. He cradled it in the palm of his hand. Sighing, he slipped his watch back into his pocket, and mounted Sonny. It was time to start another day.

It was the eighteenth of March and Amy lingered in her bed, her eyes closed, just half-listening to sounds of activity outside the confines of their wagon. She had heard her father earlier moving stealthily about so as not to disturb his sleeping family. It seemed strange to have Sally sleeping in the wagon beside her instead of Billy Joe, who was always jumping, bouncing, fidgeting, or finding ways of causing mischief.

Amy was overjoyed that Sally had decided to travel with their family all the way to Kentucky. *Just like having a big sister!* Amy thought joyously as she went over in her mind all the events leading up to Sally's decision. *How blessed I've truly been, Lord, to have a loving mother and father—and brother! It would be so hard living with the knowledge that your father would ever consider giving you away. Much less to such a poor excuse for a human being as that Cheeley person had been.*

Sally stirred in her sleep and turned over, facing Amy. She lifted sleepy lids and seeing Amy was awake she rubbed the sleep from her eyes. She sat up and looked around her. "Good mornin', Amy. You been awake long?" she whispered.

"Not long. Pa's been up and doing for quite some time, but I do believe little mischief-maker and my ma are still asleep. I haven't heard them up and around yet anyway."

For the next half-hour Amy and Sally whispered and giggled together, a happy lilt to their voices. Every once in awhile the name "Thornton" would pass Sally's lips and she told Amy that she felt a lot of admiration for him. He had been the one who had carried her to the Bradshaws' wagon the night they found her and he had stopped by the wagon to check on her several times since. Amy was certain Sally would be seeing more of Thornton Decker.

Finally the clatter and ring of cooking utensils as Margaret prepared breakfast overshadowed the muted sounds of the rolling splash of water tumbling over the rocks in the riverbed. A rooster crowed, and a cow bellowed, anxious to be milked.

Amy pulled back the curtain and saw three older boys walking through the mist on their way to water their horses at the river, just as the early morning sun topped the eastern hills. The weather the past week had remained unpredictable, one day dawning mild and sunny, and the next a northern would blow in, freezing the travelers to the marrow.

Today, Amy decided, looked to be fair but cold at the moment, and she hurriedly dressed in warm clothes.

"It's a mite chilly out there, Sally. The sun hasn't had a chance to warm things up yet. You stay in bed for a little while where it's nice and warm, and I'll bring you in something to eat in just a jiffy."

Sally smiled. "I feel plumb lazy an' useless just layin' here, Amy. Sure there ain't somethin' your ma needs help with?"

"Nothing that needs your attention right now. I'll help her. Just close your eyes and rest and I'll be back shortly."

. . .

The travelers were winter-weary, and lengthened daylight was only a taunt, not yet a reality of spring. April, however, was just a whisper away, with growth very evident—a green world in the making and the weary travelers' hearts responded.

A red-tailed hawk paused high over the edge of the river, wheeling slowly, his wings soughing in the north wind, his yellow legs tucked tightly under his belly. A hare at the edge of the water had caught his eye. The hawk turned slowly and flexed his great wings as the hare rose slowly from his crouch, trembled slightly, and then hurled himself into a frenzied flight toward the brush. The hawk made one grand swoop with talons bared.

Gilda had been watching the circling hawk, knowing all along its intentions. She shuddered and closed her eyes at the hawk's quick descent, and then cringed as she heard the pitiful cries of the doomed rabbit. She knew the laws of nature, and yet her heart cried out every time she thought of one animal dying so that another might live.

The past week or so she was finding it very hard to pray. After her encounter with Ruby Willis, she had searched her heart, trying to recapture a semblance of the faith instilled in her as a child, but memories of standing at the open graves of the Bundys and the Carpenters were still too vivid in her mind. Good people who loved the Lord and tried to live by his rules, and yet he had seen fit to take them in their prime of life, in violent death.

She had been present to hear Reverend Willis preach on God's goodness and her eyes brimmed with tears as she heard the now all too familiar words ringing in her ears: . . . *accept our prayers on behalf of the souls of your servants. If God was a God of love as Reverend Willis said, why . . . ?* Gilda pressed both hands over her eyes, and shook her head to clear it of all the gloomy thoughts. There just weren't any answers to all her questions.

Once again gloomy thoughts overrode her ability to pray. *Surely God is angry with the whole bunch,* she reasoned. *Why else would he bring the fierce storm right where they were all gathered? Why bring death to certain families and not others? And would her family be next?*

Gilda reasoned that she should be prostrating herself before an angry God, but she was in fact doing nothing of the kind. She felt only a dull, heavy weight of doubt growing within, where she supposed her soul must be lodged. Her whole body seemed to be engulfed in tides of weariness and despair.

Her attention was caught by the tinkling cries of sparrows sounding above the precise ticks of woodpeckers and nuthatches, as they drove their beaks into the trunk of an old elm tree nearby, pulling out sleeping grubs.

Gilda sighed and looked about her, trying to clear her tortured mind. There was a sweetness in the air, the smell of growing things. A few warm days had sent dogwood buds bursting into newborn leaflets and a hint of green blurred the stark outline of deciduous elms. The red maples stood majestically, their small red flowers clustered along their branches. The odd-shaped creamy flowers of the early skunk cabbage, with reddish-brown blotches had opened and were packed with drinking gnats and bees. God had a hand in such a beautiful creation. Gilda accepted that fact. She just couldn't sort out in her mind where she and her family fit into the picture.

She glanced about her again. A pair of bluebirds came silently out of nowhere and perched on a limb just above her head. Gilda caught her breath. Nothing, not even the sky after an April shower, was ever that blue. Her heart leaped as a small flock of chattering sparrows flew into the tree causing the bluebirds to take flight. Her surroundings gave her a new sense of peace and she drew in a long breath of clean fresh air and once again tried to pray.

She bowed her head humbly, folded her hands in her lap as she had been taught as a little child, and then spoke out loud to the One whom she so desperately wanted to touch her heart. "Lord, iffen yore real, iffen yore really carin' for yore people as the good Reverend says you are, iffen you really love me, Gilda Grier, then I's askin' that you . . . that you please . . ." Gilda stuttered, "let me be feelin' a forgiveness for this unbelief that still festers in . . . in my heart."

Gilda's voice broke miserably, and her young face grew suddenly piteous, as her thoughts drifted once again to the families that had recently lost loved ones. Words popped into her head unbidden: *Death comes as a thief in the night, robbin' us of everythin' we hold dear in this here life, an' I don' rightly know how to handle it.*

Her throat tightened and her head ached as hot tears coursed down her dark cheeks. "I ain't wantin' to be a unbeliever—a infidel, Lord," she uttered miserably, "but how do I rightly know me an' my own won' be next?" Gilda sobbed loudly.

. . .

Sam's caravan had been following the Wilderness Road, a route opened across the Appalachian barrier in 1775. It was the principle overland entry into the limitless reaches of the West. They had crossed the low divide, transversing the Great Valley at the headwaters of the James and Staunton Rivers; had passed over the New River at Ingles' Ferry, and had continued traveling down the middle fork of the Holston River, to within a few miles of Gate City.

On Saturday they had turned northwest, ready to leave the Holston Valley, and wind their way through a jumble of close hills, and a narrow valley drained by the Clinch and Powell Rivers. The Cumberland Gap was still over a hundred miles away, but they were making progress, however slow at times.

Sunday found them camped under an expanse of brilliant blue sky in a bottomland overgrown with green grass and wild grape. It was fed by springs, with the glassy Holston River running broad and smooth before them.

Their days and weeks on the trail had flowed together in a comfortable routine of companionship: playing cards, and singing and dancing many a night away. Often, the evenings were spent sitting around campfires, reminiscing and talking about their families and friends back in Charlottesville and other towns. Since they were nearing the Kentucky border the main topic of discussion was the ever-present threat of an Indian raid.

There were days when Matthew moved as if in a dream after his mother and father had been laid to rest. Times when he thought he heard his father's voice raised to call him to some task. At those times he felt like a lost soul. His memories for the example his parents had set in their devotion to one another as well as to him, were safely stored in his heart, to be called upon day or night, as the days would turn into weeks and slip through his fingers.

His mother had been the salt of the earth—his rock. He wanted nothing more at times than to be held once again in those safe, loving arms, like as when he was just a child—to be petted and comforted and told what to do. There was nothing of his mother left to him now, except what was locked in his heart: a life preserver in a stormy sea; her infectious laughter, and her serenely wise and beautiful love for family. But as countless others before him, Matthew learned that life, when taken one day at a time, was the only way he would be able to endure life without her.

Matthew was working through his grief and was trying to be the best help he could be to the Willis'. He anticipated Ruby's every whim. He rose before dawn to carry water, to help Ruby prepare meals, and to pack dinners. He took full responsibility with the animals and wagon, driving himself relentlessly.

Every day endeared Matthew more and more to Roscoe and Ruby and the Bradshaw family. He had made fast friends with Thornton and often relied on Ben to help him with matters too much for one man to handle.

Roscoe and Ruby took the place in his heart of his own grandparents, people he had only heard about but had never known. They had died several years before he was ever born. John and Margaret Bradshaw were like a second set of loving parents, helping to fill the void left by the death of his own. Billy Joe was a good kid, and he looked upon him as a younger brother.

And Amy—Matthew thought of her as the younger sister he had never had. He wanted nothing more than to help John protect her on this journey. She was someone special in his life. He didn't know how or in what way—but his feelings ran deep in that direction. Often reminded of the difference in their ages, thoughts of a romantic encounter with Amy were drawn up short. He felt his feelings should never be stronger than the feelings toward a sister.

CHAPTER 15

It was late Sunday afternoon and Matthew and Thornton had just ridden into camp after scouting all day for Sam. They caught sight of Sally and Amy walking to a nearby spring, oaken buckets swinging freely at their sides.

"I'm interested in Sally," Thornton quickly told Matthew. "With all the work and scouting duties for Sam I've found it awfully hard to spend much time with her though. You know, Matthew, when I entered that cave and picked her up in my arms the other night, I felt I would need nothing more out of life than to be able to hold her forever. She seemed so helpless—so small and defenseless."

Shaking his head, Thornton grinned at Matthew and his features became more animated. He cleared his throat awkwardly and ran a hand through his unruly red hair. "Don't think I've lost my head entirely or think me crazy," he said dubiously, "but I think I . . . oh, shucks, Matthew, you're going to poke all sorts of fun at me."

Matthew grinned. "I know your head is on straight, Thornton, and I don't believe for one minute you're crazy. But I can't read your mind, so spit it out—what you're thinking, that is."

Thornton's face melted into a buttery smile. "I'd like to spend the rest of my life loving Sally and protecting her from any more of life's threatening circumstances. She looks like a spring flower to me, ready to be plucked and admired. Some folks might say she's a rotten apple core because of what that Cheeley guy put her through and expectin' a baby and all and not married. But I don't rightly care what others think."

"There now, that didn't hurt too much did it," Matthew said, his eyebrows arching mischievously. "Seriously, I know what you mean. Sally has had a rough time and with a baby coming along and not married, well . . . that could tend to make folks talk. I'm glad you're open-minded enough to not hold that against her. Sally will probably be more than willing to have some attention showered on her."

Matthew paused and let Honey crop at the sweet grass covering the floor of the Holston Valley, lying wide and lush around them. "I don't know much about love, Thornton, but I feel it can happen quick or it can take a long while to find that certain girl you would like to spend the rest of your whole life with. I had a girl back in Ohio. Her name was Valerie and she was as cute as a kitten and just as soft and warm. I thought a lot of her and had I stayed in Ohio, I might have ended up marrying her." Matthew glanced at Thornton and sighed. "I guess I wasn't too serious about her though as I really can't say that I've thought that much about her since being on this trip to Kentucky. I've looked all the girls over on this wagon train but the ones I think I could be interested in are too young, and the ones that are my age . . . well, they just don't do anything for me."

Thornton's gelding neighed and pawed at the ground as a covey of quail broke and ran from cover. Thornton calmed him with a gentle pat. Then nudging his boot heels against the flanks of his mount, he said, "C'mon, Matt, the girls are about out of sight."

Breathing deeply of the redolent air, Matthew smelled the sweet grass, wood smoke, and cooking meat as he and Thornton loped easily through the tall grass, toward Sally and Amy. "I thought there for awhile that you might be interested in Amy Bradshaw, Matt. She's a fine looking girl, and I don't think you could do much better."

Matthew shook his head and grinned. "Making out a matchmaker?"

"Naw. I'm just thinkin' out loud. You don't think you could be interested in her in the least little way?"

"She's only fifteen, Thornton, and I'll be nineteen in a few months." With a heavy heart, Matthew's gaze roamed over the figures of Amy and Sally as they walked just a few yards ahead of them. "Her pa would run me clean out of Kentucky if I was to show any romantic interest in her I bet. He still thinks of her as his little girl."

Matthew slapped at the trail dust on his breeches and let his gaze fall once more on Amy as she sauntered ahead of him. He took quick note of how vibrantly alive, lovelier, if that were at all possible, she seemed today than when he had first laid eyes on her several weeks ago. With a shiver of vivid recollection he remembered her liquid brown eyes, full of beauty and promise; how her skin had looked as smooth as silk and the color of a fresh peach ripening in the sun.

The March day was unusually mild, a promise of April in the breeze that stirred the skirts of Sally and Amy's homespun dresses. The spring peepers were in full voice, filling the air with their song. Sally and Amy were so engrossed in conversation that neither of them caught sight of Matthew and Thornton as they rode toward them. Sandy bounded ahead of them, stopping every now and then to smell the ground before moving on.

"Could we have the pleasure of your company?" Matthew spoke to both girls, but gazed only at Amy, appraising her with more than a mild interest, impressed with the green flowered dress and bright green bonnet she was wearing.

Amy was so startled at the friendly intrusion that she jumped. Her heart pumped wildly in her ears and her breathing quickened as she made a quick appraisal of Matthew and Thornton sitting tall in their saddles. They looked the part of frontiersmen dressed in buckskin shirts and leather breeches. They both wore moccasins that reached their knees, and were tied with leather thongs.

The pounding of Amy's heart finally quieted and she chided

herself for staring. Stammering, she glanced wildly at Sally who was grinning profusely at Thornton. "That will be . . . just . . . just fine with me, how about you, Sally?" she finally mustered.

Sally grinned, showing bright white teeth and dimples and nodded her head affirmatively.

Dropping lightly from the saddle, Matthew stood before Amy and with an eager lift of her head she looked full into his smiling face, a tremor racing through her entire body. *She's as interested in me,* Matthew thought to himself, *as much as I'm interested in her. There has to be a way . . . God . . . please help me find a way.*

Thornton offered Sally his arm and they moved as one toward the spring. Matthew adjusted his stride to match Amy's and was enjoying her obvious struggle to recapture her composure. He looked down at her with a mischievous grin and stared once again into her beautiful eyes—eyes that he could drown in; eyes that held him spellbound. They were alive and warm, a mystical shade of brown, like warm molasses, and they now glowed with excitement.

Amy's heart was pounding as she picked her way over the uneven ground. She remained silent as they strolled leisurely along. Hungry sparrows and blue jays swept down around them to intercept insects in midair. She could hear Thornton making small talk with Sally, and she knew Sally was probably hanging on to every word he uttered. They finally reached the spring where the brush was beginning to come alive with the first feathery, almost illusionary, greenery of spring. Here the birds sang and the squirrels raced through the treetops, pausing here and there to taste the coming green of tightly furled buds.

Reaching for Amy's bucket, Matthew quickly filled it with cold sparkling water from the spring. Amy watched every move he made, comparing him to every gawky young man that had ever paid her a minute's worth of attention back home. There had been many such suitors, stumbling over their own feet, stuttering and stammering over every word they spoke. She had accepted their insipid remarks with regal poise, seriously interested in none of them, but knowing that someday she would have to make a choice.

She was never interested in landing a man some day just for propriety's sake. She only wanted to land the *right* man! She stared dreamily at Matthew. *He's a man, and he is definitely showing an interest in me today,* she thought. *And he's no pimply-faced, gangly-legged, smart-alecky youth, but all man, with strength and power emanating from him.* A meadowlark sang from the bottom branch of a huge sycamore tree and Amy thrilled to its sweet clear call. She knew it was a symbol of good luck.

After Thornton had filled Sally's bucket, he looked first at Sally and then at Amy, smiling his slow, easy smile, his red hair glistening in the sunlight. "Would you ladies like to sit a spell," he asked hopefully, pointing to a log. "Unless that is, you have something better to do?"

Smiling tremulously, Amy glanced questioningly at Sally. "Just so we're back in time for the dance tonight," Amy replied happily.

Sighing contentedly, Amy moved toward the log, sat down and carefully smoothed her skirt around her legs. She then patted the space beside her. "There's plenty of room for you, Sally," she said dreamily.

Sitting down beside Amy on the log, Sally worried a straggling strand of hair that curled about one ear. Thornton looped the reins of his horse around his saddle horn and dropped wearily down on the ground, his back against a great spreading oak. He faced them, his long legs crossed in front of him Indian style. Matthew tied Honey's reins to a nearby bush to let her graze, and then dropped to the ground beside Amy. She was lost in reverie and in seventh heaven, just being in Matthew's company.

Sandy continued to nose around the dead leaves and violets that were blooming beside the water. Two ducks swam close to the edge of the stream and Sandy bounded into the water after them. Amy laughed good-naturedly when the ducks flew off and Sandy was left standing in the cold water, forlornly gazing at their retreating flight to freedom.

Picking up a blade of grass, Matthew stuck it in his mouth, cleared his throat and stole a sidewise glance at Amy. "A penny for your thoughts."

"You'd probably feel cheated," Amy said, grinning sheepishly. "My thoughts probably aren't worth a penny."

Matthew laughed lightly and chewed nervously on the blade of grass a moment. "Will you save me a dance tonight?" he asked hesitantly, a deep longing sounding in his voice.

"I'd ... I'd be happy to," Amy stuttered as her extraordinary brown eyes blazed and glowed. She watched dreamily as a hawk circled overhead, looking for something to eat and caught bits and pieces of Sally's conversation with Thornton. Amy could tell from what they were saying that they planned on getting together at the dance too.

The sun slid slowly into a ball of crimson in the western sky and a cool breeze breathed down on the foursome. Amy shivered and rose slowly from the log she had been sitting on. She looked down at Sally. "I think it's about time we get back to camp, don't you? If we're going to the dance tonight, we better be getting our dancing shoes on."

Smiling in agreement Sally tried to rise from the log. She blushed faintly, realizing that she was helpless. Thornton quickly stood to his feet, reached out and took Sally's small hands into his larger ones and gently pulled her to her feet.

Quickly untying Honey's reins, Matthew and Thornton mounted their horses. Amy glanced up at Matthew and thought how nice it would be to always have his face to look up to. "I guess we'll see you gentlemen tonight," Amy said softly, her eyes shining and her heart beating erratically.

Matthew glanced down at Amy. He tipped his hat and said lightly, "Until tonight," and he and Thornton loped back to camp, Sandy at a full run beside them. Sally and Amy walked hand in hand back to their wagon, giggling and sharing thoughts like two ten year old kids.

Dusk had deepened and the redwings and peepers were shouting. Stars paled at the brightness of the moon now almost directly overhead. The crickets and katydids sounded their screechy songs in the silver-edged darkness, as gray smoke from a huge bonfire soared into the evening sky.

Everyone was laughing and having a good time as they sat on stumps of sycamore and locust or on blankets and large logs that had been dragged close to the fire. Food had been prepared by each family and was shared by one and all. The children were running wild within the circle of wagons, enjoying a freedom of restraint from their parents. Dogs were barking and playing fetch with a few of the younger boys.

After everyone had eaten their fill, Roscoe stood up, tucked his fiddle beneath his chin, and commenced playing. He was soon joined by Thornton on the harmonica and Howard Tippett on the banjo. With Sam calling all the moves, a circle was made and a dance was soon underway.

Sally had dressed and gone on her merry way. Amy looked critically at herself in a long rectangular mirror. She sighed in dissatisfaction as she adjusted the wide blue sash she had tied about the waist of her soft blue cotton dress. *I look like a child,* she thought dismally, turning first one way and then another. She didn't like the way her bones protruded across her shoulder line, and she felt her breasts were much too small. And to her way of thinking, braids made her look twelve years old.

Quickly Amy undid the braids, and with several quick strokes of her ivory-handled hairbrush, her hair hung in soft and rippling waves almost to her waist. She grasped a few strands of hair from each side of her head, pulled it back and tied it with a blue ribbon. She pinched her cheeks until there was a rosy glow to her skin and then she practiced smiling at her reflection in the mirror for several minutes.

Leaning closer to the mirror she studied her face soberly. *What will Matthew think?* she wondered. *Was there anything special about her that he would find attractive tonight? After all he hadn't been paying all that much attention to her since the death of his parents—up until today. Of course it could be due entirely to the fact that he was now scouting for Sam, and driving the wagon for the Willis', thus adding to his workload.*

With a sigh Amy was now in full reverie and her thoughts rambled wildly. *Lately Matthew's face had been haunting her dreams.*

Some nights he would be smiling at her as he had the first day they met, his blue eyes alert and dancing. Those thoughts faded and she would see him as he stood at the open graves of his parents, his eyes downcast, his face etched in lines of deep sadness and despondency.

Sighing, Amy made a small mocking curtsy before the mirror. Idly she glanced at the clock and knew she had been wasting precious minutes. Quickly she grabbed her woolen shawl and threw it around her shoulders and scrambled down from the wagon.

As she walked toward the gaiety, she couldn't stop from pondering the ceaseless, inward questions that plagued her. *Sally would be spending as much time with Thornton as she could tonight, but what she didn't know for sure was whether Matthew would seek her out for a dance as he had said he would. Would he be captivated by some of the other pretty young girls who would be at the dance vying for his attention? Perhaps a girl more his age than she was, more mature and . . .*

The whining of the fiddle, the twang of the banjo, and the sweet haunting notes of Thornton's harmonica assailed Amy's ears and brought her out of her reverie as she hurried nervously toward the open fire. People were clapping and stomping in rhythm and Sam was calling a square. Amy nodded at those who smiled warmly at her and her pulse pounded when she first caught sight of Matthew.

He was standing next to her father in deep conversation. When she reached them John smiled proudly and leaned down and planted a kiss on her cheek. "It's about time you were showing up, young lady. I was beginning to think you'd gotten lost, and your ma's been fussing about you missing your supper. You better hightail it over yonder and try and rustle up some grub before it's all gone. It's pretty fine fair, let me tell you."

"I couldn't eat a bite, Pa," Amy gushed. Her eyes shifted immediately to Matthew, and she felt a warm glow flow through her as he smiled at her. His handsomeness overwhelmed her. She dropped her eyes quickly and then glanced up at her father.

He winked at her and said, "Guess I'd best go find your ma and see if we can't show some of these young squirts how to do a high step or two." He turned and started to walk away and then retraced his steps and put his arm around Amy's shoulders. He gave her a loving squeeze and addressed Matthew directly. "I'm counting on you to take special care of my little girl tonight, young man."

"Oh, Pa!" Amy said, embarrassment written all over her flaming face.

"Sorry, honey, but I guess you'll always be my little girl." He smiled lovingly at Amy, gave her another hug and winked at Matthew. As he left he called over his shoulder, "You kids have a good time tonight, you hear?"

"We'll be sure and do that, Mr. Bradshaw." Matthew answered firmly, his face splitting into a wide grin. With a long purposeful step he moved beside Amy, his eyes sharp and assessing. The suggestion of nubile curves beneath her dress awakened a response deep within him, and he had a strong desire to tell her how pretty she looked in her soft blue dress.

He paused to reflect a moment. *He felt sure a man could drown in her long-lashed, liquid brown eyes, and he longed to run his hands through her thick wealth of lustrous brown hair. A fetching sprinkle of light freckles across the bridge of her nose just added to her wholesome good looks and he ached to reach over and touch her—kiss her—but not now, not in this place.*

Matthew felt he was mature for his age, partly hurried there by the untimely death of his mother and father, but none-the-less, he was a man. He was a man, with a man's desires and needs, and he had proven the last few weeks that he could do a man's work.

Fidgeting nervously at Matthew's side, Amy wondered if he would ever ask her to dance, so that she could show everyone that Matthew Carpenter belonged to her—at least for the evening—at least for one dance.

The music shifted from a rollicking square into a slower tune. Matthew pulled his thoughts together and reached for Amy's hand. He gave her a smile that sent her pulses racing and asked lightly, "Shall we?" Amy sighed deeply and moved with him into the throng of people already dancing.

To Amy's delight, Matthew danced beautifully. He skillfully guided her own awkward steps as she tried to get her feet to do her bidding. She had never been so nervous in her whole life, and her body, from head to toe, felt as if it was on fire.

Glancing up at Matthew, their eyes met and held. She felt a warm glow flow through her as his face creased into a beautiful smile. Amy relaxed immediately and leaned into him, making Matthew feel ten feet tall. He was consumed with feelings of protectiveness and desire.

The waltz finally ended and the people yelled for another square. The fiddle screeched and everyone started stomping their feet and clapping their hands. Thornton eyed the boy Sally was talking to and when the square ended and the fiddle moved once again into a slow, smoothing tempo, he put his harmonica into his hip pocket and strode purposefully toward them. He tapped the young man on the shoulder, and ignoring the look of disappointment on the young man's face, he took Sally into his arms.

Amy's borrowed lavender dress flared out around her ankles as he whirled her about. The healthy glow of color in her cheeks, her gleaming hair falling in soft curls about her face, and her eyes, deep, clear and black-lashed, made Thornton ache with a intense longing.

The movements of Sally's feet were graceful in spite of her protruding tummy, and her smile was quick and warm as she gazed up at him. Thornton was at first awkward as a buffalo calf, making terribly hard work of dancing, but with Sally's encouragement and rosy-cheeked smiles, he soon felt ready and able to dance the night away.

The tune to *Barbara Allen* filled the air as flames of the bonfire leaped high. Sparks drifted up and away from the flames that illuminated the people dancing beside it.

Sally started humming and then began to sing the familiar words: "'Twas in the merry month of May; the green buds, they were swellin'; Sweet Billy courted a fair young maid; her name was Barbara Allen.'"

"Glory be! Where'd you learn to sing like that?" Thornton asked, his luminous eyes widening in astonishment as the first verse of the song ended.

"Why . . . I don' rightly know," Sally answered. "I must of heard my ma singin' it when I was jest a wee little girl. Since I've never had nobody much to talk to, I jest fell into the habit of singin' at home jest to hear the sound of a human voice, I reckon."

"Sing for all of us, Sally, please," Thornton coaxed. Sally shyly shook her head.

"Please, Sally, just as a favor to me?" Thornton cajoled. The tenderness in his expression amazed her and with her face glowing, Sally began to sing the rest of the verses of *Barbara Allen*. She sang so softly at first she could hardly be heard. Her voice gradually gained in strength after the first measure or two, its tone and inflection clear, and the crowd settled while she sang, her sweet melodic voice carrying with the wind.

Measure by measure Sally poured her heart and soul into the haunting melody, and when the song ended, everyone clapped and began to chant, "More! More!" Sally looked at the press of people about her, at their faces so obviously filled with admiration and eagerness for another song. In wonderment, she walked over to where Roscoe was standing and whispered something into his ear. He smiled and nodded.

Amy had been listening to Sally sing, gooseflesh pimpling her arms. She listened attentively along with everyone else as Roscoe's fiddle came alive in his hands and he strummed a hymn that had been written back in 1775, and had been sung all around the country: *Rock of Ages*. Sally's sense of self-esteem was lifted to a new high as she began to sing. Listening raptly as Sally's voice rang out, clear and strong, Amy whispered to Matthew, "Isn't she just something?"

"Very nice," Matthew said, smiling warmly. "She's a beautiful girl and I can see why Thornton is so taken with her."

"Has he told you that, Matthew?" Amy asked breathlessly.

"Well . . ." Matthew hedged, not wanting to reveal a confidence. "You can see how he just glows when he's around her.

I'd take that as a sign that he cares—at least a little, wouldn't you?"

"I hope so, Matthew," Amy said animatedly. "I know for a fact that Sally is smitten with him. Wouldn't it just be something grand if they were to . . . fall in love?" Amy was glad of the semidarkness that hid the flush in her cheeks caused by her own excitement.

"Time will tell," Matthew said, his gaze enveloping her in its gentle warmth.

Men, women and children had stopped what they were doing while Sally was singing. Women clutched their husband's arms, their faces showing plainly their listening pleasure; husbands swayed in time with the music, their conversation stilled. As Sally started singing the last verse of *Rock of Ages* she coaxed everyone to join in. Amy had never seen such a wondrous, exhilarating look of bliss on another's face as she did while looking at Sally as she sang.

At last the final note was sung and Sally walked slowly back to where Amy and Matthew were now standing beside Thornton. Amy hugged her warmly and people were pushing and shoving in their eager haste to get to her side and compliment her on the beautiful songs she had sung.

Hearing the compliments floating on the air about them, Amy's heart went out to her new friend and companion. "Sounded just like an angel," one lady whispered in awe; "Good job, Sally!" echoed from several different directions.

Putting her arms around Sally, Amy hugged her and whispered, "What a beautiful voice God has bestowed on you, Sally. You must sing for us more often."

Thrilled that the people had enjoyed her singing so much Sally was further touched by all their beautiful sentiments. The most welcomed compliment of all came from Thornton. He uttered only one simple word: "Beautiful!" But it was the tone in which he said it that made Sally's heart beat so wildly within her breast, and gave her a bottomless peace and satisfaction.

Thornton looked at Sally with acute interest, his thoughts rambling. *How her green eyes danced and the dimples in her cheeks deepened when she laughed. She was a beautiful woman, unmarried and expecting a child in a few months. I'm in love; completely, passionately,* he thought to himself. His pulses raced, and by the way Sally was looking at him, he had high hopes that she just might be feeling the same way about him. "Just might be . . ."

"What's that you said?" Sally looked expectantly at Thornton.

"Oh . . . er . . . nothing. Nothing at all. Just thinking out loud, that's all." Mercifully the moonlight hid the extent of Thornton's embarrassment at his idle thoughts.

Roscoe never seemed to tire when playing the fiddle, and as he started playing again, the dancing resumed. Sally took the initiative. "Would you like to dance with me, again, Thornton?"

Thornton's quick laugh was music to her ears. "Are you sure you should be dancing so much? I mean, under the circumstances . . . er . . . ah . . . you know, the baby and all?" Thornton was so flustered and tongue-tied, that Sally burst out laughing.

"Thornton Decker, you've lived long enough in this old world to know a woman bearin' a child ain't goin' to break into tiny little pieces over a little bit of dancin'! Come on," she said happily, smiling and pulling on his arm. "Let me show you jest how fit as a fiddle I really am!"

Sam's voice rose above the music, "Swing your partners!" and "Do-si-do!" Sally and Thornton pulled Amy and Matthew into a circle and for the rest of the evening they danced the hours away.

CHAPTER 16

A V-shaped flock of Canadian geese was flying across the valley, honking and barking as Sally's boots crunched on the new-fallen snow. She was gingerly making her way to the river for a bucket of water. The temperature had plunged during the night and a skiff of snow had fallen in the wee hours of the morning. Sally was bundled up to ward off the bitter cold, and had a scarf tied over her head to keep her ears warm. It was the first week in April, but it felt like December all over again.

Pausing beside the bank where it sloped easily into the water Sally filled her bucket, shivering as the raw north wind buffeted her. She watched idly as little snow devils, picked up by the wind, whirled across her path and filled in the deeply rutted ground.

Arching her back she rubbed her burgeoning abdomen. At that moment the baby kicked violently within her and a sudden pain shot through her back. Sally caught her breath and held it until the pain subsided. Gradually her face relaxed and she rubbed her swollen belly and crooned, "There, there, my little one, don't be in such an all-fire hurry to get out into this old world."

Guarding her blossoming figure, Sally turned and walked back the way she had come, slowly and carefully. Her face was plump, her cheeks rosy red, and there was nothing about her that resembled the lost waif that the Bradshaw family had adopted into their hearts and home a few weeks ago.

The night of the dance, Sally had hopes that perhaps Thornton was interested in her—not as a traveling companion, but as a woman. But he had never approached her in any intimate way after the dance, and had never uttered a word to make her think that he found her attractive.

A pain squeezed her heart as she thought of him. "Guess I'm just too eager to find you a father, my little one," she said, talking to her unborn baby. "I was hopin' that maybe Thornton would like to become friends, an' then maybe... well, I was hopin' that some day down the line a piece he would ask me to be his wife. But I should of known he wouldn't want to take on the chore of raisin' another man's child. He probably looks upon me as a wayward woman, livin' with Cheeley an' all, an' not bein' really married to him. But you know, my sweet little baby, no matter how foolish it sounds, I love that man." Her voice quieted and in the stillness she could hear the wind teasing the treetops, and a dry rustle and rasp of branch on branch.

Reaching the wagon she shared with Amy and the rest of the Bradshaw family, Sally ended her conversation with her child. Thornton just happened to be passing by the Bradshaws' wagon when he caught sight of Sally. He looked like a schoolboy caught in some devilish prank as he caught up with her, his ears red-tipped to match his flaming-red hair and with a foolish grin on his face. "Why, hello there, Sally girl. You should have hollered. I'd have gladly fetched that water for you."

Thornton reached for the bucket that Sally was clasping. "Here, let me have that pail, girl, before you hurt yourself!" His hand closed over Sally's and immediately he was full of concern and shook his head in dismay. "Now if you haven't done gone and froze your hands!"

Setting the bucket of water on the ground, Thornton took Sally's hands into his own. He started rubbing them ever so gently, trying to bring some warmth back into them. Green eyes sparkling, Sally stood without moving, watching the play of emotions that crossed Thornton's face: concern, anxiety, and . . ." Thornton continued rubbing her hands, looking at her uncertainly.

"What's the matter with you, Thornton?" Sally finally asked. "You look so tense. Have I done somethin' wrong? Somethin' to offend you?" Sally's voice was trembling.

Before Thornton had a chance to answer her, Amy poked her head out of the back of the wagon.

Thornton released Sally's hands quickly, his face red as a beet. "I wondered where you were off to, Sally," Amy said, wagging her head. "I'm going to have to tie her down, Thornton, to keep her from doing chores. She just isn't happy unless she's finding something to do. You'd make some man a good wife, Sally!"

The words had popped out of Amy's mouth unbidden, and she hurriedly ducked back into the wagon, but not before she heard Sally's soft gasp.

"I ain't much of a prize, and not much with words, Sally, but if I thought there was the slightest chance that you . . . that you would look on me as husband material, I would ask you in a minute to be my wife." Thornton dropped his head, afraid he had embarrassed Sally, speaking so bluntly when perhaps Amy might be listening.

But a smile of pure pleasure lighted Sally's face and her spirits lifted. Her eyes sparkled and she smiled. "I ain't knowed you long, Mr. Decker," Sally said mischievously, "but from all the talk I've been hearin' about you, I think you would be good to me. An' iffen I thought you could care the least littlest bit for me, I'd be the proudest woman in the whole wide world!"

Looking like she was about to cry, Sally's words brought a big lump to Thornton's throat. His heart was overflowing with warmth and love for the simple, but sweet girl standing before him. He put his arms around her, silently begging God to still his racing heart, and help him say the right things.

Sally glanced at Thornton's face and saw the heart-rending tenderness of his gaze and she felt a tingling in the pit of her stomach. Her pulse pounded and the very air about her seemed electrified.

Sensing that Sally was caught up in his enthusiasm, Thornton plunged on. "I said it before and I'm saying it again . . . the . . . uh . . . the preacher's right handy, and if you're willing to tie the knot, then let's do it whilst we can. That is if you're sure of how you feel about me."

Sally's heart settled down to a more even beat and for a long moment she felt as if she were floating on air. Imploringly Sally gazed into Thornton's eyes. "I . . . I rightly cain't find words to say . . ."

Thornton drew Sally into a closer embrace and whispered in her ear, "I promise that I will protect and shield you from every hurt in this old world that I can. That is if you would do me the honor of marrying up with me. I can't rightly tell you what our future holds, but I do know the One who holds the future, and I'm asking you . . ." Thornton pulled away from their embrace and put his hands gently on Sally's shoulders and gazed deeply into her eyes. "Wi . . . will you be my wife?"

Before Sally could say one word, Thornton leaned down and kissed her gently on the mouth. She blinked away tears and stood on tiptoe. She wrapped her arms around his neck and returned his kiss. Stepping back she reached up and traced his lips with her fingertips. "Did you really ask me to marry up with you?" she asked incredulously.

Thornton looked down at her upturned face and smiled. "Well . . . yes, I believe that's what I asked you, Sally girl," he answered endearingly. "But as yet, I haven't heard your reply."

"If you really want to marry up with me, there's nothin' I'd rather do than spend the rest of my life as your wife. But there's one thing missin' to my way of thinkin'. You ain't said one word 'bout . . . 'bout lovin' *me*! I'd not want to think that you'd marry up with me jest because you felt sorry for me. But I surely would be proud to think that you might love me jest a wee bit . . ."

Gathering Sally into his arms, Thornton held her snugly and whispered, "Oh, my Sally girl. Remember the night I found you in the cave and picked you up in my arms? I could feel your heart pounding against mine and I knew right then and there that I loved you. More than I ever thought I could possibly love another person. And I knew absolutely nothing about you then. After spending some time with you I've found my feelings that night were true. I've never been in love before but these strange feelings I get whenever I'm with you . . . well, as sure as I know that I'm standing here shivering in my bootstraps, I know that I love you."

Thornton blushed and a big grin creased his face." Now, for a man that don't talk much, that was quite a speech for me, Sally girl."

"Oh, Thornton, I love you too. But there's jest one more thing I gotta know. That you'd love my baby too. I couldn't stand it if it he never had a pa to love an' help tend to him."

"I love your baby already, Sally . . . uh . . . our baby that is." Thornton rested his palm on her stomach. At that precise moment the baby kicked and Sally was overjoyed at the look of pure rapture that was evident on Thornton's face.

The curtains parted and Amy stuck her head out of the back of the wagon again.

"What's all this talk about love?" she asked innocently. "Don't you know that it's too early in the morning for such foolishness?"

From the sheepish look on her face, Thornton and Sally knew that she had heard every word they had said to one another. Amy smiled at them warmly then disappeared once more behind the curtains. They heard her say to her mother, "Ma, you'll never believe in a hundred years what I'm about to tell you!"

. . .

Roscoe quickly agreed to perform the wedding ceremony after talking with Thornton and Sally, and word quickly spread through the wagon train that there was going to be a wedding once they reached Martin's station.

Sam's party arrived at Martin's station late Friday afternoon, April 18, 1783. The countryside was now full of color. The bright pennants of spring and the full flowering blossoms of a fresh and burgeoning world brought a great change to the hillsides. The thickening leaves of trees with their wild flashes of color basked in the warmth of spring. Two by two, the birds were paring off, preparing for the time of nesting and raising families. Geese were on the wing again moving north in ever increasing flocks.

Captain Joseph Martin, the Virginia Agent for Indian Affairs, was the most influential person both with Indians and scattered settlers in Powell Valley. He greeted the travelers warmly as they pulled into his station amid the jangle of harness and creaking of wagon wheels. And for the very last time, the people pulled their wagons into a now familiar circle.

The weary travelers were approximately twenty-five miles from the Cumberland Gap and the bluegrass meadows of Kentucky. The Cumberland Mountains stood against the soft blue sky to the northwest, looking hard and hostile. The sun was dipping behind the mountains, and the day was beginning to cool when Sam, every bone in his body aching, finished checking on everyone and making sure they were settled in for the night. He grabbed a quick sandwich and washed it down with a cup of fresh milk that had been brought to him by Howard, then headed for Captain Martin's cabin.

The now familiar scent of wood smoke wafted around him and he breathed it in deeply. He found the Captain before his hearth indulging himself, a tin plate of rabbit stew in one hand and a steaming mug of coffee in the other.

Putting his plate and cup down on the hearth, Captain Martin stood and beckoned Sam to a chair opposite him. Sinking gratefully into the comfort of the cushioned seat, Sam stretched his long legs toward the blazing and crackling fire. Captain Martin poured a cup of strong coffee for Sam before resuming his place by the fire. "Are you hungry?" he asked Sam politely.

"No, sir, I'm not," Sam assured him.

"Some ale then?"

"No, thank you, sir. Coffee will be quite satisfactory," Sam replied.

Captain Martin's eyes flashed with interest. "Looks like you have a goodly number of people traveling with you."

Sam fastened his eyes on the face of the man with whom he was only slightly acquainted. "I'm well pleased, sir. In all, seventy-two stalwart souls started the trek west about seven weeks ago." He pursed his lips. "My heart's heavy over the loss of four of them due to the storm that blew through Virginia on the seventh of March."

The Captain leaned close and squinted into the flickering fire. "I hear these sad tales all the time." He turned and looked full into Sam's face, concern written on his own. "Just so you bear in mind not to shoulder the guilt for the unfortunate happenings on your journey thus far. It all goes with the territory."

Draining his mug, Sam's tone of voice changed, became more spirited. "It's not grim news altogether," he said, his voice holding a rasp of excitement. "We've a couple who are wanting to get married while we're here," he said with pleasure. "That is, if you hold no objections."

"None whatsoever," Captain Martin replied amiably. "What about a parson?"

"We have a parson traveling with us. We had a young girl join our group shortly after we left Charlottesville. She's been traveling with a family by the name of Bradshaw. She's expecting a baby in a couple of months and unfortunately she isn't married. That's a long story I won't go into at this time. The groom to be is one of my trusted scouts, and I feel the union will be a good one."

The Captain's face melted into a buttery grin. "I have an empty cabin I'll let the couple stay in for as long as you're here. Least I can do. Give them a little comfort and privacy."

"That's mighty decent of you, sir," Sam said easily. "I know Mr. Decker will appreciate your thoughtfulness, and after several weeks in a crowded wagon, I'm certain Miss Hawkins will be right comfortable in that cabin of yours. We'll sit tight until Monday morning. I believe that's enough time to get the kinks out before we start out on foot. Won't be the same without the wagons, that's for sure!" The Captain nodded in agreement.

"I'm proud of my Pilgrims, Captain Martin. They've been most cooperative and congenial, and for the most part they're good, strong Christian people, and will make ideal neighbors for me and my family in my valley."

Captain Martin got up and laid another log on the fire. He took a poker and stirred the burning embers, brushed his hands along the sides of his breeches, and refilled their coffee mugs before sitting down again.

"Heard tell of any marauding Indians in these parts lately?" Sam asked, squinting his eyes as pungent smoke from the fireplace drifted like gray shadows around his head and into the dark corners of the room.

Reaching for his pipe, Captain Martin tamped the tobacco and waited until he had his taper lighted and had drawn several mouthfuls of smoke before he answered. "Most of the Indian fighting in Kentucky last year was with the Shawnee coming in from the north. The Cherokee in the south were relatively quiet, but by August it seemed like Indians were all over the place!

The eyes of the Captain darkened. "Daniel Boone's son Israel was killed at the battle of the Blue Licks. I'm sure you heard the sad tale. Since then, we've had it relatively peaceful, but you keep your eyes open—don't pay to get careless in these parts. It's the surest way of being parted from your hair!"

Standing to his feet, Sam yawned deeply. "I better get out of your hair Captain and let you get to bed. Sure want to thank you again for your hospitality, and I'll pass the word on to Mr. Decker about the cabin."

"You do that," Captain Martin said, a broad smile on his face. Ain't often we get to have a wedding round here. People come and go, but they're all pretty much in a hurry. Tell that Mr. Decker to come and see me first thing in the morning. I'll have one of my boys clean the cabin and we'll see if we can't get in the spirit of things by roasting a hog or two. A wedding calls for a celebration, and a celebration calls for food—and plenty of it!" He gave out with a hearty laugh.

. . .

It was still dark in the wagon when Sally's eyes popped open. The ticking of the clock was the only sound in the quiet wagon.

From outside came the sound of a robin, its notes clear and rich in tone, singing long, loudly and deliberately. Geese were on the wing, sounding like small dogs yelping in the far distance. A new day had begun. Saturday, April 19, 1783—Sally's wedding day!

She yawned and snuggled under the down comforter, warding off the cool morning air blowing under the curtains. She wondered if sleep would claim her again.

Her baby stirred within her and she caressed the mound that seemed to grow larger and rounder with every passing day. Never had she been so happy. It was as though she was moving in a dream. She pinched her arm to prove to herself that this was no dream. At three o'clock this day, she would become Mrs. Thornton Decker.

Yawning again, Sally closed her eyes and gave herself up to the euphoria that flowed through her entire being. The baby kicked again and Sally's bladder felt like it was ready to burst. She wanted nothing more than to lie in bed, contemplating the wedding, but knew that it was impossible. She inched from beneath the covers, threw an afghan about her shoulders, and stepping over the still sleeping form of Amy, Sally opened the curtains and stepped out into the gray dawn, the cool air invigorating on her face. The camp was unusually quiet as Sally made her way as fast and as carefully as she could to the necessary house.

. . .

Thornton leaned into the mirror on the cabin wall and combed his thick red hair into place. The face staring back at him through dark blue eyes was neither handsome nor ugly that he was aware of—just a tensing of the jaw that was slowly easing into a smile. The door of the cabin opened a crack and Billy Joe hollered in, "Are you about ready, Thornton? Roscoe told me to tell you that it's just about time."

"Tell him I'll be right there, Billy Joe!" Thornton glanced about him nervously and picked up his black linen frock. The arms were a little short, the cuffs somewhat frayed, and his black linen breeches were somewhat shiny in the seat, but they would just have to do.

His white linen cravat adorned with lace on the ends, was wrapped about his throat and loosely tied in front. He wore white silk stockings and a white linen shirt. The Lord only knew he would be more at home in his buckskins, but he wanted to do Sally proud. He glanced quickly at his pocket watch. In less than half an hour Sally would become his bride. His hands trembled at the thought and his heart felt as though it was skipping beats. He stepped out into the bright April sunshine and closed the door behind him.

A crowd of people had gathered under the boughs of a great spreading oak where the ceremony was to take place. As soon as the men caught sight of him there was a rising cacophony of good wishes. Some of the remarks Thornton heard were warm and generous, some of them coarse and earthy, given in jest, but he responded to all of them with a smile. Nothing could offend him this day, nor mar his happiness.

Pushing his way through the crowd of well wishers, his face set in a wide grin, Thornton saw Matthew standing off to the side of the crowd and made a beeline for him.

He looked at Matthew in total disbelief. "I didn't know there'd be this many turn out for my wedding!"

Matthew nodded and grinned broadly as he led Thornton past the curious onlookers. "They're happy for you, Thornton, and the single ones are a bit envious. Sally's a mighty purty little gal, and if I didn't have my sights already set on a sweet little gal myself, I'd of given you plenty of competition!"

Immediately Thornton's back straightened. He walked with a determined gait, a smile of satisfaction on his face, to the spot where Roscoe was standing. He reached for the marriage license that Roscoe held out to him and swallowed hard, trying to dislodge a knot that seemed to have taken up a permanent resting-place in his throat. He willed himself to relax before he glanced at the document. He quickly signed his name with a shaking hand, then reached for Roscoe's hand and shook it.

Roscoe patted him on the back and laughed good-naturedly. "I trust you're not shaking in the knees as much as you are in the hands, young fella!"

"To tell the truth, Parson, I . . ." Thornton's face paled and he let out a gasp. "Oh, no!" he cried in disbelief as he looked helplessly at Roscoe and then at Matthew.

"What's ailing you, Thornton?" Matthew queried uneasily.

In dazed exasperation, Thornton sputtered, "I don't have a ring for Sally!"

Matthew laughed. "Is that all! For one panic-stricken moment there I thought sure you had just received direct word from the good Lord above that the world was coming to an end today at exactly three o'clock." Matthew squeezed Thornton's shoulder, spun on his heel, and sprinted away calling over his shoulder, "You sit tight and I'll be back with a ring in a jiffy, or my name isn't Matthew David Carpenter!"

Thornton let out a sigh and addressed Roscoe. "Parson, how could I have forgotten something as important as a ring? I know how women set store by such amenities. Sally's heart would have been broken if I couldn't have placed a ring on her finger today." He shook his head in disbelief. "It's a sign of old age creeping up on me I reckon."

Roscoe laughed out loud. "I have no doubt that our young Matthew will return with a ring shortly, Mr. Decker," he stated matter-of-factly. "But I do believe you sell your bride-to-be short. Although a ring may well be important to a woman, I believe Sally knows there are more important things in life than giving and receiving a ring."

Nodding his head, Thornton regained his composure and said lightly, "Suppose you're right. But be praying I can keep my wits about me long enough to get through the ceremony, would you Reverend Willis? I feel very honored to know that come July Sally and me will have us a youngun to bind us even tighter together than the vows we'll be saying before you today ever could."

CHAPTER 17

"You've got to stand still, Sally, you're shaking like a leaf!" Amy said amicably. Sally *was* shaking like a leaf as she stood before the Venetian mirror, waiting to be buttoned by Amy. She was wearing a pale yellow gingham dress of Amy's, and had been submitting numbly to the adjusting and altering that Margaret found necessary to make the dress accommodate her bulging stomach.

Amy buttoned the last button, then stood back and looked at Sally skeptically. "I think a little too much of you is showing out the top, Sally."

Sally began tugging at the bodice of the dress. Margaret scrutinized the situation and said, "I know just the thing!" She opened her sewing box and drew out a bolt of white lace with small yellow roses embroidered on it. She turned and looked at Sally smugly. "We'll just fill it in!"

Margaret tucked and pinned and when she was finished, she gazed at Sally thoughtfully, and her smile broadened in approval. Hugging her she whispered in awe, "You're absolutely beautiful, honey."

Sally blushed and tears glistened in her green eyes. "I caint believe it's me, Mrs. Bradshaw," she said softly, looking at her image in the mirror and lightly fingering a loose tendril of hair on her cheek.

The three of them stood in silence savoring the moment until Amy broke the spell. "Where's your shoes?" Sally looked blank. Amy suddenly remembered that Sally only had one pair of shoes, and they were hardly fitting to wear to her wedding. She gazed down at Sally's bare feet that were slightly swollen and exclaimed with delight, "Ma, I bet your black leather shoes would fit perfectly. If you can remember just where you packed them!"

Margaret shoved a pair of white stockings into Sally's hand. "You put these on while I try and find my black shoes. I think I can put my fingers right on them."

Amy cleared her throat and gushed, "You look simply gorgeous, Sally! Oh, how I envy you, marrying the man you love! It's all so . . . so romantic and . . . ."

Margaret was down on hands and knees rummaging through a box when she cried out, "I've found them, girls!" She hurriedly brought the shoes to Sally and insisted she sit down and try them on for size. They fit perfectly.

Looking thoughtful, Amy said lightly, "Something old, something new, something borrowed, something blue. Have you got all four, Sally?"

Sally looked down at her feet, now wearing pretty black slippers. Everythin' I'm a'wearin' is either borrowed or old, I guess, an' Ruby gave me a brand new handkerchief that she crocheted 'round the edges, jest for me. I guess that leaves somethin' blue."

Amy laughed happily. "I'm so glad, Sally! You see, I've been mighty busy the past week making your wedding gift." She pulled a package from underneath a pile of blankets, wrapped in a piece of muslin. She handed it to Sally. "I hid it to keep it as a surprise," she said, happy to see the pleasure that it brought to Sally's face as she accepted it.

Sally opened the package and gasped as she saw the beautiful light blue shawl that Amy had made for her. It was made from yarn that was as soft as a cloud. Sally buried her face in the shawl breathing in the sweet-smelling scent of rose oil. Clasping it to her breast she said, "It's truly the most beautiful thing I've ever laid my eyes on, Amy. I'll be so proud t'be wearin' it an' I'll treasure it forever!" She hugged Amy and said simply, "Thank you kindly, from the bottom of my heart."

Brush in hand, Margaret waited patiently for Sally to sit down so she could arrange her hair. Sally finally sank gratefully into a chair and fanned her face with her hand. "I'm as tired as if I'd done a whole week's worth of work!" she exclaimed, letting out with a big sigh. She cupped her swollen belly with both hands. "An' if my baby keeps kickin' me the way he's been doin' the past few days, he's gonna turn me inside out for sure!"

Looking at Sally with sunny cheerfulness, her brown eyes dancing, Amy asked whimsically, "And why, for the last few days, have you kept referring to your baby as 'He'?" she asked with a lilt to her voice. "Do you know something we don't?"

The heavy lashes that shadowed Sally's cheeks flew up and she smiled. "I . . . I guess 'cause when I think of my baby these days, I jest know he's a he."

"You're going to be late for your wedding if we don't get your hair done and be off!" Margaret fussed. Sally settled and Margaret brushed her honey-colored hair until it shone like strands of lustrous glass. She brushed each strand around her finger into curls, and piled the curls high on her head. After pinning them in place she encircled the curls with a blue silk ribbon. Ringlets twisted across Sally's forehead and curled on her nape.

While Margaret fussed with Sally's hair, Amy kept up a constant chatter. When Margaret was through, Amy looked at the beautiful girl sitting before her, sweet as a fresh-picked flower, eyes shining, and her face aglow with happiness. Feeling a rush of tenderness, Amy said sweetly, "I know in my heart, Sally, that God's hand is on you, and I wish you every happiness in life . . . always," she said sincerely.

Heaving herself out of the chair, Sally gathered Margaret and Amy into her arms. "I cain't tell you how beholdin' I am for you takin' me in when I had no one to turn to. For sharin' your wagon with me, an' fittin' me with beautiful clothes an' . . . an' lovin' me.

I'll be a good wife to Thornton, an' make you all proud. I give you my solemn vow on that," she whispered.

It was three o'clock and all eyes were on Sally as she walked slowly to where Thornton waited for her under an old oak tree. The April day was brilliant and bright with sun. To Amy, it was a good omen. "Happy the bride the sun shines on," she had always heard. Birds and insects filled the air with a cheerful cacophony and a gentle and sweet-smelling breeze wafted through the air.

Thornton gazed at a vision draped in a blue cloud. Sally was smiling serenely, grasping a bouquet of beautiful blue and yellow violets in her hand that Amy had picked for her. A rush of love for Sally overwhelmed Thornton. He reached for her hand and she looked into his eyes with a look of pure love and joy.

Roscoe smiled benevolently in their direction and said, "If you'll come and stand beside me, we'll begin." Sally listened carefully to every word Roscoe spoke that day, acutely aware of the hand that held her own, and the faint smell of rose oil. The soft breeze, the bright sunshine, and the presence of newfound friends, were added gifts, bestowed by the hand of a loving Father.

"Dearly beloved, we are gathered here in the sight of God and man..." Thornton was gripping Sally's hand tightly in his own, standing transfixed beside her. A smile claimed her lips as she repeated the vow: "I take thee, Thornton Decker, as my beloved husband, an' I promise t'love you, t'honor you, an' t'obey you..." *May I be worthy of his love, O, God!*

"I take thee, Sally Hawkins, as my beloved wife, and I promise to love you..." *I ask nothing more than to be able to spend my life loving her, Lord!* A robin, perched on a branch of the mighty oak, burst into song. It filled the air with its rich throaty notes, tossing them up into the bright sunshine.

Thornton slipped a thin gold band on Sally's finger, and repeated the words after Roscoe, "With this ring, I thee wed..." Roscoe smiled triumphantly and said, "I now pronounce you man and wife."

Thornton looked over at Matthew, at a total loss as to what to do next. Matthew grinned and shook his head, then slapped Thornton on the back. "You can kiss your bride now, Thornton!" he said enthusiastically.

Blushing, Thornton glanced quickly around the circle of friends all smiling their assent, and leaned down and quickly planted a kiss on Sally's cheek. Everyone groaned. Thornton looked about him once again, saw the grins and nods, and took Sally firmly by the shoulders and planted a sound kiss on her lips. "I love you, Sally girl," he said hoarsely.

"An' I love you," she whispered. People were suddenly closing in on them, cooing congratulations, as tears of happiness cascaded down Sally's cheeks. *It was over*, she thought. *So brief, so simple a ceremony, t'weave so strong a bond.*

That night, after all the leftover food had been cleared away and the last "Congratulations!" had been said, Thornton and Sally retired to their cabin. It was the loveliest night, the softest night, the starriest night!

Closing the door, Thornton leaned against it, looking at Sally pathetically as she limped to the bed and sagged onto the straw mattress. He saw her swollen feet and his heart went out to her. He knelt before her and gently removed her borrowed shoes, then rubbed her feet, trying to restore the circulation, his face full of concern. "I should have insisted we leave all the merry-making much sooner, Sally. You must be exhausted."

She smiled at him weakly. "I'm fine, Thornton, just a wee bit tired is all. This young'un of ours is still celebratin' though. He's jumpin' all over the place!"

"He?" Thornton questioned, a grin plastered on his face.

Sally managed a smile although her tiredness was showing through it. "That just popped out," she said, as he placed his palm on her swollen belly, feeling the movements of their child.

"Boy or girl, makes no never mind to me. I'll love it," he beamed.

Sally covered his hand with her own, the gold band gleaming on her finger. "Where'd you get my ring?"

Raising her hand to his lips, Thornton kissed her fingers. "Matthew came to my rescue. He said it belonged to his mother.

When I get a chance to buy you a ring of your own, I told him we'd give this one back."

Sally put her arms around Thornton's neck and kissed him, then whispered, "I am so grateful to all these kind people that made our weddin' day one that I ain't never goin' to forget!" She raised her hand and looked once again at the golden band. "I've never had a prayer answered more fully," Sally murmured with deep emotion. "I prayed the day I left Cheeley's home that me an' my baby would be cared for. God answered that prayer long before I opened my heart t'him.

"What's that again?" Thornton asked inquisitively.

Sally's eyes glistened with unshed tears. "I gave my heart to Jesus last night," she said softly.

Thornton cried out, "That's the best news I've heard today! Well . . . next to the best news I've heard. Repeating those wedding vows to me are the sweetest words I've ever heard in my life. But how come you never said anything before?"

"I just didn't have a chance to, Thornton. Everythin' has been so busy 'round here all day an' besides, it's sort of a weddin' gift to you, seein' as how I had no chance to get you anythin'." She smiled sweetly through her tears.

"Amy told me 'bout all the damage the storm done an' I got t'thinkin' an' wonderin' 'bout it. If that happened t'me, would I be ready t'die an' meet God face t'face? I needed forgiveness in my heart for the hate I been carryin' for my pa an' Cheeley. It's too late t'do anythin' for Cheeley, but iffen I get the chance ever, I'd like t'tell my pa I forgive 'im, jest as God has forgiven me."

Tears slowly slipped down Sally's pale cheeks. "I cain't read," Sally said forlornly, "so I cain't read his Word, but maybe you can teach me t'read when we get t'Kentucky."

Thornton laid his head on Sally's swollen belly and gave out a big sigh. "God's forgiven me for every bad thing I've ever done, Thorton, an' I'm grateful! I'm grateful t'you an' for our child, an' again I give you my solemn promise always t'love an' cherish you."

Thornton put his finger under Sally's chin, then lifted it until he was staring into her beautiful green eyes. He glared at her mockingly, "And obey?"

Sally smiled tremulously and whispered, "An' obey."

Thornton got up off his knees and gently pulled Sally to her feet and into his arms. "I'll always love you, Sally girl. My Sally girl—my wife."

CHAPTER 18

Captain Martin was up at first light on Monday morning to see the travelers off. "Mind you keep your eyes and ears open, my good man!" he called after Sam. "And the Lord be with you!" Sam turned in the saddle, removed his hat and waved it in the air.

For the first two hours, Sam, Ben and Thornton rode to the front of the line, three abreast. They were traveling on a hunter's trace that led from Martin's station through twenty miles or more of the roughest and wildest country yet, before the Gap.

Those who were walking, did so with a light, free step. There was always something interesting to look at: a flight of birds on the wing, a squirrel darting through the trees lining the trail; a bubbling brook, or violets blooming in the shelter of a rock.

The green-topped mountain peaks to the west were magnificent, reaching into a brilliant blue sky above them. At the start of the day everyone seemed to have a great amount of energy, and with spirit and harmony they sang songs as they walked or rode the trail, such as *Little Brass Wagon, Old Dan Tucker,* and *Coffee Grows on White Oak Trees.* After they tired of singing, they spoke of the good life that awaited them in Kentucky. The grass seemed greener and higher and the flowers of scarlet, bright yellow, pink and white, more beautiful, the closer they got to the bluegrass meadows of Kentucky.

The going grew worse however with each succeeding mile, and the caravan had to move slowly, single file: men, women and children, pack animals and then those on horseback. Signs of dreaded Indians soon appeared, causing concern, especially with the women.

"Seems like you're taking more and more precautions," Thornton offered.

Sam grimaced. "It's my intention to double the guard front and rear now, because the closer we get to Kentucky, the more probability of an attack. From here on out I want you and Ben to be a jump ahead of the rest. I'll feel safer knowing you two are in the lead. The other men and older boys will be taking up the front and rear positions, with our women and children and livestock in the middle. I'll be up and down the line, but I want you to report to me immediately if you see anything that arouses your suspicions. I've got Matthew and Howard riding behind to make sure no one sneaks up on us unawares."

"Do you think they knows we're about?" Ben questioned.

"I'm sure they know we're here, Ben, but as to whether they will chance an attack is anybody's guess. In the wilderness it is a wise man who prays for the best to happen, but prepares for the worst."

Most of their journey that day was spent climbing rocky trails through a primitive forest often blocked by fallen trees and numerous streams they had to ford. The trace they were on had narrowed significantly and in places was almost impenetrable. At four o'clock, when they came to a small river on a brush-and-tree-choked level, Sam called a halt for the day. They had, in his estimation, gained approximately three miles.

The pack animals were as tired as the people were, and with slow heaves of relief, they knelt and rolled as soon as their packs were removed from their backs. By the time Sam had completed his tasks and posted guards for the first watch, twilight was upon them and coyotes had begun their barking. Sam went to the riverbank and washed a day's worth of grime from his face and hands and then hurried to Howard's fire and a welcomed hot supper. Thornton and Ben had tracked on foot all day because of the wild terrain. Keeping in the shadows of drooping pine branches, they had cut through a wooded slope, fully aware of a buck and doe trotting out across a small clearing near the top of a ridge. The animals were alert and stepping uneasily. Suddenly the buck jerked his head and emitted the shrill whistle that warned his mate of extreme danger. Both animals whirled and loped over the crest of the ridge.

Thornton motioned for Ben to halt. "Somewhere on that brush-covered knob is something or someone that frightened that buck," he whispered.

Ben nodded his massive head. "Iffen a man was that close to a buck without firin' his gun, I'd say he most likely don' want to draw attention to hisself, an' is up to no good." His black eyes snapped in his ebony face.

Together they worked their way up to the rocky knob, careful not to expose themselves to an arrow or bullet from whoever just might be hiding among the rocks. After reaching the rocky summit and searching carefully they found the evidence they were looking for. Someone had lain stretched out underneath the laurel most of the day. From this vantagepoint, whoever it was could see the lay of the land for miles in every direction.

"He could have been waiting for a chance to steal a horse or he could have been spying for a war party planning to ambush any travelers coming along this way. One Indian or gunman isn't much to worry about," Thornton said glumly, "but whenever you find one, there's a goodly chance that there will be others close by."

A cloak of darkness was descending on them like a ghostly veil and it was getting too dark to see to any more tracking. By the time they found their camp, fires were burning and the smell of broiling fish and perking coffee drifted enticingly to their nostrils.

Thornton reported in detail to Sam about their find. " . . . just might have been a scout for a raiding party, wanting to pick up a few horses or an easy scalp."

"I think you're right, Thornton," Sam said.

"Ben and I will be gone by first light tomorrow and maybe we can circle around and find their camp. If there's enough of them to be dangerous, I'll head directly back to let you know."

"Now, iffen you don' min' sir," Ben offered, "I'll be gettin' on over to the wife. She's been frettin' on my whereabouts more'n likely. G'night, Mr. Tippett, sir. G'night, Thornton. See you at first light."

"He's a good man," Thornton said as Ben loped out of earshot.

"That he is," Sam said lightly. Now you better get home to that new wife of yours, Thornton. I surely appreciate what you're doing for us and hope Sally's making out fine without your help."

"She's staying with Amy's folks during the hours I'm away. I'd say they're doing a great job of taking care of her in my absence. Good night, sir. See you at first light."

After an eagerly consumed meal, John and Margaret lay beside their fire, ready to relax their aching muscles. Darkness had settled down on them like a mantle, wrapping river, forest and trail in its folds. It was strangely peaceful and the countryside held an awesome grandeur to it, although there was no way of knowing what lay hidden beneath the cloak of darkness.

"I'm glad the children have taken to doing without the wagon so well." Margaret glanced to where Amy and Billy Joe were bedded down and her throat tightened with love. "I never heard a peep out of either one of them after they ate their supper. Having to walk their horses sure put a strain on them. My oh my, if my calves don't feel as if they've been slit open by a knife. My pack straps felt as though they cut clean through to my clavicles." Margaret rubbed one foot against the other. "I've got a lot of blisters too, so I know our children must be hurting, but not one complaint out of them." She shook her head in amazement.

John laughed. "Maybe there's hope for our children yet!"

"Amy's been a bit glum not having Sally around evenings," Margaret said. "Those two have formed a beautiful friendship. But how thankful I am that God stepped in when he did, and made everything right for that girl. She's such a precious soul."

"And Thornton was just the catch for her, in my way of thinking," John added.

"By the way, did I tell you that Sally gave her heart to the Lord last night, John?" Margaret smiled to herself in the darkness.

"I believe you did, sweetheart, but news like that is worth repeating." He squeezed her hand and the warmth of his hand on hers made Margaret feel like a young girl again. With a tired sigh Margaret snuggled deeper into her bed, grateful to John that she wasn't sleeping on the hard ground. He had made a bed of boughs and leaves for them, and her aching body now relaxed gratefully into the softness.

Sometime later Margaret woke with a start, chilly and achingly stiff. A shadowy figure was moving close beside the fire that was just beginnng to crackle with renewed vigor. The light flickered across John's face, and on the fuzzy edge of sleep, Margaret sighed in contentment, feeling as safe as though she was in her featherbed in Charlottesville, Virginia. She turned over and gratefully went back to sleep.

Before Margaret opened her eyes she could smell the inviting aroma of coffee. People were beginning to stir in the pale morning light and with a groan she forced herself from her bed. Amy and Billy Joe were hunkered around the fire, eating their breakfast.

"You're an old sleepyhead this morning, Ma!" Billy Joe said gleefully, seeing that she was awake. "Pa helped Amy make some gravy with the milk that Mrs. Tippett give us. It's good, but not as good as you make!" he added on second thought.

Margaret chided herself. Never had she lain in bed and expected John or the children to fix their own breakfast! She hurriedly folded her blankets and glanced around the camp looking for John. "Where's your father, Amy?"

"He went with Matthew to water the horses. Said for me and Billy Joe to stay and help you load up."

Margaret wasn't the only one who had overslept. Sam thought half the camp had died in their beds, but he was congenial about the late start they got that morning. He knew there had been an excessive howling of wolves and hooting of owls all night, and that bodies were sore and tired from their hard day's walk. "Just don't let it happen again!' he teased.

That day Billy Joe gave the Grier children the use of Foxy and he walked with his now faithful friend and companion, Roscoe Willis. "I heard Sam talking to my pa last night and he said there's Injuns about. Have you thought much about an Indian raid on our camp, Rock? Do you really think they'll be bothering us?" Billy Joe's face was screwed up into a frown.

"It is a possibility, my lad. Sam told me so himself just last night," Roscoe said soberly. "Sam says in the wilderness it is a wise man who assumes that anything unknown is dangerous."

"But what would we do? Billy Joe asked in a small voice. What if . . ." Billy Joe swallowed, not sure of his misgivings. "If they do bother us, could you kill an Indian?"

"I'd much rather make peace with them, B.J. If we would only take the Good Book down the river instead of hundreds of men with rifles, I wonder what would happen? From what I've heard, some Indians can be tricky and mean. Others aren't no different than you and me. They want to live in peace, raise families, and do it on their own land. They don't mind sharing it, but by doggy, they aren't of a mind to have it taken away from them altogether either!"

"Can't we just tell them we ain't wanting to run them off nor cause them harm?"

"The red man can't read the thoughts in your head, B.J. All they see are great crowds of people flocking into their once peaceful hunting grounds."

Billy Joe carefully guided Roscoe through a path bordered by berry bushes. "What do you aim to do if we run into Indians and you can't see to shoot 'em?"

"My prayers will have to be my ammunition, my lad. But I'm a part of this caravan, and my loyalty lies with the people on it. If push comes to shove, I will give my life to save my comrades. But not with a rifle, my lad. I will rely solely on the Lord to lead me to do it in his own way. But enough of this talk," Roscoe said quietly. "We do not live in fear as those who do not believe and have no hope. We'll help each other through the bad spots on this trip, B.J. I have come to truly depend on you, my boy."

Billy Joe heaved a sigh and was filled with pride on hearing Roscoe's words. "They probably won't come and mess with us, Rock," Billy Joe said bravely.

"I believe you're probably right, my boy." Roscoe reached out and clasped Billy Joe around the shoulders and gave him a big squeeze.

There had been an abundance of Indian signs for days. Slowly and cautiously the caravan proceeded in a long, snaky line of men, women, and children. Everyone was alert. The men carried their Lancaster and Deckard rifles in their hands, barrels gleaming. Their powder horns and bullet pouches were full. Pistols, hatchets and knives were worn against their broad belts and were whetted keen.

Sam's growling stomach reminded him that it would soon be time for supper. He had been invited to eat with a different family every night since leaving Martin's station, and tonight he was to take fare with the Bradshaw family. They were only a mile or so away from the Gap, but he knew it was useless to try and make it before dark. The terrain was treacherous enough in the daylight hours, let alone traveling after the sun had gone down.

Tomorrow would be the first day of May. Sam shook his head in disbelief as he called a halt to their travels for the day. *Where had time gone?* He wondered. *In some ways it seemed as though they had been walking and riding through a never-never land, and there would be no end to it ever. But when he counted the miles they had covered, their delays due to the storm, and time spent at Martin's station, then he thanked his Almighty for getting them this far in so short a time!*

As the camp settled in for the night, Sam moved from fire to fire, spreading what cheer he could, while checking on the health and welfare of his charges. They were making progress of a sort, and Sam marveled at the spirit in the camp. Chins were still held high, and he heard no audible murmur of complaint, beyond the wailing of tired children, or the sigh of exhaustion that sometimes escaped the lips of the women. And praise be to God, as yet there had been no Indian attack!

That night, Howard fired upon a lurking form he swore he saw in the shadows.

The women and children slept in the innermost confines of the camp. The men and older boys had an uneasy rest while they waited the spring dawn.

Those on guard duty made their rounds, eyes glued on the dark forest mass that hemmed them in, and ears were tuned to catch the slightest sound. Sam was up all night, never relaxing his vigilance for a single minute and never really removed from the thought of an Indian attack.

Blood found the next morning on dried leaves indicated that Howard had indeed seen someone and his aim had been true. Thornton and Matthew were gone from camp before the first pale slices of light filtered through the sycamores that stretched their long arms over the riverbanks, gleaming white in the darkness like pale sentinels.

The pines of their campsite were still misted with dawn when the pilgrims entered the trace again, determined to make the Gap before dark. The sun was shining brightly and more than once it was necessary to drive snakes from before their path before they could proceed on their journey.

The routine of the day was now so familiar that Gilda had almost forgotten what her previous life had been like. She rose, washed and dressed, cooked and ate, packed, unpacked, and bedded down at night underneath the stars. In between she fed, clothed, and watched her children like a hawk. They were never more than an arm's length away from her at any given moment.

Gilda's prayer life had been growing by leaps and bounds. By now she knew everyone in the group well enough to call them by name. They were now bound together by a common goal and by Gilda's prayers. She was trail-weary and found the days monotonous, but prayed about everything that affected them all: their security, their aches and pains, their grudges and gossip, their ups and their downs.

Ben had been relieved from scouting for the day so that he could replace a shoe that Sam's horse had lost. It was shortly after midday and they had stopped for their nooning in a rocky area. Ben was busy with Sam's horse and Hattie Lou had begged to be allowed to watch him.

Gilda finally agreed. With Ben scouting most days Hattie Lou had seen little of her father the past few weeks. When Ben finished replacing the shoe, he took Sam's horse out into a little patch of grass to let him graze.

Sandy had been kept in camp that day and was lost without Matthew. He had started frolicking with Hattie Lou as she ran here and there searching through the dry grass for a stick to throw for him to retrieve.

Ben had just started back in Hattie Lou's direction when he saw her fall to her knees, Sandy growling and shoving his huge body against her. Her frightened screams brought Ben and others in the camp running in her direction. A three-foot rattlesnake was coiled about two feet away from Hattie Lou. She was still screaming, her hands tightly clenched against her mouth.

Sandy, lips peeled back in a fierce snarl, streaked back and forth in front of Hattie Lou, growling with rage. He caught the snake by the back of the neck and bit down with his sharp teeth. Giving a vicious shake of his massive head, he tossed the dead rattler down in the grass beside Hattie Lou. Ben had arrived at Hattie Lou's side just as Sandy had dropped the dead rattler. Hattie Lou now stood before her father, shaking like a leaf, tears streaming from terrified eyes. Ben grabbed her by the arm and gasped, "Where you bit, girl? I got to suck the pison out afore it starts workin'!"

Hattie Lou gulped and began shaking her head. "I . . . I ain't bit, Pa," she cried. She dropped into the grass beside Sandy and threw her arms around his massive head and buried her tear-stained face in the scruff of his neck. She hugged him and kissed his face. Sandy looked at her trustingly, whining deep in his throat as he licked at her tears.

Ruby and Gilda arrived just seconds after Ben did. They saw the snake lying in the grass and for a split second Gilda thought she was going to faint. She knelt down in the grass and pulled Hattie Lou close with one arm and Sandy close in the other. She looked up at Ruby and Ben and smiled. No screaming. No crying. Just a serene and beautiful smile on her face.

Ben put a big brown hand on Gilda's shoulder hesitantly. "Don' you go frettin' now," he said cheerfully, "she ain't come to no harm!"

"Jesus done saved my chile," Gilda said softly. "Heard her scream, Ben, an' I asked 'im to keep her safe." She bowed her head and closed her eyes and whispered softly, "Thank you, Lord, for keepin' my baby safe, jest like I asked you to. And thank you for seein' that Sandy was close by to do yore work."

Ben and Ruby could hardly believe what their eyes were telling them. What a miraculous change had come over Gilda! Ruby shook her head and patted Ben on the back. "It's the difference between unbelief and being a child of God!" she said wisely.

Ben carried Hattie Lou back to camp, Sandy following closely at their heels. Everyone gathered around them, having heard what the commotion had been about, and praises were voiced for the narrow escape from yet another tragedy amongst them.

Sandy received his fair share of hugs and praise from everyone and seeing that the Grier child was not injured in any way, the small group of people quickly dispersed and went about their business.

Ruby had witnessed first hand Gilda's calm repose in spite of what looked to be a tragedy and smiled softly. "Why do I stand amazed at your wondrous works, my Lord?" she whispered, and went in search of Roscoe, to share her wonderful news.

CHAPTER 19

Thornton and Matthew arrived back at camp just before the sun set behind the blue-misted mountains. Their shirts were soaked with sweat. Walking between them was a young Shawnee boy. He was shivering in spite of efforts on his part to appear stoical. His left arm hung limply at his side, caked with dried blood.

Sandy was wild with joy at being reunited with Matthew and pranced around him enthusiastically, vying for his attention.

"Get him a blanket!" Sam said as soon as he saw the boy. "And go get Ruby!' he added, seeing the injured arm. A blanket was quickly brought and wrapped about the Shawnee lad's thin shoulders. Although his face remained expressionless, Sam thought he detected gratitude in his black eyes.

Everybody milled around them gazing at the boy, their curiosity piqued at what a real live Indian looked like. They were all asking questions at the same time.

Billy Joe's eyes, big as saucers, assessed the boy. He looked to be about his age and was close to Billy Joe's height and build. He was clad only in leggings and moccasins. The two boys stared at one another for a moment and Billy Joe reached out to touch him, but the Shawnee youngster turned his head and paid him no mind.

It wasn't long before Roscoe and Ruby put in their appearance. Ruby had brought along her medicine box. She regarded the boy with serious eyes then started talking to him in her quiet, unassuming way. She helped dispel any ideas he might have had that she was going to harm him.

Pulling the blanket away from his left arm, Ruby examined it and said thoughtfully, "Looks like the bullet went clean through. Won't take much fixing up, lad, to make you comfortable again." She smiled at the boy sympathetically. "Had the bullet been a few inches to the right, well, all I can say is you were not alone. God's angels were at your side."

The youngster's black eyes lit up. He stared in fascination at Ruby and the stoicism left his face and was replaced by a puzzled frown. Sam felt the boy's confusion was due to the fact that these white people were being so nice to him, when in effect, he probably expected to die by their hands.

Gently cleansing the wound, Ruby applied a poultice of salve and herbs to the wound before wrapping the boy's arm in a clean, white bandage. She then fixed it into a sling. "There you go, young man," Ruby said, satisfied she had done all she could. She patted him on the hand and wrapped the blanket around his shoulders again. "Now let's go get something to fill that hollow in your stomach. She smiled down at the boy and beckoned him to follow her. He looked at Sam hesitantly, as though asking permission, and when Sam nodded his head in Ruby's direction, the boy quickly followed her.

"Where'd you find the lad?" Sam asked, addressing Thornton and Matthew.

"Thornton and I followed his trail," Matthew explained hurriedly. We know for certain that he was the one who crept into our camp last night. I believe he's been spying on us for a few days, probably wanting to steal a horse or some food. Howie got off a lucky shot and wounded him and he left a pretty easy trail for us to follow.

"Any more about?" Sam asked.

Matthew shook his head. "Thornton and I looked around good,

sir. All the tracks except the boy's were old. We're certain he was alone."

"What are you goin' to do with him?" Thornton asked, eyeing Sam seriously.

Sam shook his head. "I'd like to get him back to his people, but how we go about it is another matter. Since the boy doesn't speak English and none of us speak Shawnee, it's going to be mighty tricky trying to communicate."

"I'm thinkin' if he got here on his own, he should be able to get back with his people on his own," Thornton piped up. "Why don't we just give him some food and send him on his way now that Ruby has seen to his doctorin'?"

"Might be for the best," Sam said, nodding his head. He squeezed Matthew's shoulder and smiled. "You've done a man's job, son, and I'm proud of you. Now you fellas best get some grub and a well-deserved rest. We'll make our final decision about the boy come daybreak."

"I'm sorry we delayed you getting to the Gap today," Matthew said soberly. "I know how set you were on it."

"No apologies needed, son. We didn't make it today, but that just means we have a treat in store for us tomorrow the good Lord willing!"

Ruby was eager to help the Shawnee boy and fed him all he could eat. She was fixing him a place close by the fire to bed down when Sam appeared at her side.

"The boy will have to be tied, Ruby," he said apologetically.

"That surely won't be necessary, Sam," Ruby argued, shaking her head. "The poor lad is weak from loss of blood and lack of food, and needs a good night's rest. He wouldn't be able to rest if he was tied to a tree like some animal!"

"Sorry, Ruby, but it's in his best interest and for our safety as well. I don't have any idea what the boy might do . . ."

"I'll sit up with him all night myself, Sam," Ruby interrupted. "I promise he'll be going nowhere nor getting himself into any kind of mischief. Matthew's taking care of the animals right now, but he's going to be sleeping right here beside Roscoe and me, and Sandy will help keep close watch on the boy, I can attest to that."

Sam eyed Ruby speculatively. "It's against my better judgement, but you're a tough nut to crack, Ruby!" He shook his head and grinned. "I'll leave him in your care," he acquiesced. He looked at Ruby with admiration and ruffled the boy's hair. He didn't know if it was the flickering light from the fire playing tricks or if the boy actually smiled.

Daylight was only a scant promise in the sky when Ruby shook the Shawnee boy out of a groggy sleep. "Time for breakfast, Little Britches," she said, knowing full well the boy didn't understand a word she was saying. She held out one hand to him and dipped the other fingers into her cupped palm, then brought her fingers to her mouth and chewed.

The young boy nodded his head and smiled, his way of showing her that he understood. He looked almost like one of their own, standing there before her, wearing one of Billy Joe's faded blue shirts and homespun pants. He tried to move his injured arm and winced in pain.

"Bound to be sore for a time," Ruby said, giving the boy a light hug. Matthew and Sandy loped into view and Ruby smiled lovingly at Matthew. Sandy rubbed up against Ruby with jaws open and tongue lolling out, in what appeared for the entire world to see, was a huge grin. Ruby patted his broad head lovingly.

"You always seem to know when it's feeding time!" Ruby said, giving Matthew her full attention again.

"That proves I'm no dummy, now doesn't it?" Matthew gave her a broad wink.

"Go on with you," Ruby said, "and take the boy down to the river to wash up. I'll help Roscoe dish up the food."

Matthew sniffed the air. "Sure does smell good around here!" he said good-naturedly.

"It should! Roscoe's been up since four o'clock working on it! He spoils me rotten, but I have to admit, I love it!" Her eyes sparkled. Their camaraderie pleased them both. It impressed upon Ruby just how delightful it would have been to have had children and grandchildren, and it reminded Matthew of the happy times he had shared with his own mother and father. A day didn't pass that he didn't think of them.

The trail that day stretched before them, higher and higher to a dizzy pinnacle, before dipping into a narrow gateway, which opened the way to the wilderness frontier.

The people trudged ceaselessly, every mile seeming like three. They moved closer and closer to the great depression in the mountainside, a feeling of triumph racing through their veins. And it was with a sense of accomplishment and pride that they finally struggled through the great Cumberland Gap, and turned weary feet downward into the May-green Cumberland Valley, and toward their new homeland: Kentucky.

Everyone was in high spirits, never having seen anything as breathtakingly beautiful as the Gap. The Pinnacle Mountains to the north rose 900 feet above the Gap. The mountains rising on the south were neither as high or forbidding, but were still imposing. The blooming hills were thickly covered with laurel and rhododendron, and a fine growth of yellow pine crowned the ridges. On steep slopes and ravines there was a mixed forest growth of hemlock, tulip, magnolia, oak, sweetgum, dogwood and holly. It was a virtual paradise in spite of the dangers that hid behind their beauty.

Little Britches, the Shawnee lad so aptly named by Ruby, was still with them. No one could bear to see such a young boy go it alone in the wilderness. Sam decided, with the approval of everyone else, that the boy was to accompany them as far as he wanted to go. Sam was hopeful that along the way, he would recognize his surroundings and be able to make his way back to his people.

It hadn't taken long for Little Britches to become fully relaxed in Ruby's company, and he now seemed to trust the others in the group as well, and played happily with all the children.

Sam led the caravan of people through the Gap with some of his best marksmen at his heels. Roscoe and Ruby were next in line, tottering beneath their packs, but uncomplaining. Billy Joe, Hattie Lou and Little Britches were as close to them as their next breath. Roscoe's hand was on Ruby's shoulder, his head up, shoulders back, his steps mechanical and unvarying.

The women came next, moving one foot in front of the other, breathing hard and resisting the pull of their packs. Their younger children were in their arms or walking beside them, laughing and singing, their voices echoing loudly.

The older boys and girls were leading the pack animals and livestock just ahead of John and Matthew and the other men who were bringing up the rear.

When they finally emerged on the far side of the Gap, they found themselves in the valley of Big Yellow Creek. It was five or six miles in diameter and surrounded on all sides by mountains and hills. Here Sam called a halt.

The gentle May sun shown on bare arms and heads and sweat trickled down necks and ribs. Sam turned in his saddle and looked into the valley, and then looked back at his charge. He was so clothed in admiration for his friends and companions that stood silently around him, that chills ran up and down his spine. Providence had smiled down on them, and it was a holy and reverent moment for all.

Dismounting, Sam removed his hat and wiped the sweat from his face. "It's time we give thanks to the Almighty," he said humbly, and knelt in the grass before them. They all followed suit to the number. Men, women, boys and girls all gathered close, dropped to their knees and bowed their heads. Sam cleared his throat and raised his voice in prayer. "Father, it is with praise and grateful hearts that we now bow before you. We're grateful, Lord, that you've brought us safe thus far, and we beseech you, Father, if it's your Will, to see us safely through the miles ahead, until at last we reach our appointed place. It's in Jesus' name we ask these favors. Amen."

A chorus of "Amens" was heard. The women wiped their eyes and the men blew their noses. The younger children ran in circles, laughing and shouting, the dogs at their heels, and the older boys turned cartwheels and emitted shrill war whoops of delight.

With renewed vigor the settlers followed the Warriors Path along Yellow Creek for several miles, toiling through sloughs and canebrake marshes until they reached the Cumberland River about three o'clock in the afternoon.

"Do you hear anything?" Sam asked Ben as they approached the river. Ben cocked his head, listened for a few seconds and then gazed at Sam, a quizzical expression on his face. "I hear the clip clop of the horses' feet, the bawlin' of the cows an' the fracas of almost a hundred people, Mr. Tippett, sir. Need I hear more?"

Sam looked serious and he glanced about them warily. "That's the point, Ben. At this time of day we usually are besieged by the twittering of birds in the trees, squirrels flinging themselves from bough to bough, or rabbits bounding through the brush. It's too quiet, Ben!"

Ben was bewildered and showed it. "I don' understan', Mr. Tippett, sir. What you tryin' to tell Ben?"

"I don't want to worry the people unnecessarily, Ben, but I smell trouble brewing.

Keep a close watch, your eyes and ears open. I'll go speak to the other men." Sam turned and looked upon the shadowing hills, saw a bird or two take wing, then there was an explosion of wings lifting.

Sam took off at a gallop toward the river where he knew most of his people were already gathered. "Prepare for attack!" he shouted as he jerked Sonny's reins and doubled back to make sure there were no stragglers about. Almost before the words were out of his mouth, bloodcurdling yelps filled the air, and an ominous thunder of horses' hooves, and the howling of what sounded like hundreds of Indians, descended upon them.

An icy shiver raced through Ben's veins and a cold sweat broke out on his brow. His heart felt as though invisible fingers had clamped around it and was squeezing it in a death-grip as he sprang into action.

Together, Sam and Ben urged all the people behind rocks or trees for protection. The horses were whinnying in fear and pulling on their picket ropes, rearing clumsily in their hobbles, and fighting the young boys as they struggled with them.

"Don't shoot until I give the word!" Sam bellowed. The Indians were charging at breakneck speed, their brown faces and bodies painted crimson and their voices lifted in frightening whoops and war-cries.

At the first shout, Ruby, controlling her fear, instinctively grabbed for the three children that had dogged her heels all day. She flattened herself on the ground behind a copse of trees and pulled Roscoe, Billy Joe, Hattie Lou and Little Britches with her. She heard the Indians yowling, Sam barking orders, and the sound of gunfire.

Suddenly Little Britches jerked from Ruby's grasp, and dodging the frenzied animals and men running to and fro, burst into the open, waving his hands frantically in the air, his expression animated.

The siege was over in a matter of minutes, and no one had been injured on either side. The yipping ceased and Sam cried out, "Hold your fire!" The Indians drew back a safe distance, save one. He sat straight and proud on his painted war-horse, holding his rawhide-covered shield in his left hand. He slowly approached Little Britches, his black eyes proudly assessing his son. Every eye was on them.

CHAPTER 20

On Monday morning, May 5, 1783, the settlers moved beyond the Cumberland River into the heart of the wilderness. The gently rolling hills and thick green forests preceded them with trees six feet or more across, rising a hundred feet into the sky.

Flowers bloomed in profusion and dark green cedars studded the hillsides. Deer, bear, partridge, rabbit, turkey and quail were plentiful. The happy Pilgrims sang their way through the uncut groves of hickory, maple, cherry and oak, and willows festooned with wild grapevines, to ford countless streams.

Valleys became wider and the going became easier. Little Britches and their encounter with the Indians, had been the topic of conversation for days. Billy Joe sorely missed Little Britches. He sat glumly astride Foxy and rode for days without really communicating with anyone. Margaret had to wheedle and coax to even get him to eat.

When Sunday rolled around again, most everyone took advantage of the beautiful sunshine, bright and warm, and just lazed the day away. Billy Joe and Roscoe, his hand resting on Billy Joe's shoulder, were walking slowly toward the river's edge, in deep conversation. On the crest of a small rise above the Rockcastle River, Amy and Matthew, and Sally and Thornton, were sitting on blankets, watching Sandy bound after some of the smaller children, his exuberance matching theirs, his tongue lolling out from the joy of the romp.

A warm, happy feeling spread over Amy. "I'm so glad today is Sunday, and we have a whole day to enjoy ourselves," she said happily. "I truly love the land and the people, and the life I lived in Charlottesville now seems dull in comparison." She heaved a sigh and stared thoughtfully across the meadow, memories meandering without pattern through her mind.

Sally was watching Billy Joe and Roscoe with a soft expression on her face as they slowly approached the river, walking companionably side by side. "It's great to see Billy Joe enjoyin' hisself again, Amy. He was sorely vexed when Little Britches' father took him away, warn't he?"

Amy nodded. "He was so quiet and withdrawn for three days that I even missed fussing with him!"

Matthew laughed. "It was a stroke of good fortune!" he exclaimed. "To think we had an Indian chief's son in our very midst and didn't even know it." He shook his head from side-to-side. "Things could have gotten pretty hairy as we were outnumbered when it came to men and guns."

Amy looked at Matthew and smiled faintly. "God surely blessed us by putting Little Britches into our care."

"I was never so scared in my life," Sally said and shivered, recalling the attack.

Thornton drew in a deep breath and his eyes sparkled as he looked at Sally. He rubbed the back of his neck. "Now, Sally, you surely know that you earned a star or two in your crown for how you reacted under siege the other day."

Sally looked at Thornton with interest. "You were watching me?" she asked incredulously, "when you were so busy helpin' everybody else?"

Thornton's neck and face colored as he looked at Sally shyly. "Well," he drawled, "I guess I wasn't so all-fired busy I couldn't see how you collected the little children around you, thinking of their safety even before your own."

Sally dropped her eyes and little waves of happiness coursed through her veins. Embarrassed, but overjoyed by Thornton's praise of her, she tried to draw attention away from herself. "Amy never faltered neither," she said. "She was everywhere at once. My stomach still jumps when I think of it!"

"Everyone did just what Sam said to do without question," Amy interrupted. "We can all take pride in one another, and pray we can be as levelheaded the next time."

"I pray to God there is no next time!" Sally quailed.

"Another three weeks on the trail should do it," Matthew said encouragingly, "so take heart. Sam's not about to let anything happen to us at this late stage of the game!"

. . .

"I'm as sorry as I can be, B.J., that Little Britches couldn't remain with us longer," Roscoe said to Billy Joe sadly. "But I am happier still that he is once again reunited with his father and mother. Aren't you?"

Billy Joe looked uncomfortable, but responded. "I'm going to miss him, Rock, that's for certain!" He licked his lips. "It makes me wonder all over again, why we have to be mad at the Indians and fight them. If all Indians were like Little Britches and his father, we could live side-by-side with them, couldn't we?"

Gaining the shade of the trees, Roscoe stopped beneath a willow, and sighing with relief at the sudden coolness, sat down. The wind stirred and the branches above them swayed, making shadow patterns on the ground. Roscoe unbuttoned the top button of his shirt, and with his handkerchief wiped the sweat from his face and neck. He stretched his legs before him and coaxed Billy Joe to sit down beside him.

"Sit awhile, my boy, and enjoy that cooling breeze blowing off the river. I want to tell you a story my pappy told me when I was just a lad about your age," he said quietly, patting the ground beside him.

Billy Joe immediately sat on the ground cross-legged beside Roscoe, giving him his full attention.

"In the beginning God made a forest," Roscoe began, the timbre of his voice rich and full. "No man knew the beginning nor the end of it. Those who first entered the forest knew it had been there since the beginning of time, and they also knew they did not truly own it, but could gain from the use of it.

"There were rivers that ran hither and yon, clean and clear and undefiled; mountains, made of rock and soil, were covered with breathing, blooming plants of every description; birds of every color of the rainbow: large and small, lifted their voices to the great God who created them. Wild beasts roamed at will through the forest at that time. And then came the red man, his villages too numerous to count."

Roscoe was speaking very simply and from time to time he would pause and smile, very anxious for Billy Joe to understand everything he was saying. Billy Joe sat entranced, always enjoying his special times with Roscoe and being entertained by his stories.

"The trees were huge and round. Deer fed in the green glades, as did the mighty buffalo. There were caves where the wolves mated and peaks where the panther screamed out his rage. The forest was rich with game and natural resources, and birds beheld the grandeur and beauty of God's creation, and took to the air by the millions.

"Then the white men came. Fire and axe ate the forest and plowed the fields, and road scars began to show among the trees. The Red man found arrows were no match for muskets, and death fell among the red men, leaving quiet mounds beside the many rivers. The red man fought valiantly to preserve the forest, knowing that if the white man stayed, the game would go, and in time the Indian would have to go too. I'm afraid we're beginning to see that happen, B.J., whether we're ready for it or if we really want it to be that way. You and I would rather make friends of the Indians than fight them. But my lad, we have thrown our lot with our traveling companions and rightly so, and only God knows the final outcome."

A tear rolled down Roscoe's cheek as he and Billy Joe joined hands, and rising, made their way slowly back to camp.

. . .

Amy was still awake; her mind like a kaleidoscope that had been so shaken it could not regain its original pattern. The air, bright with sunshine all day, was now cooling rapidly with the setting of the sun. She lay huddled on a pallet under the stars, softened by a carpet of rust-brown needles. Billy Joe and her parents lay close by, and had been lost in sleep and dreams for over an hour.

Desire for adventure had never surged through Amy's veins, and no opportunity for adventure had ever presented itself until her father had informed the family of his desire to follow Sam into the wilds of Kentucky. Her grandparents' images now floated before her, as well as those of Kristy and Nikki. How precious and dear they all were.

To be parted from family and friends had been devastating to Amy, but God had so graciously seen fit to bring other dear friends into her life to make her loss easier to bear. Every moment on the trail, every person sharing in the adventuresome journey to Kentucky, had left an imprint on her.

The black, enveloping silence of the moonless night pressed upon her, and she was conscious of the gentle breathing of Billy Joe, lying beside her. She remembered the vitality of his laughter that day and smiled. True, he was a brat of a brother at times, but still a fine boy. His skin, milk and roses in Virginia, was now bronzed from wind and sun. He had matured far beyond his eleven years, and had made lasting friendships with both the young and old of their group.

The night air was chilling, and by the light from a blazing fire Amy could see that her mother had snuggled close to her father's back for warmth. Love and admiration for her parents washed over her in billowing waves.

Thoughts of Matthew tugged at her heart. They had been thrown together a lot in their travels. She was too young to know what love was all about, the kind of love her parents had for one another, but she was old enough to know that the feelings she had for Matthew went far beyond any schoolgirl crush she had previously had back in Charlottesville, Virginia. She was content in the knowledge that Matthew would be numbered with them when they reached their new homeland tomorrow.

With a deep, satisfying sigh, Amy whispered her prayers and gave in to her exhaustion, and fell into a deep and restful sleep.

. . .

Sam was taking his turn at nightwatch. The warm night air stirred the green leaves of sycamore and beech and rustled gently through the long grasses surrounding his campfire. At the moment, all was relatively quiet save for a few occasional wind-borne voices, the rustle of trees, and the stomping of horses' feet. He knew the exhaustion from their long day's journey would soon claim sleep for everyone but the guards. The sky was pitch black, and most of the fires had died out as Sam walked on moccasined feet to the edge of the camp. He paused and looked into the inky blackness, and satisfied himself that all was well.

Inching his way back to his resting-place beneath a large sycamore, he made himself as comfortable as he could, pulled a piece of jerky from his pocket, and began chewing on it. His thoughts went immediately to his family. It had been six months since he had last seen them—an eternity. Nothing, he prayed to God, would ever separate them again.

Abigail's love filled every nook and cranny of his cabin, and his beloved children, two strong and virile sons, and a dimpled-cheeked daughter, were a delight. God-fearing neighbors would now be a reality at New Hope—not merely a dream.

Sam had never been surrounded with people that he esteemed more highly than those who had made the harrowing trip through the wilderness with him did. He was particularly impressed with the courage and spirit of the women: Ruby, Margaret, Sally and Gilda, and the patience and endurance of the menfolk: Roscoe, John, Matthew, Thornton, Ben and his brother, Howard.

There would be a world of back-breaking work for them to get done before winter set in: ground cleared of trees and underbrush, cabins erected, furniture carved from their very own trees, gardens planted and fields sewn to grain. True, there would be no rest for the weary in the months ahead at New Hope, but Sam knew that as long as God lent them breath, these people would work hand-in-hand carving their niche in their new world.

. . .

Bluegrass was hurrying toward June's ripeness and trees shimmered in the freshest of new leaves as Sam and his travel-weary, but exuberant, men, women and children, rode, walked, or were carried to their journey's end. It was Saturday, May 24, 1783, at exactly two o'clock in the afternoon.

The enormity of what God had accomplished through him made Sam tremble in awe. In his own strength it would have been impossible to lead these Pilgrims to their Promised Land, but God had provided the miracle, and had given Sam an assuring promise: *I will never leave you nor forsake you . . .*

Sam rose in the stirrups and thrust his rifle into the air. The burden had been lifted from his shoulders.

CHAPTER 21

April 1785

A fire, making small, sleepy sounds, burned lazily in the fireplace, blunting the chill edge in the air. A log dropped, sending a flurry of sparks up the chimney and the unexpected crackle and pop startled Amy as she sat huddled beneath a multi-colored afghan in her favorite chair, lost in one of her endless reflections.

The Seth Thomas clock ticked rhythmically on the mantle shelf and Buttercup, Amy's yellow and white cat, purred contentedly on the braided rug before the hearth. The odor of beans, generously seasoned with chunks of ham and bacon drippings, simmered slowly on the back grate of the cooking stove, blending subtly with the more pungent smell of burning wood that permeated the air.

Heat from the flame of the fire beat on Amy's delicate cheeks, flushing them crimson. Dark circles framed her liquid brown eyes, edged by long dark lashes, and her nose was red and painful to the touch. She absently licked her dry, chapped lips and burrowed deeper into the confines of the big oak rocker, hollowed out like a nest in back and seat.

Amy's usually lustrous hair now hung in long, limp strands

about her shoulders. A cold and sore throat had kept her bedfast for two days and she was still gripped by a feeling of languor and just plain boredom from inactivity. All the windows in the cabin, with the exception of one, were shuttered. Amy now gazed thoughtfully through that one window. It faced the east and she was rewarded by a glimpse of bright blue sky, dotted here and there with thick, white clouds, and the gentle rays of an early morning sun.

Roused from her reverie, Amy sneezed, blew her nose and wiped it gently. She rose slowly, draped the afghan about her shoulders and padded on bare feet to the great oak door and swung it wide. Fresh spring air, freighted with the scent of blooming peach and apple trees and damp leaf mold, rushed in. Stretching and yawning she blinked against the glare of the morning sun as its rays reached out to embrace her.

A robin chirped from the great maple at the side of the cabin, and the call of a meadowlark lilted to her in clarion precision as she stood in the open doorway idly watching the chickens as they scratched in the yard.

Margaret's faint humming reached her ears. Her mother stood beneath the clothesline, strung from one corner of the cabin to a huge cottonwood in one corner of the yard. Her curly brown hair bounced under her blue cotton bonnet as she bustled about, hanging up her family's wash.

Chewing at the corner of her lip, Amy sighed, and then reluctantly closed the door to the chilly morning air as a rooster crowed in the distance. Returning to the rocker, Amy sank once again into its downy-soft cushions, and pulled her slender legs beneath the folds of her warm flannel gown. She sneezed and shivered slightly in spite of the warmth of the fire and the afghan that still enveloped her slight frame.

The clock on the mantle struck the half-hour just as the door burst open and Margaret, still humming softly to herself, entered the cozy warm kitchen. The air fairly vibrated with birdsong behind her. "Burrrr," Margaret said, shivering. "It's mighty cold out there this morning, let me tell you!" She drew her scarlet shawl more snugly about her shoulders with red-chapped hands.

Amy watched listlessly as her mother removed her bonnet and hung it on a peg behind the door. Margaret glanced in her direction and said, "It's good to see you up and about this fine morning, honey. Feeling better?"

Nodding her head slowly, Amy replied, "Much better, Ma. I'm just tired of lazing about in bed, that's all. Guess I'm just plain bored." Amy stirred restlessly in her chair, and unconsciously her brow furrowed. "You almost beat the rooster up this morning, didn't you, Ma?"

"Yes, I believe I did," Margaret admitted with a chuckle. She rubbed her hands together before the brightly-burning logs in the fireplace, and said lightly, "Fire sure feels good this morning." She reached up and took a small key from the mantle shelf and wound the clock carefully. Then laying aside her shawl she walked across the well-scrubbed puncheon floor and opened the shutters to let in the morning light.

"Do you want some breakfast now?" Margaret asked, hanging her shawl on the back of the kitchen door. She rolled the sleeves of her blue cotton dress to her elbows and said cheerfully, "I fixed sausage and pancakes for your pa and the boys and I've got plenty of batter left."

"I'm not hungry right now," Amy replied, yawning deeply, "but thanks anyway." Amy's dark brown eyes followed her mother as she donned her red-gingham apron and gathered up the dirty dishes and put them into the dishpan to soak. Next Margaret took the red and white-checked tablecloth from the table, opened the heavy oak door, and shook the crumbs from it. She leaned against the doorframe for a fleeting minute and watched silently as the birds and chickens quickly gathered to scratch the crumbs from the ground. Amy wondered admiringly where her mother got all of her energy as she went from one endless chore to another.

Margaret turned toward Amy, the lines of weariness that had etched her face just minutes before had been replaced by a smile. "It's sure a lovely day the Lord has given us. Doesn't seem possible that such beauty should be marred by the thoughts of troublesome Indians about."

"Has someone told Pa they've seen Indian sign?" Amy asked anxiously, petting Buttercup who had jumped into her lap.

Margaret's face clouded with uneasiness. "Your pa was talking to Sam late yesterday. Seems as though a few head of cattle have wandered away lately—with or without help, Sam says. Tracks of unshod ponies were found, but luckily no one was molested. Your pa wouldn't say much because he doesn't want to worry me, and he said he didn't want me borrowing trouble."

"I wish you were as confident as you sound, Ma. But what if . . . ?"

Shading her snappy brown eyes, Margaret lifted them toward the sky and took another deep breath, cutting Amy off in the middle of her doubts. "Just smell that air! Ummm!"

"I only wish I could," Amy lamented.

"All in good time," Margaret responded cheerfully. Buttercup jumped down from off Amy's lap and sauntered, only as she could do, to the door. Arching her back, she rubbed against Margaret's leg, before scampering outside. Margaret closed the door and the room grew silent save for the ticking of the clock on the mantle and the soft sigh of ash as it collapsed in the fireplace.

Cuttings for rose begonias sat in clay pots on Margaret's windowsills, and she picked up one of the pots and felt of the dark soil with her forefinger. Taking a dipper of water from the water bucket she carefully moistened the soil around each plant. After watering her flowers, Margaret reached for the broom.

Rising slowly from the rocker Amy gently removed the broom from her mother's hand. "Let me do that, Ma" she said sweetly, and you go sit by the fire for a spell and have yourself another cup of coffee. You can surely use it by now."

"Why thank you, honey," Margaret said, glancing at Amy. "Are you sure you feel up to it? You've been feeling mighty poorly these last few days."

Shaking her head Amy smiled warmly. "I'm feeling much better and I truly need to be up and doing something."

Reaching out, Margaret felt Amy's forehead for reassurance. Noting it was cool and dry she drew her daughter gently to her breast and planted a kiss on her forehead. "You don't have any fever, but you still look a mite peaked to me."

While Amy swept dutifully, Margaret took a clean mug from the corner cupboard and filled it with steaming coffee from the pot on the back of the stove. Her grateful sigh as she sank into the huge rocker, reached Amy's ears. Margaret slowly sipped the rich brown liquid and gazed into the blazing fire before her.

Minutes later Amy put the broom away and washed her hands in the granite wash basin. "Anything else I can do for you, Ma?"

Her eyes piercing the distance between them, Margaret said, "My, but you are feeling your oats, aren't you? I've had all sorts of help this morning." Margaret flushed with pleasure. "Matthew helped feed the animals and milked the cow, and Billy Joe, not to be outdone, fed and watered the chickens and gathered the eggs for me. Some of my hens have been hiding their eggs in all of the out-of-the-way places around here. Billy Joe found another full nest today. We'll be having us fewer eggs for breakfast, but a new brood of little chicks at this rate."

Rising stiffly from the rocker, Margaret put her empty mug into the dishpan with the rest of the dishes and faced Amy. "I guess you could go and find your pa and ask him if he needs anything from the village. After I've tidied up in here, I believe I'll take the wagon in for supplies. And while I'm at it," she said with a gleam in her eye, "I'll check on Roscoe and Ruby and see how they're faring."

"Be sure to give them my best."

"That I will do, honey. Might be I should take some of that beef stew we had left over yesterday and the extra cherry pie I baked. With Matthew staying here with us for the time being helping your pa, I don't imagine Ruby is cooking as much as she usually does."

Amy brightened at the mention of Matthew's name. "It is sorta nice to know pa is getting help with all the spring planting, isn't it, Ma?" Amy asked, exhaling a long sigh of contentment.

Margaret looked thoughtful and nodded her head in agreement. "I'm so proud of the way that boy pitches in to help your pa. Why he gets things done before John even knows they need doing." Margaret wagged her head and smiled. "What a boy—just like my own, he is."

Humming softly to herself, Margaret plunged her hands into the hot soapy dishwater. "You scoot along now and find your pa. I guess the fresh air won't harm you any now that your fever's gone. But you put your shoes on. It's no wonder you've got a cold. Some day you're going to catch your death, running around with bare feet all the time," she fussed.

"Oh, Ma, don't be such a fussbudget," Amy said emphatically running into her bedroom. She chose a peach-colored cotton dress, one of her favorites; donned shoes and stockings and tied a pretty ribbon around her hair. She grabbed her shawl that was hanging behind the kitchen door and struck out through the dewy footpath that led to the barn.

Walking jauntily, Amy swung her arms in time with her step. She longed to breathe deeply and smell the pure clean air so rich and irresistible to her nostrils, but with her nose so plugged she knew she would just have to be content to look at the beauty that surrounded her.

The rays of the sun on her face felt like a golden caress, and gave Amy's complexion the flawless translucency of fine porcelain. Catching sight of her father's wiry figure plowing a furrowed pattern behind the barn, Amy pulled her shawl close and picked up her pace. The caw of a crow split the air above her.

Duchess, John's roan mare, was dragging the plow faithfully and steadily through the long furrows, and Sandy, Matthew's dog, lazed close by, soaking up the warmth from the sun. Barn swallows were circling the air above Amy, darting in the bright sunlight, their dark blue satiny backs flashing, and their forked tails combing the air as they swooped by. Robins sang cheerily, flying out of the sweet spring distance, and silently lighting among the plowed ridges. Greedily they yanked at the big fat worms that were so abundant in the rich black soil.

"Morning, Pa!" Amy called out cheerily, grabbing for his attention. She lifted her skirts and tripped lightly over the rough ground to where her father stood. He was shading his eyes with one hand and holding to the reins and plow with the other. John peered in her direction, his brows raised in surprise, and a smile lit his whole countenance when he caught sight of her.

"Whoa! Whoa now, Duchess!" he gasped, pulling hard on the reins. The great horse came to a sudden standstill; her forefeet flung stiffly forward, her head hanging as inertly as a broken tree branch. "And a good morning to you my daughter!" John answered jovially, his eyes dancing. He pulled his watch out of his pocket and glanced at it. "What brings you out here so early in the day? Thought you was feeling poorly?"

Feeling her cheeks glow under her father's close scrutiny, Amy stood on tiptoe and her eyes widened eagerly as she kissed her father's moist leathery cheek. "I'm feeling much better, thank goodness. Ma's going to go to the village and wants to know if there's anything you want her to fetch home for you."

Sandy's tail beat softly on the plowed ground and Amy squatted and put her arms around his neck, speaking sweet nothings into his ear. Sandy swiped at her cheek with a moist tongue, raised his front right paw, and gently laid it on her knee. Amy took his large paw into her hand and shook it. "And a good morning to you, too, Sandy," she said, smiling. Rising, Amy patted Duchess on the neck and fanned at the swarm of gnats that danced around the mare's face.

Glancing over the fields that stretched beyond the barn, Amy's warm brown eyes sparkled and she said, "It's so peaceful out here, Pa."

"That it is my daughter. That it is." A flicker of animation streaked John's face as he rubbed the back of his neck and glanced speculatively about him. "God's more than gracious to his children when he spoils them with such beauty." A sly grin creased his face. "But who was it now that pulled tooth and nail to stay behind in Virginia a few years ago? I rightly recall she didn't want nothing to do with Kentucky!"

Amy tilted her head and peered up at her father's face intently. "You know that's all behind me now. I still miss Grandma and

Grandpa Johnson, more than I can say, but I feel right at home here in Kentucky. I wouldn't want to live in any other place."

"That goes double for me," John said, enthralled with what Amy had said. Sandy's tail was beating in a rhymic motion to the sound of their voices. He sighed deep in his throat and thrust his cold moist nose into John's hand. John leaned down and scratched him behind the ears. "Sandy decided to keep me company this morning for some reason. Feel mighty privileged, as he usually won't let Matthew out of his sight."

"Where is Matthew anyway?" Amy asked curiously, glancing all about her. "I thought he and Billy Joe were supposed to be helping you."

John's laugh ripped through the air and he spoke in his usual, jesting way. "You sure do a good job of keeping track of that boy, I'm here to tell you!"

"Aw, Pa," Amy said as casually as she could, "I'm just concerned with how tired and worn you look. I do wish you'd slow down just a mite." Amy scanned her father's face with anxiety. "You should let the boys shoulder more of the load around here!"

John was charged with a sweeping surge of defiance. "What in tarnation do you mean by that remark?" he bristled, his eyes snapping. "I'm not even forty yet, and I'm sure not ready to be put out to pasture—not by a long shot!"

"I didn't mean that you were, Pa. I just..."

John interrupted her, his voice now calm and steady. "I'm trying to finish with this field and Billy Joe and Matthew are planting ground west of the peach orchard. You know that in spite of his young age, Billy Joe already does more'n his share of the work around here. Why he can plow a furrow nearly as straight as I can. And I'm much obliged at Matthew's being so generous with his time. No matter how busy that boy is he's always finding time to help me out. That boy is sure something."

"We all think highly of Matthew," Amy said dreamily, remembering how he shouldered a man's responsibilities when his folks were killed on the trek to Kentucky.

"I'm so glad he decided to live with Roscoe and Ruby after he lost his parents, and I know they count their blessings every day for that decision, too. It's so nice to have him stay with us and help you out every chance he gets though." Amy never tired of singing Matthew's praises.

"I always said this family needed more boys," John said, lowering his voice. "But the good Lord didn't see fit to send your ma and me any more. Guess God knew all along that Matthew would be here pitching in and . . . ."

Amy laughed and interjected, "God knew one Billy Joe was all any family could handle, Pa! That's the truth of it!"

John broke into a grin. "Let's not be too harsh on that boy." John took his handkerchief from his back pant's pocket and blew his nose. "Billy Joe's a good kid under all his lollygaging and he's growing up mighty fast. I know it'll be awhile before he can match brain and brawn with Matthew, but two finer boys you'd have to travel this world over to find—and that's God's truth!"

John looked expectantly at Amy. "Can't say that you've complained much in having a fine brother the likes of Matthew now, have you? Or would you happen to have other interests in that boy by any chance?" John's eyes twinkled and he laughed out loud, amused by the blush that rose on Amy's cheeks.

John leaned down to dislodge a rock buried in the ground. Rising stiffly, he groaned with the effort. Amy had been so lost in her thoughts of Matthew that she jumped when she heard her father's groan. John looked at Amy sheepishly and threw the rock to the edge of the field.

It was now Amy's turn to laugh. "What was it you were saying a minute ago about being put out to pasture, Pa?" she said, reveling at the sheepish look on her father's face.

"No problem my daughter. Just need a little oil on my joints and Maggie can tend to that tonight with her bottle of liniment and magic touch." John winked and gave Amy an engaging smile as he removed his tattered hat and mopped his brow on the sleeve of his faded blue shirt.

Looking longingly in the direction of the cabin, John said, "I believe I'll just mosey on back to the cabin with you, honey. I'd like another cup of your ma's strong coffee, and maybe one of them gingersnaps she baked the other day." He picked up his Lancaster long rifle and cradled it in one arm and reached for Duchess' reins. "Let me take Duchess into the barn and give her some oats and then we'll be on our way."

Amy's long hair bounced in the spring breeze as they made the short trek back to the cabin, Sandy bounding ahead of them. The sweetly rolling countryside to where the hills rose in the distance made a gentle landscape about them. The sounds of chattering squirrels and scolding blue jays met their ears, and an eagle caught Amy's eye as it circled silently above them, scarcely moving its wings, just gliding effortlessly in the blue sky. A rabbit streaked across the path in front of them and Sandy was off and running, enjoying the chase.

CHAPTER 22

Coffee was boiling, its rich fragrance filling every room, as father and daughter entered the cozy kitchen. John leaned his rifle on the latch side of the doorway and washed his hands in the basin before settling himself comfortably at the table. Tipping his chair on two legs he watched as Amy reached for his favorite mug and filled it to the brim with Margaret's good strong coffee. She reached into the cookie jar and grabbed a handful of gingersnaps and sat down in her chair.

Taking the cookies from Amy's outstretched hand, John said, "You're getting prettier every day, honey, and all these young scalawags that have been standing knee deep at my door for the last two years courting my little girl will be asking for your hand in marriage."

A warm glow of excitement tingled through Amy as she sat across the table from her father and nibbled on a cookie. Her eyes sparkled and she wore a radiant smile. "All the boys have on their mind around here is hunting, fishing and playing horseshoes every Saturday morning, Pa." Taking another bite of her cookie, she tossed her head. "There isn't one of them I'd want to spend the rest of my life with!"

"Now I wouldn't say that was entirely gospel. I saw how you

was blushing when Jeff what's-his-name was eyeballing you last Sunday morning when he didn't think his ma was watching. Seems to me he's here more often than any other." John winked at Margaret as she walked out of their bedroom laughing.

"I heard you John William and that's enough!" she said with mock sternness, quickly striding to the table. "You should be ashamed of yourself teasing this poor girl so."

"All I been doing is sitting here enjoying good coffee and a conversation with my daughter, Maggie. You going to deny a man a chance to rest awhile in comfort?"

Margaret stepped behind John and ruffled his thinning hair. Leaning down she planted a kiss on the top of his head. Noticing that his cup was empty she said impishly, "If you've got time enough to tease, you've got time enough to hitch up the mules for me.

Now get yourself out of here and get busy before I take my broom to you!" John's laughter ripped the air as he went to do his wife's bidding.

Turning her attention to Amy, her eyes sharp and accessing, Margaret said, "If you feel up to it while I'm gone, you might shell the peas I picked this morning. I put them in the spring house." Margaret stood still in deep thought.

"Anything else, Ma?"

"I guess a new thinking cap for me," Margaret said brightly. "Would you mind bringing in the wash for me? I completely forgot about my clothes until just this minute. I'm in a bit of a hurry to stop and take them down now, and besides I'm not real sure they're all dry yet."

"I'll take care of the clothes if you'll give Ruby a kiss from me. And Ma, please tell Roscoe I'm feeling much better and that I'll be seeing him at Worship tomorrow!"

"That I will do," Margaret said evenly as she went out the door. A few minutes later she was headed for the valley, a red shawl about her shoulders, her bonnet tied neatly under her chin, and her skirts flying.

It was almost three o'clock when Amy finished with her inside chores. She picked up her sewing basket and ventured into the yard. Thick gray clouds played hide and seek with the sun as she sat in the double swing hanging from the giant maple tree standing regally beside the cabin. She leaned back contentedly and began to stitch.

Buttercup suddenly appeared out of nowhere and rubbed against Amy's leg with a luxurious purr of love. Jumping up into the swing, she settled herself in a yellow coil at Amy's side and began washing her face with one yellow and white paw. Pausing in her stitching, Amy gently stroked Buttercup's head and back. "And where have you been, young lady?" Amy asked, wisps of hair framing her face. "I haven't seen you since early this morning. You wouldn't have a boyfriend in these parts would you?" Amy was rewarded with a swipe of Buttercup's raspy tongue on her arm.

An hour later Amy looked up from her sewing to scan the landscape, and was happy to see her father headed toward the well. She hollered in his direction and beckoned to him. "Come and sit a spell with me, Pa!" she called out.

John looked longingly at her and raised a callused hand in silent salute of consent. After taking a drink of water from the long handled gourd dipper John crossed the expanse of yard that separated them. Exhaling a long sigh of contentment, he sank down wearily into the swing beside her. He reached between them to pet Buttercup, but she regarded his efforts with a haughty indifference and moved into Amy's lap.

"That cat positively adores you, but it beats the socks off me why she won't allow me to even touch her."

Amy stroked Buttercup's head softly. "Guess she knows I dearly love her and she knows you dote on Sandy whenever he's around. She's just a little jealous and offended by it, that's all." Re-threading her needle, Amy continued to stitch on her dress, pushing a thimbled fingertip against the needle, blissfully happy and fully alive. Leaf shadows moved across John's lean, weather-lined face as he gazed thoughtfully at her.

"You look more and more like your ma every day," he said simply.

Amy quickly lifted her head. "Oh Pa, I'm so glad you think so.

I think Ma's a beautiful woman. I'd be proud to think that someday I'll be half as pretty as she is."

John drew in his lips thoughtfully. "Two beautiful women in one household! Now how in tarnation do I deserve that? You know, honey, all I ever wanted in life, all my hopes and dreams, were realized when I met and married your mother. It was love at first sight for your Ma and me. I was twenty-one and Maggie was seventeen. Seems like yesterday. Can't believe how fast time flies."

John's voice died away and he reached out and took Amy's hand into his own. His gaze came to rest on her questioning eyes. "And?" Amy questioned, eagerness shining in her eyes. "Finish your story, Pa."

John chuckled with happy memories. "After you and Billy Joe came along, I knew that God had smiled on me something fierce. And to add to all those blessings, I'm now enjoying life at middle age in a country filled with tremendous possibilities. I've got me a comfortable home, hewn and carved from my very own trees."

John's gaze returned to Amy again and again in silent expectation. "I bought a hundred acres from Sam when we moved here and now we own over four hundred acres. With a garden full of vegetables and an orchard planted to apples, peaches and pears, we'll never lack for food, and that's God's truth!" John gestured widely with his arms.

"Just look at the beauty around us, Amy. Someday when you and Billy Joe are married and wanting to raise a family, you'll know the pride that comes from owning prime Kentucky soil. I can't begin to tell you how many times I've thanked the good Lord that he gave us the courage to start our lives over again here in Kentucky."

Amy giggled. "Oh, Pa, what a gloomy Gus I was back then. To think what I would have missed! You tried to tell us what an adventure it would be but I never, in my wildest imaginings, thought I'd ever be this happy. Thanks, Pa."

"My pleasure, honey."

With her dress fully mended, Amy put her needle and thread, and scissors and thimble, into the sewing basket. She folded her dress neatly and laid it on top of the basket. Thunder rumbled in the distance and Amy looked toward the sky. The clouds were darkening and getting thicker by the minute. Awakened, Buttercup yawned and stretched luxuriously. Hearing voices, Amy's mind was taken off of the gathering clouds. She grinned happily as she caught sight of Billy Joe and Matthew heading for the well.

"Here comes Matthew and Billy Joe, Pa, and just a jump ahead of the storm that's brewing. They only had cold sandwiches for lunch so they'll be starved if I don't miss my guess. I guess I better be seeing to supper." Amy glanced once more at the darkening sky as thunder rumbled once again in the distance. "But first I best get in the wash. That rain will be here before long and Ma will skin me alive if her clothes get wet all over again!"

Rising, Amy reached out and took her father's callused hand and helped pull him to his feet. She gathered up her sewing basket in one hand and Buttercup in the other and they hurried into the cabin.

John carefully propped his rifle against the wall. He laid a big log on the fire and it soon began popping and cracking, casting a flickering light on the puncheon floor.

John sat down wearily in the rocking chair by the hearth, and stretched his legs before him and folded his hands across his chest.

Amy hurried outside to take the clothes down. She knew it wouldn't be long before her father would close his eyes and fall under the spell of the anesthetizing quality in the sound of the fire and the clock gently ticking in solemn majesty above his head.

A warm glow flowed through Amy as her gaze fell on Matthew as he strode toward her. She held one of Matthew's sweet-smelling shirts she had just taken down from the clothesline up to her face.

Her thoughts ran wild: *Matthew would be twenty-one on July twenty-first, a man in every sense of the word. Every time she looked at him her heart would race, her face felt warm and her toes tingled. These feelings surely didn't mean that she was in love with him. Since knowing Matthew she had tried to force such dangerous thoughts away. Matthew would never fall in love with her. She must push her feelings aside; love another someday. But the mere thought leaves me cold and empty . . .*

Coming out of her reverie Amy quickly folded Matthew's shirt and laid it in the clothesbasket. "What'cha dreamin' about, funny face?" Billy Joe asked as he headed for the cabin, grinning and tugging on Amy's hair ribbon as he passed behind her.

Amy jumped. She had been so lost in thoughts of Matthew she hadn't heard Billy Joe's silent approach. She retied her ribbon and watched in annoyance as Billy Joe, his shirttail hanging loosely outside his breeches, and whistling off-tune, entered the cabin and closed the door behind him. *Except for his brotherly devilishness,* Amy thought in frustration, *Billy Joe reminded her more and more of their papa every day in appearance and carriage. He was getting so tall and would someday be a very handsome fellow.*

Amy was pulled from her reverie, as Matthew appeared before her, tall and straight like a towering spruce, arms well-muscled and bronzed by wind and sun. His face and thick sandy-yellow hair now glistened with water. Slowly he unbuttoned his dark linen shirt and pulled it free of his faded homespun breeches. She found herself staring at his broad chest and rippling muscles. Matthew caught her sly glances and his intense blue eyes flickered with interest.

Fumbling with the clothespins Amy's pulse raced and she felt like a naughty child caught with her fingers in the cookie jar. "I . . . I was supposed to take down the clothes and I . . . I got to doing other things, and now they'll probably get wet and Ma will be upset with me," Amy rambled.

Matthew's lips parted in a dazzling display of straight white teeth as he eased into a grin. "Well, in that case, maybe I ought to help you. We wouldn't want Ma upset with you now, would we? And the sooner you get the clothes gathered in, the sooner you can fix this starving man some vittles."

Grabbing at the clothespins that Amy held in her trembling fingers, Matthew dropped them into the reed basket at her feet. "I'm so hungry I do believe I could eat a horse!" Matthew playfully rubbed his stomach and rolled his compelling blue eyes.

"Sorry, but I'm not serving horse today!" Amy said whimsically, crinkling her nose and tossing her head impishly. Matthew reached out to tweak her nose but she quickly ducked under his arm, picked up the clothesbasket, and made a beeline to the cabin, giggling wildly. She felt his eyes on her as she rushed into the cabin.

A ripple of weakness washed over Matthew as he watched Amy's retreat. His eyes glistened, and a wealth of emotion whirled and eddied within the confines of his heart. *Amy no longer resembled the tomboy that he had grown so accustomed to the past two years. In place of boyish, straight hips, her hips had rounded out, and now emphasized her slim waist. In place of skinny arms and knobby knees, she had acquired the face and body of a beautiful young lady. She had grown up right before his eyes and he had been almost too busy to notice.*

Matthew's heart gave a lurch and pounded within his chest. Absently he picked up a stick and threw it, watching as Sandy ran to fetch it. His thoughts again ran rampant. *Having lost both parents as he did on their trek to Kentucky back in '83, Matthew had become like a son to Roscoe and Ruby Willis who had taken him under their wing. But he had also been like a son to John and Margaret Bradshaw, living and working side by side with John and Billy Joe during spring planting time, and during their months of harvest. He had come to think of Billy Joe as a brother and Amy . . . well, Amy was without a doubt the most beautiful and desirable young woman he had ever laid eyes on. He had always chided himself when he thought of Amy in any other capacity than that of a beloved friend or sister. After all he was four years her senior. But, he admitted, she was thoroughly capable of turning his world topsy-turvy.* Confused by his thoughts and emotions, and a little reluctant to enter the cabin just yet, Matthew threw the stick several more times, waiting patiently for Sandy to retrieve it.

After Amy had put away the laundry, she poured Buttercup a saucer of warm milk and filled Sandy's bowl with milk and cornbread. She started the evening meal glancing out of the east window every now and then, wondering what was keeping Matthew so long. She stepped out the kitchen door to pick a bouquet of flowers and almost collided with him. He reached out to steady her and shivers of delight followed his touch, and whipped color into her cheeks.

Matthew's pulse hummed with tension as he walked past her into the cabin with an armload of firewood for the night. Stooping down, Amy quickly picked a handful of the sweet-smelling lily-of-the-valley that grew outside the cabin door. She reentered the kitchen and filled a cut-glass vase with water, placed the flowers in the vase, and put it in the center of the table.

A loud clap of thunder shook the cabin just ahead of the sound of the wagon. John was rudely awakened and jumped as though he had been shot. He quickly made his way out-of-doors, his voice trailing behind him, "I'm coming, Maggie. I'm coming! Best you hurry inside before you get drenched!" The rain had commenced in earnest.

Margaret appeared in the doorway a scant minute later and Amy was alarmed at the look on her face. "Matthew!" she called sharply. "Billy Joe! Come quick! I need your help." Without another word she turned and made her way back to the wagon. Matthew quickly followed Margaret outside with Billy Joe tagging at his heels.

Reentering the cabin in just seconds, Matthew carried Ruby in his arms, followed by a very wet and worried Roscoe. Margaret, huffing and puffing with exertion soon entered the kitchen with a rustle of skirts. "Pull the rocking chair close to the fire, Amy," she directed.

Doing as she was told, Amy looked worriedly at Ruby's ashen face. Matthew eased his burden into the rocking chair and Margaret disappeared into her bedroom. She reappeared a few seconds later with two bed pillows in her arms. She pulled the footstool toward her, placed the pillows on it, and gently propped Ruby's right leg on the pillows.

Looking about her in consternation, Ruby said dejectedly, "My, oh my, Margaret. I'm just plumb sorry to be causing you all this fuss and bother." Her steely-blue eyes were bright and piercing, in spite of the obvious pain showing on her waxen face.

"You could never be a bother to me, Ruby," Margaret said gently. "Just quiet your fears."

Roscoe was sitting in a straight chair holding Ruby's hand,

absently patting it, a look of concern written on his face. "I'm sorry that I can't be of more help, my love. It's only in times like these that I miss... well, I miss what I don't have—my sight."

Putting a hand to Roscoe's face, Ruby patted his cheek gently. "Don't you fret now, sweetheart. You've been of more help to me in our years together than a dozen-sighted men could ever have been. Let us put our minds at ease now as Margaret has suggested."

Taking charge, Margaret started handing out orders. "Matthew, you and Billy Joe go help John with the mules, and then bring in the supplies and the basket I filled with items Roscoe and Ruby will be needing. After supper you two can help do chores and then gather up your blankets and pillows and take them to the barn. You'll be comfortable out there and I'll give Roscoe and Ruby Amy's room and she can sleep in Billy Joe's room in the loft.

"Oh, Margaret, I hate being such a bother!" Ruby cried out in dismay.

"Hush now, Ruby! You'll have to stay here with us until you're able to put your weight on that foot again." Margaret leaned over and kissed her soft cheek. Pulling Ruby's dress up over her ankle, Margaret gasped. Ruby's ankle was already black and blue and swelling by the minute.

"That's a bad sprain, Ruby, and there's just not a whole lot I can do for you. We'll keep your leg elevated and some cold compresses on it might help.

"Let me have your wet shawl, Ruby," Amy said lovingly. "We surely don't want you catching your death." Amy hung the shawl over a peg close to the hearth and then placed an afghan about Ruby's stooped shoulders and another one across her lap.

Margaret shook the rain from her own wet shawl and bonnet and hung them beside Ruby's. "Whew! I beat those mules within an inch of their lives the last couple of miles, racing them dark clouds!"

"What happened to you, Ruby?" Amy asked, looking down in dismay at Ruby's swollen ankle.

"Just the clumsiness of an old woman," Ruby said, shaking her head. "I tripped and fell going to the root cellar. Roscoe had gone over to visit with Ben Grier and Ben was bringing him home just about the time your ma found me. Ben carried me up the stairs and put me in your wagon. I was never so glad to see anyone in my life. Ben always seems to be where he's most needed. For him to show up at that exact moment was . . . well, it was divine Providence, that's what it was. Roscoe and Margaret could never have gotten me out of the root cellar without his help."

Amy was ecstatic to know that Roscoe and Ruby would be their houseguests for a spell. She felt a quick stab of guilt however, knowing she was happier with the thought that as long as Ruby was laid up, the longer Matthew would be sitting at their table.

After Ruby's foot was wrapped in cold, wet cloths and she was made as comfortable as possible, Margaret donned her apron and started putting bags of staples into the cupboards as quickly as Matthew and Billy Joe could carry them in.

Amy hurriedly set two more plates on the table. A kettle of ham and beans bubbled on the stove, filling the room with savory odors. Amy's stomach growled with hunger as she set the cornbread and butter on the table. She ran once more to the window, drawing the snow-white curtains aside and peered out. Margaret caught her anxiety. "What are you so fidgety about, youngun? You've looked out that window a dozen times at least in the last five minutes!"

Stains of scarlet appeared on Amy's cheeks. "I was just . . . just watching it rain," she said lamely. "And I was thinking about Pa still being out in the barn and . . ."

"And?" Margaret queried, smiling."

"And Matthew's still out there somewhere too. What if he gets drenched in this downpour?" Amy glanced to where Ruby was sitting comfortably by the fire and smiled sheepishly. Ruby winked at her conspiratorially.

"Matthew's not sugar, dear. He won't melt," Margaret quipped.

CHAPTER 23

At the supper table heads were bowed and John said grace, as was his custom. Plates were then filled with ham and beans and rich golden-brown cornbread swimming with fresh-churned butter. Everyone ate heartily and listened eagerly as news from the village poured from Margaret's lips. The rain continued to pepper on the windowpanes.

After she had finished eating, Margaret excused herself and disappeared into her bedroom. A moment later she returned with a white envelope in her hand. A faint, eager look flashed in her eyes as she handed the envelope to Amy. "I almost forgot in all the excitement with Ruby. This came for you today."

Amy took one look at the return address on the envelope and squealed with delight. "It's from Grandma!" she shouted, her breathing accelerating. Everyone burst out laughing at her exuberance and all eyes were on her as she tore open the envelope.

With her heart pounding like a trip-hammer, Amy began to read aloud: "'My dearest Granddaughter, Amy: I take pen in hand to tell you how much your grandmother and grandfather miss and love you all. Grandfather and I were elated to receive your last lovely letter written on January 11. It is always a pleasure to hear from you and to be able to share through your letters, of your life in Kentucky. We praise our Lord for his continued good favor on your behalf and that of the entire family.

Grandfather's rheumatism has been acting up some and also his gout, but it doesn't seem to daunt his fiery spirit. He is still able to shout "Amen" to Reverend Aker's sermons.

How is Buttercup? Our Annie presented us with five beautiful and playful black and white kittens this winter. We haven't decided yet what we are to do with so many beautiful little kittens. We can't possibly keep them all, but it would be a struggle to give any of them up.

Give Billy Joe a kiss and hug from his grandmother and grandfather, and also tell this Matthew that you mention so much in all your letters, that we send our best regards.'" Amy was reading so fast that the last sentence had burst forth from her lips before she realized exactly what she had said. She quickly glanced at Matthew, found his eyes glued to her own, and a smile splitting his face.

Popping a bite of cornbread into his mouth, Billy Joe rolled his eyes and leaned over and punched Matthew playfully on the arm with his fist. "Wonder what deep, dark secrets my sweet little sister has been telling on you, big brother?" Billy Joe guffawed and Amy turned beet red. She looked imploringly at first her father and then her mother.

"Billy Joe!" John finally admonished trying to look grim. "What have I told you, young man, about teasing your sister, especially at the supper table?"

"And what have I told you," blurted Margaret, "about talking with your mouth full?"

"Aw gee whiz," Billy Joe complained in his usual blustery fashion. "A body can't do nothin' right around this place!" He swiped at his mouth with the sleeve of his shirt and grudgingly said, "I'm sorry, sis—carry on."

With a toss of her head, Amy said to no one in particular, "Brothers are such a pain!" and continued reading aloud from her grandmother's letter. "'Kristy and Nikki both send their best wishes.

Kristy will wed the Armstrong boy this June. Nikki, not to be outdone by her good friend, has announced her engagement to Philip Fowler, and plans to be wed this fall.

My eyes are dim and my hand is a bit shaky, so I will close for now. Please write again soon, dear, and remind your mother to do the same. We miss you always and we love you dearly. Until we meet again, Grandmother and Grandfather Johnson.'"

Hugging the letter to her breast, Amy sighed. Love for her grandparents overwhelmed her, and she dropped her head as tears welled in her beautiful brown eyes and threatened to overflow. Margaret cleared her throat and started removing dishes from the table, giving Amy time to regain her composure.

Pushing away from the table John rose slowly from his chair. "Best we get to those chores, Billy Joe. Tomorrow's Sunday and . . ."

"But, Pa!" Billy Joe blurted, "I don't have all my 'rithmetic problems done for Monday yet. Maybe since Rock is here he could help me with them. That is, if I didn't have to do chores." Billy Joe gave his father an appealing glance.

"Well now maybe Reverend Willis has got other matters to attend to, like preparing his sermon for tomorrow."

Roscoe threw caution to the wind and Billy Joe drew a grateful sigh when he heard him say, "Young man, I can think of nothing I'd like more than to help you with whatever problems you think you may have with your arithmetic. My sermon, I'm happy to say, is safely tucked up here," and he tapped his head. "Come, join me, my lad, and we'll get started."

Matthew passed John his rifle; grabbed up his own gun and they walked out the door together and headed toward the barn, Sandy hot on their heels. Amy insisted that Margaret sit and visit with Ruby while she finished clearing the table.

A damp world met Amy as she went to get a bucket of water with which to rinse the supper dishes. The rain had moved on and the night was full of tremulous perfume.

Peach blossoms, green grass, sodden bark and wood smoke, strong and heady in the damp air, tempted Amy with their separate and distinct fragrances. The throbbing trill of crickets as they sang into the night air assaulted her ears as she dipped a pail of water from the rain barrel at the corner of the cabin,

Homework was done, and Billy Joe was yawning by the time John and Matthew finished with chores. Matthew picked Ruby up gently in his arms and carried her into Amy's bedroom so she could prepare for bed. Roscoe bid everyone a pleasant 'goodnight' and followed close behind.

Gently depositing Ruby on the bed, Matthew leaned down and kissed her on the cheek. He patted Roscoe on the shoulder and said, "Rest well. If you need me in the night, just stick your head out the window and holler!"

The log walls were mellow with flickering light from the fireplace as Matthew stepped back into the kitchen. He went to Margaret and hugged her soundly. "Thanks for the delicious supper, Ma. I got Ruby into the bedroom, but she just may need your expertise in getting ready for bed." Matthew kissed Margaret on the forehead.

Patting his cheek, Margaret was as thrilled as ever to hear the endearing word, 'Ma' fall so easily from Matthew's lips. "Sleep well, son. It's always a pleasure to have you sup with us. And I'll be going in to help Ruby in one moment."

Turning to Billy Joe, Margaret kissed him on the forehead and said lightly, "No shenanigans tonight, you hear? You've worked hard today and now you need your rest." Swatting him playfully on his bottom she said, "Now scoot and give Matthew no sass!"

Billy Joe gave a whistle and Sandy, dozing on the rug in front of the hearth, was immediately alert. Matthew picked up blankets and pillows for the two of them and after nodding to John he turned to leave. Reaching the door he stopped and looked back over his shoulder, his gaze reaching out for Amy. She had been watching his every move and smiled enticingly at him. "How about you and me going for a ride tomorrow afternoon? You've been neglecting Midnight Belle far too long."

"I'd love to, Matthew," Amy said breathlessly, feeling her pulse racing.

"Can I go too," Billy Joe asked plaintively, tugging on Matthew's shirtsleeve.

"No, you can't go!" Amy said, irritated by Billy Joe's request. "Why do you think you always have to tag around after me?"

"Pa, tell Amy I can go riding too!"

John cajoled Billy Joe with a "We'll see," much to Amy's chagrin.

Satisfied and looking smug, Billy Joe yawned broadly and glanced at Matthew. "Ready to hit the hay, partner?" he asked, trying hard to emulate his father. Matthew nodded and they walked out the door into the blackness, Sandy following close at their heels.

A mist, like gossamer, hung across the valley as Amy stood in the open doorway watching Billy Joe and Matthew fade into the darkness. The breeze held a chill and she quickly closed the door and bolted it. Her mother and father had retreated to their bedroom and after a quick sponge bath Amy dressed in her nightclothes. She checked the windows to make sure they were closed and shuttered and then on a sudden impulse stepped out into the velvety darkness once more. The moon cast a soft mystic glow on the world about her as she listened to the sound of the clamorous peepers chirping unevenly in the woods. Somewhere nearby a screech owl called once and then was still.

Gazing heavenward Amy saw a penciled V against the sky, high overhead and pointing northward. The geese were on the wing, their gabbling sounding like small dogs yelping. The heavens were awesome. The moon was high overhead and thousands of stars looking down, paled in its brilliance. A faint breeze blew like tender curving fingers through her hair as she looked toward the barn, now silhouetted against the spangled sky. The dim light from a lantern glowed through the open barn door, filling Amy with a sense of tranquility and peace, knowing Matthew was near.

A whiff of wood smoke stung the air as Amy quietly reentered the cabin and closed and bolted the door behind her. It had been a long day and she was tired. She tiptoed to the ladder that led to

Billy Joe's room in the loft. Kneeling beside his bed, Amy said a short prayer then climbed into bed. Snuggling into the goosedown featherbed, she waited for sleep to claim her.

The creaks and groans of the house settled down around her ears. Her grandmother's letter had brought back painful memories, and hearing that Kristy and Nikki would both be getting married soon brought tears of happiness to her eyes. Slipping out of bed, she kneeled by the window and opened the shutters and glanced up into the night sky. She fixed her sights on one particular star and started a conversation with the Lord. "I'm so glad I heard from Grandma today, Lord, and to know that Kristy and Nikki will soon be getting married thrills my heart. I know that you have someone in mind for me too. Someone that you alone have chosen; someone who will stir my heartstrings and love me forever . . . someone like . . . Matthew."

A wolf gave its mournful howl and Amy shivered and jumped back into bed.

Snuggling deeply into the confines of the mattress, Amy recalled something her mother had said over and over again when circumstances seemed to overwhelm her. *"God does not close a door, but that he opens a window nearby."* Without a doubt their departure from Charlottesville had been a wise choice on the part of her father. And if God hadn't taken a hand in her life when he did, moving her to Kentucky, she would never have met Matthew. These thoughts enveloped her like a thick, downy comforter, and she soon drifted off to sleep.

. . .

Amy knew she was going to miss the sight of the straight-backed figure in black waiting for her in the rocking chair by the fire each morning. The swelling in Ruby's ankle had finally gone down, and she was able to be up and walking about without too much pain. Ruby and Roscoe had been with the Bradshaw's for three weeks, and they were anxious to be back under their own roof.

Ruby had not been idle by any means while she spent her days recuperating from her fall. She peeled and sliced potatoes, folded clothes, and her bone knitting needles twinkled day and night, merrily producing various items of wearing apparel for the entire Bradshaw family. Amy was amazed at the wealth of Bible knowledge Ruby had stored in her head and heart, and found Ruby willing and eager to share this knowledge. Amy would sit spellbound at her feet listening to one who revered and respected God and talked to him in familiar terms. Ruby's prayers were daily conversations to a close friend and confidant.

"Pa's gone to get the wagon and Ma's in the root cellar packing up some goodies for you to take home." Amy looked at Ruby wistfully. "Are you sure you don't want to stay a few more days?"

Ruby's gaze brightened and her hands gripped the arms of the rocker. "No, my child. But it is sweet of you to ask. I have found great happiness the past three weeks, due to your family's generosity, and I feel Roscoe and I have been treated like royalty. God be thanked that we have been in such good and loving hands. But it's high time we skedaddled home. But first, young lady, there's something I've been wanting to ask you.

Curiosity has killed the cat I've been told, but in spite of that, I find that I am in a curious dither."

"About what, Ruby?" Amy asked, her interest aroused.

Reaching out and laying a gentle hand on Amy's arm, Ruby said in a low compassionate tone, "You're sweet on that boy aren't you?"

"Matthew, you mean?"

"Could there be any other?" Ruby queried gently.

"Does it show that much, Ruby?" Amy whispered.

"I'm not blind, child," Ruby said, her eyes shining. "Your love for Matthew is sweet and clean and powerful. That's what I see."

"But what if he never returns that love? Ma and Pa treat him like a son. They even think of him as a son. So I've felt shame in harboring thoughts of love for Matthew, him being almost like my brother and all. And yet . . ."

"And yet he's no kin. I understand fully, my precious one," Ruby murmured. "I can sympathize to some extent."

"You can?" Amy's eyebrows shot up in surprise.

Ruby shook her head. "Roscoe was my first cousin. We were raised in different parts of the country and I fell in love with him the moment I first laid eyes on him. He was almost thirty at the time, and I was twenty-five. I, too, felt my love was hopeless, and that love between cousins would certainly be condemned. When our parents arranged our marriage, I felt as though God himself had planned and would bless our union, and all my fears dissolved. Just trust the Lord, my child. If you and Matthew are meant to be together, and I believe you are, the Lord will see that it comes to pass."

Throwing her arms around Ruby's neck, Amy kissed her. "I love you so much, Ruby, and I appreciate how good you've made me feel. I shall remember what you've told me."

Amy's pleased look, her smile, and her kiss was a sweet reward to Ruby.

. . .

Chief Black Cloud of the Shawnee Nation sat before the night fire in a pair of loose leggings of suede-like doehide and beaded moccasins. A necklace made of bear claws and odd pieces of beaten silver hung around his neck. His straight, black hair hung loose to his shoulders, and his black eyes gleamed brightly, reflecting the firelight.

He prayed silently to Moneto, the Supreme Being of all things, to dispense his blessings and favors to his servant, Black Cloud— just as he prayed Moneto would also bring unspeakable sorrow to those whose conduct merited Black Cloud's displeasure.

Black Cloud knew he was responsible only for his conduct toward his own people—to the white man, he owed nothing, except to return in kind, the treatment his tribe had received at their hands.

To the very marrow of his bones, Black Cloud knew that there could never be true peace between the Indian nations and the white-eyes. As he had known, time had proven that the Whites would not stop at the river valleys of western Pennsylvania, but that they would spread down the Ohio River and settle in Cantuc-kee.

Treaties had been signed and boundaries established in the past, but as surely as summer followed spring, most Whites treated the Indians with unfeigned loathing, and had broken boundaries almost before they were established.

A great tribal meeting of representatives of the Shawnee, Delaware and Wyandot had met this night and had determined just what could be done about the white man, who, despite treaties forbidding it were continually crossing the eastern mountains and spilling into their sacred hunting grounds.

Since early spring there had been much bloodshed between the Indians and Whites. Three of those who had died from the Shawnee tribe would now cause Black Cloud to take up his tomahawk against the Whites. His brother, sister-in-law and young nephew had only recently been butchered during a raid, and Black Cloud had sworn revenge.

The Indian nations were being forced from the land of their ancestors. They would be pushed no longer. The Great Spirit, after all, had given the land to them in the beginning. Black Cloud had explained to his people at the Council how the white-eyes even masqueraded as Indians in order to steal horses or other possessions of their fellow man. Then they would murder and scalp them so that blame would be placed on the Shawnee and other Indian tribes.

A cold, frightening fire burned in Black Cloud's eyes. He was anxious to do his part in stemming the flood of unwanted Whites into his territory. He vowed to take ten lives for each of those that had been slain from his family. Soon, he had told his people, he would be sending scouts on spying missions, and after much prayer and guidance from Moneto, they would plan their attack on the outlying posts nearest the Great Ohio and the forests on either side of the Green River.

. . .

'83 through '85 produced significant changes in Kentucky and new settlements continued to sprout in spite of continued attack by Shawnees on river travelers. The woodland was alive with the sound of axes ringing against trees and saws ripping into wood.

July brought fireflies and the smell of sweet clover at the roadside. The meadows were frosted with Queen Anne's lace and daisies. Field corn reached for the sun and glistened with morning dew as it thrust its gold-hung spire of tassel up for the dry winds to kiss and bless. Weeds grew in abundance as did the milkweed nettle and forbidding thistles. The Bradshaws' garden matured as did the bean and squash beetles and tomato worms. They were enjoying their first ears of sweet corn and baby beets, and they had added late corn and cabbage to their garden on the fourth of July. Heat ripples radiated skyward and hot humidity lay heavy upon Margaret and Amy as they toiled unceasingly in the garden. Their muscles were tense and strained as they hoed in the crumbly, rich earth, loosening it and hitting each juicy weed with fervor.

By the middle of the afternoon it seemed as though the sun was clamped to the side of the sky, beating down on their shoulders unmercifully, and gradually their clothes had become soaked with sweat and their hair was plastered to their heads.

Amy made countless trips to the well, each time bringing Margaret a dipper of cold, sweet water to satisfy her thirst. They would then rest awhile, panting softly, lost in their own thoughts and too hot and tired for idle-chatter. The scent of young blossoms suffocated them with sweet heaviness, and birdsong rang wearily in their ears.

Amy had three blisters on her right hand and numerous mosquito bites on her face and arms. She rubbed absently at one of the blisters trying to erase the pain, but only aggravated it, making it break and ooze.

John had been busy cutting grass in the south meadow and as Amy and Margaret sat at the edge of the garden resting, they were pleased to see him ambling toward them, his clothes wet and stained with sweat.

"Gonna call it a day," John said tiredly when he came within speaking distance, absently wiping his sweaty face with his large blue handkerchief. "Too hot for man or beast to be toiling all day in this heat. Are you about finished out here?" he asked, pulling out his watch and checking the time. He couldn't help but notice the neat rows of carrots, beans, lettuce, cabbage, onions, squash and sweet corn, now almost completely free of troublesome weeds.

"Thirty minutes should do it, I figure." Margaret heaved a sigh of relief and motioned toward a row of half-eaten beans. "Our little long-eared friends were out here shortly after dawn, eating my beans and cabbage. Don't know why those dear little critters don't feast on the purslane and lambs-quarters instead."

John sank onto his heels and scooped up a handful of the rich topsoil, letting it drift through his fingers. "Means everything to you, doesn't it, Pa?" Amy questioned, catching his eye.

Nodding, John ran his tongue across his lips. "Once I put a seed in this rich ground, I know I best be ready to jump back!" he countered, his eyes bright and his eyebrows arched mischievously. He laughed heartily.

Margaret laughed right along with him, and loosened the strings of her bonnet. Great drops of perspiration ran unchecked down the sides of her face, under her neck and down between her breasts. She absently took the edge of her flowered apron and wiped her dirt-smudged face with it.

"My, my, but I do feel like I've done a good day's work out here today, but reckon I ought to go in and see about getting supper on the table." Margaret glanced at Amy. "I was hoping that we would get done long before now and could go and visit our new neighbors across the way . . ." Glancing at the sun as it made its way slowly toward the western horizon she said pensively, "guess that will have to wait until tomorrow."

"Tomorrow's fine with me. As anxious as I am to meet our neighbors I don't believe anyone in their right mind would be glad to see us today, Ma, looking so bedraggled as we do. I think a sweaty horse would smell better than I do at the moment!" Amy said, blinking perspiration out of her eyes.

Smiling, Margaret directed her attention to her husband. "It wouldn't hurt your feelings if I was to ask you to help Amy finish up out here, would it, John?"

Laughing jovially, John said, "Don't change, Maggie, dear. Don't you ever change."

"And why not, pray tell?"

"If I didn't think at the end of the day that a feisty little old woman would be waiting at home to torment me, I reckon I'd mosey into the woods and invite an Injun to take my scalp!"

"No Injun would want your scalp, John Bradshaw—not enough hair on it!" Margaret said with an impish grin.

John threw his head back and roared. "You got me on that one, darling."

Struggling to her feet, Margaret leaned over and picked a handful of half-eaten beans and put them in her apron pocket to feed to the chickens. Straightening up she moaned with the effort. "Whew! Didn't know my old bones could carry on so!"

CHAPTER 24

John and Amy watched as Margaret walked slowly toward the cabin, the sparkle of gold in her hair preventing them from seeing the tiny strands of gray that now mingled there.

Squinting into the sunlight, Amy watched her father walk to the well and drink deeply. He then poured a dipper full of water over his head and savored the coolness of it. He returned to where Amy was sitting and lay prone on the ground beside her, closed his eyes and folded his callused hands over his chest. "Guess it won't hurt your feelings none if I rest a minute or so before attacking the last of them weeds, would it?"

"Just as long as you want, Pa." Amy's eyelids closed and sunlight came in a soft, rosy glow through her lids. She wiped an errant bead of perspiration from her forehead and let her thoughts drift. *She had been so excited when her mother had returned home from a visit with Ruby the day before with the good news that a family had moved into the old Jackson homestead, no more than a quarter of a mile from their place. Amy hadn't known the Jackson's very well, but they had made the trek west with Sam Tippett's group in '80. One year of living in constant fear of an Indian attack had forced them back to Virginia. The Jackson's had no children, but this family reportedly had four: a girl seventeen, six-year-old twin girls and a five-year-old boy.*

Amy was more than eager to meet the seventeen-year-old girl. It had been so long since she had had a close friend to confide in. Sally and Thornton Decker lived about two and a half miles to the west of them and Sally's time was pretty much taken up in caring for their two little boys. They talked in bits and pieces after church services on Sundays, but had little time for long, intimate talks.

John had to call Amy twice before she was startled out of her reverie. It was after four o'clock. She jumped up and worked beside her father in the late afternoon sun until Margaret called them in for supper.

Hot and tired and with an aching back, Amy pulled her bonnet off and pushed stray tendrils of clammy wet hair away from her face as she entered the steamy, hot kitchen. Buttercup jumped down from a chair and came to rub against her legs. Amy leaned down and picked her up and buried her face in her soft fur. The muted rumble of Buttercup's purring filled her ears.

"Wash up," Margaret said cheerfully. "Supper's ready as soon as everybody else is."

Amy nodded woodenly, placed Buttercup on the floor and walked to the washstand. She pushed a few strands of hair out of her eyes and made a face at her reflection in the mirror.

Matthew, Billy Joe and Sandy came bursting through the door just as they were ready to sit down at the table. "Hello, everybody!" Matthew gushed. "Thought I best be getting Billy Joe home before you thought he'd been gobbled up by bears!" Matthew's brows arched mischievously as Billy Joe hurriedly took his place at the table.

"Billy Joe, you scoot over to the washbasin right this minute and wash your face and hands," Margaret admonished. Amy was more than delighted, and it came as no surprise, when Margaret turned her attention on Matthew and asked politely, "Won't you sit down and eat a bite with us, Matthew? We have plenty and I know how hard it is for you to resist my dumplings!" Without waiting for a reply, Margaret asked Amy to get another plate from the cupboard.

Billy Joe pushed a stray lock of hair out of his eyes and

obediently did as his mother asked. Matthew licked his lips. "Well . . . since you've practically twisted my arm, Ma. But just a bite. I don't want to spoil my appetite and get Ruby all in a dither by not being able to eat her vittles tonight." Matthew went to the washbasin and scrubbed his hands, a general feeling of euphoria filling his heart.

"Hurry and sit down, Matthew, I have something very important to tell you," Amy gushed. She could hardly wait to tell him about their new neighbors but was crestfallen when he threw up his hands in mock horror.

"That's all we need around here—more little girls!" Swallowing a mouthful of Margaret's delicious chicken dumplings he added, "What we really need are a few more handsome bucks like Billy Joe and myself. Right, Pa?"

"Right, son," John answered, a grin plastered on his face and a twinkle in his eye.

"Yes, sir, another buck to help take care of all the beautiful belles already living in these parts." Matthew's gaze settled on Amy and he added, "All the older girls around here that know when and where to sit up and take notice of us handsome fellas!"

"Bet you're in hot water now, partner!" Billy Joe said, eyeing the stricken look on Amy's face.

Matthew's remark *had* quelled Amy's excitement for the moment, and her spirits sank even lower as she made careful note of Matthew's appearance. He was all spruced up and even had on a new red shirt. She was more than a little embarrassed because of her own unkempt appearance: her sweat-stained dress, sunburned nose and arms, and a multitude of mosquito and blackfly bites.

Everyone around the table ate heartily with little conversation for several minutes, except for Amy, and she just picked at the food on her plate. Finally Amy dropped her fork and pushed aside her plate. "Why aren't you eating, dear?" Margaret asked, noticing what a dismal picture Amy made—so quiet and withdrawn.

"I'm not very hungry, Ma. I feel just dreadful," she exclaimed.

"You look dreadful!" Matthew teased.

Amy blanched and swallowed with difficulty the small bite of chicken she had been chewing on. She was puzzled at how much Matthew's remark cut her to the quick, and lashed out at Matthew. "You'd look dreadful too, if you'd worked in the garden all day under that blazing sun!" she quickly retorted, her face ashen. Matthew's disparaging words were still buzzing around in her head and she gave him a hostile glare.

"I've done my share of work today, little twerp. Billy Joe and me got all the weeds cut in the orchard, plus around the cornfield, and tomorrow we'll take vengeance on the weeds that are taking Roscoe's place. Right, Billy Joe?"

"Right, partner!" Billy Joe agreed happily. John's eyes twinkled merrily and he shared a knowing smile with Margaret as she refilled their mugs with more cold lemonade.

Amy was pouting and stinging from Matthew's remarks when he said, "You're awful quiet tonight, Amy. You're usually talking our heads off."

"That's because I don't have anything interesting to talk about," she snapped back at him.

Matthew wiped his mouth on his cloth napkin and slowly rose from the table. "Well, in that case, if I may be excused, I better head for home. I know Ruby is probably wondering what's happened to me, and I told Eleanor I'd be seeing her tonight."

"Eleanor Simmons?" Amy choked out, stiffening her back and lifting her chin.

The blood quickly drained from her face as Matthew casually answered, "The one and only."

"But . . . but, she's not as old as I am," Amy flustered, a sinking sensation knotting her stomach.

"But she's old enough to stir heartstrings, and you're just a twerp!" Matthew gave Amy a rueful grin and tweaked the end of her nose. Tears insisted on slipping out from under her long black lashes as she watched Matthew turn to leave.

"Thanks for the delicious meal, Ma," Matthew said as he started for the door. " . . . and Pa, can I borrow your scythe? Need to be getting at Roscoe's weeds tomorrow before they completely take over the place."

"It's all yours, son," John sang out as Matthew and Sandy fairly flew out the door.

"See you bright and early in the morning, Billy Joe," Matthew threw over his shoulder.

After Matthew left Amy stared at her plate in anguish. She swiped the tears from her cheeks, wishing she could sink right through the floor. *Is that what I seem like to him?* she thought to herself. *A twerp?* Amy was experiencing a gamut of perplexing emotions: annoyance, envy . . . and jealousy. Matthew was wearing a new red shirt that fit across his broad chest so smoothly and that really hurt. *All for Eleanor's benefit,* she thought ruefully. She was dismayed as tears quickly formed again, causing her to blink fast to keep them from falling.

Margaret's heart melted at seeing Amy looking so lost and forlorn. "Are you all right, honey?" she asked lamely.

"Yes," Amy answered softly; "I'm fine."

"Well then finish your supper, dear. You've hardly eaten a bite."

"I . . . I've had enough, thank you," Amy said, ducking her head and brushing at a wayward tear. "Could I please be excused?"

"Certainly. I'll clean up in here. You go on outside where it's a bit cooler. Billy Joe can help me gather up the dishes."

Amy glanced warily at Billy Joe and he opened his mouth to say something tart, but seeing the look in his mother's eyes, he changed his mind and shut it.

"Thanks, Ma," Amy breathed as she picked up Buttercup and moved toward the open door.

"Don't stray far," Margaret cautioned. "It'll be dark before you know it." Amy saw the look on her mother's face. She wanted to caution her daughter about how dangerous it was, alone in the dark, but she held her tongue. Amy was aware of the drawbacks to living in the wilds: hostile Indians, grizzlies, wolverines and rattlesnakes, just to name a few. But her need to be alone at the moment was so strong and potent within her that she threw all caution to the wind.

Once outside, she lifted her face to the sky and breathed deeply of the fresh summer air. Hugging Buttercup to her breast, she walked toward the orchard, watching the sun slowly make its descent in the western sky. She caught a glimpse of Billy Joe and her father as they left the cabin and went in the direction of the barn, faintly hearing Billy Joe as he chatted like a magpie. Her father's laughter echoed into the late afternoon air.

When she reached the orchard she eased herself down into the sweet-smelling grass and wrapped her arms about her legs. The center of her stomach was knotted and aching. Leaning her head on her arms she let her frustrations drain from her. Closing her eyes she went over and over in her mind the events that had taken place at the supper table. Her spirit had been crushed, and hot tears poured from her eyes. Heartbroken, she poured her frustrations out to the Lord.

I know I shouldn't get upset when Matthew teases me, Lord, but I'm not so sure anymore that he is just teasing. What if he never feels any differently toward me than he does right now? And what if all the hopes and dreams that I've had for such a long time that include Matthew, are for naught? What if he never gives any indication that he cares for me in any special way? How could I ever live knowing that? Amy's thoughts were suffocating and unbearable and she sobbed loudly. *God, you've always watched over me and cared for me and I'm begging you now, if you're trying to tell me something, Lord, even if it's something I don't want to hear, talk loud enough for me to hear you,* she pleaded firmly. *When Matthew is not near me I am filled with unbearable loneliness and feel as empty as if I have no life within me. But when he is near, Lord, I'm unbearably happy and so full of joy I feel at times I shall burst with it. I love him, Lord.*

He can irritate me with his indifference but there is no other like him in the whole world. In his presence the sun shines brighter, the sky seems bluer, and everything in my life is more beautiful and radiant.

Hot tears continued to slip from between Amy's closed eyelids and she lifted a slender hand to wipe them away. Her whole body was engulfed in tides of weariness and despair, and with head bowed, she continued to weep bitterly. Buttercup, seeming to sense her utter despair, rubbed affectionately against one leg, purring loudly.

Amy hugged Buttercup close to her breast and slowly rising to her feet, she retraced her steps on the path leading to the cabin, a light breeze ruffling her hair, and the familiar scent of wood smoke filling the air around her. The sun had set behind the western horizon, and the evening air was quite cool. The odor of fresh-baked bread reached her nostrils as she walked through the door.

Margaret was removing a loaf of golden-brown bread from the oven and as Amy entered the kitchen she turned toward the doorway, startled, but with a look of relief showing on her face. "Land sakes," she chided, letting out the breath she had been holding, "where on earth have you been? With all this talk about marauding Indians I hate to have you out of my sight for even a minute!"

Amy quickly apologized. "I'm sorry if I've been a worry to you, Ma, but time just got away from me." She glanced around the room. Her father was half-asleep in the oak rocker and Billy Joe was nowhere to be seen. She looked at her mother quizzically. As if in answer to her question her mother said, "Billy Joe has already gone up to bed. Poor kid was completely tuckered out."

Setting the last loaf of bread to the back of the stove to cool, Margaret stared at Amy and frowned in concern at her swollen eyes and tear-stained and sunburned face. "My, but if you don't look like something the cat dragged in! Go wash up and I'll pour you a nice cup of sassafras tea—I just boiled the roots a little bit ago. And how about a nice big slice of my bread with some of your pa's honey on it?"

Not waiting for an answer, Margaret bustled about the kitchen, slicing bread and piling it on a plate. Amy went to the washstand and found warm water in the basin. She washed her face and hands with a bar of yellow soap and ran a steel comb through her tangled hair. When she sat down at the table her eyes softened at the sight of the family Bible, opened to the book of Psalms.

When she had finished eating, Amy wiped her mouth and hands on a napkin and reached for the Bible. She pulled the lamp close so that she might see the fine print. After Margaret called John to join them, Amy read several chapters aloud. "Thanks, honey," John said as he rose from the table, took the Bible gently from her hands, and replaced it on the mantle over the fireplace. He closed and bolted the door and examined the shutters, making sure they were tightly bolted over the windows.

Satisfied that they were safely secured for the night, John leaned over and kissed Amy on the forehead. "Goodnight, daughter. The good Lord willing, I'll see you in the morning." The hand he placed on her shoulder trembled slightly. "This old man is going to take this old woman to bed—we're just plain tuckered out."

Margaret leaned down and hugged Amy. "Don't take to heart what Matthew meant as a tease, honey. I'm sure he didn't mean to hurt you so tonight."

"You always know my thoughts don't you, Ma?" Amy asked, looking up at her mother with a warm rush of love. "I wish I could say with confidence that I thought Matthew was teasing, but what if..."

John took Margaret by the hand. "Time for bed, old woman," he said tiredly. "You can finish this conversation in the morning." John and Margaret made their way slowly to their bedroom and John closed the door softly behind them.

Amy poured a kettle of hot water into the wash basin, stripped off her dirty clothes and began to bathe. After her quick sponge bath, she washed and towel-dried her hair before putting on a clean gown. Finished with her toilet Amy picked up Buttercup and extinguished the flame of the lamp. She tiptoed past her parents' door and entered her bedroom and closed the door softly. She pulled back the covers and then fell to her knees by the side of her bed, hands clasped before her.

Questions to her heavenly Father poured from her lips: *where is he now, Lord? This very minute? And what is he doing? Oh, Lord, why does being in love have to hurt so much? And why, dear Lord, did you allow me to fall in love with Matthew in the first place if you didn't intend to let him return that love?*

Once more Amy's sorrow intensified as she slowly climbed into bed. She fought desperately to hold back tears that threatened once again to fall. One torturing question after another plagued her mind: *were Matthew and Eleanor Simmons together right at the moment? Was Matthew holding her, and kissing her, and falling in love with her . . . ?*

CHAPTER 25

Indians harried the settlements in the northern section of Kentucky in early July. Families were edgy and men in these areas began riding scout through the hills. Although rumors were flying and stories were stretched and added to, the homesteaders knew it wasn't too safe to ride alone in the hills.

They went about their work with an edge of fear somewhat dimming their otherwise bright and cheery days. John followed suit with his neighbors by always having a loaded gun at his fingertips. He cautioned Margaret and Amy to always be alert, and went over and over with Billy Joe what to do in case of an Indian attack. Much to Margaret's dismay, Billy Joe carried a Lancaster Rifle everywhere he went.

It was the middle of July. Ripeness had crept across the land, hastened by the heat. Bright sunlight lit the green hills with a ripening apple glow. Margaret took a big steaming pan of chicken and dumplings from the oven and the rich, heavenly aroma filled every room of the cabin. Wrapping the dumplings in dishtowels to help keep them warm, Margaret put them into a basket. She then added four loaves of fresh-baked bread, some fresh-churned butter, a jar of strawberry preserves, and a gallon of buttermilk to the basket.

She stood in the middle of the kitchen, looking about in consternation. "If you're ready to go, I am," Amy said, impatiently tapping her foot on the puncheon floor.

"I just wanted to make sure I had everything," Margaret said in her own defense.

"You've got everything but a kitchen chair in that basket, Maggie," John chided. "You add anything more to that basket and we'll need the militia to come and tote it for you."

Ignoring John's remark Margaret looked at Amy steadily. "This is what being a good neighbor is all about, honey. It takes no more than a little food and a smidgen of neighborliness to visit newcomers to the valley and make them feel welcome."

Margaret glanced at John and saw a look on his face that she didn't recognize. "Did I say something wrong?" she asked warily.

With a know-it-all gleam in his eye, John laughed. "It wouldn't be that you're just a mite bit nosey now, would it, and being neighborly and wanting to share your food with the newcomers has nothing to do with it?"

"Well!" she sputtered, bristling with indignation. Ignoring John's question she turned on her heel and bounced out the door.

It was a beautiful day, the sun bright and hot even at the early hour. The long grass at the edge of the creek gently rippled in the warm breeze as mother and daughter easily stepped on several large rocks in the creek and made it to the other side without getting their shoes and skirts too wet. They walked briskly through a short stretch of woodlands and behind a row of feathering elms found the old Jackson homestead.

In shock Margaret and Amy stood and stared at the roughly constructed cabin and lean-to, made of chinked logs, like most of the cabins in the area. But this one looked like it would come crashing down under a heavy wind or rainstorm. The remains of a split-rail fence circled the unkempt yard, and weeds and ivy almost completely hid the dilapidated building from view. A rusting plow in the middle of the yard and a tumble of firewood beside the door completed the dismal picture. Margaret sucked in her breath and Amy closed her eyes as a shudder passed through her.

They heard a clamor of childish voices before they actually saw the two small girls break through the bushes at the side of the cabin like little wild things. The twins stopped their play at once upon seeing Margaret and Amy entering their yard. Their eyes grew as round as horse chestnuts, watching every move that they made. Their faded frocks were dirty, their dingy-gray pantalets frayed, and the fingers of one hand clutched wilting flowers. Shyly they hung their heads and two dirty little thumbs popped into two dirty little mouths at exactly the same instant. Amy thought they were pretty children in spite of their soiled faces and frocks, with their twinkling blue eyes and curling crops of yellow hair.

With apprehension Margaret approached the open cabin door and called out a friendly greeting as Amy went to make friends with the little girls. A tall woman, her face red and perspiring, appeared in the open doorway, her tousled hair framing a too-thin face. Her huge gray eyes had a haunted look, like those of a sick or wounded animal, and her left elbow extended through a great tear in her shapeless dress. In spite of her bony shoulders, it was plainly evident she was expecting a baby in the near future.

"Howdy do," she said softly, nervously wiping her hands on her frayed apron.

"I'm Margaret Bradshaw, your closest neighbor to the east," Margaret said brightly. She looked behind her and beckoned for Amy. As Amy stepped into view Margaret said with pride, "and this is my daughter, Amy."

The woman smiled shyly then nodded and said, "I'm Katherine McLin." She glanced nervously behind her and pointed to a man seated at a rickety table and said softly, "My man's name is Kenneth."

Margaret glanced into a dark and dingy room, disagreeable odors assailing her sensitive nostrils. Kenneth was solidly built with heavy shoulders and a thick, muscular neck. His shirtsleeves were rolled to his elbows and he held a knife in one dirty hand and a piece of wood in the other. Wood shavings were scattered all over the floor and the table before him.

Katherine stepped aside and bid them enter her home. Amy

took one look at Kenneth's unkempt appearance, his square, unsmiling face and strong chin, and thought to herself, *I'll bet he's as stubborn as an old mule!*

Margaret stepped to the table, held out her hand and said, "Pleased to meet you, Mr. McLin." There was no response forthcoming. Kenneth remained seated and mute, and only acknowledged Margaret's proffered hand with a cynical twist to his thin mouth. He met Margaret's smile with an icy stare, his eyes moving slowly from her face to her feet and back again. Embarrassed, Margaret quickly withdrew her hand and stepped away from the table.

"You're the first neighbors I've set my eyes on," Katherine said meekly. There was a hint of prettiness about her face and Margaret knew that at one time Katherine McLin had been a very attractive woman.

Wringing her hands Katherine said apologetically, "I hope you'll excuse the way the place looks. I . . . I haven't had time to get myself settled."

Amy vaguely heard Katherine and her mother chatting as her eyes searched the room. The weathered rafters had cobwebs hanging from them and the blackened cook stove looked as though it had never seen a scrub brush or cleaning rag. A few rough wooden shelves, a washtub, a scrub board and other assorted items were hanging on one wall. Her eyes finally came to rest on the rickety wooden table where Kenneth sat moodily staring into space. Bowls of cold mush and a big bucket of maple syrup, which had made a sticky mess on the table, were black with flies. Amy wrinkled her nose as the odors of coal oil, stale tobacco and mildew wafted through the air. She had never known anyone who lived in such crowded dirty and miserable quarters.

Pointing toward the open door, Katherine said, "Our youngsters in the yard are Bonnie and Betty," she said nervously. "They're six. Jane Marie went to the creek for some water—she's just short of eighteen. And we have a little boy, Bobby. He's five and he's . . . he's around somewhere," she said, her hands nervously flailing the air.

Katherine's face was flaming and her nervousness seemed to increase as she awkwardly pulled out a chair, removed various articles of clothing from it, and offered it to Margaret to sit on.

"Please, Katherine, don't go to any trouble on our account. We can't stay long. I just wanted to bring a little something to help out with your dinner. I know from experience how distressing it can be to move. Seems you can't find anything for days. Makes it hard to cook up a decent meal, especially with little ones around. If they're anything like mine were at that age, they're always hungry."

Amy heard her mother rattling on and on and knew that Katherine's nervousness had rubbed off on her. She was glad when Katherine suggested that she take the twins and go in search of Jane Marie.

Happy to be out in the fresh morning air, Amy and her charges started off in the direction of the creek. About a hundred yards from the cabin Amy met Jane Marie. She wore a brown faded dress and was carrying a bucket of water that looked almost as big as she did. At first glance, Amy thought she couldn't be a day over twelve. She was at least a head shorter than Amy was and it looked like a good stiff wind would blow her away. Her skin was pale, almost translucent, like she hadn't seen the rays of the sun in a long time, and her coal-black hair, wind blown and tangled, tumbled carelessly down her back.

She isn't very pretty, Amy thought to herself. And then Jane Marie looked into Amy's eyes and smiled. It was as though a ray of sunshine had been released behind her wide, cornflower-blue eyes. Her whole face lighted up, showing to perfection her teeth, so white they seemed to be made of pearl. A dimple in each smudged cheek convinced Amy that Jane Marie was indeed a budding beauty, showing lots of promise.

Jane Marie limped slowly toward Amy. After exchanging pleasantries, the twins set up a howl, each one wanting to help their sister carry the bucket of water back to the cabin. Jane Marie suggested that they each take hold of the handle and carry the bucket between them. They were satisfied and managed to carry the bucket to the cabin door without spilling too much water.

There were no awkward moments between Amy and Jane Marie. It was as though they had known each other always. They marveled at the coincidence that they had the same middle name, they were both going to be eighteen, and both of them had been born in the month of December: Amy on December sixteenth and Jane Marie four days later on December twentieth. They chatted like magpies all the way to the cabin.

"We better leave so the McLin's can be about their business," Margaret said as soon as the girls entered the kitchen. Katherine and her three girls followed their guests out into the bright sunshine.

Turning to Katherine, Margaret reached out and clutched at her hand and smiled. "Before I go I'd like to invite you all to our worship services Sunday. They start at ten and I'd be obliged if you would all come to dinner at our place afterwards."

Katherine's face flamed a bright red and tears welled in her sad gray eyes as she met the smile and the hand that was offered. "Thank you kindly for asking, Mrs. Bradshaw," she said softly, glancing toward the open door of the cabin. "I . . . I . . ." Katherine's chin quivered and she worked her mouth, but no sound came.

Margaret nodded her head in understanding. "I'm sorry, Katherine. It does seem to be a mite too soon, seeing as how you're not completely settled in yet. Maybe you can make it another time," she added quickly.

Nodding mutely, Katherine shot Margaret a look of pure love.

"And please, Katherine, since we're probably going to be seeing a lot of one another, I'd be obliged to have you call me Margaret, or Maggie if you prefer."

"I'll remember that. And about that invite to church . . . you see, we haven't been to church for several years. We don't rightly have befitting clothes." She ran her hands nervously over the mound at her waist. "Having so many mouths to feed doesn't leave much money for fancy clothes."

"Fancy clothes aren't important to the Lord, nor to me, Katherine." Impulsively she gave Katherine a hug. "But we'll talk more about that next time we meet. I'm pretty handy with needle and thread."

Katherine's dull eyes sparked to life and she sighed. "It's been so long since I had a friend, Mrs. Brad . . . uh, Margaret," she stuttered, smiling sheepishly. "Thank you most kindly for the vittles. I'll return your basket soon."

Katherine and her girls waved them out of sight as they made their way slowly home, a leaden uneasiness hanging in the air over them. Something unpleasant and unrecognizable had entered their lives.

"Enjoy your afternoon, Amy?" John asked, putting his arm around Amy's shoulders as he greeted her at the door.

Amy wrinkled her nose and gave her father a long, lazy smile, then hugged him. "For the most part, Pa!" she answered happily. I do believe I've got me a best friend again."

As Margaret and Amy worked together putting dinner on the table, Amy chattered non-stop. After she had run down, Margaret confided to John her fears about Kenneth McLin. "I could be dead wrong, and may the good Lord forgive me if I am, John, but there's something mighty strange going on in that household. Her man never said 'howdy do' nor 'kiss my foot' nor anything else when I walked in his door." She shook her head in concern. "He just sat like a bump on a log the whole time I was there giving me the evil eye. Wouldn't even shake my hand!"

Amy saw the tremble of her mother's hands as she placed a bowl of mashed potatoes on the table, and she vividly recalled their morning at the McLin's. A troubled look settled over her face. "They have no pump in the yard, Pa, and they have to carry water all the way from the creek. And I saw the way Mr. McLin looked at Ma. She's telling it true, Pa. It made chills run up and down my own spine."

Not so inclined to take much stock in first impressions, John chided Margaret and Amy gently. "There, there now, the two of you. Let's don't be so hasty to judge the man. It just might be he was ailing or something could be troubling the man that you don't have any knowledge of. There's always two sides to every story—you both know that as well as I do."

Margaret forced herself to stay calm as she placed a big bowl of chicken and dumplings on the table. It wasn't always easy for her, living with a good man like John. Her expression was somber and her face flushed, as she looked her husband full in the eye. "That's as may be, John William," Margaret said bristling. "I'll hold on to my opinion of Mr. Kenneth McLin, but mark my words, I say Katherine's afraid of that man and he'll bear some close watching! You'll see for yourself all in good time!"

Amy could see that her mother was peeved at her father's failure to understand their misgivings, and it showed as she said brusquely, "Let's eat before I lose my appetite entirely just thinking about that man and his impossible ways."

July melted into August and Amy and Jane Marie were in each other's company almost every day. They never ran out of things to talk about. One Sunday afternoon they made plans to meet each other halfway between their homesteads and spend the afternoon together. After dinner had been eaten and the dishes washed, Amy hurried in the direction of the creek. Reaching their appointed meeting place she slackened her pace. Jane Marie was nowhere in sight. The young willows screened the sun like veils of gossamer as Amy idly picked up a few flat stones and sent them skipping across the surface of the water. She chewed on a broken fingernail as she watched the ripples, looking like silver bracelets, gently fade away. The day had been a scorcher but the water felt cooling to the touch. On sudden impulse Amy removed her shoes and stockings and lifting her calico skirt, walked out into the calf-deep water. She shivered slightly as the water rushed about her legs.

The sand beneath her feet squished between her toes and bubbles of air floated to the top of the water and gently burst around her. A snapping turtle, his heavy carapace and armor-studded neck giving him the appearance of power and purpose surfaced not more than two feet in front of her, his eyes and snout barely protruding from the water.

Amy scampered quickly toward the bank. She sat down in the tall grass and started putting on her shoes and stockings. "Boo!" Jane Marie said, catching hold of Amy's shoulders and turning her around. "If I was an Injun I'd of had you for sure!"

Amy's hand clutched at her throat. "Not even an Injun could have scared me more than you did!" she squealed.

They hugged each other warmly. "I'm sorry," Jane Marie said apologetically. I didn't mean to startle you. I'm sorry, too, that you had to wait on me, but I couldn't get away any sooner. I had to hunt for Bobby. Ma hadn't set eyes on him since daybreak and . . . well . . . she was worried about him."

"Did you find him?"

"Finally. He's . . . different, Amy. Never has much to say. Just tags after Ma or runs away and hides. He's such a sweetheart, but he can be a pain too."

"I know exactly what you mean." Amy took Jane Marie by the hand and said, "Let's walk."

"Just so I'm home to help start supper," Jane Marie said. "I have to help Ma get the twins and Bobby fed and ready for bed. Ma's so tired these days, being in the . . . the family way and all," she stammered. Stains of scarlet appeared on her cheeks. Awkwardly she cleared her throat.

"Aren't you happy about the new baby?" Amy asked in surprise.

Jane Marie bit her lip and shrugged her shoulders. "I . . . I guess so. It's just that . . ." A shadow of alarm touched her face.

Regarding her new friend quizzically for a moment, Amy asked, "Is there something wrong at your house? Is that it?"

"No . . . no. Nothing wrong . . . exactly. It's just that it's so hot," she said lamely. "It makes it rough on Ma. You know." Jane Marie lapsed into silence.

A breeze rifled through the leaves of the cottonwoods and hazy sunlight rippled across Amy's face as she tried to keep her voice casual. "Do you ever think about getting married and having babies?"

"Don't rightly expect to ever get married," Jane Marie said without much thought. "Who'd want to marry me?" she asked noncommittally, a wretched look on her face.

Amy's eyes narrowed. "Horse-feathers! Why would you say a thing like that?"

"You know," Jane Marie said softly. "Men want ladies for their wives, perfect in every way; pretty, able to walk straight—not . . . not crippled like me. Someone like you, for instance." Jane Marie's voice sounded hollow and lifeless.

Stopping in her tracks, Amy faced Jane Marie. "Fiddlesticks!" she blurted. "You're pretty! You've got good cheekbones and Ma says that's important. And nobody would notice your limp if you didn't remind them of it. Someday you'll meet somebody special who won't care a lick that you limp, and you'll fall in love and get married and live happily ever after. Honest, Jane Marie!"

Managing no more than a hoarse whisper Jane Marie said, "No, I don't think I'll ever find a man who will love me, Amy. No man will ever ask me to be his wife. I'll die an old maid. Ugh! An old maid! That sounds so awful!" Jane Marie looked crestfallen.

"Yeah, pretty awful!" Amy blurted, a flicker of humor showing in her eyes.

Then she started to laugh. "Janey," she exclaimed, "you're just a sight! Worrying about being an old maid and you're not even eighteen yet. Why just look at you," she chuckled. "You have such beautiful eyes and cute dimples . . . and you have the most beautiful curly black hair I've ever seen in my life! You won't die an old maid, I can assure you of that!"

A blush crept into Jane Marie's cheeks and a smile started at the corners of her mouth. "I guess I am just a gloomy Gus." They both burst out laughing and the spell was broken.

Jane Marie wrinkled her nose and gasped. "What's that horrid smell?"

"It's Yarrow. My grandmother used to use it in a tonic. It is mighty pungent, isn't it? But the little yellow flowers are kinda pretty. I think the butterflies and bees think so too. They're mighty thick around here."

The girls had reached an outcrop of rock nearly twenty feet high. The valley floor was a mass of maidenhair fern, and short-stemmed grasses bordered the stream on both sides. A gentle breeze stirred the leaves over their heads and the air was thick with the perfume of the alder trees.

They sat and rested, leaning back on the gray-tawny rock. A

puff of air caressed their faces as they watched a robin tug at an angleworm and succeed in wrenching it from its home in the mud of the creek bank.

"Have you ever been in love?" Amy asked suddenly.

"Once. With a boy back home in Ohio."

"What was his name?"

"Toby."

"Did Toby ever . . . did he ever kiss you?"

"Naw," Jane Marie said, shaking her head. Her shoulders slumped. "I doubt he even knew I existed. I never so much as said a word to him nor he to me."

"Do you ever see your pa kissing your ma?"

"Naw. They don't do that." Amy could tell that Jane Marie was not interested in pursuing the subject, but she wouldn't let it drop.

"My ma and pa kiss a lot," Amy said with genuine pleasure. Her face turned beet red just thinking about the things she wanted to talk about.

A look of sadness passed over Jane Marie's features and she cast a glance in Amy's direction. "Have you ever been in love, Amy?" she asked quietly.

"There's only one man in this whole world I could ever love. If I ever marry he would be the one. I . . . I'm in love with Matthew, Janey. I think I fell in love with him the first time I laid eyes on him over two years ago. It just eats me up to know he's dating so many valley girls. Thinking of him holding hands or kissing them fills me so full of jealousy I can hardly stand it."

Amy's voice trailed off and Jane Marie studied her downcast features. "I guess everybody feels the pangs of jealousy sometime in their life, Amy. Ain't nothing wrong in that, that I can see."

Sighing pensively Amy bit the inside of her cheek and studied the clouds. "There's so many things I would want in life if I was married. A home of my own, with a yard where I could plant flowers and vegetables, and a kitchen with a table large enough to sit four or six or maybe even eight people around it. A clothesline to hang my family's washing on, and a swing to hang in a tall cottonwood. I'd want a husband that would find pleasure in toiling all day and come home at night, hungry and wanting to share my table; laughing and playing with our kids. I'd want a husband to help me tuck our kids into their beds at night and then lay beside me and talk far into the night."

Amy's voice grew faint. "You know, Janey. I think I just described my mother's life almost to a T." She smiled sadly. "I . . . I've said more than I should have, and you'll surely think me a silly goose with all the mooning I'm doing." She jumped up and held out her hand. "We better be heading back."

A woodpecker, high in an oak tree, set up a steady hammering as the girls silently made their way back the way they had come, arm-in-arm, each deep in her own thoughts.

CHAPTER 26

Throughout the busy summer and into fall, Amy and her mother cultivated a beautiful friendship with the McLin family. True to her word and much to Katherine's delight, Margaret had taken needle and thread in hand and turned many bolts of pretty colored cotton and calico into suitable dresses for Katherine, Jane Marie and the twins. Having finally gotten acquainted with Bobby and partially breaking through his armor of reserve, she had made several brightly colored gowns and shifts that he could wear until he would start wearing his first pair of breeches.

Having pretty dresses to wear, Jane Marie and the twins started going to church, which added to Amy's delight. Katherine begged off, however, using her unborn child as an excuse for not observing the Sabbath. No matter how Jane Marie begged, Bobby clung tightly to his mother's skirts, refusing to leave her side.

October 2 dawned bright and beautiful, but with a heavy chill in the air. The leaves of maple, poplar and sumac blazed in the valley and the fir-covered mountain slopes flamed with patches of yellow and red among the assorted greens.

John was busy gathering in the squash: russets, yellow and dark green acorns, butternuts and knobby Hubbards. He heaped them beside the pumpkins, all yellow-gold and fat as bishops.

The sugar maple in the yard stood dressed in pure gold, the leaves crisp underfoot as Margaret made her way to the garden, basket in hand, to pluck the last few remaining ears of late corn. She added a few carrots and a handful of beets and soon had her basket full. A cutting wind made her draw her shawl tightly about her shoulders as she started her trek to the McLin's.

On a sudden impulse Margaret reentered the cabin. She removed the tiny flannel baby garments she and Amy had been making in their spare time from her bureau drawer and put them in a cotton feed sack. There were scores of bellybands, diapers and swaddling blankets, soft as down and white as snow. She added a dozen tiny gowns, embroidered with daisies, ducks, and teddy bears in pink and blue to the sack. She had a box of tin soldiers that Billy Joe had outgrown years before set aside for Bobby, and she hastily added those to her sack. On a whim she put several candy canes into her basket and went merrily on her way. Grasshoppers and crickets were everywhere and the woodland in full color was awesome. The leaves were crisp underfoot and the floss of the milkweed pod was dancing in the air as Margaret met Jane Marie and the twins crossing the creek. Jane Marie was all frowns. "Good morning, Janey. And how are you today?" Margaret asked pleasantly.

"I'm just fine, Mrs. Bradshaw, but Ma . . ." Jane Marie glanced down at the twins and Margaret caught her bridled concern. She reached into her basket and produced two candy canes and held them out to the twins. They grinned and reached eagerly for the candy, sucking on the sweetness and started chasing butterflies as Margaret talked quietly with Jane Marie.

"Ma's time's come," Jane Marie said quietly.

"Praise God!" Margaret breathed aloud, her face radiating happiness. "You take the girls on over to our place and ask John to fetch Ruby. You'll find him in the barn cleaning up his harness. I'll see what I can do to make your mother comfortable until they can get there." Margaret started on her way, then stopped and threw over her shoulder, "Your pa's with her now, isn't he?"

Jane Marie looked crestfallen. "Yes, but . . ."

"But what, Jane Marie?" Margaret asked, giving Jane Marie her full attention once more.

"He . . . he won't be any help to you, Mrs. Bradshaw. He . . . he's been drinking most of the night and now he's asleep. Ma's been after him to chop some wood for several days now, but he never got it done. The fire's out and there's a chill in the house, but I didn't take the time to find firewood. She'll be fine, won't she, Mrs. Bradshaw?"

"John will chop some wood and we'll have a fire going in no time at all so don't you fret none about that. And your ma will be just fine. You just scoot on now and remember—no more fretting. Just place your trust in the Lord. He'll see your ma through this."

Margaret let herself into the small dark cabin, panting from the effort of her walk. The stench of whiskey was overpowering. Kenneth was slumped over the kitchen table, his drunken snores filling the air. A groan came from the next room and Margaret set her basket on the table and hurried to Katherine's side.

"I'm here, Katherine," she murmured, entering the small bedroom.

Katherine managed a feeble smile and sank gratefully back on the pillows with a sigh and closed her eyes. Bobby was lying beside his mother; his eyes closed tightly, tears soaking the pillow beneath his head. He was sucking one thumb and held firmly to his mother's arm with the other hand. Margaret was filled with pity for the child—so aloof, so alone, and looking so miserable.

"John and Ruby will be here very soon," Margaret said compassionately. "I'll soon have a good stiff fire going and I'll do all that I can to make you as comfortable as possible."

The room was cold but Katherine was drenched in sweat, her hair plastered to her face, her eyes glazed with pain. Margaret scurried into the kitchen and found enough water in the kettle to fill a basin. She got a clean rag and gently sponged Katherine's face and hands. She straightened the covers on the bed and plumped the pillows and propped them under Katherine's head and shoulders.

Margaret finally coaxed Bobby from the bed by promising him a candy cane if he would go with her to find some firewood. Outside, she looked about for something with which to build a fire, and her eyes rested on the remains of the split-rail fence encircling the yard. She made a game of it and soon Bobby was scurrying about the yard helping her pick up small pieces of the broken fence until the two of them had their arms full.

Back in the kitchen, Margaret quickly kindled a fire. Next she made a sandwich for Bobby and got him settled playing with Billy Joe's little tin soldiers. She checked on Katherine once more, and satisfied that Bobby was entertaining himself grandly, she ran to the creek for another bucket of water.

While the water was heating on the stove, Margaret scrimmaged in the cupboard until she found a clean cup and some tea leaves. After the tea had steeped a few minutes, she carried it into the bedroom. Katherine raised herself on one arm and her fingers clutched at the cup and tried to drink from it. It proved too much of an effort and she sank back down on the cornhusk mattress. Margaret sat down on the bed and held Katherine in her arms. She put the cup to her parched lips and finally Katherine managed to take a few sips of the strong brew.

"You're so good to me," Katherine said, her exhaustion and misery showing plainly on her pale face.

Margaret smiled reassuringly and kissed her on the forehead. "You're my friend, Katherine, and I love you," she said simply.

"I'm not afraid now. I was afraid of being all alone so I prayed hard." Katherine gasped for breath as a strong contraction hit her. Margaret held her tightly and crooned encouragement until the spasms ceased. After Katherine relaxed, Margaret laid her back upon the pillows.

"I was praying you would come. I can't rely on Kenneth. He's . . ." Her eyes filled with tears and she bit her bottom lip, trying bravely to stem the flow.

"I understand, dear. The man must be most miserable to lose himself to the strong stuff like he does."

"I'd like to believe that someday he will ask God to help him, Margaret. Help him to be a better husband and a better father. He wasn't always like this."

"I've been praying for that too, dear," Margaret said softly.

"I love my children. They mean everything to me." Katherine's face puckered up when another contraction hit her and she gasped for breath. "Will . . . you . . . you pray for me and for this ne . . . new baby?" she whispered. "You're closer to God than anyone I know. Ask him to . . . to bless my baby." Katherine closed her eyes and rolled her head on the pillow, her hands gripping Margaret's strongly as another contraction gripped her body.

As Margaret ministered to Katherine's needs, she prayed God would bring forth a happy, healthy baby, and that Katherine could safely deliver the child without danger for her own life.

Minutes passed with Katherine's groans filling the room. Suddenly she moaned loudly and arched her back, sweat pouring down her tortured face. Margaret lifted the thin sheet that covered Katherine's body and cried, "Push, Katherine! Push!"

Twenty minutes later when John and Ruby rushed into the cabin, they found Margaret standing by the side of the bed looking down with awe at the swaddled baby lying peaceably in his mother's arms. Both were sleeping soundly. Margaret put her finger to her lips and tiptoed from the room and closed the door softly.

"Looks like I lost my job," Ruby said, a large smile creasing her face.

"It all happened so fast, I can hardly believe it myself. One minute Katherine was in extreme pain, laboring to bring that precious baby into this world, and the next minute I was holding that sweet little boy in my own two hands. She wants to name him Winston after her father."

"By jiggers, a boy, eh?" John grinned and then looked at Kenneth, slumped on the table and shook his head sadly. "More's the pity that he missed out on the miracle that took place here today. And that's God's truth!" John leaned down and gently ruffled Bobby's hair as he sat contentedly on the floor playing with his tin soldiers. He then turned to Margaret and putting his arms around her he hugged her tight. "I'm so proud of you, Maggie. More'n I can say."

CHAPTER 27

The fall of '85 went by in a haze of work. The oat fields, rye, barley and wheat fields had all been clipped and thrashed of their grain. The harvest was in from the woods and the fields: filling the barn, the mow, the root cellar, the jam closet and the pantry. Wood was cut and all up and down the valley the cabins had been snugged and made ready for winter. Hopes were running high that a church could be constructed after the seed crops were planted, in the spring of '86.

The last Sunday in October found the Bradshaw family attending worship services at the schoolhouse with their friends and neighbors. It was a damp, chilly day, clouds low and gray and threatening rain. Roscoe had just intoned the final prayer but had withheld the benediction. He stood and gazed out of sightless eyes upon his congregation. A trickle of perspiration appeared on his forehead and ran down the sides of his face. He took a white handkerchief and mopped his brow then dipped his head slightly and spoke, gripping the podium tightly with both hands, his knuckles showing white.

No one in the crowded room was prepared for the news Roscoe delivered. Amy sat beside her mother, her mind like a whirligig, spinning round and round with every word she heard Roscoe utter.

Gasps and a buzz of whispers could be heard throughout the room, and as Amy glanced about her, she could see the disbelief that appeared on most faces.

Roscoe was resigning his pastorate; conceding his pulpit to a younger man. Amy heard the phrases: "... over forty years I have worshiped God with heart and hand and voice; ... taught the faith, married love-stricken couples in Virginia and here in the valley; ... baptized countless babies and converted hundreds of unbelievers. God has smiled on me indeed."

Heads were nodding here and there, but most of the congregation still looked at one another in consternation, frowns upon their faces. "But Reverend Willis," one man interjected quickly, "what are we to do without a preacher? My daughter was plannin' on gettin' married in the spring. We were countin' on you bein' here to tie the knot."

Disappointment sounded clearly in his voice and a drone of dissent was raised among the people.

Roscoe raised his hand for order. The general mood of the people suddenly brightened when they heard him say, "I haven't been your Shepherd the last couple of years to just turn tail and leave you high and dry, my friends. The Lord will provide, but it will take much prayer and the labor of all to reach the goals we set when we first stepped foot in this beautiful valley. You've already made a clearing in this wilderness, and another year will see yet a larger clearing and better garnering. You've made a splendid beginning in a hostile world, fulfilling many dreams. The wife and I have had the good fortune to share in all of this."

There was a murmuring of consent and a great shaking of heads. Complete silence reigned when Roscoe clearly stated, "I wrote back east earlier this year to a former colleague of mine, asking him to find a younger man who would be willing to make the trek west to be our pastor."

Roscoe cleared his throat and smiled. "It is now my pleasure to be able to tell you this morning that the young man is on his way and due to arrive among us any day now." "Oh's" and "ah's" were heard all over the room as Roscoe paused to let his words sink in.

"It's been hard for my wife and I to keep this secret from you. I pray you won't hold it against us. Until I was sure that my replacement was indeed a fact and not merely a whim, we stayed closed-mouthed. Stephen Cranston, the young man who will hopefully be your Shepherd, is twenty-two years old. He is champing at the bit to preach God's Word here in the valley. He's been teaching school while studying for the ministry. All you mothers who have been taking turns teaching our children the last two years, can breathe easier. Of course, the ultimate selection of a new pastor and schoolteacher will be left entirely up to you. If for some reason Reverend Cranston doesn't fit the bill, I'm sure come spring someone else can be lured to this fair valley. But until he does arrive, rest assured, I'll do my utmost to perform my duties to the best of my ability."

. . .

The rustling skitter of crisp leaves hurried toward winter. The wind could be heard in the sighing pines and whistling maples, and the days moved more swiftly with late dawn and early dusk, warm days and frosty nights. The countryside had a ragged, unkempt look to it as the temperatures dipped unseasonably low.

Wherever the valley people gathered, one topic of conversation never lagged—the coming of Stephen Cranston to the valley. His name was on everyone's lips. On the third Sunday in November there was a stranger standing beside Roscoe, and necks were craning as the young Reverend Cranston was introduced. He stood tall before them, broad-shouldered and thin-hipped with an ingenuously appealing face, his shoulders neatly filling the black coat he wore. He had a swath of wavy blond hair, tapering neatly to his collar in back.

After being introduced, Stephen gave a short but inspiring message. After the closing prayer, he walked around the room greeting and shaking hands with every person in the room. Every woman, with an eligible daughter, cast an appreciative eye in his direction, and most of the young ladies in the room fairly swooned as he shook their hands. He smiled at each one, his bright blue eyes direct as he traveled on the amiable assumption that everyone was going to like him as much as he liked them.

Matthew watched with mingled feelings as Stephen approached a group of girls that included Amy. She was altogether too pretty for his peace of mind. He was more than relieved to find her manner toward the young minister was precisely the same candid, pleasant friendliness she showed to everyone.

With mounting anxiety Matthew continued to watch the look on Stephen's face as he talked to each of the young ladies. Once again he was relieved to see that Stephen showed no more interest in Amy than he did with any of the other young ladies.

As Matthew stared at Amy that Sunday morning, he felt strange feelings in his stomach. Just looking at her, or hearing the lilt in her voice, only justified the facts: he loved her! Visions danced in his head: *he and Amy courting, building a home together, marriage and children. Could it ever become a living reality?*

No, he reasoned within himself. *Amy would never return his love. He had set himself up for heartbreak by even admitting to himself that he loved her. He must put her out of his mind and think of her only as his sister, his friend. But in his heart he felt as though there was an invisible cord, which no stretching could thin or break, binding them together.*

In an overwhelming display of acceptance and love, the valley people joined minds and hearts and welcomed Stephen Cranston with open arms. It took but a short time for them to find his religion was not a garment worn only on the Sabbath, but permeated his whole life, and all his conversations. He was a happy Christian, content with what God's providence had allotted him, and gladly consented to remain in the valley. Stephen and Matthew formed an immediate bond of friendship that brought Stephen to the Willis and Bradshaw homes more often than to any other.

The next week Amy had been surprised, but pleased as punch, when Jane Marie had shown up on their doorstep on Sunday morning to accompany them to church. Amy had told Jane Marie that a welcome dinner was planned for Stephen right after the morning worship services. Jane Marie looked as fetching as possible in her simple blue woolen dress. It accentuated her tiny waist and magnified the blue of her eyes, giving her a wide-eyed look of innocence. Her wealth of hair, black as midnight, was pulled back from her face and fastened with a blue bow. Tiny curling tendrils escaped the heavy silken mass and framed her elfin face.

The schoolhouse was bursting its seams as the Bradshaws and Jane Marie made their way slowly to a bench at the back of the room, the only seat available and just minutes before the services began.

As soon as the last "Amen" was said, tables were whisked into place and food-laden baskets were soon emptied. Amy and Jane Marie, to their utter delight, had found themselves sitting at the table next to the one occupied by Matthew and Stephen. Blessings were prayed on the food and everyone ate with great relish and abandon.

Sitting at the far end of the table with a fork halfway to her mouth, Amy felt an elbow in her ribs. She glanced sideways at Jane Marie who held a chicken leg in one hand and a rapturous smile on her face. She leaned close and whispered in Amy's ear, "Have you ever seen such a handsome man in your entire life?"

Amy chewed and swallowed, but before she could say a word, a blush crept into Jane Marie's cheeks and she whispered tremulously, "And his lips look as though they were just made for kissing." Jane Marie's eyes grew large as chestnuts as she realized she had verbally exercised her deepest thoughts.

Amy stared first at Stephen and then directed her gaze toward Jane Marie. "Why, Jane Marie, if I didn't know better, I'd say you are smitten with our young Reverend Cranston," she giggled.

Embarrassed, Jane Marie twisted in her seat and glared at Amy. Her lips puckered in annoyance and she spoke with quiet, but desperate, firmness, "If you breathe a word I've said, Amy Bradshaw, I'll never speak to you again!"

Amy grinned. "Don't worry your pretty little head. I haven't the slightest notion of saying a word to anyone—and I thoroughly agree with you. Stephen Cranston is a handsome man and he'll probably break the heart of every eligible young lady in the valley before spring."

"I know you aren't interested in him in that . . . well, in that way," Jane Marie whispered breathlessly. "You have Matthew to love. It seems Stephen and Matthew has forged a bond. They . . . they seem to get along so well together. Wouldn't it be something if the four of us could . . ." Jane Marie's smile quickly faded and she stopped speaking and hung her head sadly.

Amy looked at her friend in quiet confidence. "Yes, he and Matthew have become very close friends in the past two weeks. I can assure you, Jane Marie, Stephen is pure gold, and if I don't miss my guess, you'll be seeing more of Stephen Cranston than just at church." With a voice firm and final, Amy whispered, "Matthew and I will see to that."

After dinner was over everyone stood in line for a chance to talk to the new pastor. Amy stood behind Jane Marie and they waited patiently for their turn to greet Stephen. Amy was well aware of the feeling of shyness wafting over Jane Marie as she kept edging back, urging others to go before her. A broad-shouldered man standing directly in front of the girls stepped aside, and Jane Marie's eyes lit up like a morning sunrise as she stared straight up into Stephen Cranston's eyes.

Stephen smiled down at Jane Marie with beautiful candor. He took her small hand into his own and Jane Marie's face turned red as a beet. Her breath quickened and she stammered, "I . . . I'm Jane Marie McLin and . . . and I . . . I'm very pleased to meet you, Reverend Cranston."

Stephen's smile broadened in approval. "I'm very pleased to meet you, Miss Jane Marie McLin. Very pleased, indeed. I've heard so much about you," he said, his voice calm, his gaze steady.

After speaking with Amy, the two girls moved on, but an extremely happy smile was plastered on Jane Marie's face. All too soon baskets were repacked, children rounded up and everyone prepared to go home.

The girls helped Margaret gather up their plates and utensils, and then Amy and Jane Marie made their way to the door. Stephen was standing just outside the door and he smiled warmly at them and bowed graciously. "A good day to you Miss Amy and Miss Jane Marie, isn't it?"

He towered over them, his smile irresistible in its warmth. "I shall look forward to seeing you both again," he said pleasantly.

Amy could swear that Jane Marie floated to the buggy, blissfully happy, fully alive, and wrapped in a silken cocoon of euphoria.

. . .

The second Sunday in December dawned gray with clouds, the wind blowing cold gusts through the valley. Birch trees stood stiff and silvery, stripped of their leaves by the restless wind. The sumac lifted its gnarled, frost-blackened fingers toward the distant sun.

John and Billy Joe had finished with the chores and were dressed and ready to go to church. Margaret had insisted that Amy remain in bed as she had had a fever and sore throat on Saturday. Amy said she felt better and could stay alone for a few hours, but Margaret was reluctant to leave her alone, even for a few hours. Margaret had been told that it was unusual for Indians to plan raids during the winter months, but still felt skittish whenever her children were out of her sight for any length of time.

Matthew assured Margaret he would stay and keep an eye on Amy so that she and John could attend church and have the afternoon free for visiting. Margaret finally agreed, and with instructions for Matthew to keep the door barred and a loaded gun at his fingertips, the Bradshaws left for the day.

The morning hours passed slowly for Amy. Matthew, true to his word, had arrived on the Bradshaw's doorstep just before nine o'clock, but had gone immediately to the barn so she had not had the chance to talk to him. She tried to nap but sleep was impossible. The plump featherbed soothed her physical being, but her mind scurried from one thought to another. She read awhile and then started to embroider on a pair of pillowslips but soon tired of making endless cross-stitches and lover's knots.

With a heavy sigh Amy put the pillowslips aside and with one lithe movement she was out of bed. She had the rest of the day ahead of her and wondered idly just what the day would bring. By noon she had shed her nightgown for a simple woolen frock. Her long hair was brushed and tied back with a perky red ribbon, and though pale there was a sparkle in her expressive brown eyes.

Amy was sitting at the table trying to force down a bowl of chicken soup when Matthew entered the kitchen. He had an armload of wood and went directly to the fireplace and dumped it into the wood-box without saying a word to Amy. While he was adding logs to the fire she jumped up from the table and hurried to get another bowl from the cupboard. "I didn't know just when you would be in to eat, Matthew. Are you hungry yet?"

Matthew dusted off his hands and shrugged his shoulders. "I guess I could stand a little nourishment, but I don't want you to go to any trouble on my account." He looked at her critically. "You feeling better than you did yesterday?"

"I'm much better, Matthew. I'll have your soup ready in just a minute."

Snow began to fall about three o'clock in the afternoon, weaving a fine, white web across the countryside. It clung to everything it touched, building up on trees and stumps and whitening the distant hills so that they merged indistinguishably with the colorless sky. Buttercup was at the door meowing loudly. Amy rushed to let her in and caught sight of Matthew stooping to gather up an armload of cedar from the woodpile.

Buttercup arched her back and rubbed against Amy's legs, purring ecstatically. Shivering, Amy closed the door to a blast of cold air. She leaned over and picked up Buttercup and walked over to the window. She watched Matthew sullenly as he headed for the kitchen door.

Another blast of cold air accompanied Matthew and Sandy into the kitchen. Amy quickly closed the door behind them as Matthew dropped the wood in the wood-box. He removed his coat and gloves and tended to the fire. Sandy sank down on the rug in front of the hearth and immediately began licking his paws.

Nuzzling Buttercup against her face, Amy stared fixedly at the muscles in Matthew's forearms and back as they flexed beneath his dark woolen shirt. He was squatting before the glowing fire, his elbows resting upon his knees, seemingly lost in thought. The blaze brightened before him, strongly outlining the ruggedness of chin and brow. Amy walked over to the rocking chair and sat down, Buttercup still nestled contentedly in her arms. She studied Matthew's profile intently and the blood began to pound in her temples.

He rose in one fluid motion, turned abruptly and their eyes met in a long embrace. Stains of scarlet appeared on Amy's face and Matthew nervously ran a hand through his hair. Amy quickly dropped her gaze as thoughts of Matthew jostled for prominence in her head. Sandy thrust his cold nose into her hand and she absently began to stroke his broad head. Buttercup stopped purring and immediately jumped to the floor. Matthew hesitated for a moment and then said matter-of-factly, "Guess I'll be going out to do the milking now. Anything I can do for you before I go?"

Amy's face radiated pure pleasure to actually hear him speaking to her. She swallowed once and asked in a tight voice, "Can I go with you? I've been stuck in the house all day and I feel as though I'm suffocating."

Matthew's heart was beating up a storm. He shrugged into his heavy woolen great coat and reached for the milk bucket. To make light of the moment he said off-handedly and without inflection, "Guess you're old enough to do what pleases you." Without further word he opened the door and headed in the direction of the barn.

CHAPTER 28

A delicious ray of sunshine broke through Amy's solemnity and she leapt into motion. Running into her bedroom, she pulled her boots out from underneath her bed. Hurriedly she put them on, grabbed her woolen cloak and muffler from a peg behind the door, pulled her hood over her head and ran out the door. The December wind was howling among the pines and driving the snowflakes before it.

The day was slowly ending as Amy burst through the barn door. The interior of the barn was meshed in shadows, the strong, pleasant odors of horses, leather, manure and hay, thick and satisfying to her nostrils.

Annie was in her stall happily munching on hay. When Matthew saw Amy enter the barn he reached for the lantern hanging on a peg above his head and lighting it, handed the lantern to Amy. "Since you're here," Matthew said solemnly, "I'll let you make yourself useful. Think you can hold the lantern over my shoulder so I can see what I'm doing."

Grinning, Amy took the lantern from Matthew's hand. She stood as close to his back as she could, and held the lantern aloft. Squatting on the milking stool, Matthew reached for Annie's teats nearest him. Soon the rhythmical hiss of milk into the bucket met their ears. *Squeeze, pull, squeeze, pull,* Amy thought to herself, keeping time to the casual rise and fall of Matthew's wrists.

Matthew was aware that Annie had a sore back teat, and that she would object if she wasn't handled just right, but Amy's nearness was suffocating him, and he wanted to finish this chore as quickly as possible. Grabbing the remaining two teats he pulled—hard. Annie's response was to lift a hind foot and the milk bucket with it. Matthew drew back sharply, but the warm liquid drenched him before he could catch his balance and keep the stool from tipping over.

Amy jumped clear as Matthew sputtered, "You ornery old heifer!" Matthew was sprawled in the straw at Amy's feet, attempting to wipe the milk from off his face and out of his eyes. Suddenly he realized Amy was laughing. Laughing so hard that tears were streaming down her cheeks.

"What's so blasted funny?" he spewed, his voice clouded with anger.

Amy hung the lantern on a nail and continued to laugh. She finally managed a weak gasp and sputtered, "You're funny, Matthew! You're so blasted funny!" She finally caught her breath but it took a moment for her to gain her composure before she could continue speaking. "You can't begin to imagine what you look like with all that foam on your face, in your hair and . . ." With mischief shining brightly in her eyes, Amy doubled over again in laughter.

The humor of the situation began to grasp Matthew and he suddenly reached out and grabbed Amy's leg and tumbled her down beside him. "Funny, am I?" Matthew was laughing right along with Amy now. "Let's see how well you like it!" He started rubbing his milky white face all over her own and held her flailing arms tightly to her sides to keep her from striking out at him. She squealed and turned her head from side-to-side. Finally gasping for breath, the two of them lay back in the wet straw.

There was no longer a spark of mischief in Amy's eyes as she looked at Mathew from under her long dark lashes. Her face was aflame and she was glad of the semi-darkness that enshrouded them, and hid the flush in her cheeks. "No . . . no more, Matthew," she begged, as she tried to rise to a sitting position, feeling so alive to his nearness.

A hot tide of passion raged through both of them: a fire that burned with a clean, clear flame. Happiness welled in both their hearts and it was sweet. Pure radiance glowed from Amy's face, and her body relaxed against Matthew as he rolled over on his side and reached for her. This time she made no move to break away. His gaze was as soft as a caress as he softly whispered, "I love you, Amy."

Quickly Matthew jumped up and held his arms out to her. Taking her lifted hands, he pulled her to her feet and held her gently to his breast. He brushed her tousled hair away from her brow with gentle fingertips and absently pulled a few strands of straw from her hair. Amy was hypnotized by his touch, and tingled under his fingertips.

Sensing the awakening flames within her, Matthew leaned down and kissed foam from one cheek and then the other. He expelled a ragged breath as he felt Amy tense under his probing lips. She was standing on tiptoe, as if she was a bird poised for flight, and then they slowly melted into a tight embrace.

Matthew kissed her again and again until the tenseness left her body and her eager response matched his. She was returning his kisses with unchecked ardor. Finally Matthew pushed Amy at arm's length and studied her upturned face. Contentment and peace flowed between them as Matthew pulled her close once more. Whispering hoarsely, he said, "How I've longed for this moment— I love you so much, sweetheart." He kissed her again, fiercely, whispering between each of his kisses, "I love you . . . I love you . . . I love you," until the words were as familiar to her ears as they were to her lips, and she felt transported on a soft and wispy cloud to heaven.

Gazing up at Matthew in total surrender, time seemed to stand still as his eyes delved into her own. Leaning low he pressed his lips once more to hers in a tender, fleeting kiss, his heart beating wildly. "I love you so much, Matthew," Amy said serenely. "I just never thought the time would come when I could tell you. You've always seemed so aloof with me, always teasing, filling me with jealousy every time you dated the valley girls. That you could love me too, fills my heart with unspeakable happiness."

"There's never been anyone but you, Amy. I've never come close to loving anyone but you. All my teasing, all my aloofness, was just a cover up for my true feelings, sweetheart. I was so afraid you thought of me only as a brother of sorts, a friend . . ." Matthew's voice trailed off and he bent his head and kissed her tenderly. Lightly fingering a tendril of hair on her cheek, Matthew's face creased into a sudden smile. "Will you marry me?" he whispered, burying his lips in Amy's hair.

Startled, Amy pushed against him and looked deeply into his eyes. "You mean it, Matthew? You want to marry me?"

"Certainly I mean it! Does it surprise you so? I've wanted to ask you that question a million times or more the last two years, but I could never get up the courage to tell you what you meant to me."

"I've had the same crazy feelings, Matthew. I've been in love with you forever it seems, but I knew that it wasn't a brotherly kind of love at all, and it has caused me all sorts of pain. Loving you and not being able to tell you of that love has . . ."

"You can tell me now, sweetheart," Matthew cut in. "I'll never tire of hearing those words."

"Then ask me again, Matthew. Please . . ."

"My darling, will you marry me?"

Amy's heart sang with delight, pounding an erratic rhythm. "Yes! Matthew. Yes! Yes! A million times yes! I love you, Matthew David Carpenter, and I want to be your wife more than I've ever wanted anything in this whole wide world." Amy stepped outside the circle of his arms and gazed up at him adoringly. Taking her index finger she wiped a small dollop of foam that still rested at the side of his mouth. "Has anyone ever been so much in love?" she whispered.

"No one, darling. Ever."

"And we'll always be happy? As happy as we are right now?"

"Always." Stroking her hair, Matthew's heart jolted and his pulse pounded as he gave Amy a gentle push. "And now, Amy girl, you better be getting back to the cabin 'cause I've got me some very un-Christian-like thoughts roamin' in my brain." He laughed freely. "Go along with you now—I'll be in shortly."

Matthew's teasing tone excited Amy and her heart hammered against her ribs as she floated on clouds back to the cabin. Skipping through the newly fallen snow, humming softly, Amy's face was aglow with happiness.

They could hardly contain themselves until John and Margaret returned home that evening. When they did finally arrive home, Matthew sat them down and broke the news to them, stuttering and stammering all the way through his telling. He looked to Amy now and then for encouragement.

Billy Joe went wild upon hearing the news. "You son-of-a-gun, you," he said, pounding Matthew on the back. Billy Joe even drew Amy to him and in a rush of tenderness quickly kissed her on the cheek, bringing tears to her eyes.

John took the news with a twinkle in his eye. He pumped Matthew's hand, and he too pounded him on the back. "You rascal," he teased, giving Matthew a broad grin. At once he offered to set them up with a hundred acres of river-bottom land he had recently purchased—the richest that he owned.

"That's more than generous of you, Pa," Matthew said, relieved that John had taken their news so graciously. "As soon as this cold spell is over I'll start building us a cabin. If all goes well, we would like to be married a year from now on Amy's nineteenth birthday." He looked at Amy and winked. "That will be December 16, 1787 to be exact!"

Realizing that her mother hadn't uttered a word, Amy regarded her quizzically. "Have you any thoughts or comments on our plans, Ma?"

All eyes were turned on Margaret. She stirred uneasily in her chair and her hands twisted nervously in her lap. An edge of doubt rang in her voice as she said, "She's so young, Matthew."

Disappointment was clearly written on Matthew's face as he

kneeled down before Margaret and took her trembling hands into his own. "We can wait if you think we should, Ma," he said guardedly, but the thought tore at his insides.

The tense lines on Margaret's face relaxed. "No . . . no, it isn't that I really want you to wait, exactly; it's just that you've caught me by surprise, that's all. Living here under our own roof at times, and we never realized what was going on . . ."

"Nothing has been 'going on' as you call it, Ma," Matthew interrupted with a quick retort, looking a little embarrassed.

Walking over to her mother, Amy knelt beside Matthew, her courage and determination like a rock inside of her. "I've loved Matthew for years now, Ma. You've always known my thoughts. It's been troubling me something fierce thinking that the love I felt for Matthew would never be returned. He never let on that he cared for me in any way other than as sister or friend—until tonight. Please believe me, Ma."

"I believe you, child," Margaret said in a rush. She cupped Amy's face between her hands and kissed her forehead lightly. "I'm happy about it, really I am. I just want you to be sure—you're only seventeen."

Amy brightened. "Oh, but Ma, I'll be eighteen in just a few days and practically old enough to be called an old maid! In another year I will be nineteen. If I remember correctly, you married Pa when you were just shy of eighteen."

John slapped his knee and looked at Margaret animatedly. "Gotcha!"

Margaret looked at her husband and her face turned red. "But that was different, John. I seemed older somehow than Amy does. I . . ."

"I'm afraid she's got you by rights, Maggie. Amy's every bit as mature as you were at seventeen and I remember full well how your father and mother carried on about me 'robbing the cradle'."

Turning his attention to Matthew, John said, "I will say this much, Matthew, had I searched the world over, I couldn't have found anyone I'd rather see my daughter married to than you."

Jumping up, Amy ran to her father and kissed him on the

cheek and hugged him tightly. "Thank you, Pa," she breathed. "I love you so very much."

With a smug grin on his face John dropped his cheek affectionately against Amy's sweet-smelling hair, returning the hug. "I love you too, sweetheart." Tears of happiness filled both their eyes to overflowing.

"This is getting kinda sticky!' Billy Joe gushed, blushing profusely. His retort broke the ice and Amy and her father brushed the tears away and smiled simultaneously.

Sighing, Matthew reached for Amy's hand. "Well, sweetheart, we've braved this hurdle, now let's you and me hightail it over to my house. I want you with me when I break the news to Roscoe and Ruby."

CHAPTER 29

1786

Winter in Kentucky took a sudden flight into spring with a wild bursting of buds and a great clamor of wings and birdsong. The earth turned, and the winds eddied and swirled. Another winter had blown itself away.

But the spring brought with it a host of marauding Indians. Mostly horse stealing, but the constant danger was always present, a time when the Indians would suddenly and without warning appear. The settlers had been warned over and over again in the out-lying villages closest to the Green River to never be lulled into the thought of peace, simply because they desired peace.

Word had reached Sam Tippett and he had passed it on to his neighbors that Walker Daniel, the promising young attorney general and proprietor of the village of Danville, had recently been ambushed and killed. A little later a family of nine on the Wilderness Road had been wiped out, and a party of twenty-one badly hurt. Almost every settlement in Kentucky had been harried in one way or another: stolen horses, cattle killed, barns and cribs burnt to the ground. As yet New Hope had felt no direct threat, but they were to be ever on the alert.

Brigadier General Benjamin Logan had come to Kentucky by way of the Gap in 1775, and had built a stockade, known as St. Asaph's. He was a man esteemed, trusted and followed—perhaps the strongest man of any in the country. He had recently put out a plea for volunteers to join with his militia and be ready to move against the far distant Wabash River Indian tribes if needed.

The matter of separation from Virginia and statehood had been considered and weighed carefully. Certain conditions were imposed however: Kentucky must become a member of the Confederation at the same time that she became a separate state.

The assembly instructed Kentucky to call another convention to consider Virginia's proposals. If the convention adopted the terms, Virginia's authority over Kentucky should come to an end after September 1, 1787. Several young men from the valley had volunteered to be at the convention in Danville to assure their right of becoming a separate state, and to adopt the best measures for defense against the Indian situation. Matthew was numbered among them.

Spring and early summer found no wasted hours to Matthew's days. He woke, ate, worked, and fell into bed exhausted in mind and body. Seemingly there was no end to the things he must accomplish before departing for Danville in June.

New leaves had gradually unfurled, pale pastels at first, eventually deepening to bold, bright green. The soil warmed as wildflowers sprang to life and rushed to blossom. Amy marveled at how untiringly Matthew worked at helping her father with the early spring planting. And true to his word Matthew had started on their cabin just as soon as the weather permitted. With the help of Stephen Cranston, Thornton Decker, Ben Grier, John and Billy Joe, the cabin had progressed very well. When the day arrived for Matthew to leave for Danville their home just had a few finishing touches to be added to it.

Matthew left for Danville one bright morning in early June. Amy had been transported on a soft and wispy cloud to the heights of heaven that day as Matthew's lips slowly descended to meet her own in a warm and satisfying kiss. The surge of love she felt for him was overpowering as she buried her fingers in the crisp thickness of his hair.

She trembled with eagerness and contentedly rested against the warm lines of his body as he lightly fingered a loose tendril of hair on her cheek, a sad smile lending an almost imperceptible note of pleading to his face. He cupped one hand under her chin and lifted her face so that he might look into her eyes, so full of life, pain and unquenchable warmth. A muscle quivered at his jawline as he spoke softly to her. "I'll be back before you know it, honey. Just remember how much I love you and that you're the whole reason for my going to Danville in the first place. I'm wanting to do my share in making our world a safer place for us to live; a place where we can raise our children without fear." Tenderly his eyes melted into hers and his lips sought the moistness of her full red mouth in one last hungry kiss.

Tears formed on Amy's lashes and quivered, just short of dropping. "I'm going to miss you, Matthew. I love you so much, and I pray God will keep you safe and hurry you back home to me." Her eyes told him everything she felt, and as her words died to a whisper, the tears she so bravely tried to contain, cascaded down her pale cheeks.

Matthew saw her tears trembling upon her eyelashes and if ever tears resembled dewdrops, he thought, her precious tears did; and if ever mortal-woman was dear, then Amy was.

Reaching up with a timid hand, Amy caressed Matthew's smooth cheek, as warm tears spilled unashamedly from her eyes. Gently Matthew brushed her tears away with the tips of his fingers, and in his earnestness, captured her two small hands in his own large ones. The expression in his eyes intensified as he lifted them gently, and resting his lips against them, kissed each individual finger.

With a look of determination on her face, Amy gazed into his eyes, so palpable, that he could not look away, and he whispered hoarsely, "Goodbye, sweetheart—wait for me."

The sun gleamed through the lacy leaves of the maple tree as a brown thrasher put his whole self into song: he twitched and he jerked, almost leaping from the highest branch of the tree as he sang. Amy closed her eyes as a soft breeze, sweet with the smell of blossoms, smote her powerfully. Then hugging Matthew about the waist, she laid her head once again upon his chest and whispered, "I'll wait the rest of my life for you if need be."

Loosening his hold on her, Matthew stepped away, and a painful lump rose in Amy's throat as she watched him walk to where Honey was tethered, her small hands clenched stiffly at her sides. A faint breeze blew coolly around their heads as Matthew slowly mounted, reined Honey, and frowned into the rising sun. Looking at Matthew in all his splendor Amy wondered if he would ever tire under the load he carried.

Turning in the saddle, Matthew's blue eyes pierced the distance between them. "Make sure Billy Joe tends to Sandy's needs. He sensed something different this morning and I had to tie him to Roscoe's hitching post. First time ever he's been denied going with me."

"We'll make sure he's well taken care of, Matthew. Just pay no mind to things back here in the valley, and get your business over with. We're going to miss you, Matthew, but we're all so proud of you. Take care, and hurry home to us." Amy's voice drifted off as Matthew slowly rode away. Amy gazed forlornly down the path until he was out of sight. Long minutes after he had gone, she turned and walked slowly toward the cabin, lost in her thoughts, her sense of loneliness potent and aching within her.

Buttercup purred at her feet as the song of a mockingbird's operatic voice vied for her attention.

Entering the cabin, Amy went to the stove, poured a cup of coffee and sat down opposite Margaret at the table. She took one sip of the strong brew and about choked. "How can you stand to drink this horrid stuff?" she asked, making a terrible face.

Margaret laughed and replied, "It grows on you, honey. I could never stand the taste myself until after I married your pa. I guess I only drink it because he does. When you get married you'll understand. Being with someone day in and day out, you begin to do things like they do. Some things we do out of habit, and I guess other things we do out of love."

"Well, I certainly don't think I would ever be able to drink coffee and like it even if Matthew finds it most appealing!" Amy screwed up her nose and shoved the cup aside.

"Time will tell," Margaret said wisely.

"I'll be so glad when Matthew and I get married and move into our own place." Instantly Amy sobered and glanced at her mother. "Course I'm gonna miss living here with you and Pa and Billy Joe," she said, smiling warmly. "But it will sure be nice to be living in our very own home." A sensation of excitement arose in her like an irrepressible tide.

"Your pa and I will surely miss you, honey, and we'll also miss Matthew dropping in every whipstitch," Margaret said, frowning into her coffee cup. "Gonna be mighty quiet around here."

Amy's eyes challenged Margaret's as her voice trailed off. "But what if Matthew doesn't get home and get our cabin finished? What if we have to live right here with you and pa after we're married?" She sighed anxiously.

"You just stop all your fretting and what ifs right now," Margaret scolded affectionately. "You don't have all that much that still needs tending to at the cabin, and just as soon as Matthew gets home he'll finish it up in no time, you'll see. I know for a fact that your pa intends to do what he can while Matthew is away."

"If you say so, Ma," Amy said with quiet emphasis.

"Stephen has promised to help your pa in Matthew's absence too," Margaret countered. "And don't forget that Billy Joe is a great help and can do far more than you'd expect for his age." Margaret spoke with a sweet and candid pride in her young son.

"I miss Matthew already, Ma. So much," Amy said thoughtfully. Suddenly a warning voice whispered in her head and the color drained from her face. "What if something should happen to Matthew? And what if I never see him again?" Fear quickened her blood. "What if . . . ?"

Margaret butted in, refusing to let Amy go on with her endless 'what ifs'. "I've been praying mighty hard that the good Lord will settle your mind about Matthew," she said as casually as she could manage. "He'll be back quicker than he even thought possible.

The good Lord will be watching over that boy so quit all this needless fretting and fearing. I always say, if you pray, don't worry, and if you worry, don't pray. Worry is one burden the good Lord didn't intend for us to carry, my child."

"That makes sense," Amy said, some of the doubt edging out of her voice.

"It is truly an honor to have Matthew going to the convention and speaking up for us here in the valley," Margaret said proudly. "We surely want Virginia's authority over us to end, and if Congress forbids us to fight the Indians, excepting to protect our own kin, and in our own backyard, then the quicker we separate from Virginia and become a Statehood, the better."

"You always seem to know how to make me feel good, Ma. I'll try harder to be patient, I promise. My love for Matthew just gets in the way of my thinking at times. I do love him, Ma," she said quietly.

"I know you do, honey, and he loves you too," Margaret said softly. "That's why he went to Danville, and that's why we're going to pray he comes home with some victorious news. Now rest your mind once and for all," she said calmly.

CHAPTER 30

Amy awoke to bright rays of the morning sun dancing through her open window and across her coverlet. She jumped out of bed, gaily humming to herself and sat before the mirror in her nightgown. She gazed solemnly at her reflection. Her eyes seemed larger and darker, her skin clearer and more glowing, and her hair more lustrous than ever before.

As she dressed her thoughts included Matthew. Satisfaction pursed her temptingly curved mouth, her face pink with eagerness, and her pulses tingling as she hugged the delicious thought to her breast that in just a few short months, she would be married to Matthew. She would henceforth be known to all of her acquaintances as Amy Marie Carpenter—Mrs. Matthew David Carpenter. The bliss of her renewed vitality and well being was identical with that of springing grass and flowering peach and apple trees.

Matthew had been gone almost three months and to Amy those months had seemed a lifetime. But absolutely nothing, she vowed, would spoil this day for her. Today she would think only happy thoughts. It would be a day in which she would weave make-believe dreams about Matthew's return.

Her bare feet padded softly on the smooth floor as she made

her way to the kitchen. Pouring water into the basin she washed her face and hands. After brushing her teeth with salt and baking soda she popped a clove into her mouth and returned to her bedroom and vigorously brushed her hair. She tied a ribbon about her hair to match her lavender dress. Going to the kitchen door she opened it and stepped outside where a heavy scent of burning leaves and grass reached her nostrils. She remembered that Billy Joe and her pa were cleaning up the orchard.

Walking out into the yard Amy sat down in the swing, gazing toward the south where her log cabin was now located. It stood about two miles from her parent's cabin situated along the Green River. Limestone bluffs towered massively on one side, and drooping green ferns amassed on the lower edges of the cliffs. In the blaze of morning sunlight quartz twinkled like a thousand lights in the upper reaches of the cliffs. In the evening, when the sun had set behind the bluff, the riffles of the green water were turned into sparkling diamonds.

A quarter of a mile back from the river the land extended flatly and unbroken up the valley. It was here, in a ring of ancient beech trees, that Matthew built their log cabin. Nearby, a spring, in a rock ledge at the root of some old juniper trees, flowed perpetually cold, clear and sweet.

Late spring and early summer had been a haze of heat and work with the garden bearing bountifully. Amy almost wilted at the thought of all the work she and her mother had entailed in gathering, pickling, slicing, stringing and drying of fruits and vegetables. They had then spent hours dipping wicks into a large black kettle of hot lard hog fat and paraffin, to make candles to last through the coming winter months for both households.

Amy's wedding dress was complete and now hung on the back of her bedroom door. She had tried on her gown repeatedly and now dreamily went over every inch of it in her mind. She had chosen a gown of soft, blue-striped taffeta with side panniers. Blue lace trimmed the neckline and hem, and a row of six tiny pearl buttons adorned each sleeve. A cascade of pearl buttons, running from the high neckline to below her waist in the back, held her dress in place. With each tiny button and stitch Amy had sewn on her dress, she had offered up a prayer for their eternal happiness.

Her mind now drifted to their cabin, boasting a sitting room and bedroom at the back, a large, airy kitchen that dominated the front of the cabin and room for two bedrooms in the loft. Their cabin faced the east as Amy wanted lots of light in her home and with all the hours that would be spent in her kitchen, she wanted the morning sun to light there first. When their children started coming, they would build additional bedrooms, as they were needed.

Their furniture was all in place, complete with a goose-down mattress John had stuffed and bed linens that Margaret and Ruby had stitched and hemmed. Amy smiled, happy in the knowledge that preparations for her December wedding were progressing to her mother's satisfaction.

John was bound and determined to remain in the background, and was amused at all the fuss and bother for Amy's big day. Margaret had assured him time and time again that peace would reign again come December, and she hoped he could keep up with all the hoopla of his household until then.

Stephen had endeared himself to their entire family and they would be repeating their wedding vows to him. She had been noticing sly glances between Stephen and Jane Marie, but when questioned, Jane Marie insisted that they were just good friends.

Her stomach rumbling for food, Amy returned to the cabin and fixed herself a light breakfast. The Indian scare had diminished somewhat and the valley people were breathing easier. Margaret had gone to spend the entire day helping Ruby stitch on the quilt that she and Roscoe planned as a wedding gift for Amy and Matthew. After working in their orchard, John was going to help Jacob Swartz in his hay field and had taken Billy Joe along to help. Amy shared her breakfast with Sandy who had been left behind in her care.

Jane Marie had promised to spend part of the day with Amy, but as the morning wore on and she didn't put in an appearance, Amy became disheartened. The afternoon stretched endlessly before her and not wanting to spend another minute alone, she made herself a bread and jelly sandwich, closed the kitchen door firmly behind her and stepped out into the heat of the day. The sun blazed down on her head as she walked in the direction of the creek, preoccupied with her own private thoughts. Sandy bound ahead of her, scratching at every rabbit hole he could find and chasing half-grown rabbits as they scurried for new cover.

Amy popped the last of her sandwich into her mouth as she approached the creek, puzzled, but happy, to see Jane Marie sitting on the bank, so lost in thought, that she was totally unaware of Amy and Sandy's presence. Sandy sniffed the air and quivering, ran off to the underbrush, chasing a squirrel that had been busy among the hickories.

Amy sat down quietly beside Jane Marie in the grass. "A penny for your thoughts," she whispered, startled to see tears running unchecked down Jane Marie's pale cheeks.

"I've been praying you'd come," Jane Marie said quietly, brushing absently at the tears. "I tried all morning to work up the courage to come and talk to you but just couldn't."

"I've been waiting for you to come too, Janey. Couldn't imagine why you never showed."

Silence lengthened between them and made Amy uncomfortable. Jane Marie finally broke the silence by speaking so softly Amy couldn't understand at first what it was she was actually saying. " . . . and then he asked me if he could walk me home after the service. He told me all about his family back east and about his plans to study more and become the best preacher that we could ever have."

It was then Amy realized that Jane Marie was speaking of Stephen, and with her heart in her mouth, she listened raptly as words seemed to just tumble from Jane Marie's mouth.

" . . . course he's that already, but it's nice to know he has such drives and ambitions. He wanted to know all about me and I didn't think there was much to tell, but soon as I got started, I told him things that I've never told another living soul; things I've never told you, Amy, and you're my dearest and best friend."

Tears welled up in Jane Marie's eyes again and threatened to overflow. "I'd like to talk to you about it." Her chin quivered and her face turned white beneath her tan while drops of moisture clung to her damp forehead. "That is, if it's all right with you. And you have to promise not to interrupt me, or I'll never get it told."

Her curiosity aroused, Amy wondered what dire things Jane Marie could possibly be prepared to tell her. "You know you can tell me anything, Janey, and it will never pass my lips." Making the sign across her chest she added, "I do promise not to interrupt you—cross my heart!"

An electrifying shudder reverberated through Jane Marie and across her pale and beautiful face Amy saw a dim flush race like a fever. "I have such hate in my heart for my pa; have had for years now and it's eating me up on the inside. Stephen says I don't have to condone what my pa has done to me and the rest of the family, but he says that it's my privilege and duty to pray for him; to ask God to show him the error of his ways, so perhaps he will change. Stephen says the Lord can do mighty and wondrous things for him."

Fingering a loose tendril of hair on her cheek, Jane Marie paused and then continued in sinking tones. "I'm not happy feeling the way I do about my pa. I know the Good Book tells us we should honor our father and mother, but I just can't find it in my heart to honor my pa, Amy—I just can't!"

Amy glanced uneasily at Jane Marie and her heart nearly broke for the pain she saw etched on her friend's dear face, and she was shocked at the depth of Jane Marie's feelings.

"Yesterday I took the twins and went to Ruby's to fetch some castor oil and peppermint for Bobby as he was complaining of a stomachache and had a fever. When I got home Ma was in bed with a wet cloth on her face and Pa was passed out on the kitchen floor, drunk as usual."

With unsteady hands Jane Marie pushed her long silky-black hair from her flushed cheeks and stared for a moment at Amy out of dull, lifeless eyes. "I gave Bobby his medicine and fixed supper.

At bedtime I got out the only storybook we own and read a story to the kids and then went into Ma's room to put the kids to bed. Ma was awake. Her face was black and blue and one eye was swelled shut, but she never complained. I fixed her a bite to eat and after she had eaten and nursed Winston, she went right back to sleep."

Brushing the tears from her eyes Jane Marie cleared her throat. "I had Bobby and the twins say their prayers before they fell asleep and when we kneeled beside Ma's bed to pray, Bobby, so slow to speak always, said such a sweet prayer. He asked Jesus to not let Pa hit Ma ever again and make her cry, and he told Jesus just how scared he was of Pa. After he was finished with his prayer I let Bobby crawl in bed with Ma and I put the twins on their pallets beside her bed. Winston was already asleep in Ma's arms and I kissed Bobby and told him I loved him and to not fret. Jesus was going to answer his prayers and Pa was never gonna hurt Ma or make her cry, ever again."

Amy's heart was racing as Jane Marie continued her story. "I kissed the girls and blew out the candle and walked into the dark kitchen and sat down at the table and waited for Pa to rouse from his drunken stupor. My mind was running in a hundred different directions, Amy, and I didn't have the faintest notion of what I was gonna do or say when pa woke up. I guess I fell asleep but one sound from my Pa brought me to my feet. My hands were shaking something fierce as I reached for a candle and lit it from the fire in the stove. I couldn't see my pa too well but I could tell he was unsteady on his feet. He lurched right past me but I stopped him at the door. Icy fingers were clawing at my stomach but I faced him head on. He grabbed me by my arm and started to twist it and started cursing me and that really got my dander up."

Amy stared at Jane Marie wide-eyed, her heart thumping wildly in her chest but true to her promise she never uttered a sound.

"I'm ashamed to tell you now that I cursed him back, Amy," Jane Marie stated bleakly. "Really I did. I felt only animal hatred for the man who had fathered me. "If you ever touch ma again," I told him, "I'll kill you, Pa! If you so much as say a cross word to her I will kill you! I made no bones of it, Amy."

Jane Marie looked in Amy's eyes for condemnation. Finding none she continued. "I meant every word I said, Amy. Every word—so help me God. And I never cared a jot what Pa thought about my tirade." Amy shuddered at the force of Jane Marie's words and stared straight ahead, her eyes glued on the trees that grew on the opposite bank of the creek, but not really seeing them.

Jane Marie sighed raggedly, her black hair shining like a raven's wing. Her voice came out unnaturally high-pitched and shaky. "I . . . I haven't even co . . . come to the bad part yet, Amy." She turned and sagged against Amy's breast, wrapping her thin arms around Amy's waist.

Amy's heart twisted with pity as Jane Marie sobbed in her arms. She patted her on the back and whispered comforting words into her ear, feeling utterly incompetent to help her dear friend and yet wanting with all her heart to do something. From the circle of her arms, Jane Marie said, "I reminded Pa about that day in my Grandpa's barn back east when he . . . he forced himself on me. After he flung me aside how I ran to the hayloft to escape his clutching fingers. It was in trying to escape his drunken clutches that I fell from the loft, and I've been a cri . . . cripple ever since!"

Jane Marie's hands unconsciously twisted together and words tumbled from her mouth in a scalding rush—bursting past the constriction in her throat. "I screamed at him, Amy! Hating him with all my heart for what he's done to ma and the kids, and what he did to me that day!"

Jane Marie's tortured mind burned with the vile memories of that day. She sat up straight and wiped her eyes and blew her nose before continuing with her story. "I was only nine when my pa first hurt me but I never told a soul, not even Ma. But somehow my Grandpa Lloyd found out what Pa had been up to and drew a gun on him. He would have killed him on the spot but Pa somehow talked him out of it. Things really got bad when the news spread around town. It was hard knowing that everyone was talking behind our backs. I guess my grandpa threatened Pa again and in the middle of the night Pa loaded us up and ran like a scared rabbit all the way out here to Kentucky. I've had to live with the knowledge of what my own pa is like for so many years, Amy. I don't think to this day my Grandma and Grandpa Lloyd even knows what become of us, Amy."

Jane Marie was empty and drained with the telling, her sorrow a huge, painful knot deep inside of her. She had relaxed fractionally, but her face was pale, her eyes haunted as she turned her full attention on Amy. "Please pray for me, Amy. I don't enjoy living with all this hate burning inside of me." Jane Marie gulped back a sob, rubbed her tear-swollen eyes with the back of her fist and groped for Amy's hand.

Amy squeezed Jane Marie's hand and whispered, "I'll pray every day, Janey."

"There's been times I've wanted to die because of the hate I've held on to. I know now the good Lord don't intend for a body to have such feelings." Her eyes betrayed her concern. "Do you think he... he will still want me to be his child after all I've said and done? Can God ever forgive me for my thoughts and actions?" Jane Marie's voice broke and Amy, her emotions strung tight as a bowstring, started weeping.

She put her arms around Jane Marie and as their tears mingled she whispered, "Hush now, Janey. I love you and God loves you and he will never give you up. You're his child forever and forever."

Relief flooded sweetly through Jane Marie's whole being. She looked at Amy and smiled. "Well, you know all there is to know about me now I reckon. I always felt as though there must have been something bad in me for my own pa to do what he did to me. I felt so dirty for so long, and no amount of scrubbing could make me feel clean."

Jane Marie turned crimson. "I've always felt as though no decent person would want anything to do with me if they knew."

The flush receded, leaving two red spots on Jane Marie's white cheeks. "It was hard but I told it all to Stephen. He was so glorious about it all. Said he understands and he's going to do everything he can to help me forget the pain. I hope you can understand too, Amy, and not judge me too harshly."

"Oh, Janey, I would never judge you—never! I can never know the extent of your pain nor understand why your pa did such terrible things to you, but I do know one thing—God loves you, Stephen loves you, and I love you. And some day this terrible nightmare will all be behind you."

"If I ever do get married, Amy, I'm going to take Ma and the kids away from all their misery. Pa can live alone . . . never able to torment them again. With Stephen I feel as though I can move mountains. I love him so . . . and I do think he's beginning to fall in love with me." The look on her face turned to the incredulous.

Amy gave a happy cry and gathered Jane Marie in her arms again. They hugged and kissed and laughed and finally cried together again. "I always knew that things would work out for you and Stephen, Janey. You were meant for each other!"

. . .

Brilliant spires of cardinal flowers burst into bloom along soggy stream banks and the glades were alive with bright lacy yellow flowers. August would soon be a memory and autumn on the doorstep; days would grow shorter and the night air would take on a noticeable chill.

Chores kept Amy busy most of the morning and her mind off of Matthew's absence. There was dough on the flour board rising, bread on the back of the stove cooling, and bread in the oven baking. Amy's face and arms were flour-smudged and the kitchen was suffused with the tantalizing aroma of fresh baked bread. Taking a dipper of water from the pail, Amy poured it into the bluespeckled washbasin and washed the flour from off her hands and face.

She dried her hands on the towel that hung on the rack above the washstand and went to the cupboard, pulled open the bottom drawer, and humming softly to herself, withdrew a few, very soft, very threadbare pieces of muslin.

Taking three loaves that were already cool she neatly wrapped them in the muslin. Standing on tiptoe she reached for a basket on top of the cupboard and was putting the bread into the basket when she heard a familiar step on the porch.

"Well I'll be switched if you're not a sight for sore eyes!" Amy exclaimed, a bright expression on her face. "I was just thinking about you." She closed the distance between them and clasped Jane Marie in her arms in welcome. Jane Marie returned her smile and stepped into the stifling hot kitchen. Amy was more than pleased to note that her eyes were bright and clear and that her smile was so deep that it was showing off the dimples in her cheeks.

"Ummm, sure smells grand in here," Jane Marie said, sniffing the air and rolling her eyes heavenward.

"I made plenty and I was just wrapping a few loaves to take to you." Jane Marie sat down and propped her elbows on the table. "Thanks a heap. Ma's had her hands full this morning and she'll be tickled pink to have fresh bread to feed the kids. Nothing beats fresh hot bread—especially with fresh-churned butter swimming on it and maybe some of that crabapple jelly your ma gave us the other day. Just might cheer Pa up some too—he's been awful cranky today."

"Had your breakfast?" Amy questioned, forever conscious of Jane Marie's slender reed-like body. "You need to put some meat on them bones!"

Jane Marie laughed. "I've had plenty, thank you kindly." Amy noticed a mysterious air about her friend but she couldn't quite put her finger on it. She had the appearance of being strung tightly with repressed excitement, like a delicate musical instrument.

Jane Marie rose and walked quietly around the kitchen, her delicate cheeks flushed. She ran a finger lightly across the top of the mantel and idly glanced up at the clock that was ticking away, as though the time of day was of the utmost importance. She picked up the old family Bible and carefully leafed through its well-worn pages before she returned it to its special place on the mantel beside the clock. Humming softly to herself, and trembling in her own happiness, she edged over to the open door, stared straight ahead, hands behind her back, and rocked gently on her toes and heels. After an eternity she turned, straightened her shoulders, cleared her throat, and looked directly at Amy with dreamy eyes.

Amy had been watching Jane Marie out of the corner of her eye as she removed the last loaf of bread from the oven. Not able to stand the suspense a minute longer she blurted, "Out with it, Janey! Stop all this tomfoolery fidgeting and tell me what's eating at you!"

"I thought you'd never notice," Jane Marie answered, smiling coyly. She closed her eyes and her long, thick lashes shadowed her cheekbones. Her raven-black hair fell in soft curls about her shoulders and Amy realized just how beautiful her friend was.

The ticking of the clock measured the seconds as they dragged by. Amy was all but ready to explode under the strain when Jane Marie spun around, brought her hips to the edge of the table and leaned back provocatively. "I'm in love," she breathed at last.

The words flowed sweetly and softly from her lips. She looked anxiously at Amy, wanting to measure the reaction written on her face to this very simple, but elegant statement. Seeing none, she repeated the phrase. "I'm in love—I'm really, truly in love, Amy." She whirled around and around the room, oblivious to her limp, clutching her swirling skirts in her hands until she finally fell in a heap, completely out of breath, into the rocking chair by the hearth.

Her motions reminded Amy of the erratic flight of a goldfinch and she felt a warm glow flow through her as Jane Marie's gentle laugh rippled the air. "Silly goose! I *know* you're in love—I've known it forever, but that's not all you're holding inside, so out with it and tell me everything!" Amy ran over to her friend and sat on the floor beside the rocker. She hugged her knees to her, a thoughtful smile curving her mouth. Jane Marie had her complete attention.

"I reckon you remember how plowed down I was yesterday?" Jane Marie eyed Amy speculatively.

"You better believe I do!" Amy extolled. "I've been praying my knees down to nubbins for you!"

"Well." Jane Marie drawled, "when I left you and got home, guess who was there waiting on me?"

Amy looked puzzled and then her eyes brightened and she asked, "Stephen?"

"None other! The Reverend Stephen T. Cranston, to be exact!" Jane Marie started to giggle. "And I found out what the 'T' stands for too—Thaddeus! Don't that sound dignified and all?"

"Yes, Jane Marie. Yes, it really does, but what did he want?"

"Well . . ." Jane Marie drawled out, "he asked me to go for a walk up to Pullman's Cliff with him."

"Yes . . . yes . . . go on . . . what happened up at Pullman's Cliff?" Amy was smiling and shaking her head up and down, trying to hurry Jane Marie through her slow-moving story.

"He asked me all sorts of questions, Amy. Did I think his sermons were too long? Too short? Did I ever want to get married? How many children did I want? When did I take Jesus as my Savior?" Jane Marie paused as if in deep thought. "That last question he asked kinda threw me for a loop. I've been trying to follow your example, Amy, and living a life that Jesus would be proud of, and loving him with all my heart. I've asked him to live in my heart and feel as though he's there, but I guess I'm not smart enough to know if that's enough."

"Jesus doesn't expect more, Janey. But I know that something else is weighing on your mind."

Amy chewed savagely on the corner of her lip, and she was weak with relief when Jane Marie, blushing shyly, finally blurted, "He kissed me, Amy! It was different than I thought it would be. Wonderful, but frightening, too. It's quite different from being kissed on the cheek or forehead, I find."

"He kissed you on the lips?" Amy questioned gleefully.

"Of course on the lips!" The thought made Jane Marie giddy. "And I just about fainted dead away! I've never been so embarrassed!"

"Embarrassed? Good gravy! I've never heard tell of the like! Excited, happy, or just plumb inflamed with desire I could understand. But *embarrassed*?"

Jane Marie's expression turned woeful and she blushed the color of a wild rose. Forcing a confident air, she said, "Well, if you'd longed for something to happen for as long as I have, Amy Bradshaw, and then it finally happened, I bet you'd have been embarrassed too!"

Amy reached out and laid a steady hand on Jane Marie's arm. "I'm sorry as all get out, Janey. I sure didn't mean to hurt your feelings none. But please tell me, what did you *say*? What did you *do*?" Her heart thumped expectantly.

"I was too dumbstruck to say or do anything! I thank the good Lord that Stephen finally took the bull by the horns and I didn't have to say or do anything at the moment. He just wrapped those big, strong arms about me and told me he loved me and wonder of all wonders, he asked me to . . . to . . . he asked me to marry him!"

Amy clapped her hands in delight. "I knew it! I just knew it!" she exclaimed, jumping to her feet. She grasped Jane Marie's cold hands and pulled her out of the rocking chair. She waltzed her around the kitchen until they were both dizzy. "I just knew Stephen Cranston was gonna fall in love with you! He just couldn't help himself. You're the most beautiful, sweet and gentle person in this whole wide world, and why Stephen took so long to propose to you in the first place is more than I can figure out!"

"He's made me the happiest girl in all the world," Jane Marie whispered. "I've loved him since the first day I set my eyes on him. It sure beats all why he'd pick me to be the catch of the valley. Not that I'm kicking about it none. I've pinched myself black and blue just wanting to be sure I'm not dreaming! I'm gonna be a preacher's wife, Amy. Can you believe that? And I owe it all to you," she stated simply.

"Me? I didn't do anything," Amy said incredulously.

"You . . . you helped make me the girl I am today. You brought me out of the shell that I'd built around myself ever so long. If it weren't for you and your family, well . . . I just wouldn't have had the courage to even go to church or know I needed to give my heart to the Lord to be fit to go to Heaven. Oh, Amy, it gives me chills just to think what I would have missed, never having met you, met the Lord and—Stephen!"

"If I did anything to help you, Janey, I'm glad. These past

several months that Matthew's been gone you don't know how many times I had to bite my tongue to keep from talking about Matthew in front of you. I knew anything I said would only remind you that you had no one in your life yet. I would never knowingly hurt you, Janey. You know that don't you?"

Nodding her head Jane Marie said softly, "I know that, Amy. You're the best friend I've ever had and I love you dearly."

Jane Marie's words wrapped around Amy like a warm blanket. "I love you too, Janey. Always have and always will. Now, when's it gonna be? Your wedding, I mean?"

"We've not set a date yet, but I'm thinking we will soon." She smiled sweetly.

"If only Matthew knew," Amy said, her face suddenly creased in a frown. "He would be so happy." Suddenly a light went on. Amy cried out in a rush of excitement, "Let's have us a double wedding. Me and Matthew—you and Stephen!"

Jane Marie lowered her eyes and the smile left her face, smothered by a frown. "No, Amy. There's a heap of things I have to straighten out in my life before I can marry Stephen. All these hurts inside of me about my pa. I don't rightly know for sure that everything is right betwixt me and the Lord concerning them. You know what I mean, don't you?" She smiled wanly. "And besides, December sixteenth is your very own special day—yours and Matthew's."

CHAPTER 31

All was quiet in the Bradshaws' cabin. Margaret was braiding a rug, the bright strips spreading and twirling over her feet like snakes. Amy was hemming dishtowels and John and Billy Joe were playing checkers at the kitchen table.

Minutes before Amy had shared Jane Marie's good news with her parents and then had been drawn back into her own thoughts and dreams. One dream in particular had been dancing through her mind for several days. *Go on and ask Pa—he can't any more than say "no"*

Amy finally broke the silence. "Pa," she said hesitantly, "I'd like to ask you something."

"Ummm?"

"I was wondering if maybe our family could take a holiday? Maybe go to Greenfield? Here it is September already and we're pretty well caught up on our work. Since Matthew's not home, I'm thinking it'd be the perfect time to go." Her eyes were filled with a deep longing.

"And what would we be going to Greenfield for, pray tell?" John eyed his daughter, knowing he could deny her nothing.

"Oh, I don't know. There's a few things I'd purely be pleased to buy before my wedding. Things I haven't found at the general store in New Hope. Besides, we've never been more than ten miles from New Hope since we moved from Virginia. Greenfield is three or four times as big as New Hope. It was settled about the same time as Mr. Tippett settled New Hope excepting it's grown much faster. I heard tell that they have mercantile shops that have all the latest in fashions.

John looked up from the checkerboard and eyed Amy intently, flinching at the longing in her voice. He knew she was worrying more about Matthew with each passing day and if a holiday was what she was needing to ease her mind there was no reason he could think of to say "no" to her plea.

He glanced at Margaret and then gave Amy his full attention again. "I can think of nothing I'd like better than to take my family to Greenfield shopping." Margaret sat up and took notice. "And if it'd get this worry-wart off my tail about how poorly I'm looking these days, it'll be worth every cent it will cost me!" John gave Margaret a loving look that belied the orneriness in his voice.

"Why, John William, if that isn't just plumb sweet of you!" Margaret exclaimed. "Who'd ever thought I'd be making a trip to Greenfield? My, my. And you do need a rest from all your labors, dear, whether you think I'm daft or not!" Margaret was beaming, her braiding forgotten in her lap for the time being, her thoughts as giddy as Amy's.

Amy jumped for joy and ran and threw her arms around her father's neck and hugged him tightly. "I love you so much, Pa," she breathed, kissing him on the cheek. John was beaming—mighty pleased with himself.

"I could ask Jacob Swartz to tend to the livestock and chickens. I guess it's all settled then. As soon as you two ladies think you can get ready, we'll be off!"

Billy Joe looked at his father in absolute dejection. "Golly, gee whiz. Nobody ever asks my opinion about anything around here," he stated firmly.

"Do you have an opinion on this subject, son?" John asked querulously.

Billy Joe moved the red checker on the board and then glanced up at his father. "Just one, Pa," he said, grinning. "I don't want to go traipsing off to Greenfield or any other place. Roscoe and me made plans all summer to spend time together fishing and just enjoying each other for a change. You've kept me so doggoned busy this summer I ain't seen hardly hide nor hair of him and now that school's gonna start again in two weeks, we'll never get the chance to be together much. We done made our plans, Pa," he whined.

"Well . . ." John drawled, rubbing his chin thoughtfully. " . . . you would have to clear it with your ma, but maybe we could ask Roscoe if he would keep tabs on you for a few days."

"Do I have to go with you, Ma? Do I?" Billy Joe sounded so mournful.

Margaret glanced at Amy and grinned. "I don't imagine your sister would mind too much being separated from you for just a few days. I guess if it is all right with your pa and with Roscoe and Ruby, I wouldn't mind you staying behind. That is if you would promise to behave yourself and mind what Roscoe tells you."

Billy Joe was ecstatic. "I'll ask him tomorrow, Ma. I know it'll be all right with Roscoe though and Ruby likes having me around. She's told me so lots of times. I could help out with chores like I've been doing since Matthew's been gone too." He breathed a sigh and goaded his father, "Come on, Pa, it's your move."

. . .

Amy was tired. Bone-weary tired. Visions of her family traveling to Greenfield danced in her head all day as she helped Margaret make preparations for their early departure the next day. The cabin had been swept clean and dusted and plants on the windowsills had been watered. A box of food to eat while they traveled had already been packed in the buggy: smoked fish, several loaves of bread with ample butter, jam, honey and molasses to spread on it; cheese, apples, carrots, a dozen johnnycakes and a sweet potato pie.

John was satisfied that his womenfolk had packed enough

clothes for a month's stay. In fact Margaret was still packing, but had assured him that she would be ready to leave at the crack of dawn. John had taken Billy Joe to Roscoe's, had made arrangements with Jacob to do the chores, and was now in the barn polishing tack and bedding down the animals.

It was six o'clock and Amy was glad to be out of her sweat-soaked clothes, finished with her bath, and in a clean cotton gown and wrapper. She was comfortably seated in the rocking chair beside the hearth, dreaming of her great venture that was to start with the dawning of the next day.

Amy had asked Jane Marie to accompany them on their journey but she had declined. She explained that when Stephen had learned that her father was drinking himself to death he had offered to stay with the McLin family a few days and try and help sober Kenneth up. "He wants to present the Gospel to Pa in the worst way," Jane Marie had told Amy in a shaking voice. "Tell him how much God loves him. He has high hopes of my pa finding salvation, but . . ." Jane Marie shook her head sadly, ". . . but I don't hold out much hope, myself. Pa just doesn't care a thing about love. It doesn't matter a hill of beans to him as to the condition of his soul. Any mention of Jesus, prayer, faith or God's love, passes over him like a hot wind."

"I'll be praying for all of you while I'm gone," Amy told her thoughtfully.

"Guess I should be ashamed for not trusting God more in all this. I know Stephen depends on the Lord all the time and trusts him for everything. Whether he's happy or whether he's sad, it doesn't matter a particle to him. He says he's never once been disappointed in the way the Lord has worked things out for him. It's not that God gives him all he ever asks for mind you, some prayers aren't answered his way at all—some are. But whatever he prays for always comes out right, even if God doesn't always follow his suggestions."

"I always wondered why God revealed himself to me when I was only six years old," Amy spoke quietly. "Then I heard Stephen say a few weeks ago in his sermon how it pleases the Father to hide his truths from those who think they know it all, and reveal it to little children. He was speaking from the book of Matthew, remember?"

"Yes, I remember," Jane Marie said. "I remember every last word Stephen has ever said." She smiled with a far-away look in her eyes.

"Just think, Janey, all those comforting words were written by Saint Matthew. That's the man my Matthew was named after. Since Stephen preached on it, I read that part over and over to myself, wondering all the time what God has in store for me? I've never known much sadness or sorrow in my whole life. It's mostly been good times. Do you suppose we also have to sorrow and suffer to really know all there is to know about God and his purposes in our lives?" Amy shuddered.

"I guess our whole family has suffered with Pa the way he is. I know Ma has suffered the most. Course I'm crippled on account of Pa, but I'm trying to put that pain behind me. I truly feel I've forgiven him now. I find that I'm looking forward to the kind of man he can become when he let's God's love set him free."

Jane Marie sighed deeply and picked at one of her fingernails nervously. "If Stephen can help Pa, everything will be peaceful at our house and I won't be afraid to leave Ma alone with Pa when I get married."

"Well then I pray your house is as peaceful as a kitten on a featherbed real soon!" Amy breathed aloud and giggled.

. . .

The moon was hanging high in the western sky. A breeze moved the curtains at the windows and brought with it the rasping chorus of katydids and the whisper of the willows as the breeze sent each leaf dancing against a dozen others. Summer was passing the peak, reluctantly starting the long, leisurely glide toward frost.

Dark shadows were gathering as Amy set a lamp in the center of the kitchen table. She started to light it when she was surprised to see Stephen and Jane Marie standing outside the open door.

"My goodness! If you two don't look grand!" Amy sang out. "Come in! Come in!"

Jane Marie and Stephen entered the cabin laughing and teasing together. They sat down at the table and held hands as they joyfully told Amy they had chosen to be married on December twenty-fifth. "It's a special day anyway," Jane Marie said, as her eyes fastened on Stephen. "A day of simple beginnings: the Christ child was born for simple folks like us; and it's his simple words that still live today—words that I hope with all my heart will help turn my pa around and make our problems a thing of the past. Best of all, it's his simple words that will join Stephen and me together as man and wife."

Stephen gazed at Jane Marie appreciatively. There had been a wistfulness in her voice that had gone straight to his heart. Jane Marie's heart began to beat like a trip-hammer as she watched the play of emotions dancing on Stephen's face: pride, happiness, contentment, desire and deep, consuming love. Amy sat spellbound and listened as her two dearest friends shared their hopes and dreams for the future.

All too soon the clock on the mantel chimed the eleventh hour. Billy Joe had ridden Foxy to Roscoe's place earlier in the day, do's and do nots ringing in his ears from both his mother and father. He had been so excited about getting to spend four or five nights with Roscoe and Ruby and his happiness showed in every fiber of his being.

Stephen shook John's hand. "Godspeed, my friend, and have a safe trip. Rest assured I'll be praying for you while you're gone." Turning to Margaret Stephen gave her a hug. "Take care and don't worry about a thing back here. I'll check with Jacob and Billy Joe to make sure that nothing goes amiss."

Margaret put her hands on both sides of Stephen's face and kissed him lightly on the lips. "We love you, Stephen, and surely appreciate your kind thoughts and deeds. I promise not to worry needlessly. I know my son is in good hands. She kissed Jane Marie and told her that she would be in her thoughts during the coming week.

After paying their respects, John and Margaret retired to their bedroom for the night. Amy was still bright-eyed and bushy-tailed and reluctant to see Stephen and Jane Marie take their leave. It gave her such a good feeling to see them together, to see their love for one another shining on their faces. If ever a marriage was made in Heaven, Amy knew it would be theirs.

When she found she could delay their parting no longer Amy hugged and kissed first Jane Marie and then Stephen. She stood in the open doorway and watched them stroll away from her, arms entwined, at peace with the world and each other. The moon in the night sky was one for lovers to divulge their fondest thoughts and fancies and she heard Stephen say to Jane Marie, "A boy for you and a girl for me," as they walked out of earshot.

Amy stood on the porch awhile and then wandered aimlessly around the yard. The night breeze was cool against her cheeks, just barely moving the leaves on the trees.

Stars twinkled like a myriad of fireflies, flashing in the summer night. She glanced up at the northeastern sky and beheld a falling star. She smiled, remembering as a little girl how she had spent hours looking up into the heavens, wondering what God's house looked like; whether God slept on a feather bed at night, and if the stars were his candles.

Matthew once told Amy that a falling star meant money falling into your lap—money, money, money," he had said with a wicked gleam in his eye. Her father, on the other hand, had told her that to see a falling star meant the death of one of God's saints.

Reentering the kitchen, Amy turned and looked longingly in the direction that Stephen and Jane Marie had just taken and a chill raced through her entire body. Lately, she had little time for melancholy, but tonight it seemed to well up inside of her like a living, breathing spring of water.

She closed and bolted the door. "Why sadness, Lord?" she spoke softly to the silent room. "Tonight of all nights I should be happy." She closed her eyes and images flickered through her mind: *Matthew, home again, their wedding day just a beautiful memory, and the two of them living in their own beautiful cabin. Jane Marie and Stephen walking down the aisle, repeating their vows and . . .*

The clock struck the hour and Amy's eyes popped open, the images fading. It had been a long day and as she made her way slowly to her bedroom, she rubbed her neck muscles and stretched her arms above her head trying to ease the kink from between her shoulder blades.

On her knees beside her open window, Amy said her prayers, climbed wearily into bed, and snuggled deep into her feather mattress and pulled her patchwork quilt clear up to her chin. *Tomorrow is another day,* she thought dreamily, *but today is mine to keep forever and forever and all my life is before me—for all eternity.* And she slept.

. . .

It took some hard traveling to reach Greenfield before nightfall. Amy had been excited and thrilled but fidgety the whole trip. She couldn't relax and was as 'jumpy as a jackrabbit' to hear her father tell it. They stopped several times to rest and water the horse and to eat of the generous amount of food Margaret had prepared for the trip.

They rode over faint game trails and plunged downward into dense thickets of valley forest, following a deer path along an ever-widening stream that flowed strong but sedately past huge boulder stones. At one point they approached the ruins of what was once a settler's home. The stone foundation and toppled chimney stones still stood like small sentries amid the blackened timbers. Wild roses bloomed in profusion amongst the weeds that had taken over the clearing.

Eventually the twisting trail straightened out and they were descending into a lush green valley surrounded by ancient trees, many with their thick trunks covered in green moss. Through the verdant meadow ran a narrow silver ribbon of water wending its way toward Greenfield, the meadow margins glowing with the yellow plumes of goldenrod. Bees were as loud as they were at the height of clover bloom.

"I can't believe how this country changes in just a half a day's travel, Pa," Amy said excitedly, as she scanned the countryside. Meadows to hills, then into the valleys again and then it's back to hills." Amy's smile collapsed and her glowing youthful happiness faded. "I truly wonder what happened to the family that lived back yonder, Pa? Do you think the Indians burned that homestead down?" Amy was trembling in spite of the heat of the day.

"Expect so, honey. It's a shame that one man looking to kill another and taking away a man's dreams for himself and his family should mar beauty such as this in such brutality. Pray all the unrest betwixt our people and the Indians will soon be a thing of the past."

Margaret straightened her back and reached out and put her hand on John's shoulder. "What's that you were saying, John?" Margaret asked, tipping her face to the setting sun.

John swung his head around and looked at her. "Just passing the time of day with our daughter, Maggie. We were talking about the lay of the land around here. The whole state of Kentucky must be one vast land of beauty."

"Land sakes," Margaret said, gazing around her. "I do believe I dozed off there for a spell." She stifled a yawn. "How much farther do you suppose it is to Greenfield?"

"Probably another two or three mile I'm guessing." John answered. "You gettin' tired, sweetheart?"

"Not exactly. Just noticing that stream and was thinking it would be a nice place to make a necessary stop."

"Good idea, Maggie. I imagine Belle could do with a good stiff drink right about now." John pulled on the reins and nestled the buggy under the sheltering arms of a large cottonwood. A flock of black birds scattered across a mother-of-pearl sky as the Bradshaw family stepped from the buggy and stretched their legs.

The trees were noisy with birdsong and one particularly brilliant, chattering bird—a bird alive in color of green, gold and blue. Amy whispered to her parents, "Do you see that beautiful bird? What kind of bird is that, Pa?"

Shading their eyes from the rays of the sun John and Margaret looked towards the tree Amy was pointing to. "Why I do believe that's a parakeet, Amy. And one of the noisiest ones I've ever heard," John said softly.

Beyond the crest of a brisk rise, Amy was suddenly cheered by her first glimpse of Greenfield, seemingly a mere hole in an ocean of trees, as viewed from their position on a hill overlooking the town. It was picturesque in its beauty: a white-steepled church and tree-lined streets; gardens filled with colorful asters and chrysanthemums of gold, russet and amber hues. Yellow roses were in abundance as were sweet-smelling wild grapes growing along garden walls.

As they entered Greenfield they were overwhelmed with a cacophony of sounds: dogs barking, muted voices of men, women and children's voices in conversation as they strolled in the streets and mingled outside the shops. Loud singing and boisterous activity emanated from a taproom and the clink of iron from the blacksmith shop could be heard above the din.

"I swear if this clamor wouldn't make the cows back home give buttermilk, and cause the chickens to lay scrambled eggs!" John exclaimed jovially.

They found clean and respectable rooms in a small inn that lifted their spirits and promised great comfort to their weary bodies. The inn also had a large barn and coach house in which John could stable Belle and keep his conveyance. The two-story building seemed enormous to Amy. The lower story was made of river stones set in lime-puddled clay; the upper story of chinked logs. The beams supporting the ceiling were twice the thickness of a man's body. The upper story was divided into six small but comfortable chambers.

An open staircase, constructed of dark polished oak, led to the upper level. The surprising comfort and solid ease of the inn, its warmth and glow, gave Amy a rising feeling of exhilaration, as a young chamber maid led Amy and her parents to their adjoining rooms. Amy's eyes quickly scanned her room that was filled with charm and beauty. It was of modest size, embellished with pictures, cushions and books. She had a comfortable single bed, wardrobe, and small dressing table. In one corner stood a dry sink, where small bars of soap, shaped like miniature roses, rested in their own little dish. The soap had a dainty, pleasant fragrance to it. The chamber-pot lid was covered with a pink crocheted silencer and soft pink towels lined the rack on one side of the dry sink.

Two windows faced the square and almost reached to the ceiling. They were dressed in snow-white curtains tied back with colorful ribbons. A small table with a chair at each end was placed in front of one of the windows. Candles scented the air as did a vase of yellow roses that had been placed in the center of the intricately carved table.

The chambermaid, a young girl about Amy's age, short, plump and with a wealth of curly red hair, had welcomed the Bradshaws to the inn with tall glasses of lemonade and a platter of jumbles. The lemonade was tart, but delicious; the jumbles sweet and crusty. Amy sat on the bed and John and Margaret sat at the table and ate and talked until both the platter and glasses were empty.

"That ought to hold me until supper" John boasted, patting his stomach with a satisfied smile.

"Hold you until supper!" exclaimed Margaret in disbelief. "You won't be able to waddle to the dining room, let alone eat a bite of supper, John William! You absolutely made a pig of yourself." Margaret shook her head, her eyes bright with merriment.

"Don't you fret yourself about what I ate, dear," John said with a twinkle in his eye. "I can hold my own with the best of them. Now let's be getting to our own room and rest these weary bodies a spell."

Eight o'clock found the Bradshaw family dining in absolute splendor. A blazing fireplace and fat candles flickering in silver candlesticks illuminated the white damask tablecloths on two rows of round tables in the main dining room. A buffet table, at least fifteen feet in length, and placed between the two rows of tables, groaned beneath its load of food. Never had such an assortment of delectable food been set before them! Silver bowls held creamed onions, sweet potatoes, carrots and baby peas; platters were filled with oysters, roasted pheasant, roast beef with horseradish sauce, and hickory-cured ham, glazed with honey and browned sugar, and silver trays held macaroons in filmy sugar webbing, sponge cake filled with raspberry jam, chocolate eclairs, and apple, blueberry and peach cobbler. There were mounds of crusty loaves of fresh baked bread with sweet creamy butter, jellies and jams. Their thirst could be quenched with coffee, blackberry wine, cider or punch.

The tables were set with white damask tablecloths and napkins, gleaming silverware, and blue and white dishware. John lingered over his second helping of peach cobbler and coffee while Margaret sat looking at him with glazed eyes. "It never ceases to amaze me that someone with a spare frame such as yours could put away so much food and never gain an ounce! I gain weight just from smelling it—it just isn't fair!" Margaret, her natural exuberance bubbling to the surface, was shaking her head and grinning.

"Just makes me poor to carry it, my dear. And besides, I like my women with a little meat on their bones!" he quirked.

"John, you are impossible!" Margaret said reproachfully.

"Are you sure we can afford all of this, Pa?" Amy asked. "I've never in my life seen the like!" Her eyes were as big as saucers, taking in the room, the food and the people crowding the tables, eating and drinking in sublime comfort.

"Don't you fret none about the cost, honey. You just enjoy yourself. Your Pa can stand to splurge once in his life, and especially so when I'm splurging on two such beautiful ladies. Besides, I don't ever recollect having so much fun in my entire life."

But Margaret noticed that John's usually lively and sparkling eyes were now filled with weariness. "A good time has been had by all, John, but I think it's time we turned in." Margaret stood with great difficulty, her whole body engulfed in tides of fatigue. She folded her white cloth napkin she had draped over her knees and put it on the table. She ran her hands down the sides of her skirt to free it of any existing wrinkles and said wearily, "Tomorrow is another day."

"I guess I am purely tuckered out," John admitted. "That four-poster will sure look inviting. Ready ladies?"

Reveling in the comfort of goose-down mattresses, the travel-weary Bradshaws were soon fast asleep in their beds, exhaustion having overtaken them, and the din from below nothing more than a backdrop to their dreams.

Amy awakened early the next morning, feeling completely rested and with excitement coursing through every vein. A cock crowed in the distance and Amy thought to herself, *It's just like I was back home in Charlottesville!*

She sprang out of bed and drew the curtains. The sky was unclouded and it looked to be a perfect day. Opening the window slightly, she felt the cool air rush in. The cock crowed again and another answered, far away to the east, and she could hear the chatter of hundreds of birds in the trees. The day Amy had looked forward to for so long had just begun.

She climbed back into bed, shivered pleasurably from the freshness of the sweet morning air and stretched her strong little body in the warm cocoon of the covers. She savored the luxury of fresh linen sheets and the softness of the feather tick, and wondered idly if Matthew was awake or asleep. More than likely he was up and about. Amy was quite ready to get up now, but the inn was so quiet she felt no one was stirring around yet. She fell back asleep as suddenly as she had awakened.

There was a light tap on her door and Amy was instantly awake and alert. Thinking it was her mother she called out cheerily, "Come in!"

The door opened a crack and the maid peaked into the room. It was the same young girl who had met them the evening before. She was dressed in a simple green muslin frock covered by a white, stiffly starched, ankle-length apron. A white-lacy cap covered her curly red hair. Her full red mouth and dimpled cheeks were accented by smooth skin, and her dark green eyes were filled with eagerness and innocence.

As she edged slowly into the room, Amy saw that she was balancing a silver tray in her hands, covered with a napkin of finest damask. "Did I wake you, Miss Bradshaw?"

Amy grinned sheepishly. "I was awake much earlier but guess I drifted back to sleep." She yawned and stretched. "What time is it?"

"It's straight on eight o'clock," the maid answered as she placed the tray and its contents on the table, where the morning sun was now shining brightly on its polished and gleaming surface. She removed the napkin and immediately odors, delicate and spicy, were diffused about the room. The tray held a cup and saucer, sugar bowl, creamer and teapot to match in pink china, plus an assortment of spiced buns, iced cakes with pink sugar roses and meringues.

Amy sighed and cocked her head to one side. "It's so good to be here," she exclaimed in contentment as the sound of cooing doves reached her ears through the open window.

"By the way, Miss Bradshaw, I'm Flossie Jenkins and I'll be serving you while you're a guest in our inn." She curtsied and Amy was swallowed up in unbelievable happiness at the thought of actually having her own private maid. Then remembering her manners, she sprang from the bed, extended her hand to Flossie and exclaimed, "I'm so happy to meet you, Flossie! And please, won't you call me Amy?"

"I'll try and remember to do that. Your mother said to tell you that they'll be going down to eat breakfast at nine, but in the meantime, you can snack on what I brought you."

"Ummm, but if it doesn't smell tempting! After all the food I ate last night I didn't think I'd ever want to eat again." Amy wrinkled her nose and giggled. "Can you stay and have some tea with me, Flossie?'

"I've already eaten, Miss Amy." Flossie said courteously. "But thank you kindly just the same."

Biting into a bun, light as a feather and spiced just right, Amy's face brightened. "This is delicious, Flossie!" Licking her fingers she said, "I was born in Charlottesville, Virginia, and came with my family in 1783 to settle in a small village called New Hope."

"I don't believe I have ever met anyone from New Hope," Flossie said eagerly. "Is it far from here?"

"A long day's journey. But it is worth every mile to be in your lovely city. I can hardly wait to go shopping today."

"I was born in a little place in Pennsylvania and moved here to Greenfield back in 1778. Our town is growing by leaps and bounds. Two other inns opened up this past year and we're all as busy as we want to be," Flossie said as she began pouring Amy a cup of tea.

"We've a fort about ten miles to the north and my pa has taken me there a couple of times. It looks invincible to me. My intended, Charlie Buescher, is a soldier stationed there under Major Claybourne. Makes me feel so protected to know that my Charlie is close by in case of an Indian attack. We've been so fortunate up-to-now. No fracas for several years now. Guess that is where I'll be living when Charlie and I get married. I'll miss working here at the inn because I meet so many nice folks. But I'll gladly trade my services here at the inn to be married to Charlie and seeing to my own home, such as it will be at the fort. I never thought about Greenfield getting so big and fancy, but someday I predict we'll be as heavily populated as Danville." Now I better be getting back to the kitchen. I'll be back shortly with hot water for your bath."

"Thank you, Flossie." Flossie disappeared through the door and Amy took her napkin and wiped her fingers and slowly sipped her tea. After her snack and bath, Amy dressed in a pink dimity, brushed her hair and tied it back with a pink ribbon to match her dress. She tied the strings of her bonnet under her chin, then checked her reflection in the mirror. Satisfied that she looked fresh as a daisy she fairly danced to her parents' room.

John looked up and smiled as Amy entered their room. "My, if you don't look prettier than a May apple!" he exclaimed, giving her a broad wink.

Amy glanced at his beaming face and curtsied. "Thank you, Pa. I feel as pretty as a May apple." They shared a smile.

After a breakfast every bit as delicious as their evening meal had been the night before, John pushed his chair away from the table. "Now if you two ladies will excuse me, I'm gonna make myself scarce. I got a lot of looking over to do today. You just do whatever your hearts desire and make a great day of it. The good

Lord willing, I'll see you both this evening." John kissed each of them on the forehead and showing agility they hadn't observed in him for months, made his way out of the room.

Once out on the street, Amy and Margaret found the day very warm and muggy, the sky a hard blue, and the sun fiercely glaring on the unpaved streets. There were no sidewalks so small boys ran wild in the streets around the square, playing soldiers and Indians, with all the dogs of Greenfield scampering after them.

Amy was captivated at once with the ladies walking the streets in their beautiful attire. There were dresses of silk, cambric, lawn, linen and muslin, with full, frothy skirts and ruffled petticoats. Flounces of lace dripped from short sleeves and hems, and bonnets in every shade of the rainbow were fastened with gaily-colored ribbons. Amy gawked longingly at the ear lobes and throats that were decorated with diamond, ruby, and snow-white pearl earrings and necklaces, and marveled at the ladies' lips and cheeks, powdered and rouged.

Not to be outdone by their counter-parts, the men were a sight to behold. They were clad in breeches of homespun, broadcloth and buckskin and wore ruffled shirts, linsey shirts, checkered shirts and fringed hunting shirts. There was a wide variety of hats, mostly faded by weekday suns and rains, and many were doffed to Amy and Margaret that day as they passed by. Mountain men dressed in dirty buckskins and traders, in mud-caked boots, could be seen entering and leaving the taverns. Several soldiers from the nearby fort stood in little groups talking and Amy wondered if one of them could be Charlie Buescher.

The ladies carried fans or parasols and there was a continual flutter before their faces and under their hats and bonnets. And what a din! Children shrieked at play, babies wailed, dogs barked and a great deal of howls of laughter came from the bars.

Unhurried as they window-shopped, Amy and Margaret marveled at the merchandise they saw in each separate window. Unable to bridle their curiosity a minute longer, they entered a millinery shop. The front window was curtained in lace and it smelled of spicy flowers and scented talc. There were hats in everything from felt to straw, some trimmed and some plain. Tiny cubbyholes on one wall held ribbons, buttons and lace. Walls and counters displayed a large selection of fur tippets, feathered fans, parasols, lacy gloves and crocheted collars.

Next they made a whirlwind trek through a fabric shop, smiling at other prospective customers. Margaret fingered calico, fresh and crackling, with colors so strong, she knew even boiling wouldn't faze them. She lingered over muslin, cambric, organdy and bolts of finest linen. She ended up buying far more material than she needed reasoning within her generous heart that Ruby would appreciate having a few yards of new material for a dress. She also selected several yards of blue striped calico for Katherine, and since Jacob was so kind to be caring for their animals, she chose some pink and blue flannel to take to his wife, Mandy. It would come in handy in making some new little blankets for her baby-to-be. Next she went overboard on buying thread, thimbles, needles and a dozen other little items she thought she just might be in need of some day.

At their next stop Amy bought a dozen perfumed-candles and a box of perfumed soap for Ruby; an assortment of storybooks for Bobby, Winston and the twins, and for Katherine she chose a beautiful, blue lacy shawl. She agonized long and hard over a gift for Jane Marie. She wanted to buy her something she didn't have—something of lasting beauty. Finally she settled on a black, leather-bound Bible and had 'Jane Marie Cranston' stamped in gilt letters across the bottom of the front cover.

At a harness shop, Amy purchased a pair of boots for Billy Joe and hand-tooled, leather saddlebags for Matthew. She made arrangements with the owner to have her purchases delivered to the inn.

About two o'clock they both began to wear down and not quite as eager as they had been earlier in the day to shop. None-the-less they were enjoying their escapade. They entered a small tearoom, emptied their aching arms of their purchases, and spent almost an hour sipping tea and nibbling on an assortment of tarts and cookies.

Once more out on the street, Amy bought her first pair of pointed, patent leather, high-heeled shoes with black kid uppers. She felt both feminine and very mature with her purchase. Margaret splurged on a beautiful white organdy blouse with full sleeves, pointed collar and tucked bodice, trimmed with coral-shell buttons, and a skirt in black faille.

It was almost four o'clock when they finally limped back to their rooms at the inn. They had been gone an unbelievable number of hours. Amy's feet were sore and Margaret's back and legs ached painfully. They both heartily agreed that they needed a short nap before their evening meal.

John slipped into the room just as Margaret was awakening from her nap. He looked bright and chipper. "Laws-a-mercy, what did you find to do until this time of day?" Margaret asked, rubbing the sleep from her eyes and staring inquisitively at him.

Pulling out his gold pocket watch John glanced at the time and smiled. "It's only six, Maggie. I had to come back for supper, didn't I?"

"Oh, John!" Margaret stated emphatically. "Here I am all tuckered out and dragging my tail feathers just from an enjoyable day of shopping. I'm four years, six months and two days younger than you are and you come back looking like you've been drinking some mysterious potion from the fountain-of-youth!" Margaret grinned and wagged her head.

Better get yourself out of that bed before I show you just how youthful I am, woman!" John said, a twinkle in his green eyes.

"John!" Margaret said, blushing. "Mind your manners!" She found herself bemused and thoroughly enjoying John's antics. "Surely you can behave yourself for another few hours!" Grinning, Margaret scurried from the bed.

John murmured, huskily "Ummm, you do smell good, woman!" He made a playful grab for her. Wrapping his arms around her he gave her a soft kiss on her forehead. Margaret put her arms around John's neck and quickly kissed him on the lips. Immediately he felt a sense of peace and the sweetness of her lips overwhelmed him.

"What a remarkable man you are, John Bradshaw, Margaret whispered softly. I tell you true my dear husband, I would not trade or change one thing about you—not even one hair of your head. You are dearer to me than you can ever know."

"And you to me, Maggie darling." John lowered his head and kissed his wife with more emotion than he had shown in years. Drawing back he looked into her soft brown eyes and said lightly, "There now, wife of mine, you have been thoroughly kissed and I expect that to last you for awhile."

Margaret quickly sidestepped him and smiling broadly she dressed for supper, choosing a soft, buff-colored blouse and a brown broadcloth skirt. While she dressed, she wondered idly just what John had found to do all day.

CHAPTER 32

John had found plenty of people to pass the time of day with and had enjoyed a barbershop haircut, shave and bath. He spent many hours in the harness shop and livery, just nosing around and paid a nickel to have his boots polished. When walking around the square he spied a shingle in front of a small, white-framed house: Gerald H. Freeman, M.D. On a sudden whim, John went into the house and waited patiently until the good doctor could see him. Dr. Freeman asked John a lot of questions then gave him a thorough going over. Giving him a tonic to take once daily he advised him to slow down just a bit and assured him that following doctor's orders he would probably live to be a hundred. The doctor's words put a spring in John's step and a prayer of thankfulness on his lips.

That evening it seemed as though everybody was in town when the Bradshaws went downstairs for their evening meal. Outside, horse-drawn wagons and buggies filled the streets, dogs barked, cattle bellowed and children laughed. The local traders and merchants stood outside their business houses enjoying the cool evening air.

Inside the dining room, a number of officers from the nearby fort occupied the big tables closest to the bar. They were enjoying the finest vintages and fare the inn afforded and a cloud of tobacco smoke domed the ceiling where they sat.

Margaret ordered turtle soup, roast beef and potatoes, a piece of sour-cream raisin pie and a large glass of lemonade. Moaning aloud she said, "There goes my diet, Amy! Laws-a-mercy!"

John ate as much and although Amy wasn't the least bit hungry, she ordered a tall glass of lemonade and a brand new dessert the inn was featuring. It was a strange looking mixture to be sure. Light yellow in color, as cold as midnight to the tongue, but delicious to eat—it was called ice cream.

That second full day in Greenfield set the pattern for the two days that followed: eating, shopping and sightseeing. Amy was so totally in love with Greenfield that she had not dwelled on thoughts of Matthew or his absence from her unnecessarily. She prayed for him daily, but would then dismiss him from her thoughts, giving the Lord full charge over him, as she went about having the time of her young life.

On Wednesday evening Amy was dressing for the midweek prayer services she and her parents planned to attend. She sat before the mirror, her hair about her shoulders, curly and thick and glossy. She had arranged it first one way and then another and had studied all the effects from different angles, until her arms grew tired and she realized she didn't have long to dawdle.

A light tapping at her door caught her attention and she called out, "Who's there?"

"It's me . . . Flossie. Can I come in?"

Amy ran to the door, opened it and gave her a welcoming hug. "I'm glad to see you, but I'm afraid I won't have much time to visit. We're going to the church services tonight and I don't want to be late, but I can't seem to get my hair fixed just right."

Let me try, Miss Amy." Amy went back to the dressing table and sat down and Flossie took the hairbrush from her hand. "I'll brush it first."

Sighing gratefully Amy sank back in the chair. "If you have the time," she said simply.

Excitement animated Flossie's voice as she bubbled, "You have such nice thick hair, something the good Lord never embellished me with. I always wanted straight and heavy hair so I could do anything I wanted to with it. Mine is fine and it curls tight at the least little drop of humidity."

Amy sighed. "I wear braids a lot at home to keep from having to curl my hair. I've always thought how nice it would be to have curly hair and not have to bother with it."

"Do you think anybody is ever happy with the way the good Lord made them?" Flossie asked, her lips parting in a bright smile.

Amy laughed and shook her head. She studied Flossie in the mirror as she worked on her hair and when their eyes met she said, "You have such an air about you, Flossie. I feel as though I've always known you and you speak of the Lord so often. Do you . . . I mean are you a Christian, as I am?"

"I surely am," Flossie said, beaming. "I, too, have had a feeling that we must be kin, and we are—sisters in Christ! Ain't that something though?" She smiled sweetly at Amy and set the brush down and drew Amy's hair tight and high to the crown. She took pins from the dressing table and skillfully fastened her hair to the top of her head with little curls escaping here and there. Amy was enchanted with the outcome and studied her hairdo from every angle. She looked different somehow. Older. A difference she readily accepted.

"You are simply beautiful, Miss Amy," Flossie said, admiring her. "And hair is a woman's crowning glory!"

"Thank you kindly," Amy said serenely.

"Wish I could go to meeting with you tonight, but I have to work late. I wish . . ."

"You wish what, Flossie?"

"I wish you lived right here in Greenfield."

"I'd dearly love that too," Amy said solemnly, "but I can't be in two places at once and we'll have to be getting back home soon in case my Matthew comes home." Amy had already told Flossie of her plans to be married in December and Flossie had confided that she, too, was officially 'engaged' but her wedding date had not been decided on as yet.

Dusk was gathering and violet shadows were stealing forth from behind the trees, as the Bradshaws hurried through the crowded streets of Greenfield, borrowed Bibles from the inn clutched tightly in their hands. Their destination was a little Methodist Church located at the extreme southern end of the city.

The sweetness of September was a breeze sweeping down from the hilltops. The night sky was filled with stars and the Dipper hung low in the northwest. The moon was verging on the full, looking like a large golden pumpkin. The foliage was darkly outlined against the sky, and one could see the fanning of wings of the twilight birds. A bell tolled in the distance, announcing evening prayer meeting, and they hurried on.

Reverend Frederick O'Dell, pastor of the church, was an elderly man; tall and bending limberly under his age like an old willow. His spare body was encased in broadcloth, his dark eyes peering through spectacles. During the opening song and before he offered prayer, Pastor O'Dell cast an inquisitive glance at three strangers sitting on the front pew. He smiled warmly at them and asked John to stand and introduce his family. John obliged and they worshipped their heavenly Father in song and prayer, surrounded by a loving congregation of brothers and sisters in Christ.

After the prayer service John discussed the possibility of leaving Greenfield early the next morning. They all agreed they were homesick for the sights and smells of home. The prayer meeting on Wednesday night had only intensified their longings for familiar surroundings.

Amy was as excited at the thought of going home as she had been at the thought of traveling to Greenfield. She would miss Flossie, but she was anxious to see Jane Marie and Stephen again. She had to admit to herself she even missed Billy Joe. Her heart and soul belonged in her own valley and she would find it hard to relax until they were happily on their way.

Margaret had kissed Amy goodnight and she and John were preparing to go to their own room when Flossie came bounding up the stairs two at a time and strode into Amy's room. "I was hoping I'd get to see all of you again," she gasped, all out of breath.

"If you're ever down our way you be sure and come and see us," Amy said, knowing she would sorely miss the friendly and amiable girl after leaving Greenfield.

"I surely will, Miss Amy," Flossie said, smiling her best. "I'm purely tempted to hide in your buggy and make the trip with you."

"Come, John, it's time we went to our room and turned in. Four o'clock will come mighty early."

"If you're waiting on me, you're backing up, woman," John said humorously.

Margaret smiled fondly at Flossie. "Thanks for everything. You've been a delight!"

John handed Flossie an envelope. "To show our appreciation. You take care now." Flossie was beaming. She curtsied, and then with cheeks aflame gave John and Margaret both a big hug.

Amy was so thankful at having had the opportunity to come to Greenfield, seeing sights and people she would never forget, and yet the yearning in her heart for the familiar was overpowering. She fell asleep, the chorus of sounds below her, lulling her into a deep slumber.

Long before dawn on the morning of September 14, Amy awakened abruptly. No sound but those coming through her open window could be heard. She was aware of a tightness in her chest and stomach muscles. She lay still, staring at the ceiling and suddenly, without warning or knowing the reason why, she was crying. Hot, salty tears coursed down her cheeks and she turned her head into the feather pillow as great, choking sobs filled her throat. Foreboding of disaster was strong and potent within her.

CHAPTER 33

Shawnee Indians, burning with intense hatred toward the white man, crept into position and brown fingers tightened on tomahawks and guns. Killing innocent men, women and children was not abhorrent to them—it was a way of life. At the signal, a shrill call of a bobwhite, the Shawnee warriors, running from cabin to cabin throughout the settlements closest to the Green River, began their attack.

Long rifles cracked and shouts could be heard all over the surrounding territory.

Braves ran to and fro—their tomahawks raised in bloody battle, their pine-knot torches blazing. Settlers streamed from burning cabins, as thick black smoke blinded them and hung heavy in the cool damp air. Gunfire flickered here and there and the flames from the burning cabins glistened on the blades of the tomahawks as they reigned death and destruction in their path.

. . .

5:00 a.m.—Before the first soft light of morning hit the pines across the river, Jane Marie was adding another log to the fire. She was careful not to disturb Stephen as he slept, curled tightly in a quilt on the floor beside the stove. The rest of the family was still fast asleep behind the closed bedroom door. Jane Marie had risen early to have breakfast ready and on the table by the time everyone else awakened.

She was still in her nightclothes, reluctant to exchange her warm flannel gown and wrapper for a gingham frock. Her bare feet made no sound on the crude wooden floor as she went to the door, threw the bolt and opened it slowly. She shivered as the cool, damp air hit her bare feet. She started out of the door to get a few smaller logs to add to the slow-burning fire and heard what sounded like gun shots coming from the direction of Mandy and Jacob Swartz' cabin. Pensively she looked into the darkness, standing as quiet as a mouse, trying to hear above the frantic beating of her heart.

A smile tugged at her lips as she thought of Mandy. Jane Marie often visited with her these days, taking the twins over to play with her two little boys. This gave Mandy a few hours of much-needed rest while awaiting the birth of her third child, due in just a few short weeks.

In the distance other shots rang out and Jane Marie heard faint, muffled screams as they carried on the early morning wind. A trickle of fear danced up and down her spine and she quickly turned and closed the door. Her first thought had been to wake Stephen, but she was hesitant to do so if there was nothing amiss. She knew in her heart though that things were not just right. She took a hesitant step in Stephen's direction, closed her eyes and breathed a prayer. She licked her lips, her mouth dry and dusty, like old paper. "Please, God, don't let . . ."

While her eyes were closed and her prayer still forming on her lips, the door flew open and two dark savages, in full war paint, leaped into the room. Jane Marie's mouth dropped open and her heart pounded like a trip-hammer within her breast. Blood drummed in her ears and she drew a deep breath of air as a scream built in her throat. Her legs felt weak, as though they would give way beneath her and her fingers clenched into tight little fists as she faced her intruders. Only her eyes and the throb of her throat muscles betrayed her fear. The fetid, sickly odor of bear grease assailed her nostrils as the first Indian through the door hurled himself at her.

A guttural cry emerged from between his thin lips and with a sickly grin on his painted face and a fiendish gleam in his black eyes, he raised his tomahawk. Jane Marie's scream was cut off in mid-air as the tomahawk gave her a glancing blow to the side of her head, knocking her to the floor. The excited Indian was on the floor beside her seemingly lifeless body in seconds.

The twins were light sleepers and had lain awake since their father had crept from their bedroom a few minutes earlier. They were startled when they heard the strange noises that erupted from the kitchen. They opened the bedroom door at the same instant Stephen was so rudely awakened from his slumber by Jane Marie's screams. The twins, never having seen an Indian before, were not prepared for the sight that met their eyes.

A monstrous bear of a man, painted in brilliant colors, ran toward them, his arms waving wildly in the air, a deafening cry proceeding from his mouth. Bonnie and Betty's eyes danced from the Indian that rushed toward them to the Indian bent over the body of their sister, Jane Marie, now lying on the floor, blood pouring from a wound on her head and staining the dark floor boards beneath her.

Whimpering softly, the twins popped their thumbs into their mouths. They grabbed for one another's hands, then turned to run to the safety of their mother's arms. The Brave reached out and grabbed the twin nearest him and raised his powerful arm. It took but a second for the tomahawk to strike with deadly force. Bonnie dropped like a rag doll. Grabbing the other twin by the hair, the warrior jerked her back through the doorway and with one swift chop of the tomahawk, Betty's screams died in her throat, before they were even born.

Still groggy from sleep, Stephen grabbed his loaded musket that rested just mere inches from where his head had been resting just a moment before. With his heart hammering in his chest he jumped to his feet, a prayer on his lips.

Quickly his eyes swept the room. It had taken only seconds to snuff out the lives of Bonnie and Betty. Stephen had witnessed their brutal murders. He was torn with an urgency to help Jane Marie, but his heart also went out to the rest of her family who was now in mortal danger from the same Indian that had just killed the twins. He disappeared into the darkened bedroom, his tomahawk dripping blood.

With a strangled cry Stephen made his choice. He shook his head, filled with panic like he had never known before. "God, help us!" he cried fervently.

Instantly it seemed as though his senses sharpened, his mind cleared and with a bold and deliberate movement he advanced to where Jane Marie lay lifeless before him. Blood ran down the side of her face and collected in a pool on the bare wooden floor. A near-naked brave knelt over her body, his scalping knife in hand. As he clutched at Jane Marie's bloody hair, Stephen took careful aim with his long rifle and pulled the trigger. The gun exploded in Stephen's hands and the brave fell in a heap upon the floor, his knife falling from his lifeless fingers.

The stench of the Indian assailed Stephen's nostrils and he gulped air as tears filled his eyes and ran down his pale cheeks unchecked. He quickly grabbed up the brave's scalping knife and with one lunge he was through the McLins' bedroom door. Light from the kitchen spilled into the bedroom and Stephen's heart gave a lurch as he saw that he was too late to save Katherine and her young son, Winston. Katherine was sprawled half in and half out of the bed, Winston still clutched in her arms. Both had been tomahawked.

Bobby stood on the opposite side of his mother's bed whimpering softly. The Indian Brave jumped across the bed and grabbed his wrist. Raising his powerful arm, he was ready to reign death on the small child trembling before him. Stephen lunged across the bed and buried the knife in the warrior's back. The brave fell in a heap, knocking Bobby to the floor. Bobby screamed in terror when he saw the dead Indian sprawled across his legs. He kicked wildly and shoved frantically at the Indian's inert body.

With terror-filled eyes he looked at Stephen, and screamed out for his help.

As if in slow motion Stephen watched as the brave collapsed in a heap at Bobby's feet, wave after wave of shock slapping at him. He grabbed Bobby up in his arms and returned to the kitchen. With one foot he rolled the lifeless body of the Indian as far away from Jane Marie's body as he could, absently patting the sobbing Bobby on the back. Kneeling at Jane Marie's side he gently pried Bobby's arms from their death-grip around his neck. "Hush, Bobby," he whispered hoarsely. "Just let me set you down here on the floor and we'll see what we can do to wake Janey up. Can you be a big boy for Stephen?"

Is . . . is Janey hurt?" Bobby questioned between sobs.

"Yes, my boy, but you must be quiet now," he cautioned, "there might be more Indians about and we don't want to call attention to them."

Bobby was an obedient child and loved and trusted Stephen. He allowed Stephen to release the hold he had on him. Putting his finger to his lips, Stephen walked to the open door and peered into the murky light. After he had assured himself there were no more Indians about the cabin, he closed the door, drew the bolt and returned to Jane Marie's side.

Blood was coming from a blow to her head, oozing down over her forehead and covering her face. Her eyes were closed but she was still breathing. He quickly grabbed a towel and tore it into strips and bound Jane Marie's scalp wound as best he could, to staunch the bleeding. Tears clogged his throat and he found it difficult to breathe as he stared into her ashen face.

After attending as best he could to her wound, Stephen ran into the bedroom, grabbed a quilt from the bed and returned to the kitchen. He covered Jane Marie's body with the quilt. Holding her hand he bowed his head and prayed aloud: "Dear Lord, please let this nightmare end soon. And please, Lord, give me the strength and the knowledge to protect Jane Marie and Bobby this day, even giving my own life in their stead if need be."

Jane Marie stirred at the sound of his voice and tears formed behind her quivering eyelids. A slight moan escaped her lips. Stephen looked in utter frustration into his dearly beloved's face, faintly aware that his tears were dropping onto her face and mingling with her own.

Totally bewildered as to what to do next, Stephen turned to Bobby and his heart melted. Bobby was staring at Jane Marie, tears running unchecked down his cheeks and his mouth moving but no words were being uttered. "You sit here beside your sister, Bobby. I have something I have to do but I will be right back. Do you understand?"

Bobby never flinched, just absently patted the still form of Jane Marie, his eyes blank with shock.

Stephen went into the bedroom and quickly picked up the bodies of the twins and carefully laid them on the bed with Winston and Katherine. Then it struck him. *Where was Kenneth?*

Unbeknownst to Stephen, Kenneth McLin had aroused shortly before daybreak and had made his way outside to have a drink of corn liquor that he kept hidden in the lean-to behind the cabin. He had just raised the jug to his lips when he heard the first gunshots in the far distance and minutes later the screams of his own children. Kenneth knew his family was under attack and yet he remained huddled on the dirt floor, trying to clear his head. His gun was in the cabin and he had no way of protecting himself without it, should he be discovered. Fearing the cabin would soon go up in smoke, he hurled himself into the weeds and bushes behind the cabin. He ran sobbing, thrashing his way through the woods, oblivious to the noise that he was making.

A lone warrior running through the woods toward the river heard his sobs and stepped behind a huge cottonwood. Kenneth raced in a frenzy, running for his life, giving no thought to his family. His throat burned with the acrid smell of smoke that lingered in the air. The shooting had ceased to reach his eardrums. No bird sang. The only sound he heard was his own labored breathing and his heavy boots clomping the underbrush.

Abruptly, out of the gloom of the forest, a stocky figure stepped from behind a tree into his path, a war club in his hand. Kenneth

McLin's whiskey-washed eyes winced and he stopped dead in his tracks, whimpering. All he could see was a dark painted face, one corner of the mouth twisting evilly, a jagged scar running from the mouth to one ear. Even in his dazed condition, he knew he was in trouble and he began to curse. He cursed the red devil that loomed formidably before him and he cursed God in His heaven for bringing him to this end.

The warrior raised his club over Kenneth's head and hit him, knocking him to his knees. Kenneth's head felt disconnected from his shoulders. He heaved for air as a wave of dizziness swept over him. Blood ran into his eyes and the sound of his heartbeats in his ears, sounded like drums. In a haze he saw the Indian staring at him.

"Have wife," he panted hoarsely, "and three... beautiful... daughters. Can have all... just let me go..." Kenneth's head throbbed, his eyes were glassy and his face was turning blue.

The Shawnee warrior understood not a word Kenneth McLin said. He broke into loud cries as he brandished his bloody war club over Kenneth's head and in a tone of utter disgust he cried in Shawnee: "You mewling coward of a paleskin!" He hit Kenneth another glancing blow.

Everything went black and Kenneth McLin slumped to the forest floor. He was no braver in death than he had been in life and he died with a curse on his lips. The Indian Brave spit on his lifeless body and drew his scalping knife.

CHAPTER 34

5:30 a.m., September 14, 1786—September's blush deepened in the hills of Kentucky and the approach of Indian Summer was herald by hot sunlight and grass-scented breezes. Yellow plumes of goldenrod glowed over the meadows and the lavender and purple fencerow asters were more beautiful than ever, as they mingled their bloom of color with that of the bright spangle of bittersweet berries.

During the early morning hours fog crept in silently and laid a fine mist over the entire river valley. Bats stitched back and forth across the night sky, feeding on fat mosquitoes, oblivious to the fog creeping up the hillside.

With a rippling of movement a renegade band of brightly-painted Shawnee warriors silently slipped from a copse of whispering cottonwood saplings and entered the swiftly moving current of the Green River. Clad in doeskin moccasins and breechcloths, their faces and bodies thick with war paint, their paddles silent, they sped toward their destination, well armed with bows, muskets, tomahawks, knives and clubs.

The unsuspecting valley slept peacefully under a tent of darkness as the gentle night-breezes brought a sweet-winey smell of wild grapes down from the hilltops, mingling with the tantalizing fragrance of tall clover. Monotonous lapping sounds of river water against the shoreline could be heard as the war party, black eyes glittering, advanced on sleeping villages.

Most of the cabins in New Hope lay shrouded in darkness. Ruby Willis had risen early, her face bearing traces of fatigue and had shuffled noiselessly across the worn plank floor from her bedroom to her kitchen. She lighted her oil lamp and prepared to start her day, the glare from the lamp dazzling her half-closed eyes to wakefulness.

Ruby sniffed the air daintily, savoring the faint odor of yesterday's cabbage and a delicate breath of wintergreen as it floated in the room, full of the pale dusk of dawn. She shivered in spite of the heat from the hearth, uneasiness filling her entire being. Shaking her head she brushed at a snow-white lock of hair at her brow, at odds with herself for feeling so skittish.

Roscoe and Billy Joe were still sleeping soundly but out of the gloom and stillness there came to Ruby the sound of Roscoe's dear voice, pleasant-spoken as always. *What's got you all fired up this morning, pet? You seem a bit anxious.*

Ruby shivered, blinked her eyes and gingerly poked at glowing coals of the fire and added a log to the still bright embers. The firm ticking of the clock did little to sooth her frayed nerves. She shook her head as if to clear it and whispered, "I must be getting old and childish, Lord, looking for ghosts in a closet. Please forgive me."

Sandy stirred and rose at the sound of her voice, stretched his shaggy body and padded to the door. He cocked his head and whined softly as he scratched at its base, looking expectantly at Ruby with dark, somber eyes.

"You feel it too, my friend?" Ruby gently stroked Sandy's broad head, her arthritic fingers stiff and aching with the effort. "We'll just have a go at getting some breakfast fixed around here and see if that don't liven us up a wee bit, eh?" She drew a great shuddering sigh, her knees feeling weak beneath her, and her pulse thrummed. Forcibly she calmed herself, squelching her misgivings. She picked up the water bucket, unbolted the door and reached for the latchstring.

Sandy nuzzled her hand as the heavy plank door silently opened beneath her touch. Ruby paused and eyed Roscoe's rifle resting on two pegs within easy reach. Then shook her head and dismissing her thoughts as nothing more than the jitters, she stepped out into the chill morning air, her white shawl pulled tightly about her head and shoulders.

The cabin stood stark against the sky in the first pink fingers of dawn as she slowly made her way to the well. Her breath twinkled, a faint cloud in the frosty air. She looked to the edge of the woodland where sumacs stood like giant Sioux war bonnets and with the rising of the sun would stand brilliant against the yellowing green of oak and willow and shivered once more.

Close at her side, Sandy sniffed the air and suddenly stiffened, a low, rumbling growl sounding deep within his throat, his hackles rising. Galvanized into a hairy fury, he hurled himself into the semi-darkness. A chill struck Ruby's heart. Little given as she was to foreboding of evil, when once she was possessed of one, it became a reality. An expression of desperate resolution now came into her wrinkled, but beautiful face.

"Land O'Goshen!" she exclaimed, as she stopped dead in her tracks. She gazed back toward the cabin, to the orchard on the slope, and then at the great sweep of cleared land that reached down to the river. She looked and listened, straining both her eyes and ears.

"What is it, Lord? What has caused Sandy and me to be all in a dither?" She pressed a hand against her thudding heart and then she spied an inky form, slinking with lowered belly, across the wide expanse of cleared ground. Before she could react, a blood-curdling war cry and a pain-filled yelp from Sandy echoed across the valley. In a verge of frenzy an Indian leapt out at her, like a wild hyena.

With speed that belied her years, Ruby turned to her left and clamped her arthritic fingers tightly around the handle of the empty water bucket and with a prayer on her lips, made an attempt to gain the safety of her cabin. She stumbled over the rough ground, oblivious to the burning pain in her chest and her tortured, ragged breathing.

The swift, running warrior grabbed for her long-flowing white hair and threw her roughly to the ground, bruising her severely. He overpowered her with the stench of rancid bear grease. In terrified silence she faced her adversary, as she knew she would face her Maker in but a moment of time. For a split second silence ruled her world—no bird sang, no insect buzzed.

Ruby glimpsed dozens of black ducks, silent as shadows, skimming the naked treetops, wings swiftly beating, necks outstretched, as foul breath rushed into her nostrils and greasy brown hands clawed at her hair. A knee pressed cruelly into her stomach and a tomahawk was raised menacingly above her head.

Suddenly Sandy was at her side, deep growls rising from his throat. He lunged, throwing all his massive weight on the Indian's back and sent him sprawling. Ruby felt the weight of his body leave her and she instinctively rolled to the opposite side he had fallen. In seconds, Sandy had severed the warrior's jugular vein with his sharp teeth, killing him instantly.

Sandy whined and licked at Ruby's face as she threw her arms around his neck. "Go, Sandy," she whispered in his ear. "Go to Roscoe and Billy Joe." As she spoke a roar of gunfire split the air. Sandy made a wild dash in the direction of the cabin and as the mist began to clear Ruby could see Billy Joe's figure faintly outlined in the open doorway of her cabin, smoke from the gun he held in his hands circling his head.

Rising with great difficulty, Ruby threw the water bucket she still had clenched tightly in her hand aside and gingerly made her way to the safety of the cabin. Billy Joe squatted in the doorway, his arms wound tightly around Sandy's neck, wracked with sobs and tears flowing freely down his cheeks. Roscoe stood behind him, a loaded musket in his hands.

"Did you get him, my boy?" Roscoe asked anxiously.

Billy Joe released his grip on Sandy's neck and stood, wiping the tears from his eyes with the sleeve of his nightshirt. "I . . . I got him, Rock," Billy Joe said, heaving a dry sob. Ruby limped into sight and Billy Joe gasped. "Rock! It's Ruby! She's fine, she's . . ."

Ruby put one arm around Billy Joe and gave him a hug then reached out and put both arms around Roscoe's shoulders. "I'm fine, my darling. Really I am. A bit bruised and unsettled, but I'm fine. Now let's get ourselves behind closed doors before any more intruders show up."

Quickly Ruby herded them into the kitchen. Sandy, sniffing and nosing around the body of the Indian Billy Joe had killed, followed them into the cabin, the plank door closing securely behind them, double barred and bolted.

. . .

Days had drifted slowly into weeks then into months and Matthew had an intense desire to be home with his loved ones. After arriving in Danville back in June he had met with other delegates at the convention, time after time, with nothing gained it seemed. He was getting more frustrated as time went by with all the delays at the convention. Other young men joined ranks with General Logan's volunteers, helping the Militia, and Matthew had been persuaded to accompany them. He agreed because he was under the impression that he would be doing his country a valuable service.

The eastern part of the nation was alarmed at the rapid growth of the western country. The delegates from Kentucky that had been meeting in Danville for months were now prepared to vote for separation from Virginia and gain their admission into the Union. (Unbeknownst to Matthew and other interested parties it would be many harrowing years before Virginia's authority over Kentucky would end and they would be able to see clearly a solution to their troubled state of affairs. Kentucky would not be admitted to the Union, as a separate state, until June 1, 1792.)

General Logan's volunteers had spent months helping to destroy and plunder Indian villages. While Matthew served with the Militia, several Indian prisoners were captured and were to be taken to Danville for confinement and possible trade later on for White captives. Very disillusioned by this time with the whole set-up, the campaign now proving that it had been something of a farce, Matthew signed up for the return march to Danville.

He found himself on the evening of August 31, lying on the ground, staring up between the boughs of a sycamore tree. As twilight deepened, a warm gust of air stirred the leaves of the tree and rustled through the grass around him. In the distance a yellow gleam from numerous lighted windows could be seen flickering like huge fireflies in the deepening shadows. His two traveling companions had pestered him long and hard to join them at one of the local taverns for a bit of ale. Mathew had been adamant in his refusal, choosing instead to spend time alone, away from the gabble of human voices, dreaming of his family and of his impending reunion with them.

The busy sounds of activity in Danville had died away and women had called their children in from play and closed their doors. The odor of wood smoke permeated the air about Matthew and mingled with that of rich, savory cooking odors. His stomach growled, reminding him it was suppertime and he pulled out some beef jerky and a bag of parched corn. He ate his fill, his meager fair causing a fresh tide of homesickness to well up within him.

He had been gone from home much too long. He missed Roscoe and Ruby, John, Margaret and Billy Joe, and even thinking of Sandy wrung his heart. But most of all Matthew missed his beloved Amy. A lazy smile creased his face just thinking about her.

Every moment Matthew was not with Amy seemed empty and wasted.

Heavy clouds obscured the full moon as Matthew lay in the darkness. Thoughts of home and family rushed unchecked through his head. A foreboding persisted in his mind that something had or was about to happen. It was palpable, something he felt he could reach out and touch—something evil. Matthew shivered though it was a warm night and a mixture of concern and fear washed across his face.

Tomorrow, the good Lord willing, he would be on his way home—back to his loved ones. He pictured Amy in the open doorway of their own little cabin as he came riding into view. She would be wearing his favorite blue dress and her arms would be extended in welcome, trembling with eagerness to hold him, a smile of enchantment touching her lips.

"I'm coming home, Amy," he whispered softly into the night air. "And I'll never leave you again, darling—I promise." It wasn't until the moon was in its Zenith that Matthew's thoughts slowly dwindled and he fell asleep.

The next day Matthew and his friends traveled as fast as they could with a minimum of stops, but it seemed as though Fate intervened, putting stumbling blocks in their path at every turn. Matthew's palomino, Honey, went lame just several hours out of Danville. Matthew hoped a couple of day's rest would be all she would need before they could resume their travels. Having raised her from a colt, it was like cutting off his own right arm when her leg didn't heal and he had to do some quick trading with a farmer before he could continue his journey home.

Matthew's spirits sank even lower when one traveling companion, Hank Wade, became too ill to travel. Hank insisted on being left behind, but it had taken several days before Matthew was assured that he was comfortably settled and would be well taken care of. Matthew felt guilty leaving Hank with strangers, but he had already lost too many traveling days. His need for family overruled any thoughts he might have entertained about delaying his trip further waiting on Hank to get well enough to travel.

It was a little after midnight, September 14, and Matthew and his lone companion, Curly Daniels, made a quick camp in a thicket of scrub cedars near a clear-running stream. They were dog-tired and still several hours from home.

They unsaddled their weary and lathered horses and hobbled them in a grassy glade. Curly wrapped himself in his blanket and was snoring softly in a matter of minutes. Matthew closed his eyes, one hand holding tightly to his flintlock, and gradually the sound of his friend's snoring, the frog's clamor in the shallows, and the wind as it made musical sounds in the needlelike foliage, were lost to him.

. . .

It was an amber dawn. Clouds, yellowish-brown in color and looking like huge, winged creatures, turned the pale red sunrise in the eastern sky to amber. Buzzards glided in circles, their red beady eyes fixed upon a settlement that now lay in smoldering ruins. The shooting had stopped. The Indians had ceased their yipping. Grinning and thrusting their weapons at the sky, they sprinted away. The siege had lasted forty minutes, but for the survivors of the attack, it seemed an interminable lifetime.

The warriors had struck with deadly accuracy. The settlers had fought bravely, but taken unawares as they were, their fatalities were great. Out of 140 men, women and children now living in or near New Hope, thirty-two now lay dead. Ten more were wounded, some critically. Whole families had been scalped and homes plundered and burned. Tears stung the eyes of even the stoutest of men as they performed their grisly duty—trying to bring order out of chaos.

The restless energy of summer was about to be distilled into another season for the settlers of New Hope. Just as the leaves were beginning to fall, so fell the settlement, under a siege of death. Death had come suddenly, laden with the odor of windfall apples in the orchard and the voice of autumn echoing across the valley.

. . .

Matthew's head ached and the muscles of his back and legs were sore, but his mind was sharp and clear. The horses, having had several hours rest and plenty of grass to eat were eager to go. Matthew still felt a strong pull toward home. It was more than his dreams to be reunited with Amy; it was an urgency deep within forcing him home.

A breeze rippled the leaves in the treetops. The ash trees were loaded with red berries and Matthew recalled the old lore, that this meant a year for evil spirits. But Matthew wasn't superstitious and neither were the birds since they were busy in the rowans just now. Thoughts of Amy, the woman in her just beginning to show, had kept Matthew going for over three months. Now at last he could put those months behind him.

Matthew and Curly had been riding for three hours in and out of hills and valleys. Cattle now dotted the hillsides and everything looked beautiful and peaceful. There was a sweetness in the air, the tantalizing fragrance of tall clover mingled with that of the cidery smell of apples, fermenting in the grass. Matthew was glad to be back in familiar territory once more.

He pictured his family going about their daily chores: Margaret, humming gaily and bustling about the kitchen, cleaning, baking and spoiling everyone to death. John would be busy in the hay field or chopping wood or mending fence or half a dozen other things he always found to do about the farm. Then there was Amy. Matthew knew he was in for some pretty tall explanations as to why he hadn't written in all the time that he had been gone. He was praying hard that Amy would understand.

In spite of his delays, Matthew knew he had much to be thankful for. There had been no unexpected run-ins with roving Indians and he was hale and hearty, other than being just plain homesick.

Matthew pulled rein on his sorrel atop a rise of ground overlooking the Green River. He lifted his hat and wiped his brow on the sleeve of his shirt and surveyed the lay of the land before him. Mounded hills and the shallow but swift-moving river winding through hills lay across their path. The maples, the birch and beech trees were already turning yellow, orange and red, showing up as bright patches on a dark blanket of evergreen.

Taking his canteen from the pommel of his saddle Matthew took a sip of the lukewarm water and continued to study the terrain before him. His forehead wrinkled in concern as he stood in his stirrups and strained to see as far as he could in all directions. There was no sign of life, animal or human, but something was niggling at him, and gooseflesh rose on the back of his neck.

Just a couple of hours more, Matthew thought happily, grinning like a Cheshire cat. His spurs raked his horse's side and the animal broke into a lope. Curly spurred his own horse and kept pace.

By the position of the sun Matthew estimated it was two hours short of noon. They were close to the boundary of Jacob Swartz' spread, marked by an orchard that crowned a grassy hill. Reaching the crest of the hill, Matthew sniffed the air apprehensively. He smelled smoke. He looked towards the river and saw clouds of thick smoke hanging in the air. He could see buzzards, high in the sky, making their endless circles in the yellowish-brown sky. Matthew's face clouded with uneasiness and fear and uncertainty replaced his happiness of only moments ago.

"There's something wrong, Curly," Matthew said, as he jerked on the reins, the muscles of his face tight. Matthew stood in his stirrups and frowned as he scanned the terrain carefully in every direction. He saw nothing unusual except for the smoke and the ever-circling buzzards.

Matthew removed his hat and spanked the sorrel. He dug in his spurs and shouted, "Let's go, Curly, but keep a watchful eye!" With the sound of their horses' hooves drumming in their ears, the two friends rode hard, being watchful, surveying the lower ground in all directions as they rode.

Matthew and Curly, their faces white and drawn, were stricken at the scene they soon rode upon. Matthew's heart pounded with fear and dread as he approached the ruins that had once been the Swartz home. It was now reduced to nothing more than charred embers, smoke still rising from the ashes. Tracks of unshod ponies were everywhere.

Jacob sat cross-legged and slump-shouldered, his face white, in the space that had once held everything near and dear to him. Blood had dried on his face from a gash over his left eye and his shirt was dark-stained about the middle. A blanket, stained with blood, covered a mound before him. Jacob was so ensnared by his own thoughts and grief he failed to detect Curly and Matthew's approach.

Springing from his horse like a great cat, Matthew ran to Jacob's side. For a moment he felt light-headed, acrid smell of smoke filling his nostrils, and the smell of death in the air. He looked into Jacob's face. His eyes were clouded with confusion and shock and intolerable pain that brought tears to Matthew's eyes.

"You hurt bad, Jacob?" Matthew gasped as he kneeled beside his friend, the morning sun beating gently upon their heads.

Jacob blinked, his dark eyes wide and unfocused. "Wha... what?" he croaked, his face pasty white rather than the usual bronzered.

"How bad are you hurt?" Matthew repeated.

Jacob's eyes rolled and he drew in a slow, shuddering breath. "Not bad... ain't bad at all... do believe I'll make it."

Matthew examined the cut above his eye. It wasn't as bad as it looked except for all the dried blood. He opened Jacob's shirt and saw a deep, rather ragged gash running from under his right arm to his waist. This wound was still bleeding slightly. Matthew quickly ran to his horse and got his canteen and a piece of muslin. He gave Jacob a drink of water and then poured the rest of it over his wound. He tore the muslin into long strips and bound Jacob from just under his arms to below his waist. "That ought to help stop the bleeding, Jacob. Can you tell me what happened?"

"It was first thing this mornin'... they was on us, Matthew... 'fore we even knew they was about!" Jacob looked at the mound before him. "They're gone, Matthew. They're all gone—Mandy an' the babe, Johnny an' Ethan. Oh, God, Matthew, my whole family's gone!" He burst into tears, the sobs shaking his whole body.

Rocking gently on his heels Matthew squeezed Jacob's shoulder. "I'm sorry, Jacob. I'm truly sorry." Jacob's eyes narrowed and he looked at Matthew out of pain-filled and tear-washed eyes. "I hate to leave you like this, but... I have to go and find my own family, Jacob. Do you understand what I'm saying?"

"Yes, my boy," Jacob said in a daze. "But I imagine your family is just fine. They... they wasn't here when those red devils... when those murderin' red devils..."

Matthew hunched forward and grabbed Jacob by the shoulder. "Not here? If they aren't here, then where are they?" he interrupted his heartbeat faltering.

Jacob blinked slowly. "Why... they... they was in... in Greenfield, Matthew." Jacob fixed his eyes on Matthew's face. "John asked me . . . ." Jacob's voice sank so low Matthew could barely understand him. "I was . . . tendin' your place . . . don't know if they burned it or not."

Matthew sighed. He had no idea what his family was doing in Greenfield, but he thanked God for the fact that they hadn't been home at the time of the attack. Looking helplessly up at Curly, who had been sitting astride his horse, Matthew said, "I imagine you want to be off to your own place, Curly. Go on and as soon as I get Jacob settled I'll be off myself. God bless you, Curly. I hope . . . I pray you find your family is . . ."

Curly tipped his hat, spurred his horse and rode off, not waiting for Matthew to finish his sentence. "Thanks, Matt," he called back over his shoulder, "I'll be in touch."

Over the loud buzzing of flies, Matthew opened his canteen and filled it at Jacob's well. He handed it to Jacob and said, "I hate to be traveling on, but I must go and check out the neighbors. I'll be back to help . . ." He glanced helplessly to the blanket-shrouded mound and back again to Jacob.

"Don't you fret 'bout me, Matthew. I'll take care of my own," Jacob said tonelessly. "I . . . I've got a lot of . . . of fight in me yet."

Matthew nodded and anxiously took his leave.

CHAPTER 35

Until now, Matthew had always thought he had been a fair man, looking at both sides before forming an opinion. He had felt a certain sympathy for the red man, feeling that he had been betrayed and lied to repeatedly. Treaties had held little meaning to the white man, especially when it came to the land the Indians lived on. But Matthew's here-to-fore sympathy started fading and was replaced by a cold fury as the day progressed.

Riding through the countryside, it was difficult for Matthew to realize that Death had lurked among these sunlit woods earlier in the day. Tanagers, bluebirds, cardinals and an infinite number of warblers now whistled and sang while flitting from tree to tree. Here and there a cottontail and an occasional deer bound away before him as he made his way through myrtle and honeysuckle tangles to his homestead.

It was almost more than Matthew could have dared hoped for. John and Margaret's cabin was still standing. The Indians had set fire to it, but miraculously, only the better part of the kitchen had burned away. The phlox was like a flame in the garden and zinnias and chrysanthemums were ablaze with color in various flowerbeds that Margaret had so lovingly tended all summer.

Nothing seemed to be missing from the barn and the chickens

were still scratching away in the dry grass. Matthew assumed the Indians had been in too much of a hurry to steal their belongings and livestock.

Buttercup had been lying curled up into a ball when Matthew came riding in. She lazily stood and stretched then walked on silent feet to where Matthew stood. She rubbed up against his leg, arched her back and looked up at him and mewed as if to welcome him home. Matthew reached down and picked her up and nuzzled her head under his chin. "Glad to see me home, eh? Well, I'm glad to be here, let me tell you." He rubbed her gently. "How many lives did you use up during the attack, Buttercup?" Buttercup purred contentedly in reply. Gritting his teeth, Matthew set her on her feet, remounted, and rode at a gallop toward his own cabin. His thudding heart told him it was probably gone.

"But not my family, dear Lord. I thank you for that miracle! I can accept what I find done to my home, just knowing my family is safe."

Reaching his own clearing, Matthew realized the Indians had missed his cabin all together. He could hardly contain his joy. He bent his head reverently and again thanked his heavenly Father who had spared him the anguish so many others were feeling that day.

His cabin stood as it had long months before. Standing before the garden gate he closed his eyes and drank in the smell of flowers, grass and the ripeness of the land.

Opening his eyes he looked about him: at the shine of goldenrod in the fence corners; the glow of little white asters in the meadow; the scarlet gleam of dogwood berries and sumac clumps twined in the aspens along the river.

Snowy white clouds moved in the blue sky and the flowers in the fields dipped with the breeze. Matthew was home again—and it was intoxicating. He could not resist going into the cabin. The cool interior invited him into an alluring emptiness. Amy's presence was everywhere. He felt her presence in every room where he walked, in each piece of furniture they had put in place. The smell of spice and herbs and lavender permeated the air that he breathed. A fire had been laid at the hearth, only waiting to be lighted to make the house come alive. And soon they would light that fire—together, as God had intended from the beginning of time.

Matthew was tired—bone-weary tired. He would have liked nothing better than to lie across the feather mattress, kick off his dusty boots and sleep for a week. But he realized he had wasted too much time already. He had so many people to check on. His thoughts included Roscoe, Ruby, Billy Joe, and the McLin's and Stephen. "I pray Lord, that Stephen has been looking out for them all . . ."

The quietness surrounding the cabin produced its own calming effect on Matthew. He rode out at a more leisurely pace across a meadow, through a shallow brook toward Roscoe's cabin about a mile from his own, as the crow flies. Reaching Roscoe's spread, Matthew spied the bodies of two Indians lying in the yard, a few feet apart, partially covered with blankets. Only their arms and moccasins were showing. His face blanched. Already the bodies were attracting attention of huge numbers of wheeling turkey buzzards and black flies.

For a fraction of time, Matthew felt he was now a part of the death and destruction that lay all around him. His hand tightened its hold on his musket. Living would never again be taken for granted. It would be cherished as a gift from God and each day would be savored. Time stood still for no man and Death awaited one and all.

But he was young and strong and he felt optimistic. He would soon be reunited with his family and together they would look to a brighter future.

Hesitantly Matthew walked toward the door that was tightly closed against the warm day. He heard no sound from within. He reached for the handle just as the door burst open and Billy Joe threw himself into Matthew's waiting arms. Joy filled Matthew's heart as he spied Ruby and Roscoe sitting beside the hearth, from all indications, hale and hearty. Sandy almost bowled him over in his eagerness to reach him. There was bedlam as everyone started talking at once.

After spending time with Roscoe and Ruby and learning all about their harrowing experiences and flirtations with death, Matthew left Billy Joe with the Willis' and made his way to the McLin home. He agonized over what he might find. He was too tired and numb by this time to pray. He only whispered "God, help me," over and over as he rode toward his destination, fearing what savage things had been done to his friends.

He was overjoyed to see the McLin cabin still standing. He could see two bodies in the tall grass in the front yard, but again he was met with a stillness that was immeasurable. He wiped the sweat from his eyes with the sleeve of his shirt and flung himself off his lathered horse. Gripping his musket tightly in his hand he skirted the bodies in the yard, fanning at the bluebottle flies that buzzed around his head. Bone-weary and more discouraged than he had ever been in his entire life, he armed himself with a boldness he didn't really feel and pounded on the door.

The door slowly opened and in an unabashed display of affection, Matthew was grasped in Stephen's strong embrace. "Thank God you've come, Matt," Stephen breathed. He pulled Matthew into the small kitchen and closed and bolted the door behind them. As Matthew's eyes became adjusted to the dimness in the small kitchen he saw Bobby sitting on a chair, chewing on a dry biscuit. Stephen motioned Matthew into the bedroom.

Jane Marie now lay on her mother's bed. She was pale, white as bleached muslin and so still—still as death. Stephen knelt on the floor beside the bed and took one of Jane Marie's hands into his own. He groaned and looked up at Matthew. Matthew read the pain in his eyes.

"Today has been a nightmare, Matt, and I need your help. I would like to borrow your horse and get Janey into the village. She needs a doctor in the worst way."

Matthew crossed the small space, the loose flooring creaking under his weight, and looked into Jane Marie's face. She lay quietly beneath the folds of a quilt, her head swathed in torn strips of bloody cloth. Matthew's belly muscles tightened and he flinched as though he had been hit.

"I've got to get her to a doctor! She's never really gained consciousness and I'm so scared, Matt." Suddenly, Stephen was sobbing, the tension of the last few hours having taken its toll on him. "Oh God, Matt, why did this happen? How . . . ?"

Not knowing what to do or say, Matthew patted Stephen's back comfortingly. "Thank God I was here, Matt, or . . . or . . . they would have all been killed. "Thank you, God," he said hoarsely as fresh tears burned his eyes and throat then slowly made their way down his cheeks. He was hosting a day's growth of whiskers that showed up darkly on his pale face. Stephen brushed awkwardly at his tears with an unsteady hand and slowly regaining composure, rose from his knees.

"Where are the others?" Matthew's eyes roved the room. It was strangely devoid of life. "Katherine and Winston? And the twins, Stephen?"

Stephen shook his head sadly. Wrapping the quilt around Jane Marie's unconscious form, Stephen picked her up tenderly in his arms, hardly feeling her weight, and made his way to the kitchen door. "They're . . . they're gone, Matthew. All of them. Except for Kenneth, and I haven't seen him all morning. He's probably out in the woods sleeping off a good one. I put Katherine and the children in the lean-to, until . . ." He looked helplessly at Bobby who was staring at the two of them, barely aware of his surroundings, and strangely quiet.

When Stephen walked out the door with his precious bundle, the sun was shining brightly and the birds were chirping merrily. He took a quick glance at the bodies lying in the yard. "I'll help to bury them when I get back," he said, "and I'll bring your horse back just as soon as I can." Without another word Stephen rode off with Jane Marie held tightly in his arms.

Zachary Reynolds, the doctor from the nearest fort, was tending to the wounded in the back of Philip Harman's barbershop. Stephen didn't want to leave Jane Marie's side once he got her into the doctor's hands, but he had been dismissed from the room while the doctor examined her.

Forty-five agonizing minutes later, the doctor walked quietly out of the room and closed the door behind him. He removed his spectacles and absently cleaned the lens with his handkerchief. "Reverend Cranston," he said with quiet dignity, "I won't belie the fact that your friend is in critical condition. I've examined the wound to her head and I must be truthful in telling you that I've never seen a wound such as this that didn't . . . well, that didn't end in death."

Stephen gasped and started for the room where his beloved lay. The kindly doctor grabbed his arm and pulled him away from the door. "I must forbid you to enter, young man. If she has any chance at all, she must remain quiet. Go home now and return in a few hours. I should know one way or the other by then." He shook his head sadly and went about his business of tending to the other wounded and dying.

Stephen walked out of the building in a daze. He knew he had a job to do. There were countless other people who needed his consoling words of comfort and help was badly needed clear across the valley. As he surveyed the carnage of his flock, he realized there were few families that hadn't lost at least one loved one or had one injured. No one had been spared—men, women and children alike had been injured or slaughtered unmercifully.

Despondent in heart and soul, Stephen rode back to the McLin homestead. After taking Bobby to the Willis' for safe keeping, he and Matthew worked several hours side-by-side helping those in direst need. Soldiers from the fort were everywhere at once. They had found Kenneth McLin's body and buried it where it had fallen—mute testimony of his futile attempt to reach a safe haven from the Indian attack.

At three that afternoon, Stephen found himself back at Jane Marie's side. She had just regained consciousness a few minutes before he arrived. He kneeled beside her cot, holding her hand and prayed aloud: "Please dear Lord, let my darling live, if it be thy will. And help me, Lord God, to trust you not only in good times but also in the darkest hours of my life. I can't imagine life without her, Lord. I need her beside me and covet her gentle ways and appealing laughter. Her faith in you alone should merit thy mercy, Lord."

Jane Marie stirred at the sound of his voice and a soft moan escaped her lips. Her face was black and blue and her eyes were just tiny slits in her swollen face. She winced as she slowly turned her face toward the presence beside her.

"I'm here, sweetheart," Stephen said anxiously. "Please, darling, speak to me." He waited anxious moments and slowly she tried to focus her eyes on his own.

"Stephen?" she whispered hoarsely.

"Yes, sweetheart. I'm here."

"Wha . . . wha . . . ha . . . happened?" In a space of just a moment full realization hit Jane Marie and she screamed out a long, wailing cry. A cry so piteous in its sound that Stephen's heart broke all over again.

Doctor Reynolds came running and moved quickly to the cot Jane Marie was lying on. He took her hand and felt of her pulse. He merged slender, silvery brows and heaved a deep sigh. Straightening slowly he rested a blue-veined hand on Stephen's shoulder and grimly shook his head. He had been schooled to exercise total self-control. He had been practicing for thirty years and still found it difficult to accept such senseless waste of life. The Indian attack on New Hope and other outlying settlements bordered on madness. He brushed at a tear as he walked away.

Stephen gathered Jane Marie into his arms and gently rocked her back and forth, crooning to her, "Hush, my darling. I'm here. I love you so much and you need all your strength to get well for me."

Jane Marie's sobs finally subsided. She put her arms around Stephen's neck and he gently kissed the tears from her swollen eyelids. He then kissed each cheek and finally rested his lips gently on hers, trying to impart his strength into her with his kiss.

"Is Ma all right?" she asked in a tormented voice. "And the twins and Bobby and Winston? Stephen . . . tell me . . . are they . . . ?"

Stephen's heart skipped a beat as he laid her gently back onto the cot. He pulled the blanket up to her chin and whispered, "They're all . . . all fine, Janey," he sobbed, unable to go on. He rested his hands on his knees, bowed his head and great sobs shook him.

Jane Marie stared at him. "Please, Stephen, tell . . . me . . . the tru . . . truth."

Stephen raised his tear-swollen eyes and looked into Jane Marie's eyes sorrowfully. "They . . . they didn't make it, honey," he said quietly. "Bobby is the only one left. But please, don't think about it, just concentrate on getting well. I love you, Janey—I need you . . ."

Jane Marie put one small finger to Stephen's lips. "Le . . . let me speak, Stephen. I haven't much time. I . . . I have to make you understand how much I . . . I love you. I want to thank you for the happiness you've given me. I'm . . . I'm just sorry . . . ." Her voice was getting faint and her eyelids closed. " . . . sorry . . . I . . . have . . . to . . . leave you. But I have to go and meet Ma and the . . . others . . ."

Stephen stood, lifted her once more into his arms and walked through the door and out into the bright sunshine. His tears dropped on her cheeks as he sat down beneath a huge willow tree, Jane Marie's small form held tightly to his bosom. He could feel her flesh quivering through the thin blanket and held her tighter. "Please, God . . . please," he begged as a look of despair washed over his face.

Jane Marie opened her glazed eyes once more and seemed to stare beyond his own. She lifted one shaking hand and traced the outline of Stephen's mouth with one finger. Her eyes opened wider and seemed to gain luster. Just a flicker of a smile creased her lips as she stared straight ahead of her. "Ma will never suffer at . . . at Pa's hands again. She's at home . . . with God. And the little ones," she barely whispered, "I see them. I wish you could see it, Stephen. It's so . . . so beautiful, and I hear the tinkling laughter of the angels . . ."

The quivering stopped and Stephen heard a little gasp. In the twinkling of an eye, his beloved's soul was reunited with her Maker. Whippoorwills were calling and deep-voiced frogs sounded like the continuous beat of faraway drums.

Stephen sat perfectly still, holding Jane Marie tightly in his arms as the warmth slowly slipped from her body. He gazed into her face, so serene now in death. She looked like a sleeping child and he brushed at the smudges his tears had made on her cheeks and the words of St. John beat strongly within him: *The Lord giveth, the Lord taketh away—blessed be the name of the Lord.*

Stephen spoke aloud, "Let not your heart be troubled: ye believe in God, believe also in me. In my Father's house are many mansions: if it were not so, I would have told you. I go to prepare a place for you. And if I go and prepare a place for you, I will come again, and receive you unto myself; that where I am, there ye may be also . . . ."

CHAPTER 36

The sun was sinking in the west and a faint breeze was sweeping down from the river when John, Margaret and Amy walked through their charred kitchen on Thursday evening, September 14, 1786. Their reunion with Billy Joe and Roscoe and Ruby was nothing like what they had pictured it would be. It had been heartbreaking to learn of the senseless deaths of so many people who had died at the hands of marauding Shawnee Indians.

Ruby praised Sandy and Billy Joe and credited them with saving her life as well as Roscoe's during the raid. Margaret would agonize for days over the realization of just how close she and John had come to loosing their beloved son. But pride in Billy Joe now flowed throughout her entire being as first Ruby, then Roscoe and finally Billy Joe gave their accounts as to what had happened to them on that dreadful morning.

Stephen was the one to tell Amy about Jane Marie's injuries that led to her death. No mention was made of his quick thinking and bravery that had saved Bobby's life. The story Stephen told was in praise of those dear souls who had given their all during the horrendous battle and of those who fought bravely and still lived to tell about it.

Being reunited with Matthew after so many months of being

apart had been a blessed experience to Amy. Just to know that he was home safe and sound brought praises from her lips. They had so little time together that she had not yet learned much about his trip to Danville, nor he of her trip to Greenfield. Stephen and Matthew had been working around the clock, burying the dead, helping to repair homes as best they could, and consoling those who had lost their loved ones in the raid.

John and Billy Joe immediately set about making repairs on their cabin, their spirits tormented because of so much grief and heartache surrounding them. But the Bradshaw family thanked God many times a day that it was just material things they had lost when it could have been so much worse. Their family was together again, complete and whole and that was all that mattered.

It was a perfect Indian-summer day—as bright as a bittersweet berry. The woodland was full of color. The maples stood regally, their crispy red and brown leaves blending with the yellow birch along the river. Southbound, broad-winged hawks were gliding above the ridges in seemingly endless parades.

It was Sunday morning, October 1, almost three weeks from the time of the attack that Stephen conducted the Memorial Service for all the dead of New Hope. From the village people came, and from the outlying homesteads within easy riding distance they came. The schoolhouse was packed and those that found no room inside stood quietly assembled outside the open door. They were dressed in the best that they had; some, having lost everything but the clothes on their backs, sat in borrowed clothes. Their eyes were hollow and sunken, their mouths grim, but they had assembled themselves together for one purpose: to honor their dead and to find hope and inspiration for living.

When the singing of hymns began, tears fell and lips quivered. When Stephen stood to speak, every eye was upon him. He opened to the book of Psalms and taking as his text, Psalm 116:15, he read: *Precious in the sight of the Lord is the death of his saints.*

Stephen held his head high, his gaze steady and his voice calm. The only visible sign of the stress he was under was in the slight trembling of his hands and the paleness of his face. "My friends," he began in an even, conciliatory voice, "we live such a short while on this earth and most of us will readily admit that we are reluctant to die—simply because we do not know what 'Death' is all about. We view it with fear and trepidation, not certain what is around the bend in the road for us. Death seems to be the finality of all that makes us a mortal being, and yet, if we could but see what lies beyond, the beautiful life that God has prepared for those who love and trust him, we would run with hurrying feet and open arms to meet our Master and Maker. As the deer pants for water, so we should long for the living God. Eye hath not seen, nor ear hath not heard or even imagined the wonderful things that God has prepared for those of us who love him.

"They who have gone before us now walk with God beside sacred streams, amid beauty that here on earth we can only guess at. They behold a peace beyond any man's dream. Death should not be a sad time for the Christian—it should be a time for joy and thanksgiving. But, my friends," Stephen said, his jaw tensing visibly, "it is only human to shed tears in times of sorrow. Christ also shed many tears of grief during his short lifetime. God has collected all the tears we have shed these past few days and has preserved them in a bottle and has recorded every one in his book. But he also tells us, 'with the morning, should come joy.'

"Death is a joyous transition for God's chosen people—from a world filled with sorrow and pain, to a place where the soul never dies, and is freed to live with God throughout all eternity. God's saints are very precious to him and he does not lightly let them die. He counts the stars and calls them all by name; he numbers the very hairs of your head and he sent his only son to die on the cross, so that anyone who believes in him would not perish, but would have eternal life. The great 'I Am' has lovingly sent his Holy Spirit to dwell amongst us and it is that blessed Presence that will sustain us in the days to come. God's greatness is beyond discovery; beyond our wildest expectations and . . . beyond the coming spring."

Stephen raised his hand and gave the benediction and everyone silently filed out of the schoolhouse. Matthew knew his beloved

Amy and his dearest friend, Stephen, needed time alone with their thoughts of Jane Marie. He went about shaking hands with so many of his dear friends who had come to pay their respect, and then led Bobby over to the shade of a large Maple tree just south of the schoolhouse to wait.

Stephen escorted Amy to the small cemetery located on the hillside behind the schoolhouse. Those who had lost loved ones during the attack followed close behind.

Amy was dry-eyed as she left the service. She clutched tightly to Stephen's arm, oblivious to the stares of understanding villagers, as they made their way slowly to the grave. Jane Marie had been buried alongside her mother, brother and twin sisters under an ancient beech tree, its sun-gold glow awesome in its beauty.

Slipping to her knees beside the fresh-turned earth, Amy bowed her head and her body slumped in despair. Grief and despondency tore at her heart. The sobs finally came, wracking her small body with spasms. Tears coursed down her pale cheeks and splashed to the ground. Stephen stood behind her, his hands gripping her shoulders tightly. He looked skyward and prayed aloud: "God, I know you are up there in all your glory, and I know that you hear me. I am confident, Father, that you are giving Jane Marie all the love and peace she so desperately sought while living here on earth. A love that outshines by far the love that I could have ever given her. I am satisfied that she now walks with you through those streets of gold in your Eternal City."

Stephen gently lifted Amy from the ground. She turned and buried her face in the folds of his coat as his arms gently enfolded her. "She's safe now," Amy cried, a flash of wild grief ripping through her, "and nothing will ever hurt her again."

Stephen nodded as words of the ancient prophet, Isaiah, echoed through his heart: *When you pass through the waters, I will be with you; and through the rivers, they shall not overwhelm you.*

"God is with us today, Amy," he whispered. "The rivers may run deep that we are required to walk through, but we do not have to go through them alone. God will not forsake us. He is here, walking beside us and our tomorrows are secure in his loving hands."

. . .

Amy sat bolt upright, her heart beating like a trip-hammer in her chest, gasping for breath. Although her room was cold and drafty she found herself sweating profusely. Fearful images of brown greasy fingers, covered in blood, had been reaching for her—terrorizing her. These anxious scenes faded slowly as she reminded herself it had only been a dream—the same dream that had haunted her for weeks.

She shivered, snuggled more deeply into the confines of her feather mattress and tried to relax. She had been fighting to erase the memory of all that she had heard about the massacre from her troubled mind, but she knew the night demons would always be lurking in the dark shadows of her mind—waiting to pounce when she least expected them.

A shaft of pale sunlight pierced the darkness of her soul as she listened intently to the sound of the hurrying wind as it raced through the branches of the big maple outside her bedroom window. Its huge, bare limbs scratched like frozen fingers at the windowpane now thickly covered with frost from within.

She was reluctant to leave her warm bed, but from the clatter of crockery, the tantalizing aromas drifting upward, and the slam of the kitchen door, Amy knew everybody else in her household must be up and about. Since moving to Kentucky her family had usually followed a given order of a morning ritual. Her father was up first, lighting a fire and putting a kettle to boiling. He would then head to the barn to do the milking and feeding of the livestock. Margaret rose, bathed and after starting breakfast would then rouse Billy Joe. When Billy Joe went to feed the chickens and gather the eggs, Amy would hurry to the kitchen and have her privacy to bathe and dress.

Margaret was now busy fixing her special 'birthday breakfast' and her toes wiggled in anticipation. Flinging back the covers she swung her feet over the side of the bed and slipped out of its warmth. The icy air chilled her to the bone. Yawning, she reached for her wrapper that lay over the bottom of her bed and shrugged into it. She went to her window, knelt before it and began scratching in the icy coating on the pane. AMB she wrote. Then with great flourish she added MDC followed by 12-16-86.

She shivered and her gaze shifted to a blue jay sitting on the branch of the maple tree outside her bedroom window, his feathers fluffed against the cold. She giggled. It looked to her as though the jay was actually scowling.

"Oh no you don't, Mr. Jay," she said lightly, "you'll not spoil my day with your scowls!" Excitement started mounting in the pit of her stomach. Today was her nineteenth birthday and her wedding day. A day made for living, laughing and loving!

After breakfast was over Margaret started removing dishware from the table. In spite of her mother's protests Amy wanted to help with tidying up the kitchen. "I've got some things I'd like to talk over with you, Ma. We can talk while we work. Our time together doing chores is about over." Amy's eyes grew large and liquid.

Margaret smiled and shook her head in silent agreement. A comfortable silence reigned between mother and daughter for several minutes, the only sounds emanating from the room was that of the ticking of the Seth Thomas clock on the mantel, the hissing and cracking of the flames devouring yet another log in the fireplace, and the clinking of dishes in the dishpan.

Tears burned and blinded Amy as she stood with her hands in hot soapy water. "I promised myself this morning that this day would not be spoiled with thoughts of Jane Marie. But, Ma, I can't seem to help thinking about her." Amy wiped her hands on a towel and then wiped the tears from her cheeks. "I was so happy the night before we left for Greenfield. Now I'll never see Jane Marie again in this world. Never see her glossy black hair curling about her beautiful face; never hear the appealing laughter in her voice as she gazed into Stephen's adoring eyes as they shared their hopes and dreams of marriage and motherhood. Death claimed all of that, Ma." Amy's voice broke miserably as pain ripped through her again.

"Come and sit at the table, dear, and we'll have a cup of sassafras tea. It'll soothe your nerves and quiet the churning in your stomach. I usually find it so anyway."

"Thanks, Ma. You always know of ways to ease my woes." Amy sat down woodenly in a chair and Margaret went to the cupboard and drew out two clean cups.

Amy sipped her tea. "Ummm, nice and sweet, just the way I like it."

"It breaks my heart to see you grieving for Jane Marie, honey. But yet you need to work through your grief slowly. You mustn't keep it all bottled up inside you where it would most certainly build and fester. I've had my own problems grieving for Katherine and her new babe and the twins. It's heartrending"

Margaret pushed back a wayward strand of hair and took a sip of tea. "As you know, as soon as you're married your pa and I will be taking care of little Bobby until other arrangements can be made for him. Sally thought it only fitting that she care for him until after the wedding. I've been over to Sally's place to see him several times since his mother's death. He seems to be handling his grief well on the surface but that child is certainly going to test the waters. He's a bright child for his age, and normally I can look into a person's eyes and figure out what's going on with them. But for the life of me, Bobby's eyes reveal nothing."

"He's all we've got left of the McLins, Ma. I haven't talked it over with Matthew yet but I think I would like to care for Bobby. Let him live with us if he'd want to. I believe Jane Marie would have liked that."

A pain squeezed Margaret's heart and a look of sadness passed over her face. "I do believe you're right, honey. If your pa and I was a wee bit younger, we would gladly take on the job of raising him. If you and Matthew do raise the child, your pa and I will do everything we can to help you." The tense lines on Margaret's face relaxed somewhat.

"Every day I thank God that if it hadn't been for you wanting to take a few days out of our hectic schedules to go to Greenfield, we could very well have lost our lives too. And if it hadn't been for Billy Joe . . ." Margaret shook her head and nervously picked at a loose thread on the sleeve of her dress. "Roscoe and Ruby are such precious souls and I don't believe I could have handled their deaths as well as you are handling Jane Marie's. We're all tested and tried in our walk through life, but for all those souls who came through this scathing, I'm humbly grateful. God is good and he can bring solace to our wounded spirits if we but let him."

. . .

Cold nights, chilly days, frost on the grass and snow in the air—and December sixteenth had indeed arrived. The wind hurried over the hilltops and down the valleys and the leafless trees held little restraint. It had snowed during the night, transforming the meadow into a shimmering wonderland and the woodland into a place of magic—a beautiful backdrop for a home wedding, Amy decreed.

"Something old, something new, something borrowed, something blue." Amy was standing before her mirror, repeating the old adage as she fingered one of the few treasures of her own girlhood: a small gold locket that Kristy had given her when she was twelve years old. It now hung around her neck on a blue velvet ribbon.

She had them all she concluded: Kristy's locket, her wedding dress, Jane Marie's Bible that Amy had so painstakingly chosen in Greenfield and a beautiful white linen handkerchief with tatted trim of small blue stitches made by her Grandma Johnson—a special gift for her wedding day.

Amy's heart gave a lurch as she pressed the handkerchief to her face, smelling the scent of lavender, and thoughts of her grandmother and Jane Marie filled her entire being. Two very special people in her life that would not, could not, be with her to share in her happiness. God had not seen fit to let Jane Marie stand beside her this day, listening to her repeat her vows to love, honor and obey Matthew. But inexpressible happiness welled in her breast and she trembled with the knowledge that Jane Marie would be looking down on them from heaven, showering them with her love. She may be absent from her in life, but forever in her heart and mind. And her beloved grandmother, so many miles away, would be with her in thought, if not present in body.

. . .

Margaret slipped into her bedroom where Amy was dressing. She brought with her a little chaplet of her carefully tended pale pink geraniums to adorn her smooth, tawny-brown hair and a pretty knot for her breast.

Arrayed in her wedding attire, Amy looked like a beautiful flower herself. She had pulled her hair tight and high to the crown of her head, letting little curls escape down over each ear and at the back, trying very hard to arrange it as Flossie had done while she was in Greenfield.

After pinning flowers on Amy's dress, Margaret pinned the chaplet in her hair, stepped back and looking into her big brown eyes said softly and sweetly, "My beautiful daughter—I love you so. I will keep a picture of what you look like today in my heart forever." She kissed Amy tenderly and careful not to wrinkle her dress hugged her gently.

"I love you too, Ma," Amy whispered.

There was a light tap on the bedroom door and when it opened a crack Matthew said simply, "It's time." Amy watched as Margaret rushed to the door, turned and looked lovingly at her once more, tears lighting her eyes. She blew her a kiss, which Amy returned with a beautiful smile.

Chairs were crowded as closely together as possible before the hearth. Bobby was sitting straight as a little tin soldier in the chair next to John. As arranged, Billy Joe was sitting between Roscoe and Ruby Willis, and the remaining chair, next to John, was for Margaret.

Behind them sat Thornton and Sally Decker with their two little boys, Tommy and Tyler. Ben and Gilda Grier were attired in their very best. Hattie Lou was all smiles and little Arliss was sound asleep in his mother's arms. Sam and his family had not been able to attend the wedding but had sent their best wishes along with a beautiful quilt that Abigail had stitched for the happy couple.

Matthew stood in front of the blazing fire beside Stephen. He felt awkward and self-conscious in the new clothes he had purchased while in Danville, but bore himself proudly as to conceal it. He had chosen a tailored frock of dark blue woolen cloth with breeches two shades lighter in color. His short waistcoat was made of a dark, flowered-blue satin. A white shirt with delicate cambric ruffles on the wristbands and a white linen cravat completed his attire. His hair, a shade darker than when he was a boy, was brushed carefully into a thick crest over his forehead. His cheeks were glowing and his blue eyes were brilliant with the joy of youth.

Amy took one last look in the mirror and pinched her cheeks for color. Lifting her skirt with one hand and clutching Jane Marie's Bible and her handkerchief in her other hand, she glided through the door and across the spotless puncheon floor. She looked like an angel, her dress billowing around her legs and her hair shining like spun gold.

She glanced lovingly at her family seated before her. Margaret was beautifully attired in crimson and gold-shot silk, and the glow of her smile warmed Amy from across the room. John, scarcely at home in his grand apparel, was radiant. Seeing Amy standing before him in all her grandeur John's eyebrows rose in amazement. His smile widened in approval and he winked at her. Amy reveled in his open admiration of her.

Billy Joe, his hair neatly parted and slicked back on the sides, had a wide grin on his face as he looked first at Amy and then at Matthew admiringly. Bobby sat straight as a poker between her mother and father, holding tightly to one arm of each, his eyes dark and haunted, seeming much younger than his seven years. Roscoe was beaming and Ruby was dabbing now and again at her eyes, wearing a happy smile.

Amy walked slowly to where her parents sat, leaned down and kissed first her father and then her mother. She smiled warmly at all her guests then straightened and turned toward the hearth. She raised her eyes to find Matthew watching her, his eyes brimming with tenderness and passion. She took one step in his direction and Matthew bent toward her, his arm crooked, through which she slipped a trembling hand. As one they turned toward Stephen.

He stood before them, elegantly erect in his broadcloth and linen. His pulse quickened as he gazed at Amy. He felt as though he had come to the brink of a dread abyss. Instead of Amy's face he seemed to see Jane Marie's face, and his eyes glowed over the memory of her for the space of a moment. He could almost hear her soft laughter rippling gently about the room; could see her gazing at him with undying love and feel her gentle touch.

He shook his head as if to clear the memories from it and smiled at his two dearest friends warmly. Margaret dabbed at her eyes and John hoped no one would notice the tears in his eyes as Amy placed Jane Marie's Bible into Stephen's trembling hand. Stephen glanced at the name inscribed on the leather-bound cover and ran his fingers lightly over it as a shadow moved across his eyes.

"We are gathered in the sight of God . . ." Stephen's words rang out brightly. Amy stared at Matthew with grave and innocent wonder, a soft blush creeping over her face and neck.

Matthew looked at Amy as Adam might have looked at Eve, the world empty save for the two of them. He never knew how long he stood there beholding her beauty before he felt Stephen's hand on his shoulder, his voice saying softly, "Repeat after me."

With a thrill of pride Amy looked deeply into Matthew's eyes. This was the man she loved with all her heart and she knew he returned her love. She felt no fear, only infinite peace in her heart—knowing she had been waiting all her life for just this moment.

"I, Amy, take thee, Matthew . . ." Her voice rang out sweet and clear.

After the brief ceremony Stephen reached out and took a hand of each into his own. The warmth of his smile echoed in his voice as he said simply, "God bless you both—today and always. Don't ever look back or think of what might have been. Think only of the wonderful life ahead of you—a life blessed by God. Jane Marie would have wanted you to be happy today and I want you to know that I have accepted fully what the Lord has chosen to serve me."

Stephen pulled them to him and the three embraced. Stephen whispered just for their ears alone, "God gave me strength this morning as I was reading in Isaiah 60. '. . . *my sun shall no more go down neither shall my moon withdraw itself for the Lord will be my everlasting light and the days of my mourning shall be ended.*'"

Releasing them Stephen backed away and said in a lighter tone, "Happiness always, my friends—and remember, I love you." Tears were coursing down his pale cheeks as he slowly made his way out of the cabin. No one tried to stop him.

Margaret looked at first one and then the other of her two dear children. She picked a thread from Matthew's coat then stood on tiptoe to hug and kiss him. "Be happy, my son," she murmured, her eyes misting with tears.

Matthew held her close, caressing her hair and the smile he gave her pierced her heart with its sweetness. "Thank you, Mother, for the precious gift that you have entrusted to me this day," Matthew said with a coaxing smile.

Everyone ate heartily of the generous bounty of food that Margaret, with the help of Ruby and Sally, had so lovingly prepared for the wedding supper. But under the circumstances, no great amount of merrymaking had been planned. No music, no dancing. After the meal was finished and well wishes bestowed on the newlyweds, their friends departed to their own homes.

John followed Matthew and Amy outside, his breath a shimmering cloud in the brittle cold. He had found it hard all day to say what was in his heart. Finally, with shaking fingers, he drew a cloth pouch from his coat pocket and placed it in Matthew's hand. Matthew drew a beautiful gold watch from the pouch. He released the catch of the case and looked at the black-numeraled face.

"That belonged to my own dearly departed father and I want you to have it, son. Billy Joe will receive my own upon my death," he added. "My pa always told me the watch kept perfect time. He would have bet his life on it—right to the second."

Slowly Matthew wound the stem and it started ticking, clear and steady. He would wind it faithfully from that day on. "Thank you, Pa," Matthew said, and hugged him fiercely.

John reached out with both arms and drew Amy gently to him. "You are my first born pride and joy. I would not attempt to try and tell you what you mean to me my child. But I know in my heart that you know of the bond between us as well as I do. Intangible, yet so strong that nothing could ever break it. I'm cutting the cord now so to speak, and you are no longer bound to your mother and I, but have become as one with Matthew. Go in peace, my child, and may God always bless and keep you." John could say no more because of the lump in his throat.

"I love you, Pa, more than I can ever tell you." With one last kiss Amy brushed at the tears that slipped down her cheeks and watched as her father turned and made his way slowly back into the house.

As Matthew opened their cabin door, he glanced up into the heavens at a friendly velvet-black sky, littered with a myriad of crystal-bright stars. High up, in one corner, hung a crescent moon. The whole sky was glowing, silhouetting the trees and the hills in their whiteness. The stars leaned so close Matthew felt that if he stood on the highest hill he might be able to grasp one. An old oak tree, standing regally behind their cabin, not yet completely naked, rustled crisply and two barred owls, their repeated notes rising with questioning intonation, hooted at each other.

Matthew ushered his bride into their cabin then locked and shuttered the door. After lighting a lamp he set it on the kitchen table. He had been to the cabin earlier and had a blazing fire going in the fireplace. The wind was rising and Amy could hear it whining about the corners of the house. She stood before the hearth enjoying the welcome warmth and cheeriness. "Sure feels good," Amy murmured, shivering slightly.

Matthew stoked the fire and added three more pieces of apple wood to the brightly burning embers. He turned slowly and wrapped his strong arms around Amy. Leaning down, his mouth covered hers hungrily. Amy quivered at the sweet tenderness of his kiss, breathing in the sweet scent of his cologne. Blood pounded in her brain, leapt from her heart, and made her knees tremble as Matthew captured her lips once more. His warm male scent was intoxicating.

Releasing her lips Matthew touched one cheek with his fingertips. His blue eyes caught and held her own. Amy at once thought of their oak tree as she looked at Matthew: tall and sturdy and dependable.

Matthew drew a deep breath, tasting tears as they kissed and clung together and he wondered whether they were Amy's or his own. He kissed her hair, her cheeks, her lips and sighed deeply. "My dearest one; oh, my dearest wife, how very, very much I love you." He gazed at her serenely as she looked up to him and worshipped him with her eyes. "I will make you happy always and you'll never want for a thing that is in my power to give you—I promise."

Amy pressed his fingers to her lips and kissed them one at a time—her eyes caressing him. Matthew slowly unbuttoned Amy's wedding dress and slipped it over her smooth shoulders, letting it fall to the floor, his hands lingering over her trembling body. She moved close against him. "I was born to love you, Matthew, and I shall love you forever." Before his appealing smile, Amy's defenses melted away. "I want to please you, my husband. I want to grant you your every desire." Her voice was little more than a whisper.

Matthew could scarcely breathe as a knot, big as a boulder, constricted his chest. Amy's soft endearments and her pledge of love was just the encouragement he needed.

Amy felt a soaring moment of triumph in the first moment of possession by her new husband, words they had uttered during their wedding ceremony ringing in her ears: "... to love and to cherish, 'til death us do part."

THE END

BVG